THE QUIET SISTER

ALEX STONE

Boldwood

First published in Great Britain in 2025 by Boldwood Books Ltd.

Copyright © Alex Stone, 2025

Cover Design by Head Design Ltd.

Cover Images: iStock

A CIP catalogue record for this book is available from the British Library.

Paperback ISBN 978-1-80280-342-6

Large Print ISBN 978-1-80280-341-9

Hardback ISBN 978-1-80280-340-2

Ebook ISBN 978-1-80280-343-3

Kindle ISBN 978-1-80280-344-0

Audio CD ISBN 978-1-80280-335-8

MP3 CD ISBN 978-1-80280-336-5

Digital audio download ISBN 978-1-80280-339-6

This book is printed on certified sustainable paper. Boldwood Books is dedicated to putting sustainability at the heart of our business. For more information please visit https://www.boldwoodbooks.com/about-us/sustainability/

Boldwood Books Ltd, 23 Bowerdean Street, London, SW6 3TN

www.boldwoodbooks.com

For Ahl.

1

NOW

October

What have I done?

I fought my way through the crowd that had gathered on the once familiar street. I'd never seen so many people here before. Sunday evenings were usually quiet. Calm. Not like this.

I scrunched my nose at the strong scent of smoke filling the air. It reminded me of bonfire nights as a child, where the night air had carried the smell of burning towards us long before we'd even reached the park.

That was wrong too. It was still October. Too soon for bonfires.

When I'd left almost two hours earlier, I'd breathed in the damp autumnal evening air but now...

Bile rose in my throat, and I swallowed. I had to keep going. I craned my neck to see properly. Blue lights flashed against a glow of red and orange. I could feel the heat on my face even from here. But I still wasn't close enough. I couldn't see. Couldn't be sure.

I reached the front where the crowd of curious locals with their mobile phones held high recording the action were held back behind a makeshift tape barrier.

I ducked underneath it.

'Miss!' a police officer called to me before I was even fully on the other side. 'You need to keep back.'

I shook my head at him. A piece of tape wasn't enough to deter me. Nothing was.

My rebellion seemed to ripple through the crowd and the police officer's attempt to follow me was thwarted by the reporters who surged forwards in my wake.

I veered up the street around the corner and my eyes widened as my feet froze in place. I'd known it already. From the second I'd seen the smoke billowing upwards above the rooftops something inside me had known. And yet, now as I stood here, my gaze transfixed on the burning building ahead of me, I realised that I'd still hoped I was wrong.

After all, I usually was.

I started walking again, drawn to the building despite the danger. The voice of caution in the back of my head screamed at me to stop. It was the voice I usually listened to.

Until today.

'Miss!' The police officer's voice was louder this time and followed by a strong hand that grasped my arm, drawing me to a halt. 'You can't be here.'

I turned to him this time. My eyes barely seeing him through the blur of my tears. 'It's my...' My voice croaked before giving way.

He turned his head, and I followed his gaze back to the building that had once meant so much to me.

I gasped as a fireman emerged through the broken front door, a lifeless body in his arms. Even through the smoke I recognised her. I knew her better than I even knew myself.

I took a shaky step forward, but the police officer blocked my path.

'She's my sister,' I whispered.

Understanding softened his professional expression.

I clung to his arm as paramedics rushed towards the fireman and they lowered my sister onto a stretcher. They leaned over her, checking for a pulse, slipping an oxygen mask over her face and trying to resuscitate her. But I could tell from their expressions it was already too late.

They kept trying. Hoping. I knew how it worked. I'd been here before. A different place. A different time. But the result had been the same.

I'd ended up alone.

A uniformed officer ran towards the paramedics and his hand flew to his mouth as he reached them. Ethan, I realised as I squinted at him through the smoke and tears. I could feel his sadness as he reached out and stroked her left hand as it lay beside her on the stretcher. The intensity of his action surprised me. I'd introduced them only days before, but I could see she'd already mattered to him.

Jealousy spiked within me. She always mattered.

I pushed that thought away as guilt engulfed me. It felt as though those two emotions were in constant battle. I'd always known they would destroy me one day. I just hadn't realised they would destroy her too.

'I want to go with her,' I said softly as the paramedics wheeled the stretcher towards the waiting ambulance.

The police officer at my side nodded and guided me forwards. Ethan turned and his eyes met mine. 'Mia!'

Mia.

The name ricocheted through me.

He rushed towards me. 'I can't believe it's Chloe.' He glanced back over his shoulder, and I stared at the ring on her left hand. 'Do you want me to call Scott? I can get him to meet you at the hospital?'

I froze.

'Mia?' Ethan touched my arm gently.

'N-no,' I stuttered. 'I-I'll call him.'

'Are you sure?' Ethan studied me uncertainly.

I nodded. 'I should be the one to...' My voice gave way again, but Ethan nodded. He understood.

At least, he thought he did.

2

THEN

August

I snuggled against Scott on my faded grey sofa. It was just what I needed after a long week. Just him and me.

Us.

I let out a contented sigh. I loved that word. Loved being part of it. Part of something.

Scott shifted as he turned to look at me. 'Are you okay, Chloe?'

The concern in his tone was like a warm blanket wrapping around me. My sigh was only soft, barely even audible over the action movie playing on the TV screen in front of us. But he'd heard it. He'd noticed. More importantly, he'd cared enough that his attention had been diverted from the movie he'd been so eager to watch and he was now completely focused on me.

I smiled. 'I'm good.'

The word felt insufficient. I was better than just good. I was happy. *We* were happy.

Scott grinned at me as though confirming my silent declaration. 'Yeah, you are,' he murmured, as his gaze travelled gradually down my body.

Heat rushed to my cheeks as he snaked his arm around me, pulling me even closer until my body was pressed against him. I closed my eyes as his lips met mine.

Upbeat music suddenly played, loudly battling for attention above the sounds of explosions coming from that TV. I ran my hand through Scott's hair, determined not to let the noises distract me.

'Ignore it,' Scott murmured breathlessly, between kisses. 'You can call them back later.'

The ringing persisted.

With a groan I wriggled away from Scott. 'I'll reject the call,' I said, reluctantly unwrapping myself from his arms as I reached for my phone on the coffee table.

My eyes widened as I saw the caller's name displayed on the screen. 'It's my sister,' I said, my heart pounding as I leapt to my feet. 'I'll be right back,' I called over my shoulder and raced out of the room. A WhatsApp video call from Mia required my undivided attention.

'But what about—' Scott started to ask, his voice full of surprise at my sudden departure.

I waved my hand dismissively as I cut him off. 'Keep watching, I'll catch up,' I assured him as I focused on the phone in my hands.

I tapped the answer button as I slipped into the kitchen and closed the door behind me.

'Hey, Chloe.' Mia's smiling face greeted me from an unfamiliar room.

I beamed. 'Hi, it's *so* good to see you. How's Rome?'

'Hot,' Mia said, fanning herself with her hand. 'Why do I never get sent to a hotel with air conditioning?'

I shook my head and murmured sympathetically. She smiled in satisfaction. Sympathy was what she'd wanted. What she always wanted.

This time it was the heat. Last trip it had been the noise. Next time it would be something else. There was always something. And yet, I knew, it wasn't really about the heat or the noise. It was about needing to feel heard. Our lives were complete opposites and yet she wanted exactly the same thing that I did: to feel like she mattered.

'So, what's new with you?' Mia asked, when she had finished telling me about the latest drama at work. 'Still on your own?'

I flinched at her question. 'I told you, I'm dating—'

'Oh right, the paramedic,' Mia said with a nod.

'Policeman,' I corrected.

Mia shrugged. 'I knew it was a guy in a uniform of some kind.'

I hated the way she did that. Dismissed things as though they were trivial. As though Scott was trivial.

She tipped her head to the right. 'I'm glad you finally have someone else in your life, besides just me.'

There was a sisterly warmth to her words, but despite that they sent a chill through to my bones. They were a not-so-subtle reminder of how empty my life was. That all I had was her.

Until now.

'Let's just hope this one is more reliable,' Mia added. This time she didn't even bother to mask the coarseness of her words.

My skin bristled. I didn't need her of all people reminding me how my previous relationships had ended. But Scott was different. I trusted him completely. I trusted him with my life.

He'd already proved I could.

'He is,' I replied with a steely certainty.

Mia smiled. 'Great, then I can't wait to meet him when I see you next month.'

My heartbeat quickened. 'You're coming back?'

'Yep, my contract here is nearly over. So I'm going to come back to England for a bit. I thought I might visit you in London while I'm there.'

Mia was coming to London. To see me.

Despite the gulf that existed between us I couldn't help feeling hopeful that this was it, the moment I'd been waiting for. The chance for us to reconnect. For Mia to see me differently. To finally see me as an equal.

I had to restrain myself from jigging up and down with excitement. I couldn't allow myself to get too carried away. Not until she was actually here. Mia's plans always had a habit of changing at the last minute. Today she might be planning to come home, but tomorrow her contract could be extended, or she could be offered a new one in Milan, Madrid or Paris. With Mia, you just never knew what would happen, or where she would end up.

'It will be really good to see you,' I said with restrained enthusiasm. There was an art to finding the right balance between excitement and realism. She needed to know that I was looking forward to seeing her, that I missed her. But I wouldn't be desperate. I couldn't need her.

I couldn't afford to need anyone.

* * *

'You were a long time,' Scott said solemnly as I slipped back onto the sofa beside him.

I glanced at the blank TV screen, my eyes widening in surprise. 'Did I miss the end?' I hadn't realised I'd been talking to Mia for that long.

He shrugged. 'Nah, I just turned it off. It wasn't really the movie I was interested in.'

I cringed inwardly. I'd neglected him. We were supposed to be spending a lazy evening together, and I'd ditched him for my sister the second the phone had rung.

Perhaps I should have ignored it and called Mia back later. But when Mia called, I answered. It was the way we worked.

'Sorry,' I said, snuggling up to Scott. 'It's just so hard to catch Mia these days.'

Scott grunted an acknowledgement, but his body was still rigid and tense.

'You have my undivided attention for the rest of the night, I promise.'

He turned his head towards me. 'Really?'

'Really,' I assured him.

Scott smiled slightly. 'I'm sorry, babe. I know it's selfish of me, but I didn't want to share you with anyone tonight.'

He wrapped his arm around me, and I let out a relieved breath. He was okay. We were okay.

'But I should be more understanding. I know it's not easy for you with Mia so far away.'

I grinned broadly at him. 'She might not be far away for much longer.'

'Oh?'

'She's planning to come home next month.' My cautious realism evaporated as I voiced Mia's plans aloud. 'You'll finally get to meet her.'

Would it be good to see her though? Doubt niggled at me. The idea of Mia's visits somehow always ended up better than the reality. I wasn't sure if I actually wanted her to visit, or just wanted *her* to want to. I needed the sense of acceptance that her desire to see me gave. Even if that was short lived.

'That's awesome,' Scott said, but his voice lacked enthusiasm.

I tickled his ribs. 'No need to be nervous, she's going to love you.' I wasn't entirely sure that was true either. Mia had a tendency to disapprove of the guys I dated.

Though that was preferable to the times when she liked them too much.

Scott nodded. 'Yeah, 'course she will.'

I kissed his cheek, feeling a warm rush of affection for him. It was cute to see him so unsettled. It showed that meeting my sister mattered to him.

I mattered to him.

I wrapped my arms around him and squeezed him tightly. 'It's going to be amazing to finally have the two most important people in my life with me at the same time,' I announced with a conviction I didn't entirely feel. 'We're all going to have such a great time together.'

I crossed my fingers as I spoke and offered up a silent prayer. I would take all the help I could get to make my declaration true.

3

NOW

October

The taxi turned right, and my lungs contracted as I stared down the hill at the view of the wide stretch of sand and sea ahead.

'Isn't it beautiful, honey?'

Mum's voice echoed in my memory. I'd only been five years old on that first visit to Bournemouth, but Mum's excitement was still so vivid.

'You're going to love it here.'

My breathing became laboured as the past continued to replay in my head. Mum had been right. I had loved it.

At first.

'Impressive, isn't it?' the taxi driver asked, mistaking my gasp for awe.

'Y-yeah.' I struggled to speak.

'This your first time in Bournemouth?'

I shook my head. 'My family and I spent our summers here when I was younger.'

'Nice,' he said, with a nod of approval. 'You must have some lovely childhood memories.'

I hesitated.

He was right, I did have some lovely memories. But they were distant and faded. Buried beneath everything that had happened. Even the good times were painful to think about now.

It was why I'd vowed never to come back.

And yet here I was.

I lowered my head and focused on my hands in my lap, refusing to look at the sea any longer.

Bournemouth.

Why did it have to be Bournemouth?

I rocked back and forth, the seatbelt pressing against my chest. What was I doing? This was the last place I wanted to be. Clearly this had been a bad idea. But then I'd always known that, right from the second it had occurred to me. And yet, what other choice did I have?

I racked my brain for an alternative. Even at this late stage I was still praying for a bolt of inspiration, a solution which I hadn't already thought of. But the reality was there had only ever been two options, stay in London or return to Bournemouth. As bad as this was, it was still the most favourable.

My sister was gone. And if anyone discovered what I'd done... I swallowed, refusing to allow myself to finish that thought. Bournemouth had one thing in its favour: it was safe. At least for Mia.

'There you go,' the taxi driver said as we stopped in front of large metal gates.

I stared up at the pastel colours of the vast apartment complex that towered above them on the other side. Its elegant grandeur hadn't diminished in the years I had been absent. It was one of the things that had appealed most to Mia, and ironically what had made me uncomfortable. The modern chicness of it was in a different league to the flat we had owned before.

'Hey, look,' Dad said as we walked along the promenade. 'It looks like they've almost finished building the new flats.'

I gazed up at the construction work that was taking place where the car park used to be. It was always interesting to see the changes that had been made between our annual summer visits.

'Wow! Wouldn't it be so cool to live there?' Mia said, her eyes wide. 'Look how close they are to the beach.'

'We already have a flat in walking distance to the beach,' Mum pointed out.

Mia scrunched her nose. 'But you can't see the sea from ours. Besides, it's really tiny and old.' Only twelve years old and Mia always wanted more. Wanted better.

I saw Mum's shoulders slump slightly and I veered towards her. 'Well, I love our flat,' I announced as I linked my arm through Mum's. 'It's special.' Mia and I might be twins, but there were times when I felt so much older and wiser. Or perhaps just more considerate.

Mum smiled down at me and patted my hand. I could feel her gratitude, her love, radiating from her expression.

'It's all a moot point anyway,' Dad said, with a shrug. 'There's no way we would ever be able to afford one of those apartments. The only reason we have a flat here at all is because your gran left it to your mum when she died.'

'It's a shame she couldn't have left us a better flat, though.' Mia pouted.

I felt Mum's body tense beside me. 'She left us everything she had.'

I glared at Mia as my mind raced, searching for the right words to make her understand how much her dismissal of our cosy flat was *hurting Mum. My lips parted as I summoned my courage to stand up to her.*

'Can we get an ice cream, Dad?' Mia asked, and I realised the moment had passed. I'd been too slow.

'It's a bit early for ice cream,' Mum said.

Mia stared up at Dad with big pleading eyes. 'P-l-e-a-s-e.' She dragged the word out with sickening sweetness that made me wince.

Dad chuckled and rolled his eyes. 'Come on, then.'

I caught Mum's sigh. Soft and quiet, no one else heard it. But I did. I always did.

I shook my head sadly. One year later Mia had got her wish for the new flat. Even now, that still jarred against me.

According to Dad, moving here was a fresh start. But the problem with starting over was it meant something else had to end. I hadn't been ready for that. Not then.

But right now, it was what I needed. A new home. A new start. But most of all, an end to everything that had happened in London.

'We made good time,' the taxi driver said, in a tone that implied he thought I would be happy to have reached my destination faster than expected.

'That's great,' I said with forced enthusiasm.

I took a deep breath, counting slowly. One. Two. Three. Four. I held it for two beats and then exhaled slowly as I counted to four again, attempting to summon the strength to open the door and step out of the taxi.

My fingers hesitated as they rested on the door handle, my gaze still locked on the colourful building. For so long this had been the place I was trying to evade, but now it was the place I was escaping to.

It went against every instinct. Every part of my body protested, screaming at me to leave. I didn't belong here.

No. I froze as realisation dawned on me. Chloe didn't belong here.

I pushed my shoulders back and raised my chin.

But I wasn't Chloe any more.

4

THEN

August

I let out a weary sigh as I scowled at the heavy clouds that were moving closer over the unusually quiet park.

Sales had been down all day. I'd been counting on the typical boost from the after-work foot traffic this evening. I pivoted the bucket of roses closest to me, rotating it a quarter turn, as though that small adjustment would cause a sudden surge in sales.

The problem was much bigger than that, though. The only thing my little tweaks and adjustments to the display achieved was to give me something to do for a few seconds. A sense of purpose. Control.

In reality of course, that was the very thing I didn't have. My day, my entire business, was largely dependent on the weather.

'Hey, Chloe.'

'Scott?' I swung round and stared at him in surprise as he approached my stall, before hurriedly checking my watch. 'I thought we were meeting at the restaurant later?'

'We were, but I heard the weather forecast was for heavy

showers this afternoon and I thought you might need a hand packing up, before the downpour.'

My surprise melted away and I beamed at him. 'You did?'

'I knew you'd still be here,' he said as he wrapped his arms around my waist and pulled me closer to him, 'trying to squeeze in a few more sales until the last minute.'

'Hmm,' I murmured as he kissed my lips lightly. 'You know me so well.'

'I do.' He nodded, without hesitation.

My smile grew even bigger.

Scott chuckled softly. 'Plus, it was a good excuse to see you sooner. I missed your smile too much to stay away any longer.'

I laughed. 'Well, I'm glad, because I've missed these arms,' I told him as I let myself sink into them, exhaling deeply. There was something so special about Scott's hugs. They had a way of making me calmer, as though nothing else mattered. Just us.

'Been a long day, huh?' Scott asked.

I groaned into his shoulder. 'It was so slow. And I have a throbbing headache.'

Scott stepped back and tilted his head down to look at me. 'We don't have to go out tonight, if you'd rather just go home—'

'No,' I said quickly. 'I want to spend the evening with you.'

Scott chuckled. 'You still can. I was about to suggest we got a takeaway, curled up on the sofa, and watched a movie together.'

I eyed him suspiciously. 'Do I get to pick the movie?' Our taste in movies was one of the few things we disagreed on.

'Naturally.'

'And you really wouldn't mind?' I asked hesitantly. I hated it when I let my uncertainty show, but I couldn't help it. I had to be sure that he was okay.

That we were okay.

'Hmm, I think I can survive one movie,' Scott said playfully.

I rolled my eyes. 'I meant, are you sure you don't mind changing our plans?'

'We were only going for dinner. The restaurant will still be there tomorrow night.' Scott took my hand in his.

I let out a sigh of relief. I loved how adaptable he was. He never objected if things didn't quite go to plan. He just revised the plan.

Maybe I could learn how do to that too.

Maybe.

'Come on, you can tell me all about your day as we get this lot loaded into your van.' He pulled the little fold-out cart from under the trestle table and started loading the almost full buckets of flowers into it.

I shook my head, as I copied him. 'You don't want to listen to me moan about work.'

We fell into a steady rhythm, manoeuvring the flowers like a well-choreographed dance. I loved it when he came to help me. It showed he cared about my business. About me. I wasn't going to ruin that by complaining about bad sales.

'You're not moaning,' Scott said, steering the full cart down the path to the entrance of the park. I fell into step beside him, carrying a couple more buckets. 'You're simply sharing your day with me. It's what couples do.'

Warmth emanated deep inside me. Scott's words were as comforting as his hugs. Understanding. Supportive. Interested.

Those were qualities I hadn't experienced for so long; I'd almost forgotten how they felt.

But I remembered how it felt to lose them.

I swallowed, attempting to shift the lump that had formed in my throat. 'You rarely even talk about your work. And you have a far more difficult and stressful job than I do.' I couldn't let this supportive relationship be one-sided. The best way to keep Scott was to make him feel as accepted and wanted as he made me feel.

'Are you kidding? I could never do your job, Chloe. Sitting in this park all day, smiling and chatting to everyone no matter how cold and miserable you actually feel.' He shook his head. 'To be honest, I don't understand why you do it.'

We reached my van and I set the buckets on the floor as I rummaged in my bag for the keys.

'And after what happened, it's hardly any wonder that none of your staff will work out here,' Scott continued as I clicked the remote and he opened the van door.

'What *almost* happened,' I corrected. 'Everything was fine, thanks to you.' I kissed his cheek.

Scott shook his head. 'We got lucky.' He stepped away and started loading the flowers into the back of the van. 'Anyway, it's not like you even need it. You own your own shop so why torture yourself with this tiny little stall?'

Tiny little stall.

Those three little words welded me to the spot. Was there an undertone of disdain to them?

'I love my stall,' I mumbled quietly.

Scott froze with buckets of flowers in his arms. 'Sorry, babe.' He cringed. 'I know you do.' He set the flowers down in the van and turned back to face me.

I shook my head. He didn't get it. He didn't understand how important the stall was. 'It's the only thing I have that's really mine. Totally, completely mine.'

He rubbed my arm. 'Just because you have mortgages for your house and shop, it doesn't make them any less yours.'

I squirmed. 'Yeah, but...'

'Don't worry, babe.' Scott planted a kiss on my forehead. 'I know what's really going on here.'

My jaw dropped. 'Y-you do?' Panic bubbled in the pit of my stomach.

He knew.

What must he think of me? Of my lie? My failure?

And yet, at the same time I felt a weight lift slightly. Part of me wanted him to know. The part that regretted that I'd ever deceived him in the first place.

'You'll never amount to anything.'

Dad's words sprang into my head. He'd spat them at me so often, I could hear his intonation and see his expression as clearly as if he'd been standing in front of me.

He might be gone now, but his words lived on.

I had to be better. Be *something*. Guys like Scott weren't interested in women who didn't amount to anything. They were attracted to smart, successful, confident women. The kind of woman I'd made him believe I was.

'Of course. It has sentimental meaning,' Scott said.

'Oh.' The word came out almost as a sigh, as my shoulders slumped.

'It's where your business got started before you opened your store.'

I plastered a smile on my face. 'Right.' But as I looked at Scott grinning at me full of pride, my smile withered. Instead of pride, all I felt was guilt.

He wasn't even close to the truth.

I didn't own a store. I never had.

I'd been lying to Mia about owning a store for years. I'd known she'd report that news back to Dad. I'd wanted her to. Perhaps then he would think I had amounted to something. Perhaps he'd be proud of me. Perhaps they both would.

But no amount of success, whether real or not, had ever changed their perspective of me.

So what had possessed me to tell Scott the same lie? It had been stupid. And now I was trapped.

Perhaps it was time I told him the truth. If we had any kind of future together, surely it needed an honest foundation. At least about this.

'That's not really it, though.' I swallowed. 'The flower stall is—'

'Is where we got started, too,' Scott finished for me with a wink. 'It's special to me too, because of that,' he added gruffly. 'But you don't need to stand out here six days a week to hang on to that.'

He was right, of course. I didn't need to hang on to the flower stall out of sentimentality. I had him now.

But my attachment to the stall was far more practical than that.

'I worry about you out here on your own all day. I can't be here to protect you all the time, and I don't know what I'd do if...' Scott's voice trailed out, and he shook his head. 'Our memories will still be here even if the flower stall isn't.' Scott's cheeks flushed as he turned away and busied himself with the flowers.

I watched him with adoration. Scott wasn't usually the sentimental type. For him to speak like this our meeting must have meant a lot to him.

I meant a lot.

The problem was, that realisation increased my need to tell him the truth. He deserved that. Our relationship deserved that. But that was precisely the reason I never could.

Being honest now would mean admitting I'd lied in the first place. That knowledge would undermine our relationship. Once he'd discovered one lie, he'd be on constant alert looking for more.

And if he looked hard enough, he would find them.

I'd always been safe before because no one cared enough to notice. That would have required them to take an interest in my life. To pay attention. To ask questions.

Nobody did.

At least, not until Scott.

Yet, he was the person that should have been hardest to mislead. The one who was trained to recognise the signs.

That should have been enough of a reason for me not to have even gone on one date with him. And yet at the same time it was also part of his appeal. He was good.

Maybe I could learn that from him too.

Pink still tinted Scott's cheeks as he avoided my gaze. Then again, they always say love is blind. Scott was proof of it.

'Okay,' I heard myself say. 'I'll give up the stall.'

A broad grin spread across Scott's face, and he seemed to grow another inch as he straightened his back and turned to me. 'That's great news.'

For a fraction of a second, I couldn't help but wonder what he was most happy about: that I wouldn't be spending my days in the park, or that I'd listened to him.

I shook myself. Of course it was about his concern for me. Nothing else.

It wasn't fair to judge him by someone else's behaviour.

By Mia's behaviour.

Besides, it wasn't as though I actually *had* listened to him. I'd never intended to keep the stall, not in the long term, sentimentality or not. I just couldn't give it up immediately. The problem was how to tell Scott that without explaining why.

'It's for the best,' Scott assured me.

'It is.' I nodded. 'Just as soon as I get relocated to the new store and it's all up and running.' I grabbed the handle of the now empty cart and started wheeling it back to the stall for the second load. At least that part was true. I was planning on opening a new store. Admittedly I'd told Scott it was a relocation. But in a few more months I would genuinely own a store, and then my lies would all be irrelevant.

At least the ones about my business anyway.

'Why wait?' Scott asked as he slammed the van door closed and hurried after me. 'I hate thinking of you alone in this park. It's not safe. You're not safe.'

'I—' My brain whirled searching for an appropriate answer. 'I can't let all this stock go to waste,' I said, waving my hand at the van.

'Fair enough, but these will be gone in a few days.'

'I have standing orders with the suppliers. I can't let them down. I need to keep the good relationship with them.'

'How much longer until you can buy a place?'

'Mia said it would be soon,' I said as we reached the stall and started the process of loading the flowers again. I paused. 'But she's been saying that for a while. Probate cleared weeks ago.'

Scott let out a frustrated sigh. 'I still don't understand why your dad made Mia an executor but not you.'

I kept my head down and focused on the task at hand with more concentration than it required.

'I mean, you said she's rarely in the country, right? Whereas you're right here, and you have experience with finance.'

I scoffed. 'It's only a flower st—' I cleared my throat '—shop.'

'A flower shop that's so successful you're expanding into bigger premises.'

I squirmed. 'Only because of the inheritance I'm getting from Dad's will.'

Scott shrugged as though that detail was irrelevant.

But it wasn't. My shoulders slumped. Without that inheritance I wouldn't even be able to contemplate opening a store. I couldn't even afford to rent the space, let alone buy it.

'Sorry, Chloe,' Scott said, suddenly wrapping his arm around my shoulders. 'I didn't mean to make you sad reminding you about your dad.'

I swallowed. 'You didn't.' At least not for the reasons he thought.

'Just keep focused on how proud he must have been of you and everything you've accomplished.'

I felt like I should agree, even with just a tiny nod of my head. But I couldn't. It wasn't true.

Scott gave my shoulder a gentle squeeze before flipping the table onto its side and he leaned over it to fold the legs in.

I let out a weary sigh. 'Dad ceased being proud of me a long time ago.'

Scott's head jolted up and I knew from his expression that I'd said that aloud.

'That can't be true.'

This was my chance to take it back. To say I'd exaggerated. That I was being melodramatic.

But I couldn't.

'Chloe?'

'Dad and I didn't have a very good relationship,' I said hesitantly.

'Really?' Scott blinked. 'I know he only died a few months before you and I met, but you'd seemed so upset, you still seem so upset, that I assumed you were really close.'

'You're right, I am still sad. It breaks my heart to know I'll never get a chance to make things right between us now.'

Not that I ever could have done. After all it was Mum I owed the biggest apology to. One I would never be able to give her.

5

NOW

October

'Mia.'

My head jolted to the left as I stepped out of the taxi. A man wearing a dark uniform leaned out of a doorway of a small building beside the driveway to the apartment complex.

I stole a quick glance at my reflection in the car window as I ran my hand through my hair, checking I looked the part even if I didn't feel it.

'H-hi.' My voice shook as I replied. It felt wrong to answer to that name. Like trying on a pair of the most gorgeous shoes that were too small. They might look perfect, but it didn't mean they would fit.

I cleared my throat. 'H-how are you?' I asked, squinting as I checked to see if he was wearing a name badge whilst purposefully keeping my distance. If he knew Mia's name, then that meant she probably knew his.

I should know his.

Time seemed to freeze as he walked towards me. I couldn't

breathe. Couldn't move. What if he could tell that something was different? That I was different?

Uncertainty flashed across his face and my heart rate quickened. But then he smiled. 'I'm doing well, thanks,' he said, as time restarted with a jolt. 'It's good to see you again.'

His words sounded genuine and yet there was something about his smile that felt off. It was friendly and welcoming but there was an uncertainty to it.

You always overthink everything.

The sharpness of the voice in my head was like a charge of electricity jolting me back into action.

'T-thanks, it's good to be back.' I silently cursed the hesitation in my voice that made my statement sound more like a question. I quickly turned away from him and focused my attention on the taxi.

I caught the taxi driver's confused expression as he lifted my suitcase out of the boot and wheeled it towards me. From the way I'd spoken earlier, he'd no doubt assumed I hadn't been back here for years.

But then *I* hadn't.

'Thanks,' I said, taking the case from him as I avoided eye contact. The last thing I needed was for him to start asking questions. I just wanted him to leave and avoid any more awkwardness.

'No worries,' he said as he closed the boot.

I watched as he clambered into his seat and drove away. A sudden sense of abandonment washed over me as I stared after him. His unspoken questions might have departed with him, but so had my means of escape.

'You're back earlier than we anticipated,' the stranger behind me said, and I shifted awkwardly as I turned to face him. 'We don't usually see you down here in the winter.'

I shook my head. 'No, I had an unexpected change of plans, so—' I shrugged '—here I am.'

My breath caught in my chest as I stared at him, silently dreading his next question. What if he asked what had changed? It wasn't as though I could tell him. I couldn't tell anyone.

'Do you need any help?' he asked, nodding at my suitcase.

My body seemed to deflate with relief at the ease of his question. I shook my head. 'I'm good, thanks.' The words felt wrong coming out of my mouth.

I was anything but good.

'It's no trouble,' he said, reaching for the suitcase.

My grip tightened on the handle. I just needed to be alone. 'I'm fine.'

His hand jolted back from the suitcase instantly and I realised my tone had been too sharp. Apologies formed on my tongue. I had to make amends.

'Of course, Ms Philips,' he said as his entire manner morphed from friendly to professional. 'Would you at least like me to open the gate for you?'

I hesitated for a moment, thrown by his reaction. He didn't seem fazed by my outburst at all. Perhaps he was used to ill-mannered residents. Or perhaps, more specifically, he was used to Mia.

I started to nod meekly, still remorseful for my tone. But I stopped. Mia wouldn't behave that way. She wouldn't be apologetic or meek. And neither would I.

I lifted my chin. 'That would be appreciated.'

He led the way to the pedestrian access, tapped a security fob to a panel beside the gate, and held it open for me.

'Thanks,' I said and slipped through the gate.

It closed behind me with a clunk that seemed to vibrate through my body.

I was in.

He nodded at me with a polite smile, before heading back to his office. I turned and surveyed the courtyard as I edged forwards.

You don't really believe you can do this, do you?

I tightened my grip on the handle of the heavy suitcase that I tugged along by my side and lengthened my stride, in an attempt to outrun that voice of doubt. But, just like the suitcase, it continued to follow me. I couldn't escape the weight of either.

My heel caught on the block paving, and I stumbled forwards. Perhaps the high-heeled boots had been too much. They weren't really necessary. And yet somehow even the tiniest detail felt important, just like the designer jeans and leather jacket. Things that would have been out of budget on my salary. But they were all part of the image I was creating.

And I needed all the help I could get.

My gaze drifted up at the eight separate buildings that made up the apartment complex surrounding me. I read familiar the names on the signs outside the entrances, as my feet instinctively guided me towards the block directly ahead. The six years since I had moved to London seemed to instantly dissipate.

I was home.

6

THEN

August

'Sorry, you don't have to talk about it, if you don't want to.'

I tipped my head to the side. Scott was giving me an out. An easy way to avoid talking about my past without it being a reflection on how close we were as a couple. Without me having to lie. Or evade.

'It's okay,' I said finally. Mia was coming back soon. At some point she and Scott would meet. Our childhoods, our pasts, would undoubtedly come up in conversation. If I didn't tell him, Mia would.

She would relish doing so.

I took a deep breath. 'I think I want to talk about it. I want to share that with you.'

Scott smiled and his whole face seemed to light up. My words had done that. My willingness to let him in had made him feel important. Valued. It felt good to be able to do that for someone. To do that for him.

I pushed the cart back down the path towards the van. If I

was going to talk about the past, then I needed movement. Something to distract me from the pain. I heard Scott scrambling behind me to pick up the folded table and hurry after me.

'Things changed after we lost Mum,' I told him as we reached the van. 'Dad wasn't the same. Especially not with me. I know it's tough for anyone to grow up without their mum, but—'

Scott drew back as he stared at me. 'You said you'd lost your mum, but I didn't realise you meant when you were a kid. How old were you?'

His question hung in the air as the street seemed to close in around me. Even though I'd told myself I wanted to do this, there was a reason I hadn't done so before. A reason I didn't talk about my parents to anyone. Didn't think about them. Or at least, I tried not to. Because even after all these years, it still hurt to do so.

'We were twelve when we lost Mum.' I tried to shrug, but my shoulders felt heavy and uncooperative.

'Oh, Chloe.' Scott propped the table against the side of the van and pulled me to him. My body felt rigid and tense as I hugged him back awkwardly.

It felt wrong to accept sympathy. I didn't deserve it.

'Wait, "we"?' he said, stepping back to peer at me, confusion etched into his forehead. 'You said "we were twelve".'

I stared at him. 'Yeah, Mia and I are twins.'

'Seriously?'

'I told you that before, like right when we first started dating.'

Scott shook his head. 'No way – I would have remembered that. It's so cool.'

I laughed uncomfortably. 'You said that then too.' I couldn't believe he'd forgotten. He was as bad as Mia.

That thought was like ice to my veins. Cold and sharp. It

wasn't fair of me to liken him to Mia. He treated me better than she did.

He loved me.

'Sure, babe.' Scott kissed my forehead. 'If you say so.'

It was an affectionate move he did all the time. A little kiss to show he cared. But this time it felt different. Disbelieving. Condescending.

I didn't like it.

And yet, he hadn't actually done anything wrong. Had he?

I pulled away and opened the van door.

'Sorry,' he said behind me. 'I never asked about your parents before as I got the feeling you didn't want to talk about them. I shouldn't have asked you now either.'

Remorse oozed from his voice. I'd made him feel bad.

A familiar sense of guilt descended around me. I always made people feel bad. So bad that it hurt them to look at me. To be around me.

I couldn't let that happen with Scott too.

'It's fine,' I assured him a little too brightly. 'I'm fine.'

The lie jarred against me. I wasn't fine. I hadn't been for a long time.

'Yeah,' he agreed. 'You are so strong. Much stronger than you realise.'

I studied him curiously. He really believed that. He had no idea how much I struggled. But then that was my goal.

My life was a pretence now. A well-rehearsed performance to mask the person I truly was. Perhaps it was selfish. To hide the real me. To deceive. But what was the alternative?

A chill spread through my body. I already knew the answer to that. I'd lived it before.

Scott slipped his hand in mine, our fingers automatically entwining. I didn't deserve him either. I didn't deserve his comfort. His love. Every part of me knew it. Knew that I should walk away. I should do it for him.

But I couldn't.

My fingers tightened around his as I clung to him, never wanting to let go. I might not deserve his love, but I craved it.

I let him pivot me around and we perched on the edge of the van surrounded by flowers.

'We were on holiday in Bournemouth at the time. Mum grew up in a flat not far from the beach and she inherited it from her mum when she died. We used it as a holiday home. Every sunny weekend. Every school holiday. It was perfect.'

Scott sat silently beside me giving me space. And yet somehow it also felt like an expectation. He was waiting for the rest of the story.

'She wasn't feeling well the one day. She stayed home to rest. We thought it was just a bug and she'd be fine. But...' My voice cracked. 'She wasn't fine.'

'I'm so sorry.' I tried not to flinch at the word. More pity. More sorrow.

'Dad—' I cleared my throat '—never got over it.'

'What did you mean, "especially with you"?'

'Huh?' I feigned ignorance.

'You said earlier that your dad was different, especially with you.'

I squirmed awkwardly. Apparently Scott wasn't going to let me escape that question.

I lowered my gaze, as I chose my next words carefully. 'Mia and I are identical twins, but only in our appearances. In every other way we are complete opposites. Mia has Dad's confidence and sense of adventure, whereas I'm like Mum. Quiet, shy, sentimental. But I guess after she died, our similarities meant that I was a reminder of her. Of what had happened. One Dad couldn't bear to face every day.'

I felt a heaviness descend upon me. Every word I had said was the truth. And yet, it wasn't the whole truth. It was deceptive in its incompleteness.

'That sounds so hard.'

I scoffed. 'It was torturous for him.' I understood. I felt the same way about myself, except for me there was no escape. I was trapped with my own company. My own thoughts. My own memories.

'I meant it must have been hard for *you*.'

'Oh.' I blinked. A warm glow emanated deep within me. His concern was for me. No one else, just me.

And he was right. Understated, but right. Hard didn't even begin to describe how it had been to live without Mum. But then it hadn't really been living. Just existing.

'Mum's death seemed to bring Dad and Mia even closer together. They became this tight-knit little duo, and I just didn't seem to fit any more.'

It had simply been a matter of surviving one day to the next. Going through the motions of going to school, eating, sleeping and then repeating it all again. It was pointless. Empty. And agonisingly endless.

'I had to get away. To make a change.' My gaze drifted around the park and beyond. 'So I moved here. London was so vast, and I just wanted to get swept up in the noise and busyness of it.'

I let out a deep sigh. 'I thought Dad would object.' I frowned. 'Or maybe I hoped he'd object. He'd always wanted Mia and I to go to university. Build solid careers for ourselves. But he never said a word. I went home to visit a few times a year, still hoping things would change. That he would accept me. Eventually I barely went home at all.' I watched a little girl squealing with laughter as her dad pushed her on the swings. 'I guess part of me secretly hoped that he'd miss me when I wasn't there. That he'd come after me and bring me home. That he'd tell me I belonged there. With him.'

I glanced at Scott and saw pity etched into his features as he stared at me. Perhaps I had been too melodramatic. Too emotional. I shouldn't have revealed that. I'd said too much.

'I've never told anyone that before. Not even Mia,' I admitted quietly as I lowered my gaze back to my hands in my lap. 'Besides, it's irrelevant. Dad's gone now too, so...'

I shrugged as though the finality of knowing his acceptance would never happen didn't matter. But it did. At least when he'd been alive there had been a possibility. Albeit an unlikely one.

Scott reached out and covered my hands with his, as though he wanted to protect them. Protect me.

Except it was too late for that.

'No wonder you're lonely.'

My head jolted up and I stared at him. 'I didn't say I was lonely.'

Scott smiled slightly. 'I've known it from the moment I met you.'

A rumble of thunder silenced my words and we both looked upwards at the darkening sky.

I flinched as raindrops landed on my cheek and I leapt to my feet. 'Come on, before we get soaked.'

Scott helped me pack everything in the van in silence. My revelations had made the mood sombre. I didn't want that. I wanted fun and laughter. I wanted distraction from the past. From the guilt that still weighed heavily on me.

Maybe it was a good thing that the storm was starting now. It had saved me from telling him any more. From telling him the things that there would be no coming back from. Not for me. Not for us.

7

NOW

October

The elevator pinged as it arrived on the fourth floor. I stepped out slowly and glanced up and down the short corridor, checking the numbers on the doors. I turned to face the door at the end. This was it. I was here.

I rummaged in the bottom of my Gucci handbag and fished out a set of keys. I stared at them, mesmerised by the magnitude of what they represented, as they dangled from my fingers. They had unexpectedly become more precious than anything I had ever owned in my life.

I slid the key into the lock of the flat and pushed the door open, stepping in apprehensively. It felt strange, as though I was trespassing in someone else's home.

You are.

I shook my head. No, it wasn't like that, I told myself as I closed the door behind me with more force than necessary. This was just how things had worked out.

And now, the flat was mine.

I set the keys down on the table by the door, disrupting the thin layer of dust that coated the surface. I left the suitcase in the hall and edged further into the flat. Tingles of familiarity prickled my skin.

I pushed the bedroom door open and peered in, surveying the master bedroom. The walls were decorated with nautical-themed pictures and the large window opened out onto a balcony with a partial sea view. I sucked in a deep breath. It was so different from the plain whitewashed walls and mini-malist furnishings that I remembered from the last time I was here.

It was one of the things I'd always hated about this flat. The stark emptiness of it. It had jarred against the homely cosy flat that we'd had before. That flat had been filled with Mum's deli-cate tasteful touches, family heirlooms and precious memories. Whereas the absence of her presence had always been notice-able here.

But then, like Dad said, that was exactly the point.

A colourful collection of Elemis lotions and OPI nail varnishes lined the far edge of the dressing table beside a small mirror. They were Mia's favourites.

My gaze darted around the room again. It wasn't just Mum's presence that was absent here. It was Dad's too.

I knew Mia had spent a few days in the flat after Dad's funeral in March, but she'd been in Rome since then. That meant she must have cleared Dad's stuff out straight away. I folded my arms across my stomach as I hunched forwards. She'd eradicated every trace of him. Just like they had done with Mum.

The flat was clearly Mia's now.

Dad and I might have spent the last twelve years as virtual strangers, but he still deserved better than that. They both did.

I walked towards the mirrored wardrobe and lifted my hand,

pressing my fingers to the edge of the sliding door. I froze as the unfamiliar reflection caught my attention.

It was me and yet it wasn't.

The wrong clothes. The wrong hairstyle. Even the wrong make-up. But all of it was required now. My choices were no longer mine to make. They were defined by her.

I let out a weary sigh as I realised that to a degree they always had been.

My fingers lingered against the wardrobe door. It felt wrong to open it. To snoop inside something that didn't belong to me. And yet, it should have felt freeing. A levelling up of twenty-four years of imbalance where she had taken whatever she'd wanted from me.

I pivoted on my heel, turning my back on my reflection and resumed my exploration. I opened the door to a second bedroom and memories collided into me.

This had been our room.

Our single beds that had once lined the opposite sides of the room, marking our territories, had been replaced with a double bed. The posters of Taylor Swift, who we'd both desperately wanted to be, were gone too. Our continued love of her music was one of the few things we still had in common. I studied the pictures that had replaced the posters. More subtle nautical images. Our bedroom felt more like a show home now, just like the rest of the flat always had been.

It wasn't just Mum who'd been erased here. It was everything. Including me.

I slammed the door closed. This was going to be even harder than I'd anticipated.

And yet, perhaps there was a way to put my own stamp on it now. A few subtle touches that no one else would notice as being out of place, but would make it feel more like Mum's flat had. More like a home.

The living room lay at the end of the hall. My pace slowed as I approached. There had never been any doubt about the attraction of this flat, the view from the main window was just as spectacular now as it had been back then.

What would Mum have thought of it if she'd ever got to see it? It was the question that had tormented me for fifteen years.

The window opened out onto a larger balcony and the view was even more impressive than the first. Miles of sandy beach stretched out to Hengistbury Head in the distance. It was stunning. The kind of place that dreams were made of.

Or at least other people's dreams.

I tipped my head to the left. The beach seemed bigger than I remembered. I lowered my eyes and the long row of beach huts lining the promenade below caught my attention. There had been one good thing about our move to this flat. It had brought me closer to Aaron.

At least for a little while.

I counted along the row of huts. One. Two. Three. Four. I stopped and frowned as my gaze settled on what should have been the familiar rooftop of the beach hut Aaron's family owned, but was now a sheet of blue plastic. It was another reminder that everything changed.

I turned my back on the view and the memories it brought with it, and focused my attention on the living room. Two small turquoise sofas faced the TV and a glass dining room table with cream chairs was tucked into an alcove. To my right lay a tiny kitchen, which could be crossed in about two strides, but it was all I needed.

With my exploration complete I suddenly felt lost. It was done. I was here. Starting my new life.

Except, how was I really supposed to do that?

Make yourself useful, the voice in my head instructed and I nodded slowly. It was the first helpful thing it had said in days. I knew how to be useful. Productive. Organised.

I marched to the kitchen and rummaged in the cupboards, searching for cleaning supplies. I pulled out a couple of disposable cloths and an almost empty bottle of disinfectant. But it was enough. In fact, right now it was exactly what I needed.

I turned the tap on and heard the boiler kick in. I let the water run to heat up before realising I was still wearing my leather jacket. I shrugged it off, threw it over the back of one of the sofas in the living room, peeled off the boots from hell, and returned to the kitchen in my socks.

I grabbed a bucket from the cupboard, and positioned it in the sink as I squirted in a generous amount of disinfectant and filled it with water. I turned the tap off and the flat fell silent.

An eerie sense of isolation washed over me. I never used to mind the quiet, but now...

I peered over my shoulder at the empty living room behind me as I listened to the silence. Until recently, I'd lived alone for years. It had never bothered me before. I liked the space. The freedom. Perhaps that was the problem. I wasn't really free. Not now. I was on borrowed time.

My move here was just an illusion of escape. I was trapped in the lie that I had made.

I grabbed my phone and tapped the Apple Music icon. I opened the playlists and froze as the title of a playlist jumped out at me.

Chloe & Mia.

We'd made that list together. It was filled with songs that had been the soundtrack to our lives. Mia's favourite boyband in our teenage years. A reminder of gigs in our early twenties. The breakup songs she'd cried to. And the party anthems she'd played too loud as she danced without caring how stupid she looked.

It was all there. Preserved like a time capsule. One of the few surviving mementos of our lives together. The good parts at least.

I was surprised that Mia had gone along with making it in the first place, let alone kept it for all these years. She'd never really been the sentimental type.

Especially when it came to me. My finger hovered over it. It was so tempting to hit play and allow myself to step back in time. But I didn't. I couldn't.

Instead, I scrolled down the list and selected one entitled 'pop'. It was innocuous. It lacked any connection and yet somehow that was both its appeal and its disappointment.

I sighed and hit play. It was better than the silence.

I perched the phone on the worktop as Pink's 'Never Not Gonna Dance Again' filled the tiny kitchen. I nodded my head in sync with the fast-paced rhythm and focused on the lyrics as I dipped a cloth in the bucket of water. I winced at the steaming heat. It's fine, I told myself as I started scrubbing the worktop, even though it didn't look dirty. Everything was fine.

I just needed to wipe away every invisible trace of Mia. I needed to make the flat feel like mine. To feel like home. But at the same time, I knew that it wouldn't. It couldn't.

Perhaps nowhere could now. Especially somewhere that I wasn't supposed to be.

8

THEN

September

'Welcome home.' I grinned at Mia across the table as we clinked our wine glasses together.

'You say that every time I get back.'

I laughed. 'Of course I do. I'm always delighted to have my sister back home.' Or at least, part of me was delighted.

'You know I don't actually *live* here, right?' Mia asked, arching her eyebrow.

I took a sip of wine and shrugged. 'London's still home. Or as close to it as either of us have, anyway.' Perhaps it had been the wrong thing to say. To remind her, remind us, of everything we didn't have. Everything we had lost.

'I have my flat in Bournemouth.'

My flat.

I tried to hide my grimace as I pressed my glass back to my lips.

'Oh, you're not still upset about that, are you?' There was an impatience to Mia's tone as though I should be over it by now. But how could I be?

'It was our family holiday home,' I reminded her.

'That you hadn't visited in years. Dad knew how much you hated Bournemouth, so it made perfect sense for him to leave the flat to me.'

I scoffed. 'Dad didn't know anything about me. He didn't want to.'

'You're the one who left,' Mia reminded me.

'What choice did I have? He treated me as though I'd ceased to exist long before I walked out that door. I just—' my voice caught in my throat '—hoped one day he'd want me in his life again.' I choked back a sob. 'His death was so sudden; I didn't even get chance to say goodbye.'

Mia lowered her gaze and stared at the table between us. A familiar sense of guilt churned beneath my sadness. I shouldn't have mentioned Dad's death. Not to Mia. It had only been six months, not long enough for the pain of loss to even begin to heal.

I sniffed and shook my head, as I attempted to shake off the darkness that closed in around me any time I thought about the past. 'Besides,' I forced my voice to sound bright, as I tried to shift the conversation. 'I don't hate Bournemouth.'

'Riiight,' Mia dragged the word out, showing she didn't believe me.

'I don't,' I repeated. 'It's just kind of bittersweet to go back there without Mum. That was her place. She loved it so much.'

'That's why *I* go back every Christmas,' Mia said haughtily. 'Dad and I wanted to be close to her.'

'Really?' The word slipped from my lips in surprise. Mia's attachment to Bournemouth had never seemed to be about Mum, but more about the beach. Otherwise, surely she wouldn't have been so keen to sell Mum's cosy little flat and persuade Dad to buy the gorgeous new beachside apartment after her death. But what if I was wrong?

'Just because I'm not all depressed and moping, it doesn't mean I don't miss her.'

'No, of course not.' I shook my head. 'I didn't mean th—'

'I might not have been as close to Mum as you were. You were always her favourite. For all the good that did her.'

The wine glass trembled in my hand, and I set it down on the table, focusing all my attention on not spilling it as I tried not to allow my thoughts to slip back into regrets of the past. It was a dangerous path. All the things I wished I could change. The 'should have dones'. The 'if onlys'.

But it was too late for any of that. Mum was gone. And now Dad was too.

I looked up at Mia as the corner of her mouth twisted upwards. It was only a fraction, but I saw it. She'd wanted to hurt me. To lash out and remind me of my failings. She didn't realise that I didn't need her to do that. I managed it perfectly well all by myself.

I couldn't blame her, though. My mistake had cost us all. And Mum had been the one who'd paid the ultimate price.

Sometimes I wondered why Mia and I stayed in each other's lives. The only thing that united us was our loss.

We were the only family either of us had left.

It was just a shame we despised each other.

9

NOW

October

I stood in the centre of the living room. I'd run out of places to clean. It had been a distraction. But without it...

'What am I doing here?' I asked the empty flat.

Running away.

The familiar voice in my head answered. The worst part was, I knew it was right.

Dizziness blurred my vision as my breaths became quick and shallow. I staggered towards the balcony, tugged open the door and stepped outside.

'You can't heal in the place that broke you.'

Mum's words sprang into my head. Last time those words had driven me to leave Bournemouth, and yet now they had ended up bringing me back.

I was running away again.

I thought starting over in London had healed me. That I'd put the past behind me and moved on. But now I was back in Bournemouth, unable to ignore the memories that I'd tried so hard to push aside, I realised London had simply been a distraction. A place for me to bury myself in work and pretend I was okay.

But if I'd really been okay, I wouldn't have sought out Scott.

The irony was, Mum was the one person who would have understood.

* * *

'How come we live in Reading, and not here in Bournemouth near Grandma?' I asked, letting the cold salty water lap over my feet as Mum and I paddled along the shore.

'It's complicated,' Mum said, with a small shake of her head.

'You mean, I'm too young to understand,' I objected with a pout. 'I'm not a little kid any more, Mum.'

Mum chuckled. 'I see, now you've turned twelve, you're all grown up, are you?'

I sighed and put my hands on my hips. 'I'm almost a teenager.'

'Oh, honey.' Mum pulled me to her and hugged me tightly. 'Don't be in such a rush to grow up. Have fun being a kid while you can.'

I tipped my head back and peered up at her. 'I can be grown up and still have fun, can't I?'

Mum chuckled again as she held her hands up in the air. 'I give up.'

I smiled triumphantly. 'So does that mean you'll tell me?'

Her smile withered away, and she nodded mutely. 'I was only a teenager when I lost my dad. It—' Her voice cracked and she took a deep breath as she started walking again. 'It was too painful to stay here, living each day in the places we used to go together,' she continued as I fell into step beside her and slipped my hand in hers. 'As soon as I was old enough, I moved away.'

'But you left Grandma here? Alone?' I stared at her stunned. She'd abandoned her.

'*She understood.*' Mum's voice was firm, but her grip tightened as she clung to my hand.

I let out a deep breath. Mum's reaction had confused me as a child, but I understood it now. She'd needed to believe she'd done the right thing, that her mum truly had understood and supported her decision. And yet, part of her felt just as I had done at twelve, that she had abandoned her family.

I'd judged her for that. I'd seen her as fallible for the first time. Perhaps it was a natural part of growing up, that the childish idolisation of a parent dimmed over time. Back then I had no idea that in a few short years I would do exactly the same thing.

I inhaled deeply, letting the salty sea air fill my lungs. The sad part, I realised now, though, was I wasn't sure it had worked for either of us.

'*Your grandma asked me to consider moving back when you girls were born.*' Mum's voice was so quiet I wasn't sure if I was really supposed to hear. '*She wanted to be a bigger part of your lives, but she couldn't bear to leave Bournemouth and move closer to us. The flat was a link to Grandpa. It was their home.*' Mum swallowed. '*But I refused,*' she said almost apologetically. '*Spending our summers here had been a compromise.*'

* * *

I wondered now if either of them had truly been happy with that arrangement.

Staying away involved guilt. Coming back involved painful memories. It didn't seem as though either was easier to live with.

Of course there was one fundamental difference. Mum hadn't been responsible for the grief that engulfed her. Unlike me, she hadn't caused someone's death.

10

THEN

September

I glanced around the noisy hotel bar. 'You know, you could have stayed with me?' I told Mia, desperate to shift the conversation away from Bournemouth and on to something safer.

And this *was* safer. Because no matter how many times I offered, I knew she would never actually take me up on my invitation.

Mia screwed her nose up. 'And play third wheel to you and your new boyfriend? No, thanks, that's not my style.'

'He's not that new any more,' I said, grinning. 'We've been together almost three months now.'

'It's going well, then?' Mia smiled tightly, and I squinted as I tried to read her expression. Her tone still sounded light and upbeat as though she was happy for me. And yet there was something else, something beneath the surface.

'Very,' I replied firmly. I was being ridiculous. It wasn't as though Mia would be envious of my relationship. She was adamant that she wasn't going to settle for anyone. And the trail of short-lived relationships she left in her wake were proof she meant it.

'Does that mean I'll get to know his name at some point?'

'You mean you've forgotten it.' My voice was brittle. It wasn't surprising and yet, it still hurt.

Mia froze. 'Wait, have you already told it to me?'

I arched my eyebrows.

'Okay, I'm taking that as a yes. Give me a hint, what letter does it start with?'

'S.'

'Simon?'

I rolled my eyes.

'Steve?'

I sucked in a deep breath. 'Are you seriously just going to go through every name starting with S?' I tried to keep the frustration out of my voice. But she was my sister. She was supposed to pay attention and remember the things that were important to me. Just like I did for her.

But then our relationship had always been unbalanced.

'Not every name.' Mia grinned mischievously. 'I know he's a guy so that narrows the list a little bit.'

I groaned as my frustration stated to ebb away. It was always hard to stay mad at Mia for long. At least outwardly.

'Oh, come on. You know I'm bad at names. I can barely remember the names of the guys *I've* dated, let alone someone else's.'

I laughed. 'To be fair, that is kind of a long list.' But even though I was laughing, there was still a heaviness in my chest. 'Okay, okay. I'll let you off,' I said, holding my hands up in surrender.

Just like I always did.

Mia's radiant smile beamed at me with satisfaction. 'Seriously, though. I might be rubbish on some details, but you can count on me when it matters. You know that.' Mia's smile wavered. 'Don't you?'

There was a hesitancy to her question that lacked her usual confidence and certainty.

I nodded firmly. 'Yeah, I know.' Except I couldn't help but notice she still hadn't asked Scott's name. 'Well, anyway, my point was that you're always welcome to stay with me if you ever want to. It would be good to have you around.'

I debated the truth of my words. Good wasn't really a word that applied to how it felt to be in close proximity to Mia. And yet, I still needed to be. Still hoped that this time would be different. That we would connect. That she would… I swallowed. That she would like me.

'I *am* around.'

I twizzled my wine glass on the table. Grudgingly I had to admit that she was right. She was back in London for the first time in months. And yet…

'It's not the same,' I muttered, aware that my voice sounded small and lost.

Mia laughed. 'I'm in Hammersmith, Chloe. Your house is like ten minutes' walk from here. I can practically see it from my room.'

I lifted my head, and my eyes met hers. 'But—'

'Honestly,' she cut me off. 'I'm fine in the hotel.'

My objection withered on my lips. She thought my concern was for her being stuck in a hotel.

I shifted awkwardly in my chair. If I was honest with myself, my invitation for her to stay with me wasn't really for Mia's benefit at all. It wasn't even as though I particularly wanted her to stay with me. But something deep inside me told me that her acceptance would have meant everything.

'You spend too much time in hotels,' I said, refocusing my attention on Mia's well-being like a good sister should.

'I'm used to it.'

I shook my head. 'That's what worries me.'

I waited for Mia to brush my concerns aside with her usual breeziness. But she didn't say anything, she just studied her wine glass with far more attention than it deserved.

Her silence was unfamiliar. Perhaps she was tired of my judgement. She didn't need me constantly nagging at her.

'Sorry,' I said. 'I know you love being an interpreter, and the lifestyle that comes with it.' I slumped in my chair; it was time that I learnt to accept that just because it wasn't the same as mine that didn't give me the right to criticise it.

'I'm not sure that I do,' Mia mumbled into her glass.

'What?' I stared at her. I couldn't have heard right. It wasn't possible. Mia loved her life. She loved the travel. The adventure.

'I'm not sure it's for me,' she said more loudly. But there was still a hesitation to her voice. 'Not any more.'

'But...' I stared at her. 'What would you do instead?' Beneath my surprise, excitement bubbled. I almost didn't even care what her answer was. It didn't matter. As long as whatever she chose to do involved staying here. Staying close.

Choosing me.

I hated the paradox of emotions that Mia always brought with her. I wanted to be able to cling on to my resentment of her. That anger made me stronger. And yet, beneath it, there was a big part of me that wanted her in my life. She was my family. My sister. No bond was stronger than that.

If Mia was around more then maybe, just maybe, we could fix what was broken between us. We could learn to like each other again. To support each other.

And yet, at the same time, I knew how disastrous it could be.

Mia shrugged helplessly. 'I have no idea.'

'Wow.' I flopped back in the chair.

She chuckled ruefully. 'Yeah, wow.'

'I guess I just can't picture you without your jet set lifestyle.'

Mia frowned. 'Aren't you the one that's always telling me not to leave it too late to settle down?'

'Well, yeah, but I didn't think you'd actually listen to me. You never have before.' I winced as soon as the words left my mouth. They had been too blunt. I was usually more careful. More tactful.

She rolled her eyes. 'Well, maybe it's about time I started listening to you, then.'

Our eyes met and we both laughed.

'Geez, that's a scary thought,' Mia said, and I nodded.

'It completely goes against twenty-four years of sibling rivalry.'

Mia cringed. 'Don't get too used to it.'

I shook my head. I wouldn't. I knew better than that. No matter how much I longed for this outward display of a friendly, sisterly relationship to be real, it was only surface level. At least for now.

I knew what lay beneath.

The question was, would Mia ever allow me to forget it?

'I'm bored of this place,' Mia announced suddenly. 'Let's go somewhere else.'

'Er, okay. Sure.' I nodded as though I was ready to move on too. But the truth was I'd been perfectly content and comfortable exactly where I was.

I gulped down the last remnants of my wine. I should be used to Mia's abrupt changes by now. I liked plans and consistency, whereas Mia was impulsive and indecisive.

It was destabilising and I felt as though I never quite knew where I stood.

But then, perhaps that was the point.

She picked up her Gucci bag that was hanging on the back of her chair. 'Oh.' Her shoulders slumped. 'I left my jacket in my room.'

I reached for my purse. 'Do you want to go—'

'Here.' Mia cut through my words as she pulled out her credit card and dropped it on the table in front of me. 'You take care of the bill while I run back upstairs. My PIN's still the same.'

'Sure, but I can use my—' I started to say as I held my own credit card up.

Mia rolled her eyes. 'Put that away. You're with me.'

There was an edge to her voice that I knew better than to argue with. 'Thanks,' I said, as I slid my card back into my bag obediently. 'I appreciate it.'

This was how it worked when we were together. Mia always paid. And I always cooed over her, grateful for her generosity.

And yet, something inside me told me it wasn't about generosity. It was about reminding me who was in control.

11

NOW

October

I retreated from the balcony and paced the living room, desperate for movement. Stillness was my enemy and meant I had time to think. And thinking always led back to the past.

But it wasn't just my childhood that I had regrets about now. It was the recent past too. So recent that it was still raw, the wounds fresh.

It's too late for regrets.

I snorted. That pesky voice was right again. And yet, I was good at regrets. I collected them like Mum and I used to collect seashells on the beach. They served no purpose, other than to act as a reminder of what might have been. But I couldn't discard them. I kept hold of them, pulling them out from time to time to examine them, before packing them away again as best as I could.

But their presence was always with me. Always making me wonder.

I vowed to be better. But I wasn't.

It was only later that I started to question. Started to have doubts. What if I'd done things differently? What if I'd been more patient? What if I'd been stronger?

Now I had another regret to add to the collection.

Mia.

But this one was bigger, more prominent. Not because she had mattered more. Not because her loss was felt more sharply. But because I should have known better. Once was a mistake. But twice...?

Twice was a problem.

I puffed out my cheeks and let out a long slow breath, as though hoping to dispel the memories.

It didn't work.

It never worked.

My solution back home would have been simple. I'd pull on my trainers and head to the park. A walk always cleared my head and calmed my nerves.

But here...

I peered out of the window. Frustratingly, I had to admit the promenade along the beach would be perfect for a long walk. Flat and spacious. It was ideal.

I'd hoped that enough time had passed for things to be different now. That being back here would be easier than I'd thought. It wasn't.

If I'd had another place to go, I would have done. Even now it was tempting to call a taxi and leave immediately.

But this town, this apartment, could give me the one thing I needed most of all right now. Time. Time to lay low and regroup. Time to make a new plan. To decide where I wanted to be. What I wanted to do.

My foot tapped as though my body was impatient. Maybe a walk on the promenade was worth a try. After all, it wasn't as though I could ignore the fact I was back in Bournemouth. I'd tried that since I'd arrived, and I was failing miserably.

I glanced at my watch. It was already 4 p.m. There wouldn't be time for a long walk today before the sun set. But it would have to do.

Retrieving the suitcase from where I had abandoned it in the hall, I dragged it towards the master bedroom. I paused outside the door before veering to the left and stepping into the guest room. At least that room had once been partially mine.

I hoisted the case up onto the bed and my fingers automatically spun the dials of the lock. I slid the catch, and the zips released with a satisfying clunk. I paused for a moment, sucking in a deep breath before dragging the zips around the case and flipping it open.

I ran my fingers across the neatly folded designer clothes, knowing that I really ought to hang them up. But instead, I rummaged beneath them and pulled out the practically brand-new Nike Air Max trainers from the case. They weren't my usual choice, but then what about my life these days was? I shoved my feet into the shoes, grabbed the leather jacket from the back of the sofa, marched to the hall and strode out into the corridor. My eagerness to be out, to be moving, carried me with a momentum that to anyone else would have looked like eagerness to go to the beach.

Once outside I sucked in deep breaths of fresh salty air. Ahead of me lay the driveway and the security office. The idea of passing it again didn't appeal. The guard had been friendly and welcoming, but I wasn't really in the mood for making small talk. What if he asked what had brought me here?

I would have to lie.

Again.

12

THEN

September

My pace slowed as I approached the basketball court and I lingered at the edge beside a heap of bags. I smiled as Scott skilfully weaved between two heavier-set guys and took a shot. He whooped and punched the air as the ball flew perfectly through the net. Suddenly he was surrounded by exuberant teammates, all cheering as they slapped him on the back. It seemed I had arrived just in time to witness the winning shot.

The circle around him started to dissipate and as Scott turned, his eyes met mine. 'Chloe!' He sprinted towards me. 'Did you see that?'

I stepped back, avoiding Scott's arms as he reached out to hug me. 'You're all sweaty,' I objected with a squeal.

Scott laughed. 'Sorry, I forgot about that. But did you see?'

I grinned. 'I did. That was an impressive shot.'

He beamed at me full of pride.

'I'm glad I was here to see it,' I said sincerely. There was something so special about sharing moments like this. Small but important.

'Me too,' Scott said, but then his brow wrinkled. 'But why are you here? You don't open the stall on Sundays.'

'Oh, I—' I shuffled as I remembered I'd intended to be more discreet with my stalking. This was his time with his friends, how would he feel about me encroaching? 'I was just doing some shopping on the high street.' I held up my Primark bag as proof. 'I decided to walk home through the park. And then I spotted you and...' My words trailed off, but Scott didn't seem to notice.

'Cool,' he said with a nod.

I smiled. My presence had been accepted. Not that there was any reason why it shouldn't be. I was simply walking home. The fact that I'd gone shopping purely so I *could* walk home through the park where I spent almost every other day working was irrelevant.

I swallowed.

Wasn't it?

I was just being interested in Scott's life. His life outside of the time we spent together.

'Hey, how did it go with your sister last night?' Scott asked me suddenly.

I smiled, touched that he'd remembered. It seemed he was interested in my life outside of the time we were together too. 'Good, thanks.'

'Are you sure?' Scott asked, looking at me inquisitively. 'You sounded rather hesitant about that.'

I shook my head. 'No, it was good. Really good, actually. Mia's thinking of making some changes. She says she wants to be more settled and travel less.'

'That's great. So you'll be able to see her more often, then.'

I glanced at Scott; his tone sounded almost as apprehensive

as I felt. I knew what was behind my doubts. But what was behind his?

'Yeah, hopefully.' I nibbled my lip. I did want to see her more often, didn't I? Despite our differences she was my sister. There was a bond there that couldn't be denied. I'd tried. It had never worked. I needed her in my life.

Unfortunately.

I let out a deep sigh. It might all be irrelevant anyway. 'Mia didn't say *where* she was thinking of settling down.'

'You're afraid it won't be in London?' Scott asked.

'I'm afraid it won't even be in the UK.'

'Ah.' Scott nodded with understanding and his shoulders relaxed.

I frowned. That felt an odd reaction, almost as though he was relieved. But that didn't make sense. Whether Mia stayed or left it didn't make any difference to him, to us. Only to me.

Then again, my feelings were so confused, perhaps I was deflecting my anxieties on to him.

'Yeah.' I scrunched my nose. 'It's just with all the amazing places Mia has visited over the years, I'm not sure where she'll end up. It might be that I see her even less than I do now.'

Scott reached for my hand. It was incredible how his touch, even when disgustingly sweaty, made me feel stronger.

'You know, whatever happens with Mia, you're not alone. You have me now.'

I nodded firmly as I blinked rapidly, determined to hold back the tears that threatened to form at the magnitude of that declaration. I wasn't alone any more.

Scott gave my hand a squeeze before letting go. 'And when we have kids—'

'Kids?' I stared at Scott as he grabbed a bag from the pile by my feet, pulled a towel from it and wiped his face.

He paused and peered over the top of the towel. 'Yeah. You do want kids, don't you?'

I nodded. 'Yes, I do, I just—'

'Don't know if you want them with me.' His hands fell to his sides and the towel draped along the dried soil as though it was too heavy for him to hold.

'No, that's not what I meant.' I shook my head adamantly. I'd be lying if I said I hadn't fantasised about it. The chance to be part of a family again.

But did I want it *yet*?

A few months together felt too soon to have those answers. It even felt too soon to be asking those questions. At least out loud.

'I've thought about the possibility of us having kids someday,' I admitted, lowering my gaze. It felt risky to share that confession. It was too soon. *Much* too soon.

And yet, I wasn't the one who'd raised the topic.

Scott's fingers stroked my skin as he lifted my chin. 'Someday is good.' He smiled and my heart pounded. Of course he wasn't trying to rush me. He was just sharing his hopes for the future.

For *our* future.

'Life is short, Chloe. It's important to know what we want and chase after it. And I want you, Chloe.'

I stared at him, stunned by his declarations. His certainty.

And yet, wasn't that what I was doing here in the first place? Chasing after what I wanted. A future with him.

A babble of voices pulled me from my thoughts as Scott's teammates crowded around us, retrieving their bags.

'Hi,' one of them said, grinning as he glanced from Scott to me and back again. 'So, are you going to introduce us?'

'Er...' Uncertainty clouded Scott's features and for the briefest moment I wondered if he was going to say no. 'Yes, sorry,' he said, smiling. 'Chloe, this is Ethan.'

Ethan wiped his hand on his shirt and reached out to shake mine. 'It's great to finally meet you, I've heard so much about you.'

'You have?' Heat crept into my cheeks. I felt at a disadvantage. Scott may have talked about me to Ethan, but he hadn't even mentioned Ethan's name to me. 'So, how do you two know each other?'

Ethan shot Scott a quizzical look.

'Ethan is my oldest and closest friend,' Scott announced, flinging his arm across his shoulders. 'I told you that, remember?' He grinned at me expectantly.

'R-right.' I nodded unconvincingly.

Scott's smile dimmed.

That wasn't good.

I slapped my hand to my forehead dramatically. 'Of course, how could I forget, you're the one who knows all of Scott's deep, dark secrets.'

Ethan laughed. Either he believed my pretence of a sudden recollection, or he was just amused by the prospect of getting to spill the beans about his best mate.

'Yeah.' Ethan winked at me. 'You and I should definitely talk.'

'Hey!' Scott objected as he gave Ethan a playful punch in the arm. 'Where's the loyalty here?'

His words were jovial, but I couldn't help but notice he looked a little pale.

'Right.' Ethan suddenly grew serious. 'The guys and I are heading off for post-game drinks, if you want to join us?'

'Absolutely,' Scott replied without hesitation. He turned back to me. 'You'll be okay on your own, right?'

I nodded automatically. 'Of course,' I replied in surprise. It felt like a strange question to ask. I was quite capable of being on my own. I'd had plenty of experience of it.

I shook that thought away. Scott was probably just being thoughtful and feeling bad that he was ditching me to hang out with the guys.

And yet, the fact remained that he was ditching me. He'd chosen *them* over *me*.

'Great.' Scott slung his bag over his shoulder and gave me a quick kiss on the cheek. 'Let's go, then,' he said to Ethan.

'It was good to meet you,' Ethan said, as they turned away.

I watched as they jogged after the rest of the guys who were already walking down the path to the pub. Part of me hoped Scott would glance back. But he didn't.

13

NOW

October

With a groan at the thought of another encounter with the helpful security guy, I turned to the left as I exited the pedestrian gate, grateful when my gaze fell upon a familiar path. My feet instinctively changed course down the slope that curved to the promenade.

I reached the bottom and stopped. I glanced left then right, my gaze following the miles of promenade that lined the sandy beach as I debated which way to go. As my gaze settled on the pier not far away on the right, I felt another sudden wave of familiarity.

Boscombe pier.

Mum had loved the pier, especially at sunset.

* * *

'What are you doing?' I asked as Mum clung to the railing, her shoulders rising and falling in the orange light as she sucked in deep

breaths of the salty sea air.

'Making a memory,' she said with a smile. 'Here, you try it.' She reached out her hand and guided me in front of her, cocooning me between her and the railing. 'Focus on the feel of the warmth of the sun on your face and the sound of the waves crashing against the pier below and let your gaze travel far out onto the horizon. Doesn't it feel as though you are almost part of it?'

'Part of what?' I asked, squinting as I stared obediently at the horizon, desperately trying to feel what I was supposed to.

'Everything,' Mum replied.

* * *

I found myself walking to the pier in a daze, drawn to it by some desperate need to occupy the same space, as though it would somehow enable me to step back into the past.

But then the pier hadn't just been special to Mum. I'd made other memories there too. Memories with someone who really had made me feel as though I was everything.

At least for a little while.

I lingered at the open gates but the warm sense of belonging I had felt back then was noticeably absent. And yet, despite my reluctance to be back in Bournemouth, now that I was here there was a strange calmness to it.

Slowly I walked along the pier as hues of orange filtered into the sky. The memories the sea brought in like the tide were from another era. The ghosts of the past were almost more tolerable than the new ones.

Almost.

Time had a way of dulling the sharpness, but never erasing it. Or perhaps it was just that I was used to that pain. I'd lived with it for more than half a lifetime. I was used to the weight of it. It was part of me. Part of who I'd become. In a way, I would have felt more lost now without it.

But there was no escape from the dead.

I approached the end of the pier and stopped in front of large chain-link fence panels that blocked my path. I peered through the gaps at the deserted pier. Pieces of the railing were missing on the left-hand side, and red and white tape was interwoven across the gap.

I scowled as I stepped back, assessing the fence that was preventing me from reaching Mum's favourite spot at the end of the pier.

Chloe would stay behind the fence and obey the rules. But if I was truly going to be Mia, then I needed to start embracing her philosophy of doing what she wanted regardless of the rules. I glanced behind me, before squeezing between the panels. That tiny insignificant action felt rebellious and I walked with renewed confidence to the end of the pier. Although I still had enough caution to stay to the right, away from the missing railings.

I reached the end of the pier and took a deep breath as I stared out at the horizon. It was vast and unending. I shivered in the cool late afternoon breeze. I was so small in comparison. So insignificant.

You are irrelevant.

I shook my head. No, I wasn't. I mattered.

But to who?

I froze. It was just a simple question. At one point in my life there would have been a list of people who I had mattered to. A short list. But the people on it had been important.

And now...

Tears trickled down my cheeks before falling into the salty

water below. There was no one left now. No one to matter to. No one to know me. To see me.

Not even Scott.

But then, not even he had really seen me. I was just a shadow. Present but unimportant.

If I wasn't here now, who would even notice? I peered over the railing at the frothy white water below as the waves broke against the pier. If I disappeared it wouldn't matter. The world would go on without me.

It already had.

14

THEN

September

'I'm taking you to lunch tomorrow,' Mia announced, the moment I answered her call.

I blinked. It was the first time I'd heard from her since we'd met for drinks a week ago, and yet her call sounded more like a demand rather than an invitation.

'Erm.' I searched my memory, trying to recall if I already had any plans for my Sunday. Not that it mattered. This was Mia. Everything could be cancelled for Mia.

'At 1 p.m. at that pub I like on the riverbank.'

'Sure,' I replied, even though my acceptance felt superfluous. Compliance was always easiest.

Although there was something I could do differently this time.

'I'll bring Scott.' My announcement stunned me. I hadn't asked for Mia's permission.

'Scott?'

I bristled silently at Mia's question.

'It'll be a great opportunity for you two to meet,' I said, as though I hadn't heard her question. I wouldn't let her know she'd hurt me. Not this time.

'Oh right, that guy you're seeing at the moment.'

At the moment.

My jaw tensed. There was something so dismissive, not just to Mia's words, but the tone as well. She still thought my relationship was temporary.

Or perhaps she hoped it would be.

Guilt stabbed at me the moment that thought occurred to me. I was being disloyal to my sister. And yet, it didn't diminish the certainty I felt that my thought was right.

Perhaps that was why she never remembered Scott's name. Not because she'd forgotten it. But because saying it out loud it made him more real. More important. Right now, she could dismiss him as 'that guy'. Trivial and fleeting.

'You don't mind calling the pub to make a reservation, do you?' Mia's authoritative voice interrupted my thoughts.

'Oh, er—'

'You know how busy I am.'

'Of course.' The words left my lips instinctively before I'd even registered what I was saying. Not that I minded making the reservation. But how busy could Mia really be, given she wasn't actually working right now?

But I was.

'Besides, I know how much you love organising things.'

I tipped my head to the left as I debated the meaning of her words. Part of me felt a tingle of pride. Mia trusted me to take control of the arrangements. And yet, somehow it felt like I was more of a PA than her sister.

My grip tightened on the phone in my hand. After all these years nothing had changed. Mia was still manipulating me. Playing on my need for her approval. Her acceptance.

What was even worse was that it still worked.

15

NOW

October

'Are you okay?'

I jumped at the voice behind me and swung around, my gaze darting down the isolated pier, an instinct to run overwhelming me. 'Sorry, I didn't mean to startle you.'

I hesitated. My body was still braced to run, but rational thought flickered in my brain.

That wasn't Scott's voice.

I turned to face the guy who'd spoken, my panic easing as our eyes met. I was safe here. Or more accurately, *Mia* was safe here.

No one would be looking for her. They had no reason to. She'd never been a threat to anyone.

Unlike me.

'Only no one's supposed to be down here and you just looked so...' His forehead creased as he squinted at me in the fading light. 'Mia?'

I blinked. I hadn't expected anyone to recognise me. Especially not here. Mia had never had time for the small, quiet pier.

She preferred to hang out at the beach or congregate with her friends around the kiosks, indulging in cheesy chips and ice creams.

But then I guess it had been a long time since we'd been here together. Maybe she'd changed.

I forced a smile on to my face; it was time to step back into my role again. 'Hi, how ar—' I squinted at the man who was still staring at me. 'Aaron?'

His eyebrows lifted as corners of his mouth turned upwards in a bemused smile. 'Yes?'

My mouth opened and closed, but I couldn't find my voice. It was him. It was really him. I'd never expected to see him again. And yet, here he was, right in front of me. 'It's, er, it's good to see you again,' I muttered finally.

He nodded as his smile became more natural. 'Yeah, you too.'

A rush of warmth flooded through my body, sending tingles to every part of me. He was happy to see me.

Flashes of the summers we'd spent together raced through my memory. Even our phone calls, video calls, emails and text messages held a special place in my heart. They'd kept our relationship strong during the long months of separation between the holidays that brought my family back to Bournemouth each year.

'It's all going to be okay, Chloe. We're in this together,' Aaron promised me as he held me tight. He drew back and gazed into my eyes. 'I'll always be here for you, even when we're miles apart.'

He'd been so sincere. I'd believed him wholeheartedly.

Until he dumped me for Mia.

And then just like that, the warm fuzzy feeling was gone. Because even now it wasn't really me he was happy to see at all.

It was Mia.

I swallowed, as I tried to push away the pain that realisation caused.

After all this time, his betrayal shouldn't matter to me. *He* shouldn't matter.

And yet, I knew he still did. Beneath the hurt and the anger, I still cared.

16

THEN

September

Scott's gaze darted from me to Mia and back again. 'That's incredible.'

Mia and I smiled at each other as we sat side by side opposite Scott in the busy pub. We were used to this reaction whenever we met someone who hadn't seen both of us before.

'Seriously,' Scott continued as he edged forwards in his chair, analysing us. 'You have the same colouring and the same brown eyes. Change your hairstyle and you would almost be indistinguishable.'

Almost.

There was always an almost.

'Except Mia's the pretty one,' I said with a shrug. I tried to act as though that detail didn't bother me. But it did. It always had.

It was hard to pinpoint it. Our features were practically indistinguishable. The same shape of our faces. The same accentuation of our cheek bones. The same noses that we had inherited from Mum.

We looked so similar and yet at the same time we were so different. Like the before and after of a makeover. But it didn't matter what make-up I wore or how precisely I replicated her smile, her poise; there was always something missing.

I wasn't her.

I never could be. No matter how much I wanted to be.

She dug me in the ribs with her elbow. 'That's not true, is it, Scott?'

We both turned to face him.

Scott shook his head slowly. 'You're both beautiful,' he said.

I frowned. Was it my imagination, or did his gaze linger on Mia just a second too long as he spoke?

'So, Chloe tells me you're an interpreter,' Scott said. 'That's amazing.'

'Mia speaks three languages,' I informed him proudly, grateful for the shift in conversation. 'French, Spanish and Italian.'

The awe in Scott's expression deepened as he shook his head in disbelief. 'You really are impressive.'

His words were like a wave of icy water washing over me. What was I doing? Mia didn't need my help to sound better than me. It was already clear that she was.

Mia shrugged. 'It's just a job.'

'Are you kidding?' Scott said. 'Not many people can speak multiple languages.'

'Certainly not Chloe,' Mia said with a chuckle. 'Languages really aren't her forte.' She leaned forwards closer to Scott. 'I think they all sound the same to her,' she whispered loudly, ensuring that I heard.

I bristled. I might not know enough to actually hold a conversation in another language, but I could tell them apart. Usually.

'We all have our strengths,' Scott said affectionately, and I smiled.

Scott didn't care if I couldn't speak another language. He and I communicated perfectly well in just one.

'*Tout le monde n'a pas l'oreille pour les langues*,' he added with a shrug.

My smile withered as I stared at him in disbelief. He'd spoken in French to her. I didn't even know he could speak French.

'Ah, *vous parlez français!*' Mia exclaimed in delight.

'*Juste un peu, et pas très bien*,' Scott replied with a chuckle.

My gaze shifted back and forth between them, as though I was watching a tennis match. What was happening here?

Mia shook her head. '*Vous êtes trop modeste. Votre accent est parfait.*'

I grasped for words that had a vague familiarity. Something about being modest and a perfect accent.

Tinges of red crept into Scott's cheeks and he lowered his gaze. But it didn't stop the wide grin that spread across his face. He was pleased. Flattered even. I might not understand all of their words, but I knew his body language. I knew him.

I wanted to join in. To say something impressive. To regain his attention. His approval. But I couldn't.

Tightness gripped my chest. I'd been here before. On the outskirts of conversations I couldn't understand. Mia had relished my ineptitude. She and Dad had chatted in French while I'd lingered on the sidelines. Not just of their conversations, but their lives too.

Once again, I cursed my inability to master other languages. I wasn't stupid. I'd had my own academic strengths. I knew that. And yet, this was the one that mattered. To Mia. To Dad. And now, it seemed, to Scott too.

But Scott's fluency in French wasn't the problem here. What counted was his loyalty. And right now, it seemed to be severely lacking.

I felt Mia shift beside me as she leaned towards Scott a little more. She was relishing his attention.

I dug my nails into the palms of my hands as I glared at Scott. He was letting me down. I'd thought he was different. That Mia wouldn't sway him. That I was the only one who held his attention. His love.

I could see now that introducing them had been a mistake. One I should have known not to make.

I frowned. If I was honest with myself, perhaps some part of me had always known. The part that wanted to test him. That wanted to disprove what I already knew. That wanted him to choose me.

After all, what better way to test him than with my twin. Especially when that was Mia. I'd never known a guy who wasn't interested in her. If he passed this test, then I'd know for sure that our relationship was solid.

Instead, jealousy rippled through me. It was a feeling that was so familiar to me now. But I still hadn't mastered how to handle it. I couldn't even blame Mia. Not really. It wasn't as though she'd tried to upstage me. It was unintentional. And yet, it was also inevitable.

Mia was always going to outshine me.

'But we mustn't be rude,' Mia said, turning her attention to me.

'True,' Scott agreed, chuckling softly. 'Poor Chloe will feel neglected.'

There was something about the way he said, 'poor Chloe', that grated against me. Perhaps he meant it to sound tender or concerned. But all I heard was him mocking me. Belittling me for my lack of ability to converse at their level.

I fought to keep my breathing steady. It felt like Scott was siding with Mia. Teasing me. Laughing at me. When he should have been defending me. Protecting me.

That's what he was supposed to do.

That's why I'd picked him.

Mia studied me with a broad grin, and I waited for the next dig. 'But we still love her anyway,' she said, her tone suddenly serious.

I waited for the insult that would follow. The punchline of the joke that I couldn't understand. But there was nothing.

'Of course we do,' Scott agreed, smiling at Mia.

I clung to their words. They loved me. Despite my failings, they loved me.

I frowned. So how come I felt so empty?

17

NOW

October

'Why didn't you let me know you were back?' Aaron asked as we stood on the pier with the sun fading in the distance. There was a twinge of hurt in his voice. It was a tone I knew well.

'I-I only arrived a few hours ago,' I stuttered as he enveloped me in a hug.

His arms felt strangely safe and familiar, and I found myself instinctively wrapping my arms around him as I breathed in his deep, musky scent.

'Ah, okay,' he said, stepping back, and I reluctantly let my arms fall back to my sides.

There was a familiarity to that as well. The sense of something missing. I'd felt that way when our hugs had ended.

I swallowed, as I searched for something to say. Anything to distract myself from the ache in my chest. 'I can't believe you're here.' I studied his face. We'd been eighteen the last time we'd seen each other. His skin was more tanned now, and fine lines appeared in the corners of his eyes when he smiled, but the years we'd been apart suddenly felt like no time at all.

Aaron frowned. 'Didn't we already have this conversation back in December when I first moved back to Bournemouth?'

December.

Aaron had been back almost a year.

'Right, yes.' I nodded a little too enthusiastically. 'Of course we did. That's not what I meant...' My words evaporated. It was exactly what I'd meant. I'd had no idea he was back in England, let alone in Bournemouth.

But Mia had known.

Why hadn't she mentioned it to me? It wasn't as though I was a threat to her. She'd already won that battle.

And as a consequence, Aaron had taken our planned trip without me.

* * *

'I can't believe we're actually doing this.' My voice trembled as I stared at the visa in my hands.

'If you're having second thoughts, we can postpone the trip,' Aaron said, his brow furrowed as he studied me uncertainly.

I shook my head. 'No, I don't want to postpone.'

'Are you sure? You know our parents would prefer if we waited a couple of years. They've always said we're too young to take a gap year before uni. And Australia is so far away...' Aaron's words trailed out.

Panic churned my stomach. What if his suggestion wasn't out of concern for me, but simply a way to back out himself. 'Don't you want to go?' I asked hesitantly.

I couldn't blame him if he'd changed his mind. Aaron had a life here. A university place waiting for him. Parents who would miss him. Whereas me... I swallowed. There was nothing here for me.

A gap year in Australia was my chance to get away. Start over. I'd be free from my memories and mistakes that lingered here. And perhaps best of all, I would finally be able to step out of Mia's shadow.

Aaron grabbed my hand and pulled me to him. 'Of course I want to go.' His voice was firm, full of certainty. 'We've been dreaming of this for years, ever since your mum told us about her gap year.'

I nodded, his embrace calming my racing heartbeat. 'I wish Mum could have been part of it. She'd have loved to help us plan the trip.'

Aaron drew back and lifted my chin, so our eyes met. 'She is part of it, Chloe.'

I blinked back the tears that threatened to fall. It was hard to believe within one short month everything had changed. I guess it wasn't the trip he was having doubts about. It was me.

'I, er...' I realised Aaron was staring at me and I fought to bring my thoughts back to the present. 'I was just out here reminiscing about Mum and the old days with you, and then—' I waved my hand at him '—there you are.'

'Ahh.' He nodded with understanding. 'I guess it must still be hard being here without her. I remember how much she loved it down here. Especially the pier.'

Warmth emanated from deep within me. He really did remember.

I nodded. 'It's why I never wanted to come back,' I admitted sadly.

'Really?' I heard the surprise in Aaron's voice. 'It was no secret that Chloe felt that way. After all that was why your dad changed his will. But you—'

I frowned. 'Changed his will?'

Aaron gazed at me uncertainly. 'To leave the flat to only you.'

'It wasn't always that way?'

Confusion furrowed Aaron's brow. 'Not until Chloe told him she didn't want it. I thought you knew that?'

My stomach lurched as I stared at him. 'I—' I stopped myself just in time. '*Chloe* never said she didn't want it.' A tremor vibrated through my body. 'She was just never given the option of it.' It was just another way Dad had cut me out of his life.

'But your dad told me she had.'

I drew back. His words were like a punch to my gut. Dad claimed I'd rejected the flat? Why would he do that? It didn't make any sense. It was him who'd abandoned me, not the other way around.

I shook my head. No, Aaron must have misunderstood. Or he was simply lying. 'Why would Dad talk to you about Chloe?' That didn't seem right. Both of them had done everything they could to avoid actually talking *to* me, so why would they talk *about* me?

'He spent a fair bit of time down here at the start of the year, before—' Aaron stopped abruptly, but we both knew the words he was trying to avoid.

Before he died.

Aaron swallowed. 'He'd stop and chat whenever he saw me. I always asked about you both.'

'Both?' I repeated the word, stunned. 'You asked about C-Chloe?'

'Of course I did.' Aaron looked so surprised that I'd asked that question. As though I should have known he would ask. That he would still care. But why would he?

I shook my head. Aaron's reasons didn't matter now. Dad was the priority here. What he'd done. What he'd said.

'What exactly did Dad tell you?' I demanded, carefully keeping my tone even.

'He said after his diagnosis, Chloe had gone to see him and...' Deep lines creased Aaron's forehead. 'Mia, are you okay?'

I heard his words, but they sounded muffled and far away. Somehow, I managed to nod my head mutely. But I wasn't okay. I was anything but.

What diagnosis? Dad's death had been sudden and unexpected. There hadn't been a chance to clear the air and make peace before he died.

Had there?

The air felt thick and heavy as my breathing became more and more laboured.

I'd certainly never been to see Dad to tell him I didn't want the flat, which meant... I shook my head. Surely not even Mia would do that.

Would she?

Fire raged inside me. I knew the answer to that. The past few weeks were evidence of how far Mia would go to beat me.

To break me.

It was who she was. Or at least, who she'd been.

I reached for the railing to steady myself, barely able to catch my breath as I realised one inescapable truth. I'd done worse to her.

Far worse.

'I'm sorry, I didn't mean to upset you bringing up your dad. I know how hard it was for you when he died.'

I nodded again. It had been hard. Hard to grieve for a father who'd long ago ceased to care that I existed. Who even in death had cut me out.

Except perhaps it hadn't really been him who'd cut me out at all.

18

THEN

September

I slid my hand across the table towards Scott. 'I'm so glad the two of you are finally meeting,' I said with exaggerated brightness. This was what I'd wanted, I reminded myself. The chance to show my successful relationship off to my sister. But at the same time, there was part of me that wanted to impress Scott too. The part that needed to feel as though I still had family who cared about me. That wanted him to believe it too. To believe I was lovable.

My hand lingered, empty and exposed in the centre of the table as I silently willed Scott to take it. Surely, he wouldn't leave me hanging there. Not in front of Mia.

'Me too,' Scott said, finally diverting his gaze from Mia. He blinked as he seemed to register my outreached hand and hurriedly grabbed it, almost knocking over his beer in the process.

I let out a relieved breath and turned to Mia with a beaming smile. 'Now you can see for yourself how good Scott and I are together?'

Our gazes locked and time seemed to slow under the intensity of her stare. Her expression was unreadable. Even to me.

And then suddenly she smiled.

'I'm thrilled you've finally met someone who makes you happy.'

There was a sugary sweetness to her words that felt as fake as my own smile.

'It's so important to find someone who can accept us as we are. Flaws and all,' Mia added with a wink.

Scott shook his head. 'Chloe doesn't have any flaws.' He squeezed my hand. 'She's perfect.'

My head jolted back, and I stared at him stunned.

Perfect.

Scott thought I was perfect.

I'd never been called perfect before. Not even when I was good. But the idea of it now was inconceivable. Especially when I was sitting right next to Mia. The same Mia, who until only a moment ago, Scott hadn't been able to take his eyes off.

'No one's perfect,' Mia said.

My stomach lurched. She was right, no one was perfect. I knew my imperfections. And so did she.

I waited for her to expand on her statement. It would be so easy for her to shatter the idolised image that Scott held of me.

I wouldn't blame her for doing so. Part of me even felt as though she should. Scott deserved to know the truth that I would never be able to tell him myself.

Scott shrugged. 'Maybe not, but Chloe's perfect for me.'

A weight lifted from me. Scott didn't expect me to be perfect. He understood I had flaws, just like everyone else. It didn't even matter to him what those flaws were.

'It *was* pretty special,' Scott said quietly. A glimmer of hope flickered inside me. I was winning him over.

'It was heroic and romantic,' I assured him and smiled at the tint of red that coloured his cheeks.

* * *

'Thanks, Pat,' I said as the barista handed me my coffee from the kiosk at the entrance to the park. I wrapped my hands around my take-out coffee cup, feeling the warmth seep into my fingers as I ambled the short distance back to my flower stall. I scrunched my nose as I examined the dark clouds overhead. It was hard to believe it was actually June.

Pat's coffee was the one thing I'd miss when I opened a proper store. Perhaps I'd buy myself one of those fancy coffee machines and make my own. It would be an investment given how much money I'd save each day. And the luxury of being able to sit inside in the warm and dry to drink it, would make it enjoyable regardless of whether it tasted as good.

I smiled as a familiar jogger passed me and nodded. Our tiny silent greeting was insignificant and irrelevant and yet at the same time it wasn't. It was an acknowledgement of my presence. I was accepted here.

Perhaps I'd miss more than just Pat's coffee after all.

The tantalising aroma of my coffee was too tempting to resist, and I pulled the plastic lid off, allowing the liquid to cool for a moment before taking a tentative sip.

Footsteps pounded against the path behind me. I knew that sound. Another early morning jogger. I moved to the side of the path, to let them past. I'd never seen the appeal of running, especially on a Saturday, but I had to admire the determination of those who did it.

I turned my head as they drew near, ready to smile my usual greeting. But my brow creased as I caught sight of him. A teenager dressed in jeans and a dark jacket; he didn't look like he was out for a Saturday morning jog.

Our gazes met and, in that instant, he charged at me, his hand outstretched. My eyes widened as the scream that built inside me caught in my throat.

I felt a tug on my shoulder as his hand grabbed the strap of my bag. Instinctively I jerked my hand up to stop him, sending my cup of coffee flying.

'Argh!' His hand fell from my bag as the hot liquid splashed across his face. He staggered backward, his hand pressed to his cheek.

'Hey!' I heard the cry ahead of me and saw a guy sprinting towards us. 'Get away from her!'

My feet sprang into action as I broke into a run towards him, my hand gripping the strap of my bag as it swung on my shoulder. I shot a glance behind me, checking to see if the teenager would follow. He seemed to hesitate for a second, before fleeing in the other direction across the park.

'Are you okay?' the guy asked as he grew closer. 'Did he hurt you?'

My pace slowed to a halt as we met. 'No, I'm fine.' But my voice trembled, casting doubt upon my reply.

He reached out, his fingers resting upon my arm. 'Are you sure?'

I took a shaky breath. 'Yeah, I'm just...' My words trailed away.

'It's okay, you're safe now,' he said reassuringly.

I fought back the smile that tugged at the edges of my mouth. This wasn't the time.

'I'm a police officer,' he added.

'You are?' I asked, as though I didn't already know. He might not remember me, but I remembered him.

'PC Scott Barnes,' he said as he pulled his ID from his pocket.

Scott.

I turned away and stared at the retreating back of the teenager. 'He got away,' I stated flatly. Scott pulled his phone from his pocket and tapped on the screen. 'I'll call it in to the station. Did you get a good look at him?'

'Erm...' I hesitated. 'He was a teenager, I think. But...'

'It's okay,' he said before pressing his phone to his ear. 'Hi, this is PC Barnes.' He stepped away and I tuned out his conversation as I tried to prepare myself for his inevitable questions. What colour was his hair? His eyes? What was he wearing?

'Okay.' I spun around as PC Barnes approached. 'So, I've reported the incident and they are going to keep an eye out, but to be honest...' His grim expression finished his sentence for him.

'You're not going to be able to find him,' I said quietly.

He shook his head before running his hand through his dark hair as he stared across the park, where the kid had disappeared. 'I'm sorry, if I could have got to you just a little bit quicker—'

'Hey,' I interrupted him. 'It's not your fault. I'm just grateful that you scared him off when you did.' Yet, even as I spoke, I couldn't help but feel curious as to why he'd chosen to stop to speak to me instead of running after the kid.

'So am I,' he said as he turned back to face me. 'You're sure that you're okay?'

I nodded automatically.

'Really?' he asked, clearly unconvinced.

'J-just shaken,' I assured him. I pressed my hand to my chest. 'My heart is pounding.'

'It'll be the adrenaline from the shock. There's a kiosk a little way back there, we can get you some sweet tea. It'll help.'

I shook my head. 'I need to get back to my work,' I said, gesturing to my stall a couple of metres away.

He smiled. *'I thought I'd seen you before. I bought flowers there for my mum for Mother's Day a couple of months ago.'*

'Oh.' I did my best to act surprised. 'Yeah, actually, you do look kind of familiar.' I frowned, pretending to search my memory.

Not that I really needed to.

I already knew who he was.

19

NOW

October

I stepped back into the now dark flat and fumbled for the light switch. Things that had once been instinctive had been lost after a six-year absence.

'I want to go back to the old flat.' I pouted as I stood surrounded by boxes in the middle of the living room, refusing to allow my gaze to drift to the window. Appreciating the view of the beach as it curved towards Hengistbury Head felt like a betrayal of Mum.

'It's gone, Chloe,' Dad said. 'This is our holiday home now.'

'But it was Mum's.' I knew I sounded like a whiny child, but I didn't care. How could he sell Mum's flat? How could he replace it so easily? It felt as though he was trying to erase it from our memories. To erase her.

'She's gone too, isn't she?' He glared at me. It was the first time he'd

looked directly at me in weeks. I'd wanted him to see me. To notice me. But now that he had I just wanted to disappear.

I couldn't help but wonder if he wished he could erase me too.

'I couldn't go back to that flat,' Mia said, her voice croaky and pained. 'Not after...' She choked back a sob and Dad turned to her, wrapping his arms around her protectively.

'It's okay,' he whispered. 'You don't have to. Your mum wouldn't expect you to.'

'She'd be happy that we bought this flat, wouldn't she?' Mia asked, peering up at him tearfully.

'Of course she would.'

'Chloe said she wouldn't. She said Mum would be upset that we sold Gran's flat. She said we were selfish to use Mum's life insurance money to buy something Mum wouldn't have wanted.'

'No, I didn't say it like that,' I said quickly as Dad glared at me again. 'I might have asked if she would be upset, but—'

'Well, Chloe is wrong. Again,' Dad said firmly.

I drew back. I knew what he meant. I had been wrong before. A mistake so huge there could never be a way back from it. No apology would ever be big enough.

And yet, somehow, I still had to live with it. That knowledge. That guilt. That grief.

Mia flung her arms around Dad's waist. 'Elle me manque telle-ment, papa.'

'Je sais, ma chérie,' Dad said soothingly as he stroked her hair. 'Moi aussi.'

I listened to their exchange in silence. Another reminder that I didn't fit.

'Come on, Mia. I'll buy you an ice cream to cheer you up while Chloe finishes unpacking.'

I stared after them as they abandoned me in the empty flat. The worst part was I couldn't even blame them.

I would leave me too. If only I could.

* * *

I slumped back against the door. I hadn't been back here since I was eighteen. I'd vowed never to come back. And yet, now I'd chosen to do just that. A shrill ringing beside me sent me staggering forwards away from the door, as my heart rate quickened. I turned and stared at the intercom as the ringing continued.

Someone was outside.

I edged closer to the screen, trying to make out the grainy black and white image. It was indistinguishable.

Who would be ringing the bell? No one knew I was here.

At least, no one should.

I picked up the phone and pressed it against my ear with a shaking hand.

'Hi Mia,' a woman's voice greeted me.

I let out a breath. I still didn't know who it was. But at least I knew who it wasn't.

Scott.

'Hello,' I replied hesitantly.

'Are you going to buzz me in?'

'Er, w-who...?'

'It's me.' There was a weighted pause as though she expected that to mean something to me.

It didn't.

'Rachel,' she said with a chuckle as though I was foolish not to have known that.

Rachel. My stomach lurched. Mia's friend.

I remembered her. She was hard to forget. In fact, the whole group of Mia's friends were. A tight little clique of girls Mia had managed to join when we were kids even though she didn't live here. Somehow, even after all these years, they'd stayed friends.

'It's freezing out here.' There was an edge of impatience to her static-filled voice from the intercom.

'Sorry,' I said automatically. I peered at the buttons beneath the screen, searching for the right one. I spotted one that looked like a key and pressed it. I heard a buzz and she disappeared from the screen.

I swallowed. Rachel was now in the building and on her way up to see me.

No. I shook my head. She was on her way to see Mia. I sucked in a deep breath and let it out slowly. This could be a problem.

Could be?

I almost laughed out loud at my understatement. There was no way this was anything other than a huge mistake. I should never have buzzed the door open; I should never even have answered the intercom. Better yet, I should never have come here in the first place. This plan had always been foolish.

I knew Aaron well enough to navigate my way through a conversation as Mia. But Rachel? The only thing I knew about her was how much I disliked her. And now I was supposed to be her friend.

20

THEN

September

'You don't mind getting me another red wine, do you, Chloe?' There was a tone to Mia's voice that made it clear it she wasn't asking but telling me.

'Another pint for me, while you're up, babe,' Scott said.

I pushed my chair back silently, biting back my irritation. There wasn't even a pretence of it being a request. Somehow that felt worse.

'Here, these are on me,' Mia said, handing me her card.

'But you already bought us lunch,' Scott objected. 'We can get these.'

I stared at him stunned, anticipating him reaching into his wallet for his own card. I'd never heard Scott object to someone else offering to pay before.

'Right, babe?' he added, turning to me. And I realised, 'we' meant me. He wasn't offering to pay. He was volunteering me.

'Nonsense.' Mia wafted his objections away with a wave of her hand.

I stood beside the table waiting to see how it played out. Although I suspected it would go the way it always did where Mia was involved.

She would win.

'Well, thank you, Mia. That's really kind of you,' Scott gushed.

I tried to remember when he'd thanked me with such conviction when I paid for anything. But now that I thought about it, I couldn't even remember a time when he had actually thanked me at all.

Perhaps it wasn't necessary. Not between us. Some things didn't need to be said out loud.

Did they?

Mia on the other hand *did* need to hear my gratitude. I pasted on my biggest smile. 'Yes, thank you so much, Mia.'

I joined the queue at the bar and glanced back at the table. Mia and Scott were engrossed in conversation. I strained my ears, desperate to hear what they were saying, but the crowded pub was too noisy to enable me to decipher a single word.

I let out a heavy sigh.

On the one hand, I wanted Scott to be accepted into my family. That was normal. It was what most people wanted for their partners. But that didn't stop resentment bubbling up inside me like a volcano ready to erupt.

I was jealous. There was no doubt in my mind about that. Jealous of how captivated Scott was with Mia. But also jealous *of* him. Mia treated him with a genuine warmth and enthusiasm that I had always longed for from her.

I shook my head. No, Mia was incapable of such feelings. Everything about her was superficial. It was always about what she could gain. And right now, that was being the centre of attention. I nibbled the inside of my cheek. Of course, making me jealous would be an appeal too.

An image of Aaron six years ago sprang into my brain, with Mia stroking his arm and beaming at him. I could still see his expression as he saw me, a mixture of embarrassment and concern. At least he'd had the decency to feel guilty. Not that it made his betrayal any less painful.

'What would you like, love?'

I turned to face the bartender. 'A better life.' My eyes grew wide as I realised what I'd said.

'Sorry, what?' His eyebrows drew together in confusion as he leaned forwards across the bar, straining to hear over the noise of the crowed pub.

'A pint of bitter, one red wine and one white, please,' I said, trying to keep my tone even as my face burned.

He nodded as his shoulders relaxed. He looked visibly relieved at my revised order. As least these were things that were actually in stock.

I wasn't even sure why I'd said what I had. I didn't want a better life. Mine was good. Scott's presence in it had already made it better.

'Paying by card?' the bartender asked.

I nodded and held Mia's card up to the card reader. I let out a silent breath of relief as it beeped its approval. It didn't care which twin I was.

'You not having anything?' Scott asked as I set his pint of bitter and Mia's glass red wine down on the table between them.

'It's still at the bar. I couldn't carry all three drinks.'

'Ah.' For a split second I thought he was going to fetch it for me. And then he took a swig of his beer.

I rolled my eyes and went back for my drink.

'Thanks for your card,' I said as I sank back into my chair

with my drink in hand. I slid Mia's card across the table to her, grateful to be rid of it.

Mia smiled as she put it back in her bag. 'Still afraid of getting caught, I see.'

I swallowed. I hadn't realised my discomfort was so easy to see. But then again, Mia had always been able to read me too well.

'What's this?' Scott asked.

'We used to switch places when we were kids, but Chloe always screwed it up by acting so guilty that it gave us away.'

'Not always,' I said, my words icy and sharp.

Mia looked at me blankly. 'Really? Are you sure about that?'

I gritted my teeth. I was sure. But I also knew there was no point in pursuing it. Mia had clearly chosen to conveniently forget that I had been so convincing in my portrayal of her, she had passed her GSCE in science. To admit it now would be to admit that she wasn't as smart as she liked everyone to believe.

'That must have been so much fun,' Scott said, oblivious to the undercurrent of our conversation. 'Pretending to be each other and messing with everyone's heads. You had so much power.'

I arched an eyebrow as I studied him. He always seemed so serious and sensible. Messing with people's heads wasn't something I'd thought he would approve of. Or, for that matter, *should* approve of.

'It was.' Mia shot him a mischievous look.

I frowned. I had the distinct impression that I was missing something, but what? I shook my head. What power did a couple of teenagers really have?

'It's fun to break a few rules sometimes,' Mia said, pivoting her wine glass on the table. 'It keeps things more interesting.'

Scott leaned back in his chair. He looked deep in thought, as though assessing her words.

Perhaps it was just professional curiosity. Maybe he was trying to profile her. Determine the severity of her rule breaking.

I swallowed. Or perhaps he was just intrigued by her.

I knew from experience how disastrous that could be for me.

21

NOW

October

Pacing the hallway waiting for the knock that I knew was coming, it still made me jump when it happened.

I reached for the latch, and I hesitated as I took another deep breath. I'm Mia, I reminded myself, before pulling the door open. I'm Mia.

'Rachel, hi.' I grinned at the stranger as she stared back at me. 'How are you?'

'How am I?' She put her hands on her hips. 'I'm offended, that's how.'

'Y-you are?' I'd only been here a few hours and somehow, I'd managed to offend someone I hadn't spoken to in years. What the heck had I done?

'I had to hear it from Daniel that you're back.'

'Daniel?' I cursed silently as soon as the name left my lips. Mia wouldn't need to ask who she meant. She would know.

Rachel had only been in the flat a few seconds and I was already messing up. I had to be more careful.

'The concierge.' Rachel spoke slowly as though I was a child.

'Oh, right.' I rolled my eyes as though I'd known that. 'Come on in,' I said, debating the wisdom of inviting her inside, against the risk of appearing rude if I didn't.

My whole body felt jittery. I just wanted to slam the door and hide alone in the flat. But I couldn't.

Mia wouldn't.

I stepped back and she walked down the hallway towards the living room. Clearly, she had been here before.

'Can I get you something to drink?'

'Red wine would be great, thanks.'

'Sure, I'll just see if I have any.'

'If you have any?' Rachel laughed. 'Mia, I have never known you not to have wine.'

I laughed awkwardly. 'True.' Except was it true? I had no idea.

As her sister, shouldn't I have known details like that? But then I'd never visited Mia at the flat. She'd rarely even visited my house. On the rare occasions we met it was in hotel lobbies and restaurants. Anything else would have implied a closeness that simply didn't exist.

And now never would.

An unexpected wave of sadness swept over me. I'd long ago accepted that Mia and I would never have a close relationship. Not that it had stopped me hoping. But there was a finality to it now. This time it really was too late to make amends.

I gave myself a silent shake. Standing in the hallway dwelling on what couldn't be changed wasn't going to help anything. It would just make my visitor suspicious.

I glanced across at Rachel as she lingered by the window in the living room, staring out into the darkness. I walked to the kitchen and quietly opened and closed the cupboard doors, peeking inside, searching for wine. Rachel was right, I realised, as I found a neat row of bottles of red.

I pulled one out and resumed my search, this time for wine glasses.

'It's a shame you're at the back of the complex,' Rachel said as I carried the wine and glasses into the living room.

I focused on pouring the wine as I bristled at the criticism of Mia's flat. It was ironic given I had always resented it myself. But not for the view. The view was indisputably spectacular. And yet even that small acknowledgement felt like a betrayal of Mum's flat and her memory.

'I have an unobstructed view from my apartment.'

'Ah.' I nodded. Rachel's criticism made sense now. I vaguely remembered Mia saying Rachel had moved into the apartment complex a couple of years ago, though thankfully she must at least be in a different building.

It had been inevitable really. Rachel had never liked the fact that we'd moved here. She didn't like to be outdone. So of course she would buy an apartment with an even better view. 'That must be impressive,' I said, remembering that Mia always cooed over Rachel in a way that I had never understood.

Rachel shot me a bewildered look as I handed her a glass of wine. 'You know it is.'

'Right, of course I do.' I rolled my eyes, as I let out a feeble chuckle. Obviously, Mia had visited Rachel's flat. She would have relished every opportunity to show it off and remind Mia that she was better than her. 'I don't know where my head is today. I guess I'm a bit tired from the long journey here from London.'

Rachel frowned. 'Long journey? It's only two hours. I'd have thought you were used to longer journeys than that with all the travelling you do.'

I tried not to wince.

22

THEN

September

'Well, he's *definitely* an upgrade on the guys you've dated in the last few years.' Mia announced as we stood outside the pub watching Scott walk away.

I nodded. 'Yeah, he really is,' I replied with a grin. I caught the wistfulness in my tone, and felt my cheeks grow warm. I was acting like a lovesick teenager. But even that realisation couldn't dull my smile.

'He's very charming and attentive, but there's also an intriguing quality to him,' Mia continued, seemingly oblivious to my excitement at her approval.

'He likes you too,' I told her.

'You think so?' she asked hopefully.

There was an uncharacteristic edge of insecurity to her manner.

'I do,' I assured her, touched by her desire to have made a good impression on the person who was so important to me.

I let out a contented sigh, feeling a shift to our relationship.

Mia had never needed my reassurance about anything before. And she certainly never cared what my boyfriends thought of her.

Except one.

I shook that thought away. This was different. Completely different.

'I know we got along well, but that could just have been him being nice to me because I'm your sister. But—' Mia's smile was radiant as she beamed at me '—we did seem to really click, didn't we?'

Her question unbalanced me. There was a difference between liking someone and clicking with them. Wasn't there?

'I haven't had that with a guy in a while,' Mia continued excitedly. 'Someone who really gets you, you know what I mean?'

'Of course *I* know,' I replied coldly. 'Scott really gets me.'

Mia's expression shifted, as her brow crinkled. 'Oh, I'm sure he does,' she assured me. 'To a degree, at least.'

'What does that mean?'

'Oh.' Mia's eyes widened innocently as she shook her head. 'I'm sure it's nothing.'

'What's nothing?' Tension tightened my muscles.

'It's just...' Mia paused. 'You don't really seem to have that much in common with him.'

An unspoken 'unlike me' hung in the air.

I swallowed. What if Scott didn't just like Mia as my sister? What if he *really* liked her? I gritted my teeth. Everyone always liked Mia.

How could they not?

My eyes narrowed and I realised I was scowling at Scott's retreating figure. Usually, I'd have been offended by his excuse to ditch me at the pub the second Ethan called. But today I was glad he had. Glad it wasn't just me he'd bailed on. It was Mia too.

A slow smiled formed on my lips. Perhaps he wasn't as smitten with her as she thought.

'It was good to finally meet him,' Mia said. 'You've been dating for months, and I feel like I barely know anything about him.'

I snorted. 'If you'd come home more often you could have met him sooner.'

A flash of surprise passed over Mia's face and I realised that my tone had been too barbed. I'd only intended to gently tease her about her extended absences.

Hadn't I?

'I'm here now.' Mia's voice was barely a whisper.

She was right. The past didn't matter now. It was irrelevant. Gone. *Now* she was here.

I reached out and squeezed her hand. 'I'm really glad you are.'

A familiar sensation stirred in the pit of my stomach. It was the truth, but it wasn't the whole truth. Part of me was glad she was here. But another part...

'Me too,' Mia replied, giving my hand a squeeze too before we both let go. 'It's a shame Scott had plans with his friends this afternoon. It would have been good to spend more time together.'

I felt jealousy prickle my skin. I shook my head. I was being ridiculous. I couldn't afford to allow myself to have doubts like this. I wouldn't survive it. Not again.

I lifted my chin and took a deep breath. There was nothing between Scott and Mia. My jealousy was unfounded. Neither of them would hurt me like that.

They were better than I was. They were good.

Or at least Scott was.

'We'll all get together again soon,' I said with a shrug, as I turned away and started walking. But even as I said it, I wondered how true it was. Soon wasn't a word that applied when it came to Mia.

For the first time, her unreliability was a relief.

'Aww, you're crazy about him, aren't you?' I could hear in her tone that Mia thought it was cute, maybe even amusing. It made me feel as though she viewed it as a schoolgirl crush that would fizzle out in a few months. But I knew it wouldn't. It was different. He was different.

'He's everything.' I cursed silently the second the words left my lips. I knew better than to be so open with Mia. I wanted her in my life, but I knew her well enough to know we worked better with distance between us. And not just physically.

Mia's eyes widened. 'Everything?' I heard doubt in her tone. She didn't believe me. How could she? She'd never been in love. Never let anyone get close enough to be loved by them. She didn't know how it felt to be this connected. This wanted.

'It's like Scott said—'

'He's perfect for you,' she finished firmly.

I smiled. Occasionally, our sisterly connection actually functioned. Mia got it. Somehow that mattered more than it should.

'I think...' I hesitated. 'I think we could have a future together.' It was the first time I'd said those words aloud.

'Wow.' Mia stopped, as though my revelation had caused her to forget how to walk. 'It's a bit quick to be thinking like that, isn't it?'

I laughed. 'It's not like I'm about to run off and elope. You know me, I never rush into anything. I'm just saying it's a possibility.'

Mia licked her lips, and I could see from her serious expression that she wasn't convinced.

'I *like* having it as a possibility,' I interrupted before she could put her concern into words. I knew her stance on relationships. She kept everyone at a distance. Even me.

I understood it. Losing the people you love made you cautious about letting anyone get close again. I did the same thing. To an extent.

But the difference between us was that I wanted to feel close to someone again. I wanted to let my guard down. To be loved unconditionally. If that was even possible for someone like me.

'Scott's the first person who's come close to making me think about a future outside of my rut.'

Mia tutted. 'You're not in a rut.'

I shrugged. 'I am, and it's okay. I've known it for a long time. I just didn't really know what to do about it. I go through the motions of each day. Get up, go to work, go home, and that's it. Each day is a carbon copy of the one that came before. Meeting Scott was like injecting life back into my day. I feel different when I'm with him.'

'You don't need a man to change your life. If you're not happy or fulfilled with how things are, change it yourself. Now that Dad's house has sold, you'll be in a better financial position to do so.'

'The sale has gone through?' I couldn't hold back the excitement from my voice.

Mia nodded. 'We've exchanged contracts, and completion is scheduled for a week on Wednesday. The funds should be in your account by the end of that week. So there's nothing holding you back now. You can start that new business you wanted to.'

'Business expansion,' I corrected. 'I already have my own business.' One that would soon live up to my claims, I added silently.

Mia shrugged. 'Or maybe this is an opportunity for a bigger change.'

'What kind of change?' Mia's comment sparked my curiosity. Did she think I was capable of something more?

'Maybe close your business and get a normal job instead.'

'A job?' I was wrong. Mia didn't think I was capable of more. She thought I wasn't capable at all. 'I don't need the inheritance to get a job. I could have done that already, if I'd wanted to.'

'Okay, then move somewhere new. Travel. Have an adventure. Whatever you want.'

'Scott's job is here.'

'Who says he has to go with you?'

Every muscle in my body tensed. 'And why wouldn't he?'

'I'm just pointing out that you don't need a guy in order to have an adventure.' Mia shook her head. 'Getting tied down to a guy because he makes you feel better about yourself isn't the answer.'

I bristled. 'I shouldn't have said anything. I just thought you'd understand.'

'I do understand. You want to be part of something again. You want a family. You think I don't miss that too?'

I stared at her. 'Do you?'

'Of course I do. But there's a difference between wanting it and needing it. I don't need other people to enable me to be myself, and neither do you. You are so much stronger than you think you are.'

The corner of my mouth turned upwards. Scott had said something similar too. That I was strong. Strong enough not to need anyone. Perhaps they were right. I was capable and independent. I'd had to be.

But that didn't mean I *wanted* to be. Not all the time. Not every moment of every day. Sometimes I just wanted someone there with me. Someone to share things with. Laugh with. Be with.

Dependency was overrated, I knew that. I knew what happened when you were solely reliant on someone, and they disappeared. I knew what that did to you. What it had done to me.

But you could still be independent and not be isolated. Still be strong and also loved.

Loved even when things were tough. Loved in spite of your flaws.

Loved the way that Scott loved me.

23

NOW

October

'It was so good to see you,' I lied, as I followed Rachel down the hall towards the door. The only thing good about the entire evening was that it was finally ending.

'Are you sleeping in here now?' Rachel asked as she did a double take whilst passing the guest bedroom.

I cursed myself silently. Why hadn't I moved the suitcase? Or at least shut the door?

But then I hadn't expected visitors. Especially inquisitive ones.

'I was just unpacking in there.'

I studied Rachel's movements as she lingered in the doorway, her gaze trailing around the room. Had she believed me? I didn't know her well enough to be able to tell. But then from her perspective, why would I sleep in the guest room when I had a perfectly useable master bedroom with its own ensuite?

'O–kay,' Rachel said slowly before finally moving on.

I made a mental note to keep the bedroom doors shut from now on. Or better still, avoid Rachel all together.

She turned to me as we reached the door. '*Câlins et bisous.*'

I froze. What was that? French? I forced a smile on to my lips. Was I supposed to reply? But with what? Any attempt I made would show my inadequacies. And yet Mia wasn't supposed to be inadequate at languages. She was supposed to be fluent.

I was supposed to be fluent.

* * *

'*Switch with me.*'

'*Huh?*' *I looked up from my revision notes and stared at Mia as she leaned against my bedroom door. 'Switch what with you?*'

'*Switch places,*' *she replied. 'Take my Chemistry practical assessment for me and help me pass my GCSE.*'

I shook my head. 'No way.'

'*Why not?*' *Mia put her hands on her hips. 'Are you too scared?*'

'*Yes, of course I am. We would be in so much trouble if we got caught. Besides which, it's wrong.*'

Mia rolled her eyes as she marched across my room and dropped down on the bottom of my bed next to my desk. 'You're always such a goodie two shoes.'

I bristled. She had a way of making being good, being responsible, sound so bad and boring.

'*Come on, you'd not only be helping me, but you'd also be helping the entire school.*'

I laughed. 'How does me doing your Chemistry assessment help the school?'

'*You're saving everyone from the very real possibility that I could burn the building down.*'

I rolled my eyes. Mia was always so dramatic. 'You won't burn the building down.'

Mia arched an eyebrow. 'Do you really want to take that risk?' She leaned towards me. 'You know that I could.'

I frowned as the hairs on my arms stood on end. Her voice was so flat. So serious. It felt like a threat. But she couldn't. She wouldn't.

Would she?

'Besides, if you take my Chemistry assessment, I'll do your French speaking assessment.'

I laughed, feeling relieved. Now I knew she wasn't serious. 'There's no way anyone will believe it if I suddenly start speaking fluent French like you.' Mia's plan was completely flawed. We couldn't possibly get away with it. 'And no one would believe it if you aced Chemistry either.'

'That's why we don't ace anything. We take the tests, but we do them badly. Our version of bad in subjects we each excel in, is going to be better than our best attempts to do well in subjects we are useless at.'

I hesitated. She had a point. 'But it's still cheating.'

'But we're not cheating on the final exam. Just the practical stuff. And it's not like it actually matters. You're never going to speak French after we leave school. And I'm certainly never going to need to know which chemicals to mix together.'

'So if it doesn't matter, then why even bother to cheat?'

'Just because the subjects don't matter, the grades do. Do you really want to have an F on your college applications?'

'N-no,' I said hesitantly.

'Those bad grades will follow us for life. University applications. Job interviews. We will be putting ourselves at a disadvantage. But we have the opportunity to rebalance the scales. All we need is a pass. Something believable. But something better than an F.'

I nibbled my lip. It sounded so reasonable. 'It still doesn't seem fair.'

'Don't you think anyone else in our position would do the same *thing if they could? We've had years of putting up with people mistaking us for each other. Isn't it time that we make use of it for once?'*

'What if the teachers realise?'

Mia snorted. 'Mr Jones has never been able to tell us apart. He calls me Chloe half the time anyway.'

'But Madame Dumas will know.'

'I won't wear make-up, I'll hunch my shoulders, shrink into the background and I'll stutter over every word. I'll be just like you.'

I bristled. Mia's description of me sounded so pitiful and yet I couldn't dispute that it was accurate.

'It's easy to be you. Everyone always falls for it.'

I nodded slowly. She was right, they did. Mia had a way of being so believable. Even when she was pretending to be me.

At least the difference this time was she wanted to help me, instead of making me take the blame for something she'd done.

'We can do this, Chloe.' Mia grabbed my hands and squeezed tightly. 'I believe in us. I believe in you.'

I stared at her, stunned, as a warm fuzzy feeling emanated from somewhere deep within me. 'You do?'

'I do,' Mia said as she nodded firmly. 'We know each other better than anyone. We can be each other.'

Mia's words repeated in my head. She was right. We could be each other.

Even if it was just for a few hours. I could finally be what I'd always wanted to be.

I could be Mia.

* * *

For a moment I felt that same excitement course through my veins. I *was* Mia now.

I straightened my spine and rolled my shoulders back. '*Au revoir*,' I said dramatically, channelling my new found confidence into the few words I actually remembered.

Rachel's smile slipped. Clearly my response was not what she'd expected.

I swallowed. 'It's been a long day,' I added, in a feeble attempt to justify the error I'd clearly made.

'Yeah, sure,' Rachel said, but crease in her forehead didn't lift. She started to turn towards the door but paused. 'Why did you really come back?'

'I told you—'

'Yes, I know,' Rachel said impatiently. 'A career break.' She waved her hand dismissively as she spoke. 'But you could do that anywhere, and yet you chose Bournemouth.' Her eyes narrowed. 'I know you better than that, Mia.'

24

THEN

September

I tucked my feet under me as I snuggled against Scott on his sofa and tried to push all thoughts of yesterday's lunch with Mia from my mind.

It was just the two of us now. The way it should be.

'You're quiet tonight,' Scott said as I rested my head on his shoulder. 'Everything okay?'

I nodded. 'Yeah, all good.'

Scott pulled back, causing me to lift my head as he studied me dubiously. 'I know that tone. It means "everything's not really okay, but I don't want to burden you with my problems".'

I stared at him stunned. 'How do you know that?'

He kissed my forehead. 'I speak Chloe language.'

I chuckled softly as my heart swelled. I liked that. The knowledge that someone understood me well enough to know the meaning beneath my words. That someone cared enough to even question it.

'Come on,' Scott prompted. 'Out with it.'

'I guess I'm just feeling a bit...' I hesitated. I wasn't used to sharing my feelings. It made me feel vulnerable to start now. Especially with this.

'It's okay,' Scott assured me. 'You can tell me. You can tell me anything.'

The sincerity in his voice was like a blanket wrapping around me, cocooning me inside. Safe and warm.

'I feel a bit jealous.' There, I'd admitted it. The words were out there. I couldn't take them back now. And yet, that's exactly what I wanted to do.

'I mean, I want you and Mia to get along, I really do. You're the most important people in my life. But—' I clamped my mouth closed, refusing to let the accusation that was bubbling inside me escape.

'But what?' Scott's eyebrows lifted.

'You got along a little bit better than I'd—' I searched for the right word '—hoped.'

'She's your sister,' Scott said, his tone implying that statement was all the response that was needed.

Perhaps he was right. The simple fact that Mia was my family was naturally reason for Scott to be charming, funny and attentive. Any partner in a loving relationship would do the same.

'Did I do something wrong?' Scott's voice was uncertain and worried.

He'd been trying to do something good. Something for me. And I'd made him doubt himself.

'No,' I responded quickly. 'It's not you. It's me.'

Scott arched an eyebrow. 'Or is it Mia?'

My heart pounded a little lounder. 'What do you mean?'

'You've never had concerns about how well I get on with other people usually. And it feels like this is very specific to Mia.'

I swallowed.

'Am I sensing some history here?'

Admitting the truth felt disloyal to Mia. The problems we had were kept between us. It's how our relationship had survived as long as it had despite the resentments. We simply didn't talk about them.

'Yeah,' Scott said, nodding knowingly. 'That makes sense.'

'I didn't say anything,' I objected.

'You didn't need to; I can see it written all over your face.'

Guilt washed over me. I'd betrayed her. Not with my words, but my expression. It was still wrong. Still bad.

'It was a long time ago.'

Scott didn't respond, and yet somehow the silence spoke volumes. He wanted to know more. Perhaps he deserved to know more.

'Aaron, my first boyfriend, and Mia...'

'He cheated on you with your sister?'

'I—' I wanted to deny it. To defend Aaron. But could I? 'They got together after we broke up.'

'But I'm guessing the break-up wasn't your idea?'

I shrugged. 'I guess I still hoped I could fix what had gone wrong between us. But then they started dating.'

'And you didn't stand a chance with Mia in the picture,' Scott said with certainty. He was right. I hadn't. But the fact that he knew that felt like a betrayal.

'She's always been more outgoing and confident than me.'

Scott nodded. 'Yes, I can see that about her. I can understand why you'd feel a little insecure around her. Especially given the way she was flirting with me when you were at the bar.'

I clenched my jaw together. It wasn't as though it was unexpected.

Scott grimaced. 'I wasn't sure whether to tell you. I mean, I don't want us to keep secrets like that from each other, but at the same time, she is your sister. I don't want to make things difficult between you two.'

I shook my head. 'You're not the one who's making it difficult.'

Scott reached for my hand and held it tightly. 'Promise me you're not going to let this come between you? We can all just forget it and pretend it didn't happen, right?'

I wanted to say no. I was tired of brushing things under the carpet and pretending they hadn't happened. It didn't make it better. It didn't make them hurt less.

But he was right, I couldn't let it come between Mia and me. At least not yet.

You catch more flies with honey than vinegar, Mum used to say. And right now, I needed to keep Mia onside. Or at least as onside as she ever was.

'It's not like it meant anything,' Scott added, when I didn't respond.

I gritted my teeth. He was wrong. It did mean something. It meant Mia hadn't changed.

The question was, had I?

25

October

I locked the door and leaned back against it, exhausted from Rachel's visit. Being Mia was more tiring that I'd remembered. But then the last time we'd switched it had been in an environment I'd excelled in.

*   *   *

'How did it go?' Mia asked as she met me at the school gate.

I grinned. 'Mr Jones totally bought it. He really thought I was you!'

Mia flung her arms around me. 'That's awesome.'

I clung to her. I'd made her happy. I'd had to lie to do it, but it was worth it. That lie had brought us together. United us.

'I can't believe you actually pulled it off,' Mia said as she stepped back and studied me.

I flinched. She sounded so condescending. 'You were the one who told me I could do it.'

Mia snorted. 'Yeah, but I never actually thought you would. To be honest I thought you'd chicken out before you even got in the classroom.'

I lifted my chin. 'Well, I didn't. I took your test and did well enough to get you a passing grade. Now it's your turn.'

'Yeah, about that.' Mia sucked her teeth. 'I think you're right. There's no way Madame Dumas will ever believe I'm you.'

'What?' I stared at her stunned. What was she doing? She couldn't bail on me now.

'My French is just so good.' Mia shrugged apologetically. 'She'll totally be able to tell that I'm faking being bad at it.'

'It was your idea. You said it was easy to be me. You've done it before. Even Dad falls for it.'

'That's different. It's not French.'

'But I took your Chemistry test.' My words were barely audible.

'Aww.' Mia patted my arm. 'I'm so grateful.' She shrugged again. 'But you were right, this wasn't a good idea. And you'll do fine on your own.'

'But the test is in a few hours, and I haven't studied for days because you said I didn't need to.'

Mia cringed. 'Yeah, you might want to cram a bit, then.'

'Mia, you can't do this to me.'

'I'm not doing it to you. I'm doing it for you. If we get caught, we'll ruin everything. It will destroy our chances of getting into college. Of having a good career. Trust me, Chloe. This is for the best.'

She gave me another hug, but this time it felt different.

'I'm helping you,' she said as she stepped away. 'It's my job to protect you, even when it hurts.'

'No!' I snapped. She wasn't going to get away with this. I was tired of her manipulating me. 'You roped me into this, and now you're going to stick to the plan. You're going to take my French exam, and you're going to pass it, like you promised you would.'

I paused, hoping Mia would be reasonable and see the error of her ways.

She shook her head. 'I can't.'

'You can. And you will. Or—' I swallowed, summoning my courage '—I'll confess to taking your Chemistry exam.'

Mia shrugged. 'You won't,' she replied, unphased. 'You wouldn't want to destroy everything...'

* * *

We'd never switched after that. I'd learnt my lesson.

Or so I'd thought.

I'd pulled it off back then. But could I now? This time was different. The stakes were higher, and I was out of my element. Bournemouth was Mia's turf. And Rachel's.

I swallowed. Mia was no longer my biggest threat.

If Rachel figured out the truth, I knew she wouldn't hesitate to expose me. I couldn't afford to let that happen. Mia had convinced me of the destructive power of getting caught cheating on an exam, but that was trivial compared to what would happen if I got caught this time. The stakes were much higher now.

One way or another, my life would be over.

26

___

THEN

September

'Ethan!' Scott leapt to his feet as the front door opened and the guy from the basketball game stepped into the hall. 'I didn't expect you back yet,' Scott said, glancing at his watch.

'I'm on the early shift this week,' Ethan replied as he strode across the short hall and joined us in the living room.

I stood up beside Scott, glancing back and forth between them. Why had Ethan just let himself into Scott's flat?

He smiled at me. 'How are you doing, Chloe?'

'I'm good,' I replied hesitantly.

Scott's eyebrow arched as he noticed my bewildered expression. 'Did you forget Ethan's the mate who's letting me crash here until I find my own place?'

'This is *Ethan's* flat?' I couldn't keep the surprise from my voice.

Scott laughed. 'You can't really blame her,' he said to Ethan. 'You and I are on such different schedules these days, you're never home when we're here.'

I tried not to let my confusion show on my face. Except nothing about this was right. I'd had no idea anyone else lived here. Let alone that it wasn't even Scott's flat.

I glanced back at Ethan, suddenly aware that I was an unexpected guest in his home. 'Sorry, I, er...' I fumbled to find the right words to apologise for my intrusion.

Scott and I had been together for four months; how had I not known something so important?

But then, it wasn't as though we came here that often. We usually went back to my house. I thought it was because Scott was thoughtful and knew I liked my own routine. My own structure.

'No worries,' Ethan said with a shrug. 'We met so briefly in the park the other day.'

I forced my smile back on my face and bit back the desire to explain that my apology wasn't for not realising he was Scott's flatmate, but for not even knowing he had one.

I suddenly felt like I was trespassing.

We stared at one another awkwardly. I couldn't think of anything else to say. All I wanted to do was get out of this stranger's flat. Out of this awkwardness.

'I should get going,' I said, picking up my bag from the beside the sofa.

'You don't have to rush off on my account,' Ethan said. 'You're welcome here any time.'

Scott shook his head, with a smile. 'No, Chloe's right. I promised to take her out for dinner.'

I blinked. When had he promised me that? We'd planned on having a quiet evening in front of the TV. Just like normal.

Clearly, he was trying to get us out of here. Was that for my benefit? Or did he feel as uncomfortable as I did?

Ethan chuckled. 'You're just eager to whisk Chloe away

before I have chance to share all your embarrassing stories that I promised her.'

I smiled, feeling a little bit of tension slip away as Ethan joked.

Except, what if he wasn't joking? After all, I hadn't known the truth about whose flat I was currently standing in.

Scott's smile dropped and for a moment my eagerness to leave waned.

'Careful,' Scott said with a brittle laugh. 'Or I might just tell her some of yours too.'

The smile faded from Ethan's face and the two men stared at one another silently.

I glanced back and forth between them. What was going on here?

With a sharp nod, Scott broke the stare, wrapped his hand around mine and led me to the door.

'It was nice to see you again,' I called over my shoulder as Scott ushered me out of the flat. Despite my earlier eagerness, the abruptness of our departure made me feel even more uncomfortable.

'Sorry about that,' Scott said as we walked down the stairs. 'I really thought we'd have the place to ourselves all evening.'

I stopped, yanked my hand free from his and glared at him. 'That's what you're apologising for?'

Scott frowned. 'Yeah, why? What else is there?'

'Seriously?' I couldn't believe it. How could he stand there and feign innocence?

'What did I do?' Scott asked indignantly.

'You never told me you were crashing at someone else's flat.'

'Of course I did,' he said, sounding surprised by my accusation. 'Ethan's an old school mate who I work with.'

I shook my head. 'I thought it was your flat.'

'Oh, I see.' Scott drew back. 'And that matters to you?'

'Yes, it does.'

His shoulders slumped. 'I am trying to get my own place,' Scott said quietly. 'I just can't afford it yet.'

Guilt tugged at my heart. I'd made him feel bad for not being able to have his own flat. I, of all people, knew better than that. 'I didn't mean it as criticism. I don't care that it's not your flat,' I assured him quickly. 'I care that you pretended it was. You should have just told me the truth.'

Even as I said it, guilt swelled within me. I was a hypocrite. I expected him to be truthful with me, whilst I lied to him.

Perhaps now was the time to come clean. He'd understand. This proved that he would get it. The pressure. The sense of failure that caused a tiny omission.

For Scott it was his flat. For me, it was my business.

'But I never said the flat was mine.'

'You—' I froze as I searched my memory, trying to remember exactly what he had said.

I swallowed. He was right. I couldn't think of a moment when he'd actually claimed he owned it. But still, it had been implied. Hadn't it?

'You acted as though it was yours,' I stumbled.

'If I did, then I'm so sorry. I would never intentionally mislead you.' Scott pulled me towards him. 'You are the most important person in my life. I never want to be anything but completely honest with you.'

I nodded. 'Me too.'

It was a misunderstanding, that was all. Scott hadn't lied. And yet the uneasy feeling in the pit of my stomach intensified.

He hadn't lied. But I had.

27

NOW

October

I stared at the clock as the numbers changed: 01:00. I rolled over and buried my head under the pillow. I was exhausted and yet I still couldn't sleep. Even in my old bedroom, I couldn't block out thoughts of Mia.

I'd never felt like I belonged here and now I felt more untethered than ever. I was an imposter in a world where nothing was mine. Every single thing that I owned had been lost. What the fire hadn't taken, I'd had to walk away from. The result was the same; it was all gone.

All I had left were memories and guilt.

With a groan I swung my legs out of bed, grabbed the pillow and duvet and dragged them along the floor as I padded to the hall in my bare feet.

I paused at the doorway of the master bedroom. I edged forwards, tempted to step inside, but I knew it was a bad idea. Nothing good could come from going in there. Mia's presence was too strong.

But then, her presence wasn't confined in a room, or even within the walls of the flat; she was everywhere I went. In truth she always had been.

The difference now was, I knew there would be no escaping her. Before, I'd had the hope of someday being independent from her. At least emotionally. But now... I hugged the pillow to my chest as I lingered in the doorway.

I learnt a long time ago that putting physical distance between myself and my problems didn't make them dissipate. The guilt lingered.

And yet being back here intensified it.

'I didn't have a choice,' I told the empty room.

Everyone always has a choice, that voice in my head chided me.

It was right of course. I could have done things differently.

Just like last time.

I let out a weary sigh. It would be so easy to shrink to the floor and just give up. To allow the past to engulf me.

I'd travelled that path before. It was familiar. It felt as though there was a kind of safety to that. The predictability of it. The dependability. And yet I knew it wasn't safe at all.

It would destroy me.

I forced myself to turn away and sauntered to the living room. Snuggling beneath the duvet, I cocooned myself on the sofa, grabbed the remote control from the coffee table and pressed the power button. Whenever I couldn't sleep at home, I watched old sitcoms to distract myself, maybe that would help. I clicked the Netflix icon and waited for the screen to load.

A half-watched episode of *New Amsterdam* caught my attention in the 'continue watching' list. My breath hitched in my chest, and I jabbed at the power button, frantic to make the image disappear.

Tears streamed down my face unchecked, and I pulled my

knees up to my chest, circling my arms around them as I rocked back and forth.

It was such a trivial thing; a part-watched episode of one of her favourite series. And yet, it's innocuousness was exactly what made it so devastating. She'd never get to see the end of that episode, let alone the series.

Mia's fascination with medical dramas had always bewildered me. I consciously avoided them, instantly flicking the channel if I stumbled across one by accident. It would never be entertainment to me, because I'd already experienced its reality.

* * *

Blue lights flashed through the living room window as I reached for Mia's hand.

'She's going to be alright, isn't she, Chloe?' Mia asked, clinging to me.

It was the first time I'd ever heard Mia seek my reassurance. Instinctively, I wanted to say yes, it was Mum, of course she would be fine. She had to be. But I'd seen the look on Dad's face as we waited for the ambulance.

'What if she doesn't wake up?' Mia asked, giving voice to my own fears.

I shook my head. I couldn't think about that. A life without Mum was inconceivable.

The sound of feet shuffling across the tiled floor caused my head to jolt towards the bedroom as my stomach lurched. Dad staggered into the doorway; his eyes met mine as his body crumpled against the wooden frame.

I stared at him. He seemed like a stranger to me. His usually neatly combed hair was matted from the salty water and stuck out in random directions. But it was his face that made him almost unrecognisable.

Pained and haggard, he looked decades older than the man who'd left the flat a few hours earlier.

'Daddy!' Mia dropped my hand, raced the few steps across the tiny living room, and flung herself into his arms.

He hugged her to him, as though trying to draw strength from her. But his eyes never left mine.

'How could you?' He spat the words at me with such hostility that I stumbled backwards. 'I'll never forgive you for this.'

28

THEN

September

'How about a girls' day on Saturday?' Mia's bubbly voice greeted me as soon as I picked up the phone. There was never any small talk with Mia. She was always direct and said what she wanted.

Or demanded.

'I work on Saturdays,' I replied, grateful for the excuse to avoid spending time with her.

And yet, I knew I wasn't really avoiding it. I was just postponing it. The fact remained I needed to see her. Needed to finalise things if I was ever going find a way out of the situation I had got myself into.

I had to put Mia's flirting out of my mind. Pretend as though everything was fine.

Just like always.

Mia sighed. 'Sunday, then.'

'Oh, erm...'

'Well, that wasn't the response I was expecting. You used to love our girls' days.'

'I still do.' It caught me by surprise how true that statement was. Despite everything, spending time with Mia still meant something to me. More than it should. 'But I already have plans,' I added firmly.

Mia grunted. 'With Scott, I suppose.'

'Yes,' I replied, feeling as though somehow that was the wrong answer.

'But it's been ages since we had a day together. I miss hanging out with you.'

'I miss it too.' I wished I didn't. It would be easier that way. But she was my sister. My twin. And I couldn't help hoping that one day that would mean as much to her as it did to me. No matter how unlikely that was.

'So, tell Scott something more important came up.'

'I can't do that.'

'Why not? He knows we don't get to see each other much, right? So if he loves you, he'll want you to do what make you happy and spend time with your twin sister.'

Twin sister.

It was funny how Mia only referred to us as twins when she wanted something. And right now, she wanted attention.

I knew she was using it to manipulate me, but it still felt good to hear. It felt like I was part of something. That I belonged. Even if it was only for a moment.

'Of course he loves me and wants me to be happy, but that doesn't mean I can just ditch him at the last minute.' Unlike Mia, Scott always treated me like a priority. And he deserved no less from me.

'It's not the last minute. It's Sunday.'

'We have plans, Mia,' I said firmly.

'To do what?'

I bit my lip.

'Chloe?'

'I'm not sure what we're going to do yet, but the point is that we're doing it together.'

'So you don't really have plans, then. Though,' Mia paused, her triumphant tone suddenly hesitant and concerned, 'why don't you? Your relationship is still too new to have become stagnant.'

'Spending the day together *is* the plan,' I replied defensively.

Except was that enough?

Was Mia right? There was nothing wrong with simply spending the day together. But why didn't Scott and I have actual plans to do something or go somewhere? Had our relationship stopped being new and exciting? Had we become complacent and boring?

I rolled my eyes. I was letting Mia do what she always did. Make me question. Doubt.

It was bad enough that she could make me unsure of myself, but I wouldn't allow her to make me question my relationship.

Scott and I both worked long hours. We were tired by the time Sunday finally rolled around. But no matter how exhausted Scott was, he still showed up. He was still present. Still there.

Unlike Mia.

'I can't believe you made other arrangements when you knew I was back in town,' Mia grumbled.

'How was I supposed to know you would want to meet this weekend? It's not as though I can keep my entire calendar free on the off chance you might at some point feel like a girls' day with me.' Except that was exactly what I used to do. Every time she was in town, I turned down every other invite and cancelled anything that was already planned.

But things were different now. I had Scott.

He was solid. Dependable. Present. All of the things that Mia would never be. Could never be. And I wasn't going to risk losing him for someone who may or may not even turn up on Sunday.

'I'd booked something special for us.' The disappointment in Mia's voice pierced my heart.

'What?' I asked. I knew I shouldn't, but I couldn't stop myself.

'It was a surprise,' she said quietly. 'I just wanted to do something nice for you.' She let out a long sigh. 'It doesn't matter now. I'll have to cancel.'

My stomach lurched. What had I done? Mia was finally reaching out and I'd shut her down.

I opened my mouth, the desire to tell her I'd go with her was overwhelming. But the words wouldn't come.

Going with Mia meant cancelling my plans with Scott. One way or another I'd upset someone.

29

NOW

October

'Hey,' a familiar voice called across the promenade as I headed back toward the flat and I turned my head to the right.

'Oh, hi.' My eyebrows lifted as I saw Aaron standing at the top of a ladder that was resting against a bright pink beach hut. The plastic sheet had been removed, exposing the empty space where the roof and side should have been.

My stomach tightened at the sight of him. I wasn't prepared to see him again. At least not so soon. After six years apart, two encounters in less than twenty-four hours felt too much.

And yet the butterflies in my stomach, as he smiled broadly at me, implied the opposite.

'I'll come down,' Aaron said, and I watched as he clambered down the ladder and crossed the promenade to me.

I felt cornered. I couldn't just walk away, but I didn't really want to stop and talk. Not to him. Not to anyone that knew Mia.

All it would take was one wrong word, one slip, and he could realise I wasn't who I claimed. I should tell him I was in a hurry.

That I couldn't stop and chat. And yet, the words wouldn't come. My voice betrayed me.

But I knew that deep down, whilst my fear of being exposed urged me to leave, some part of me was exactly where I wanted to be. Where I'd always wanted to be.

With him.

'How are you?'

I nodded. 'I'm good. It's great to be back.' I realised as I spoke that it wasn't entirely a lie. Bournemouth might not have been somewhere I had planned to return to, but it did have its appeal. It was hard not to be captivated by the stunning coastline. Though if I was honest with myself, my love of Bournemouth when I was a teenager had been more about Aaron than anything else.

Aaron tipped his head to the left as he studied me. 'Did you change your hairstyle or something?'

I ran my fingers through my hair. 'No, why?'

'I don't know, something about you seems different.'

I laughed nervously. 'It's been a long time since we've seen each other.'

Aaron chuckled. 'March wasn't that long ago.'

I shuffled awkwardly. 'March?'

'When you came back to Bournemouth after your dad's funeral,' Aaron said, looking at me curiously.

'Oh, I—' I clamped my mouth closed. I hadn't known Mia had come to Bournemouth then. She'd been in a hurry to leave after the funeral, insisting we had to clear out his house quickly as she had to get back to work. And yet she'd come here. To Bournemouth. To Aaron.

Jealousy simmered inside me. Mia had seen Aaron six months ago, whereas for me it had been six years.

'I'm glad you let me help you with the flat. I couldn't bear the thought of you having to go through all your dad's stuff alone.'

Tightness gripped my chest. 'Right.' My voice was thick and rough. That was how Mia had cleared Dad's belongings out of the flat so quickly: Aaron had helped her. 'It was really good of you to help out like that.'

My words felt hollow. It was good of him, and yet that didn't stop it from feeling like a betrayal. He'd been there for Mia after Dad's death, but what about me?

Aaron shook his head. 'It was the least I could do. You know I would have come to the funeral too.' He shrugged weakly. 'But I understand why you felt that wasn't a good idea.'

I stared at him. What was he talking about?

'It would have made things harder for Chloe,' Aaron said slowly, seeing my surprise. 'Right?'

I froze. Clearly, I should offer some sort of agreement, but I couldn't. Aaron had wanted to go to Dad's funeral, but Mia had stopped him. For me.

Questions whirled in my brain. Why had he wanted to go? To say goodbye to Dad? To support Mia? Or— My lips parted. Was it possible he had wanted to be there to support me?

30

THEN

September

My gaze was locked on Mia as she stood at the bar chatting to the bartender. She hadn't fully forgiven me yet for not cancelling my Sunday plans with Scott. But she had been pacified with Saturday night drinks and the promise of my undivided attention all evening. The same rule, however, did not appear to apply to her.

She flicked her hair back over her shoulder as she laughed at something he'd said, and his smile grew. He was beaming at her now. His eyes drawn to her. Our drinks neglected.

She'd always had that effect on people. The ability to make them feel as though they were the centre of her world. But it never lasted.

Perhaps I'd been too quick to judge her the other day. It was hardly surprising Scott thought Mia had been flirting with him. By a normal definition she probably was. But when it came to Mia, normal definitions didn't apply. She was the exception to every rule.

The bartender finally finished pouring out two pints of cider and slid them reluctantly across the bar.

I watched his expression fall as Mia picked up the glasses and turned away. His gaze remained on her, as though hoping she would turn back. But she didn't.

She never did.

To Mia there was no point in looking back. The past was behind her and that's where she was determined it would stay. It didn't matter if it was a brief moment with a bartender, or something much bigger. The past was done with.

I was the only person she had ever returned to. I was the only tie she had. The only thing that tethered her to anything.

She might not come out and say it, but she needed me. Part of me rejoiced in that. But another part found the tether increasingly suffocating.

Sometimes I couldn't help but wish I could sever all ties.

Mia sat down opposite me and handed me my drink. 'Cheers,' she said, still beaming from her flirtatious encounter.

'Cheers,' I repeated, twisting in my chair so I didn't have to see the bartender's gaze constantly drifting to our table.

'I'm so glad you managed to fit me into your busy schedule,' Mia added after taking a sip of her cider.

Despite her smile her voice dripped with sarcasm.

An instinctive need to apologise bubbled to the surface but I clamped my jaw closed, preventing it from escaping. I shouldn't need to apologise for having plans that didn't revolve around her.

'Seeing as you're ditching me tomorrow, I've decided to go to Reading, and take a last look around Dad's house to make sure we've got everything.'

'Oh, you're going alone?'

Mia shrugged. 'You're busy.'

'Yeah, but...' My objection trailed away. It wasn't as though I actually wanted to go back to the house. Before Dad's death I'd managed to avoid going there for years. He and I had both preferred it that way. And yet the fact Mia hadn't even thought about asking me to go with her cut deeply.

Perhaps that was the intention.

'That's a good idea,' I replied instead, with a half-hearted attempt at enthusiasm.

Dad and I hadn't been close in a long time, but it was still heart-wrenching knowing he was gone. The finality of it was crushing.

Before, there had at least been a chance he might forgive me some day. A slim chance, admittedly. But now there was nothing.

'You don't mind if I borrow your car, do you?'

'I have a van,' I corrected.

'Oh yeah.' Mia scrunched her nose disdainfully. 'Oh well, I guess it will do, thanks.'

I blinked. 'I didn't—' My attempt to point out that I hadn't actually said yes was cut off abruptly.

'I knew you wouldn't let me down twice in one weekend.'

She was manipulating me. I knew she was. And yet, I felt powerless to stop it. I hadn't really let her down.

Had I?

A part of me wanted to object. To tell her I needed my van tomorrow. Not because I actually did need it, but just to spite her. To say no.

For once.

'I'll collect it in the morning,' Mia decreed, and I knew the moment for objection had passed.

A familiar sense of compliance descended over me.

And yet this time there was something else too. Disappointment. I was still allowing Mia to control me.

'So...' I said, scrambling for a distraction. 'Is everything still on track for completion on Wednesday?'

Mia nodded. 'So far, so good.'

I took a grateful swig of cider. A few more days and everything would start falling into place.

'You look relieved,' Mia said, eyeing me curiously.

'Just excited,' I lied. 'The timing is perfect. My stall is seasonal. The weather is already getting colder, so I won't be out in the park much longer. That means I can spend the time focusing on the new store.' My explanation sounded reasonable even to my own ears, but the truth was, Mia was right: I was relieved.

I always took on temporary work during the winter months when the stall wasn't viable. But I hadn't been with Scott then. There was no way I could get another job this year without Scott realising I'd lied about owning a store.

Everything had become so convoluted and difficult. All because of one stupid little lie.

Although did it still count as a little lie now? It had when it started. A flippant comment to Mia, leading her to assume that I owned a store had seemed so trivial at the time.

But somewhere along the way it had ceased to be just an implication that I was a successful businesswoman, it had become an outright lie. And not just one, but a precarious patch-work of lies that could come unravelled at any moment.

The only blessing was that Dad would never know the truth.

'And what about you?' I asked, determined to redirect the focus. 'Do you have any plans for your share of the inheritance?'

'Actually, I have.' Mia sat up straighter. 'I'm going to travel the world,' she declared proudly.

I hesitated. 'Isn't that what you've already been doing?'

Mia pouted. 'No, silly. That was just work.'

I stared at her, my mouth opening and closing, while I struggled to speak. I'd never heard Mia be so dismissive of her job. Her life.

'I'm talking about seeing the world.' She drew a circle in the air with her hands, as though to demonstrate the scale of her plan.

'I've been looking into world cruises. I've always wanted to do a cruise, and this would be perfect. Just think how much I could see in four months.'

'So, after the cruise...' I let my half-formed question hang between us.

Mia shrugged. 'Who knows. Maybe I'll do another cruise. Or maybe I'll go back to one of the countries I'll have visited.' She wafted her hand. 'That's for future me to worry about.'

I pasted a smile on my face. 'That's awesome.'

And it was. For her. Then again, maybe it was for me too. After all, wasn't this exactly what I wanted? To be free of Mia?

31

NOW

October

'Are you okay?' Aaron's voice sounded faint and distant.

I nodded automatically. 'I'm fine.'

'Are you sure?' he asked doubtfully. 'You've gone really pale.'

I pasted on a smile, determined to reassure him.

'Here, have a seat,' Aaron said, grabbing a folded deckchair from the doorway of the pink structure behind him. He opened it out and thrust it towards me. 'And I'll make us some coffee.'

I sank into the chair gratefully, but my smile felt a little less fake. It had been a long time since anyone had seen behind my pretence of being fine. A long time since they had cared to look close enough. At least without their own agenda.

But with Aaron there was no hidden motive. He simply cared.

I peered through the doorway, watching as he clattered around in the small hut, boiling a kettle of water on a small camping stove. His actions brought back memories of winter breaks cocooned inside, snuggled together with mugs of hot chocolate as we watched huge waves crash against the shore.

My body relaxed against the faded deckchair, as a gentle sigh escaped my lips. 'I'm glad your family still kept the beach hut, even after you all moved away,' I admitted quietly.

'Yeah, I think they felt bad about selling up the family home the second I'd left for Australia.'

Australia.

That one word felt like a punch to my stomach. It had been my idea. My dream. And he'd gone without me.

'Keeping the beach hut was their way of keeping a foothold here, so we could at least come back for holidays,' Aaron continued, oblivious to my reaction.

I nodded stiffly. 'And do they come back much?' I fought to keep my voice even as I stuck to the safer topic.

Aaron shook his head. 'I'm trying to lure them back more often now that I'm living here again, but apparently Portugal has greater appeal.'

My eyes widened. 'Oh, wow. So they actually did it, then? They moved to Portugal?'

Aaron nodded. 'I thought you knew that already.'

'Oh, erm...' I was going to have to be more careful. I was supposed to be Mia, which meant I was supposed to know what she knew.

The problem was, I didn't.

'I remember it was their dream,' I said hesitantly. 'But I guess it just slipped my mind that they'd actually done it. It was a long time ago.'

Aaron nodded. Accepting my lie as though it was reasonable. Believable.

But I hadn't known where his family had gone. After Aaron dumped me, I avoided his family. I wasn't part of his world any more. And that meant letting go of his family too.

Aaron's absence was another reason why my own trips to

Bournemouth had ceased. Without him or Mum, the place had been flat and empty.

Lonely.

At least when he'd been here there had been hope. The possibility that one day he would see Mia for who she really was and his obsession with her would fade. That one day he would realise he was in love with the wrong twin.

But he never did. He never would.

He would always prefer Mia.

32

THEN

September

'Hey,' I said, smiling as I pressed my phone to my ear, while I rummaged in my bag for my keys. 'You have good timing; I've just got home.' I caught the slight slur to my words and chuckled to myself. Perhaps the second bottle of wine on top of ciders had been a bad idea.

'A bit late, isn't it?' Scott's gruff tone made my smile wither instantly.

'Well, a-a little bit, I-I guess,' I stuttered, feeling like a naughty schoolgirl, when Dad had caught me sneaking in two minutes past curfew.

I swallowed at the memory. He'd always been so strict. So protective.

I shook my head, refusing to allow my thoughts to go there.

With a deep breath I slid the key in the lock and pushed the door open. 'But it's Saturday night. It's not like I have to work in the morning.' My voice was firmer. I was old enough to decide what time I got home.

I stepped into the hall and kicked my shoes off as I nudged the door closed with my hip.

'I thought we were spending the day together tomorrow.' Scott sounded dejected, as though he thought I'd forgotten him.

A familiar tug of compassion pulled at me, eroding my resentment. 'Aww, we are. Of course we are.'

'But now you'll be tired and grumpy all day.'

I blinked, stunned by the abruptness of his accusation. What was happening here? I'd spent an evening catching up with my sister who I barely saw these days and yet, somehow, I felt as though I'd done something wrong. 'Am I usually tired and grumpy when we spend time together?' I fought to keep my tone light, and resisted the urge to point out that right now it sounded like he was the tired and grumpy one, not me. Although that was rapidly changing.

'You don't usually stop out until after midnight before our dates.'

'Ha,' I taunted, as something rebellious kicked in. 'How do you know? I might.' That would make him wonder, I gloated inwardly, feeling an unfamiliar sense of smug satisfaction.

'I know,' Scott replied, his voice strong and serious. 'I know *you.*'

Something about the way he said it sent tingles through my body. Even on a phone call I could feel the connection that existed between us.

That sense of connection had a way of quelling my uncertainties. Somehow, they seemed less important than they had a moment ago.

'You're mad because you care,' I realised suddenly. His objection to my staying out late wasn't about controlling me or dictating what I did with my time. It was just a reminder that we were a partnership now. The decisions we made individually impacted both of us. That needed to be factored in.

When I thought about it in those terms, his bad mood was no longer irritating. It was endearing. It showed he cared. Showed he wanted to be with me. To treasure every moment. And not let our time be disrupted by anything, or anyone else.

'Of course I do,' Scott confirmed. 'Don't you know that by now?'

'Yes,' I replied. It wasn't a lie. I did know. 'But maybe I hadn't realised how *much* you care.'

I know you.

His words repeated in my head. He was right. He did know me.

Mostly.

But there was a side of me that I couldn't share with anyone. Even Scott.

Not if I wanted to keep him. And I *really* wanted to keep him.

I knew the alternative only too well. I'd already lived it. The isolation. The loneliness. Never really fitting in.

But with Scott I did.

Even if that meant I needed to change to do so.

33

NOW

October

'How come you're out so early on a Saturday morning anyway?' Aaron asked as we sat on the decking in front of his beach hut, sipping mugs of hot coffee.

'I'm an early riser,' I said with a shrug.

'Since when?' Aaron stared, his jaw gaping.

'Since, er, since today,' I said hesitantly. How could I have been so careless? Working in the flower trade had made me an early riser, but Mia never had been.

'Ah.' Aaron nodded. 'For a moment there I thought you were turning into Chloe.'

I tried to laugh, but it sounded fake and forced. 'You're up early too,' I said, shifting the focus on to him.

Aaron glanced over his shoulder. 'Yeah, I'm trying to get all the repairs done before the winter weather sets in.'

'How come it needs so much work?' I asked, studying the beach hut. Compared to the ones either side of it, it seemed to be in a pretty bad state. The roof was missing, along with several side panels. 'Did it get damaged in another storm?'

Aaron's head jolted back and he stared at me, his eyes wide. 'You remember that?'

'Of course, we'd come down early that year for the half term break, and I, er, Chloe,' I corrected quickly, 'spent most of it helping you and your dad repaint the hut.'

Aaron laughed. 'Yeah, and somehow she talked us into letting her choose the paint.'

'You know she was only joking when she suggested pink. She didn't actually think you would agree to it.'

'I know.' Aaron nodded slowly. There was a sadness to his voice as he spoke. 'But I could never say no to Chloe. I couldn't bear to disappoint her.' He smiled wistfully. 'Not even when it meant ending up with a bright pink beach hut.'

His words sounded so sincere. For a moment I almost believed them. But he had disappointed me.

The day he'd chosen Mia over me.

* * *

'Aaron,' I called, waving eagerly as Mia and I walked towards Aaron's beach hut. His head jerked towards me, and he froze. I tried to decipher the expression on his face. Surprise? Anger? Whatever it was, it wasn't his usual reaction to my arrival.

Suddenly he scrambled out of his deckchair, his eyes darting left and right as his gaze shifted between Mia and me.

'What's going on?' I asked, as my pace slowed.

For a split second he looked confused, and then suddenly his jaw tensed and he marched forwards.

'I'm sorry about last night,' I said earnestly.

Sacrificing my date with Aaron had been painful, but Dad had needed me. That was huge. He never needed me. Not any more.

'I hoped you'd understand.' I held my hand out, reaching for him as he drew near, but he shook his head and veered past me.

'Aaron?' I turned, watching his back retreating from me, with my mouth hanging open. He'd shunned me. No explanation. No apology. It was as though I'd simply ceased to exist.

I turned to Mia beside me, my eyes wide as I stared at her helplessly. 'You said you'd explained to him why I couldn't meet him.'

'I did,' Mia assured me.

'Then why is he so mad at me?' I waved my hand after him. 'I thought he'd be pleased for me. Dad hasn't asked for my help in years. I know it was only to get rid of a virus on his laptop, but it was something.' Something I could do that Mia couldn't, I added silently. Something useful. 'I couldn't say no.'

Mia nodded. 'Of course not. You did the right thing. And Aaron should be happy that you and Dad are finally starting to reconnect. Even if it is just as his technical support.'

I swallowed. She was right. For all my hopes that Dad coming to me meant things between us were improving, the truth was, he only saw me as an IT helpdesk.

'I'll find out what's happening,' Mia said as she gave my shoulder a squeeze before running after Aaron.

As she closed the gap between them, she reached out, tugging on his arm. I expected him to shake her off and storm past her. But instead, he stopped and turned towards her.

I blinked. Aaron and Mia usually merely tolerated one another for my sake. And yet, he'd stopped for her and not me.

Mia's lips moved and I strained my ears, desperate to hear what she was saying. And then she lifted her arms and wrapped them around Aaron's waist, pulling him to her.

Everything else seemed to fall away. All I could see was them. Mia was hugging my boyfriend. And he was letting her.

I took a step forward, scrambling to find my voice to scream my objections. And then Aaron moved. I froze, waiting for the inevitable. He would push her away and come back to me. Of course he would.

But he didn't.

Instead, he hugged her back. Clinging to Mia as though he couldn't survive without her.

I couldn't move. Couldn't breathe.

Every part of me screamed, and yet I didn't make a sound. I couldn't. I couldn't do anything except watch them walk away, their arms wrapped around each other.

I cleared my throat. 'How come you never painted over it later?' I fought to keep the tremor out of my voice. I had to act normally. I couldn't let him see how much his betrayal had hurt me. Not then, and certainly not now. 'You must have had to repaint it since then.'

Aaron shrugged. 'Kind of got used to it, I guess.' He stared at the beach hut; there was something so wistful in his expression. And then suddenly he shook his head. 'But, no, it wasn't storm damage this time. There was a fire a few weeks ago.'

'A f-fire?' My voice cracked as I drew back in the chair. Even the mere mention of the word caused images to play in my memory of Mia's body being carried from my burning home.

'Not a big one,' Aaron added quickly, sensing my discomfort. 'Thankfully it was extinguished in time before it spread to the other huts. But it's needed a lot of repair work.'

'That's awful.'

Aaron nodded. 'Yeah, but it was lucky no one was hurt.'

Tremors rippled through my body as I stared at the hut. It was lucky.

This time.

I felt tears forming and I blinked them away rapidly. I couldn't let him see how much his revelation had affected me. He would ask questions. Ones I couldn't answer. Not now. Not ever.

We stared at the beach hut in silence for a moment. But I wasn't here. Not at this building. This fire.

The memories were so vivid. The air so thick with smoke that it made me nauseous. The crackles and pops of the fire that was tearing my world apart in front of me.

And Mia. Her lifeless body as the fireman carried her out to the waiting paramedics.

It felt like something I'd seen on TV. Dramatic and intense. It couldn't have been real. It *shouldn't* have been real. And yet, it was.

'I've ripped out all the burnt wood already, now I just need to rebuild it,' Aaron said, interrupting my thoughts.

I nodded slowly as I stood up. 'I should let you get on with it, then, and stop distracting you.'

He turned back to me and smiled. 'It's too late for that, I'm afraid. You've already distracted me with that incredible smile of yours.'

I lowered my gaze to the ground as I shuffled awkwardly.

'Sorry.' Aaron's cheeks flushed as he stood abruptly. 'I don't know why I said that.' He seemed genuinely surprised by his own words.

I tried to laugh. 'It's fine, just...'

'I should stick to carpentry?'

This time my laugh was small but genuine. 'Maybe,' I said

quietly. And yet, even as I said it, I hoped he wouldn't. I liked his corny chat-up line. It meant he still liked me.

Even if I wasn't really me at all.

34

THEN

September

I opened my front door and was confronted by a huge bouquet of flowers. 'I'm sorry,' Scott said, peering over the top of them. 'I totally overreacted last night. You were just out with your sister, having a good time, and you didn't need me getting over-protective.'

My heart felt like it would explode from the surge of love I felt for him in that moment. This was exactly what I'd always wanted: someone to buy *me* flowers. The disagreement before-hand didn't matter. It was natural that we'd disagree occasionally. That one of us would be moody, bad tempered or say the wrong thing.

What mattered was what happened after. What happened now.

Scott held the flowers out towards me. 'Can you forgive me?'

I nodded without hesitation. 'Thank you,' I said, accepting the flowers and ushering him inside. 'They're beautiful, and so was your apology.'

I held the flowers to my left and wrapped my right arm around his waist, inhaling his sandalwood cologne. He leaned forwards and his lips met mine. Soft but intense, his kiss felt charged with emotion more powerful than I had known before.

Finally, we separated, and our eyes met. 'Mmm,' I murmured. 'Maybe we should disagree more often when you apologise this well.'

Scott laughed and shook his head. 'I prefer it when we're on the same side.'

I stepped back, casting him a puzzled look. 'You know, just because we have a difference of opinion, it doesn't mean we're not on the same side. No one can agree 100 per cent of the time. And if they did, how boring would that be?'

'True,' Scott said, closing the front door behind him. 'But it's just...' He took a deep breath. 'Well, you have to look at it from my perspective. I know you're used to being on your own. Used to being independent. To not having anyone in your life to care or worry about you. But when you're out until all hours, I worry.'

The flowers suddenly felt like lead weights in my hands. 'I have people who care about me.' I set the flowers down on top of the cabinet at the side of the hall, wanting to be free of them and the painful memories Scott's speech had stirred within me.

'Who? Mia?' Scott snorted. 'She doesn't count.'

I stared at him. How could he think that, let alone say it? He dismissed her as though she was irrelevant. And yet, he'd been so charming to her the other day. Was he faking it? Being attentive and interested because he felt compelled to be, rather than because he actually liked her?

'Mia would rather spend her life galivanting in another country than being there for her own twin,' Scott continued.

'She's there for me. We talk. We WhatsApp. We—'

'She's not present, Chloe. She's just using you, so she doesn't feel completely alone. That's not love.'

'Mia loves me.' I hesitated. 'In her own way.'

I wasn't entirely sure which one of us I was trying to convince: Scott or myself.

I knew our relationship wasn't a typical one. Being twins changed the dynamic. It was destabilising to see another version of yourself each day and know you fell a little short. Our sibling rivalry operated on a different level, even before our world fell apart. And now we were left with painful parts in our pasts. Parts Scott couldn't understand. No one could. But however much resentment we harboured for each other, we were still sisters. Still family.

Although Dad had taught me: being family didn't guarantee being loved.

Scott reached for my hands and pulled them close to his chest. 'I love you, Chloe. I love you so much that it scares me sometimes because I don't know how I would cope if I lost you too.'

Too.

The word seemed to fill the narrow hallway.

'Loss leaves a void inside you,' Scott said slowly. 'It's like a jigsaw with a missing piece. I'm incomplete without her.'

'Her?' Jealousy battled with concern. Scott's anguish and grief were practically tangible. Easing his pain should have been my only focus. And yet, my body tensed as some part of me fixated on that one word: her.

He'd never mentioned losing anyone before. He'd had months to have done so. Months he had remained silent.

His silence felt like a betrayal. He hadn't trusted me enough to share his past with me.

Scott hung his head. 'I should have told you sooner. I wanted to but I never quite found the right words to start. But I want to talk about her now. I'm ready.'

'Who?' I asked hesitantly.

'My fiancée.'

'Y-your f...' I couldn't even say the word. I couldn't breathe. Couldn't think. 'I-I didn't know you were engaged.'

'We'd been together for so long; she was my whole world. I thought we had our whole lives to look forward together. And then one night she was just gone.' Scott's body crumpled as he shrank onto the bottom stair. 'There was an accident and she...' His voice cracked.

The sound of it broke through my inner turmoil and I rushed to him, wrapping my arms around him tightly, as though a hug could hold him together.

I wanted to ask what had happened. But this wasn't about me and my curiosity. This was about Scott.

Questions didn't make things better. I knew that. Being expected to relive the worst moments of your life on demand was torturous.

'It's okay, you don't have to talk about it. But I'm here if you ever do,' I whispered, the words I'd always wished someone would have said to me.

Scott mustered a small smile, and I could see the gratitude in his watery eyes. 'It was almost two years ago now,' he said, as though two years was a long time. That it should have been long enough to soften the pain. To move on.

But it wasn't. Two years was nothing.

'Grief knows no time limit,' I said gently.

Scott nodded. 'That's because grief is just love which has lost its recipient.'

'That's a beautiful way of looking at it.'

'I find grief comforting in a way. Not the pain of it exactly, but the presence of it.'

I nodded. I understood. There was something reassuring about knowing you still cared enough about the person you'd lost to feel the pain of it. There was a constant fear that if it dimmed, so would they. I knew what it was like to stare at old photographs, trying to embed their images so deeply into my memory that I would never forget them. And yet, still being fearful that one day I would. That one day, Mum's image would fade, that I would no longer be able to recall the sound of her voice.

'My grief means Sasha's still with me. That the love I carry for her is still strong. Still real.'

I wrapped my arms around him and hugged him tightly. His words were so beautiful, so heartfelt. And yet, my sorrow for his pain, didn't stop the jealousy that niggled at me.

He'd been engaged before.

There had been someone else. Someone so important to him that he'd wanted to share his life with her. Someone he still loved. *Sasha.*

There was a familiarity to it. I'd spent my whole life in second place. I'd thought with Scott I was first. But I couldn't compete with a memory. Sasha was frozen at a perfect moment in time, with the promise of a future together lying ahead of them. Scott would always remember the best things about her.

How would I ever be able to measure up to that?

'That's why I was so hurt by your actions.' Scott's voice was stronger now, edged in accusation.

I blinked. 'My actions? You mean, by me going out for a drink?'

'Not just a drink. Several. I could hear the slur to your words on the phone. You were drunk.'

'Not drunk, just a bit tipsy, maybe.'

'Because of Mia.' Contempt dripped from his words.

'It's not like she made me drink,' I pointed out indignantly. I resented the implication that Mia had that much control over me. Even if it was true.

'She's a bad influence on you,' Scott insisted. 'Just like Sasha's friends were a bad influence on her.'

'Is this why you've suddenly changed your view of Mia? You seemed to like her the other day, but now—'

'I will protect you from anyone who risks taking you away from me. Even your sister.'

'Mia's not going to take me away from you. She couldn't.' It was the one thing I knew with absolute certainty.

Scott arched an eyebrow. 'Really? How did you get home?'

'I-I walked,' I replied defensively. I wasn't stupid. I knew not to drink and drive.

'You walked.' Scott shook his head disapprovingly. 'You walked home alone after midnight, having had too much to drink. Anything could have happened to you.'

My indignance gave way and I lowered my gaze.

'Did Sa—' I clamped my mouth shut preventing me from finishing that question. I couldn't ask him if that was what had happened to Sasha. If she had gone out with her friends and had too much to drink. It wasn't fair to put him through the agony of reliving that pain.

Regardless of what had happened to Sasha, he was right about me. I'd thought I was being careful, but I'd overlooked the risks.

Again.

'Love comes with an obligation, a commitment. You have to think about the consequences of your decisions. You have to consider how your actions affect the people who love you.'

'I-I...' I wanted to object. To tell him that I'd spent years thinking about the consequences. The problem was it was all too late. The consequences had already happened and all I could do now was live with them.

'I'm sorry,' I murmured, embarrassment stifling my voice. 'I'll be more careful in future, I promise.'

Scott's love for me was so immense, he cared about what happened to me. That knowledge was like a warm hug. I mattered. And yet, somehow that hug felt restrictive.

Was it possible that Scott loved me too much? I shook my head slightly. Of course not, I just wasn't used to it. For the last six years Mia had been my benchmark. Compared to that no wonder Scott's intensity felt a little overwhelming.

So why couldn't I shake the feeling that I was being controlled again? Just like with Mia.

Scott nodded. 'Good, because I need you.' He wrapped his arms around me and hugged me tightly. 'I'm never going to let you go.'

35

NOW

October

I peered out of the living room window at the row of beach huts below. Aaron was back at the top of his ladder, hammer in hand, working on the roof again.

I studied him from the safety of my flat, confident that he wouldn't spot me up here. He was so focused on his work that I had no doubt I had already drifted from his mind.

And yet, for a brief moment I'd had his attention. I'd felt like I mattered. I inhaled slowly, allowing the air to fill my lungs, desperately trying to recapture that feeling and hold on to it.

But it was too late. It had already gone.

That feeling never lasted.

I shifted my weight from foot to foot. There was a fine line between mattering to someone and something more. Something darker.

Being with Scott had taught me that.

And he wasn't the first.

* * *

I sat on the bottom of my bed. I wasn't sure how I'd got there. I wasn't sure of anything. I felt like I was caught in a nightmare. Everything seemed hazy and distant. I was present. And yet I wasn't. Not fully.

What I'd witnessed on the promenade couldn't have been real. Aaron wouldn't shun me like that. I refused to believe it was possible.

And yet...

'Chloe?'

Mia's voice sounded muffled. I shifted my gaze, attempting to bring her into focus. But all I could see was the image of her hugging my boyfriend.

'Chloe?' Mia nudged me this time. 'Talk to me, Chloe.'

'Talk to you?' I spat the question at her as Mia's words broke through my daze. 'You left with my boyfriend, and you want me to talk to you?' Pain and anger bubbled up within me, the emotions that had been overwhelmed by shock were suddenly erupting.

'I went after him to find out what was happening, just like I told you I would.' Mia's wounded tone did nothing to quell my anger.

'You went to talk to him. Not hug him.'

'He was upset.'

'He was upset!' I leapt to my feet as I hurled her words back at her. 'What about me? Your sister?'

'Staying with you wouldn't have helped. What was I going to do? Give you a hug, buy you an ice cream and tell you to forget about him?' She shook her head. 'I knew you needed answers. I wanted to get them for you. It was the best way I could think of to help you.'

I blinked. Her reasoning sounded plausible. Mia had never been very good at offering emotional support. She was better at taking action. At doing something. Anything other than talking about feelings.

'D-did you...' I hesitated. 'Did you get answers?'

Mia nodded as she rested her hand on my forearm and guided me back to sit on the bed. 'Aaron said that you and he had grown apart and weren't in the same place any more.'

I frowned. 'What are you talking about? We are in the same place.' Her words didn't make any sense. 'We want the same things. The same future.'

Mia shuffled awkwardly beside me. 'I think he's just got cold feet about the trip.'

I froze. 'He doesn't want to go to Australia with me?'

How was that possible? We'd been talking about taking this trip for years. He'd always wanted to go with me.

'It is a big thing to expect him to go to another country with you. You can't blame him for wanting to go to university with his friends instead.'

'You don't even like him, and now suddenly you're talking about him as though you understand him.'

'I just know how fixated you've been on this idea.' She gave a feeble shrug. 'And I guess I can see why he might have felt pressured to go along with it to make you happy.'

Was that what I'd done? Had I pressured him into taking a gap year with me? To defer his admission to university and travel to the other side of the world with me?

'We're only eighteen,' Mia added, as though our age explained everything. 'He was scared to tell you. He knew how hurt you'd be.'

'So instead, he treated me like that?' I swallowed.

Mia gazed at me, her expression full of pity. 'I think he was just overwhelmed and didn't know how to handle it.'

I pushed myself up off the bed and turned toward the door. 'I need to see him. I need to tell him it's okay. That we don't have to go to Australia.' My words tumbled over themselves in my eagerness to fix my mistake. I shouldn't have suggested Australia. Just because I wanted to escape, it wasn't fair to expect Aaron to.

I reached for the door handle, but the second my skin touched the cold metal I froze.

If we didn't go to Australia, then what would we do? What would I do?

I'd been clinging to this dream for so long, I hadn't thought of anything else. Aaron had his parents to support him and a university place waiting for him. But me?

I had nothing.

My family merely tolerated my presence. They were as eager as I was for the day that I finally left. If I wasn't going to Australia, then I still had to go somewhere. Anywhere but here.

'Maybe you should give him some time.'

'But he needs to know it's okay. That we don't have to go. That he doesn't have to break up with me.'

Mia placed her hands on my shoulders and pivoted me away from the door. 'Let me talk to him again. I'll explain it to him.'

'But—'

'The worst thing you can do right now is crowd him. He already feels pressured. What he needs now is to see that you can give him time and space.'

I wanted to object, but how could I? Mia was right, I'd been so focused on what I needed, I hadn't paid enough attention to what Aaron needed. It never occurred to me that he might want a different future than the one we had mapped out at fifteen.

'It's going to be okay,' Mia assured me. 'I'll win him back for you. You know no one can resist me.'

* * *

I grunted. With hindsight I couldn't understand why I'd listened to Mia. I'd trusted her, and she'd let me down again.

Resentment bubbled inside me. Back then, I'd given her the

benefit of doubt. But knowing what I knew now, it was hard not to suspect she had intentionally deceived me. She'd never had any intention of helping me win Aaron back.

I turned away from the window. I shouldn't be standing here spying on Aaron, or letting my mind drift back to the past.

Both were slippery slopes.

Yet, even as I resolved to put the past behind me, I couldn't help thinking that I finally had the upper hand. I was Mia now. Everything she had taken from me was now within my grasp.

I was the irresistible one now.

36

THEN

September

I tipped my handbag upside down, scattering the contents across the living room carpet.

'Everything okay?' Scott asked from the sofa.

'I can't find the van keys.'

'When did you last have them?' Scott asked as he stood up and glanced around the room.

'Last night. I did a couple of flower deliveries before I went to meet Mia. But I always keep them in my bag.'

'Maybe you got distracted and put them down somewhere else?'

'I've checked the hall already, as well as the kitchen and upstairs.'

'What about your jacket pockets?'

'I've checked those too.'

'Well, I'm sure they'll turn up. They must be in the house somewhere.'

'Yeah.' I scratched my head. 'I guess so.'

'Can't you manage without the van today? You don't open the stall on Sundays.'

I shook my head. 'I told you earlier, I'm letting Mia borrow it today to go to drive to Dad's house in Reading.' I glanced at my watch. 'She'll be here any minute to collect it.'

'Don't you have a spare key you could give her?'

'I can't find that either.'

'You've lost both keys?' Scott stared at me in disbelief. 'How did you manage that?' He tipped his head to the side as he studied me. 'You have been really tired recently.'

'Have I?' I hadn't noticed feeling any different. I stepped in front of the decorative mirror that hung on the wall in the hall and studied my reflection.

Scott nodded. 'You've been working even longer hours than usual recently.'

I frowned as I turned back to face him. 'I haven't been working *that* much more. I've been making a few more deliveries thanks to the online orders finally picking up, but that's all.'

'And then you've been slotting Mia into every spare minute as well,' Scott continued, as though he hadn't heard me.

'I haven't seen much of Mia,' I objected indignantly. Except I wasn't sure which bothered me more, his accusation, or the fact that despite Mia being only ten minutes away, she was still keeping her distance.

'All I'm saying is that it's hardly any wonder you're exhausted.'

'Mia's return has been somewhat draining,' I acknowledged. 'Not because of the amount of time we've spent together, but because of how much energy her presence in my life consumes.' I clamped my mouth shut. I'd said too much. Scott didn't know I felt as though I was in a constant battle with myself: the part of me that wanted Mia to be here, to reconnect, to be real sisters, and the part that hated her.

'Perhaps it's taking a toll on your health,' Scott suggested.

I studied my reflection again. I still looked the same as I always did. At least to me. But perhaps Scott could see something I couldn't.

Perhaps he cared enough to notice.

Scott put his hands on my shoulders and guided me away from the mirror. 'Why don't you put your feet up and I'll put the kettle on?' he said, steering me towards the sofa.

'But I still need to find the keys. I don't know where else to look.' I shook my head. 'I just don't understand what could have happened to them.'

'Mia will just have to make other arrangements. A train maybe, or a taxi.'

I screwed my nose up. 'Yeah, but I feel like I'm letting her down.'

'I'm sure she'll get over it. There's no point getting yourself all stressed out over it. Besides, it's not like you've lost them on purpose, is it?'

'No,' I said, but I heard the wobble of doubt that edged into my voice. I couldn't have done, could I? I might have conflicting emotions about Mia, but I wouldn't actually try and sabotage her day, would I? Not even subconsciously?

Would I?

37

NOW

October

The morning sunlight peeked through the grey wintery sky as I reached the bottom of the slope and paused. Turning left would take me straight past Aaron's beach hut. I knew he was there. I'd watched him from the window again.

I felt my body shift slightly to the left. It was so tempting to go in that direction. To casually stop and chat. To fall back into the friendship we'd once had.

But it wasn't that simple.

I turned right and marched forward, afraid that if I slowed my pace, I might change my mind.

My gaze locked on the pier, but now instead of just bringing back memories of Mum, it also reminded me of Aaron. Of his smile. His concern.

I felt a familiar tug in my chest. I longed for that. To have someone who cared about me. Really cared about me. Not just for the short term, or until someone more interesting came along. I wanted someone genuine. Someone good.

Was Aaron good? Was he the one?

* * *

'You can do this,' I told myself for the tenth time as I walked down the slope and veered to the left towards the beach huts.

I shouldn't have listened to Mia. I knew she was trying to help, but she didn't know Aaron like I did. Staying away from him wasn't the answer. We needed to talk. It was one of the things I loved about us: no matter what the topic, or how hard it was, we could always talk things through together. This was no different.

If he'd changed his mind about Australia, I could accept that. We would simply make a new plan. Together.

Squeals from a group of girls approaching ahead caught my attention. My gaze narrowed as I squinted at them in the August sun. It sounded like Mia.

Just then Mia broke away from the group and ran a few steps ahead towards me, grinning broadly.

I blinked. I'd never seen her so excited to greet me before. A warm rush radiated from my chest as I lifted my hand to wave at her.

Suddenly she veered to the right. My gaze followed her, and I watched as she leapt up the small step in front of Aaron's beach hut and flung her arms around his neck.

My body went limp as my hand fell to my side and my feet stopped moving. What was happening?

Aaron lifted his hands and rested them on her waist. The noises of the beach beside me fell away. I waited for him to push her away. But he didn't. He stayed there. Her arms around his neck and his hands on her waist.

I wanted to look away. I needed to. But I couldn't. My body wouldn't comply. All I could do was stand and stare.

* * *

I shook my head, pushing the memory away. I wouldn't get my hopes up over Aaron. Not again. Not after the last time.

I needed to be more careful.

I *would* be more careful.

Music disrupted my thoughts, and my gaze dropped to Mia's handbag hanging from my shoulder.

I'd kept her phone charged, because it seemed best to continue as normal. Act as she would. But now it was ringing, I actually had to answer it.

I reached into the bag and pulled the phone out. I stared at the name displayed on the screen.

Ethan.

They'd only met once and yet his number was already in her phone. I wasn't sure why that surprised me.

The question was, why would he be calling now? To talk to Mia? Or to talk about me?

My stomach lurched. Did he know what I'd done?

I fought to keep my breathing under control. I couldn't fall apart. Not now. There was too much at stake. But that didn't stop my thoughts from spiralling.

There was no coming back from something like this.

And yet, if Ethan had figured out the truth, surely he wouldn't be calling. The police would be banging on my door instead.

Or Scott would be.

So what *did* Ethan want?

I frowned at the phone in my hand. There was only one way to find out. My finger hovered over the answer button.

'You know you do actually have to press the button to make it stop ringing.' Rachel's voice startled me, and I nearly dropped the phone. 'Sorry,' she said, though she sounded more amused than apologetic.

A baby squirmed in Rachel's arms. 'She's teething,' Rachel informed me, sounding rather frazzled. 'She's been awake almost all night. I took her for a walk on the beach, hoping some fresh air would make her sleepy.' Rachel let out a weary sigh as the baby whimpered. 'So much for that idea.'

'I'm sorry,' I said, and I realised I actually meant it. Rachel might not be my favourite person, but that didn't mean I couldn't be sympathetic.

'They'll hang up, you know?' Rachel said briskly, seeming unnerved by my empathy.

'Huh?' I murmured, unable to shift my gaze from the baby in her arms.

Beneath my sympathy, there was another emotion. One that was far too familiar. How was it that someone like Rachel had managed to get everything I'd ever wanted? A husband. Kids. A family.

All the things I'd thought were finally within my reach until just a few days ago.

'The phone,' Rachel said.

I blinked. 'Oh, right. I should answer it. I'll just go...' I pointed towards the side of the promenade where I could take my call away from everyone else. 'Nice to see you both.' I mumbled as I turned away.

I took a few steps and hit the hang up button. I didn't want to talk to Ethan. I didn't want to talk to anyone.

Glancing back over my shoulder, I realised Rachel was watching me. Her curiosity had been piqued.

That wasn't good.

Rachel was like a shark. Once she smelled blood in the water, she started circling, ready to strike. I had enough people I had to be careful of already, I didn't need her getting involved as well.

I turned away quickly, trying to push the image of her curious expression from my mind. I didn't want to think about Ethan or her.

And yet, I knew from experience ignorance wasn't always better.

38

THEN

September

'I guess you found your keys, then.'

I swung round at the sound of Mia's voice behind me, a bucket of roses in my hands. 'Yeah.' I cast a sheepish glance back at the van. 'I did.'

'Where were they?'

I busied myself loading the roses into the cart, keeping my head down. 'In my coat pocket.' My cheeks burned as I spoke. 'I could have sworn I'd looked there. I just don't understand how I missed them.' I glanced up at Mia. 'I'm really sorry.'

She eyed me suspiciously. I knew she wouldn't believe me. I couldn't blame her. I wouldn't have believed her if our roles were reversed.

Mia shrugged. 'As Mum would say, there's no point crying over spilt milk. Or in this case lost keys.'

I flinched at the unexpected mention of Mum. I couldn't think of a time when Mia had quoted her before. She barely spoke of her at all.

'I'll give you a hand,' Mia announced as she grabbed a bucket from the back of the van.

What was happening? First Mia wasn't holding a grudge, and now she was helping me? I didn't even think she knew what park my stall was in, let alone expect her to actually be helping me set it up.

'Is everything okay?' I asked cautiously. If Mia was being this nice, then something was wrong.

'Everything's great,' she replied, shooting me a bright smile.

My heart raced. She was definitely up to something.

'I just thought I could keep you company for a bit. I've never seen you in work mode.'

'It's the same as my usual "mode",' I said with forced brightness. 'It just involves a lot more flowers.'

Mia chuckled.

Mia never chuckled at my sarcasm. She never offered to help. And she certainly never showed any interest in my work.

'Why are you looking at me like that?' Mia asked, pausing as she reached back into the van for more flowers.

'Like what?'

'Like I have two heads or something.'

I rolled my eyes as though she was being ridiculous. 'I'm just surprised, that's all.'

'Is it really so unbelievable that I would want to come and help you?'

'Yes.'

We both froze as we stared at each other. I waited for the fall out. The indignation. The drama.

I should have lied and said no, just to keep the peace. And yet, for some reason I hadn't.

Mia suddenly started laughing. 'You have a point.'

I blinked. She wasn't mad at my bluntness. She wasn't even offended. Who was this woman in front of me?

'Come on,' Mia said, handing me more flowers. 'You're never going to sell anything if you stand there gaping at me all day.' She slammed the van doors closed, grabbed the handle of the cart and started pushing it towards the entrance of the park. 'You might want to give me directions,' she called back over her shoulder to me, 'otherwise, your stall is probably going to end up in a new location today.'

My body jolted back into action, and I hurried after her. Whatever Mia was up to, right now she was clearly staying.

* * *

'Are you sure you don't want to sit down for a while?' I asked, shifting my weight ready to stand up and vacate the stool for her.

Mia waved her hand as she paced in front of the stall. 'No, you stay put. It's your stool.'

I sank back reluctantly. I wished she would have sat down. All her pacing was making me nervous.

'Are you going to tell me what's on your mind?' I asked finally, unable to bear the suspense any longer.

Mia paused her pacing and turned to face me. 'I had a lot of time to think when I was doing that long journey in the taxi yesterday.'

The taxi.

I nodded slowly. Of course, that's what this was about. I knew Mia's acceptance of me letting her down had been too easy.

'I feel like you and I aren't as close as we used to be.'

Close.

That word didn't fit. We had never been close. Not when we were kids, and certainly not as adults.

'We don't spend as much time together these days,' Mia continued.

Her words sounded so heartfelt, but I knew her better than that. The distance in our relationship was her decision, not mine. Curiously, it had never concerned her before. So why would it now?

I rolled my eyes. The answer was obvious. She was playing games again. Manipulating me by tugging at my emotions. Or at least, she was trying to.

'It's hard to spend time together when we are in different countries,' I pointed out flatly.

Mia nodded. 'That's true. But we're not in different countries now. And yet...' She shrugged, leaving her statement unfinished. 'I mean, I get it; things are different now. You have a boyfriend. Of course he takes priority over your twin sister. But, well, I guess I just miss you, that's all.'

'You do?' I couldn't keep the dubiousness out of my voice. Since when did Mia miss anyone?

'And then I started thinking about the cruise, and how that's going to be another four months apart.'

'Okay,' I acknowledged hesitantly. Mia was building up to something, I knew she was. Something bad was coming...

'And do you know how much they charge for a single supplement?' Her eyes widened. 'I mean, I might as well pay the extra and just take someone with me.'

'So you're not going on the cruise?' I asked hesitantly. Emotions bubbled inside me, so many that I wasn't sure which was strongest. Hope? Fear?

Mia cast a puzzled look at me. 'It's the trip of a lifetime. Of course I'm still going. Weren't you listening?'

I managed a half nod. 'I was, but...' I shrugged helplessly, completely confused.

'But I'm not going alone.'

'Oh.' I nodded fully this time. That's why she was rambling about the single supplement.

'You're coming with me.'

39

NOW

October

It was tempting to turn around and retreat back to the solitude of Mia's flat. Except, I didn't dare turn around in case Rachel was still standing there, watching me.

I ambled forwards. At least this way I knew I was safe.

A store on my right was just opening up for the day, and I watched as a young woman wheeled a rack of colourful beach toys onto the promenade. She smiled and nodded, before disappearing back inside.

My pace slowed as something niggled in the recesses of my memory. There had been a shop here when I'd come with my parents too, but it was... I froze as the woman returned but this time, she wheeled out a rack of surfboards.

A surf shop.

My breathing was fast. Too fast. The short gasps of air were making me feel lightheaded. But then again, maybe that was the memories.

I was being ridiculous. They were just surfboards. And yet I knew, they were so much more than that.

Mum paused in front of the surf shop as we waited for Dad and Mia to catch up.

'Mum?' I followed her gaze to the line of surfboards she was staring at as though she was transfixed by them. 'Mum?' I repeated, touching her arm when she didn't reply.

She turned to me with a jolt. For a split second she looked confused, as though she'd forgotten I was there. And then suddenly her smile was back in place. 'Sorry, honey, did you say something?'

'Are you okay?' I asked, edging closer to her. There was something about her behaviour that worried me. Despite her smile she seemed so lost and sad.

'Yes, I'm fine.' Her voice was bright. Too bright. It sounded forced and unnatural.

'You were staring at the surfboards.'

'Oh, was I?' Mum shrugged. 'I guess I was just lost in old memories.'

My eyes widened. 'You used to surf?'

'I did indeed. My dad taught me.' She lifted her chin, and her eyes shone with pride. 'I was pretty good at it too.'

'That's so cool.'

She nodded but she still didn't seem to be fully present as she lifted her hand and traced her fingers across one of the boards. 'I grew up here, you know?'

'Until you moved away for university, right?'

She blinked and turned to me. 'Yes, that's right. Someone has been paying attention to their old mum's boring stories.'

'You're not old.' I rolled my eyes. 'And your stories aren't boring. I love hearing them.'

She put her hand on my shoulder and gave it a gentle squeeze. 'And I love sharing them with you.'

'But you don't talk about them very often.'

'No, I guess I don't.' Her attention drifted back to the surfboards. 'I miss those days,' she said wistfully. 'The simplicity. The excitement.'

My eyes lit up as a brilliant idea formed in my head. 'You should go surfing.'

'What?' Mum laughed. 'Me? Surf?'

'We could hire surfboards, and you could teach me.'

'I couldn't.' She cast a sideways glance back at the surfboards.

'Why not? You know you want to.' I could see it in her eyes: the wistful longing of wanting something so badly it hurt. I glanced at Mia over my shoulder. I knew how that felt.

'I haven't been on a surfboard since Dad died,' Mum said, her voice brittle and strained. I turned back and noticed tears forming in the corner of her eyes.

'I'm sorry, Mum.' I reached out and stroked her arm gently. 'You don't have to teach me to surf.'

'Are we going surfing?' Mia's excited voice demanded behind me.

I cringed. Why had Mia had to arrive just then? 'No,' I said firmly. 'Mum doesn't want to.'

'But I want to.' Mia pouted. 'Dad will take me, won't you, Dad?' She turned her back on Mum and smiled sweetly at Dad.

'Well, I—' Dad started.

'Pleeease,' Mia begged.

Dad looked across at Mum, and she gave a slight shrug. It was inevitable. Mia always got what she wanted.

'Yes!' Mia cheered.

She grabbed Dad's hand and tugged him towards the shop. 'Come on, let's go now.'

'Chloe, are you coming?' Dad asked, holding his other hand out to me.

I shook my head. 'I'll stay with Mum.'

'Don't be silly,' Mum said, her voice stronger now. 'You don't want to miss out on all the fun.'

I glanced uncertainly back and forth between Mum and Dad.

'I'll be fine,' Mum whispered in my ear, giving me a nudge towards Dad. 'Go surfing.'

Tremors vibrated through my body. Why had I had to go and ask Mum to teach me how to surf? If I hadn't, maybe she would still be alive.

40

THEN

September

'Chloe!'

I paused with my hand on the door handle, about to close it. I leaned forward in my seat, and peered out of the open doorway, to see Scott running toward me.

'Hey,' he greeted me as I stepped back out of the van and gave him a hug. 'How come you've packed up so early tonight? That's not like you.'

'Oh, I just felt like calling it a day.'

He pressed the back of his hand against my forehead. 'Aren't you feeling well?'

'No, I'm fine,' I assured him. 'I'm just a little preoccupied, that's all,' I added.

'Hmm,' Scott murmured. 'I know just the thing for that.' He took the van keys from my hand, closed the door and activated the central locking. 'Come on,' he said, slipping his hand in mine. 'I'm buying you a coffee and you can tell me what's on your mind.'

* * *

'I upheld my part of the deal,' Scott said, as we wandered through the park, coffees in hand. 'Now it's your turn.'

'It's Mia,' I admitted.

Scott nodded. 'I figured it would be. I knew she'd give you a hard time about not lending her your van yesterday.'

I cast a sideways glance at him. 'You said it wasn't a big deal.'

'It isn't, but I get the feeling your sister is used to people doing things her way. Especially you.'

I rubbed the back of my neck. This was so different to what he'd said to me yesterday. He'd made me feel like I was being overly anxious worrying about Mia's reaction.

'It'll all be fine, babe. You girls just need a little time apart and it'll blow over. I know she's your sister, but it's for the best, trust me.'

I shook my head. 'No, you don't understand,' I said, turning to face Scott. 'Mia isn't mad at me. We don't need time apart. In fact, she wants me to go with her on her world cruise.'

Scott ran his hand through his hair. 'She wants what? But you can't.'

I flinched at the abruptness of his words. 'Why can't I?' I asked defiantly.

Scott blinked. 'You're not serious, are you?'

I started to shake my head. Of course I wasn't. The idea of actually accepting Mia's invitation was too ludicrous to even consider. There were countless reasons why I couldn't possibly go. Why I wouldn't want to go.

And yet, something stopped me.

'What if I actually did go?'

Scott and I stared at each other speechless.

'It's like a six-month trip,' Scott said finally.

'Four,' I corrected him.

'Oh, only four? Well, that makes all the difference, then,' Scott scoffed.

'I can't talk to you if you're going to be like this.' I turned on my heel and started marching back towards the van.

'Chloe, wait.' I heard Scott's footsteps following behind me. 'I'm sorry. You just caught me off guard. I mean, it's four months apart from each other.'

I drew to a halt. 'I know,' I said quietly.

'I'd miss you so much if you go away for that long.'

I nodded. 'Me too.'

'But you haven't ruled it out. So I can't help wondering if you've really considered me.'

'I have. Of course I have. I'm not really thinking of going. Or at least I wasn't. But then...'

'I made you mad at me?'

I smiled slightly. 'Yeah, kind of. And then I just started wondering. I mean, it's a world cruise! When am I ever going to get that kind of opportunity again?'

'A world cruise *with your sister*.' Scott grimaced.

'What's wrong with my sister?'

My tone surprised me. It sounded indignant. As though I was offended at his disdain for Mia. When really, I was just curious.

I wanted him to voice all the thoughts I'd never been able to say aloud. To list her flaws. To acknowledge her manipulative, controlling behaviour. Her intention to hurt me.

Because if he said it, maybe it would finally make me face it. The truth that I worked so hard to deny. That I would be better off without Mia in my life.

'Nothing,' Scott replied, a little too quickly. 'I like her. I do. But I'm not really sure that you do.'

I ground my toe into the dried mud path. 'That's not tr...' My objection withered on my lips. How could I claim it wasn't true? I didn't *like* Mia. Sometimes I questioned if I even loved her. And yet, if I didn't, why hadn't I cut ties with her like I'd done with Dad?

Did I want her in my life out of a desperate need to hang on to the last remaining thread of family I had, no matter how frayed the relationship was? Or was it unrealistic hope that drove me? Wistful thinking that maybe one day things could be different between us? Maybe she could accept me? Forgive me?

'Maybe this is exactly what we need. Time away, just the two of us. Maybe we could reconnect. Rebuild the relationship.'

'Maybe,' Scott said doubtfully. 'But if you haven't been able to do that in twenty odd years, what makes you think you're going to accomplish it in four months on a boat in the middle of the ocean?'

Silently I had to concede he had a valid point. Sharing a room had been a nightmare as kids. What made me think it would be any better sharing one again now? Especially on a ship where there was nowhere to run away.

'I know it's a crazy idea. I guess I got kind of swept up in the excitement that she even asked me to go. She's never asked me to go anywhere before.'

'I know she's important to you. And I really want things to get better between you two and for you to see her more often. But I'm just not sure this is the solution. In fact, I have a bad feeling that it could be the opposite.'

I nodded. He was right. 'But the fact that she's even suggested this, is huge. It could be a real game changer for us. And I can't help feeling like my decision here could make or break our relationship. Saying no when she's holding out an olive branch...' I shook my head.

The implications of my unfinished sentence hung between

us, as Scott wrung his hands together. He looked as unnerved as I felt.

'It all seems rather sudden though, doesn't it? Why would she suddenly make an offer like this?'

I frowned. 'She did say the single supplement was expensive.'

'Ah, of course. It would be cheaper for her if you go too.'

'Yes, but surely that couldn't be the only reason she asked me. Could it? She has friends she could have asked instead.'

'Maybe she already did. Maybe they said no. Not everyone can just put their lives on hold for four months.' Was Scott, right? Was I a second choice? Or more likely the last choice once she had exhausted her list of people she actually liked?

And did it matter if I was?

Part of me wanted to believe it didn't. The key thing to focus on was that Mia had invited *me*. But another part knew the naivety of thinking like that. I'd been used by Mia before. She always had an ulterior motive. It was foolish to believe this would be any different.

She hadn't changed. And, it seemed, neither had I. I still let her get in my head. I let her manipulate me. Confuse me. No matter what she did or how badly she betrayed me, somehow, I never learnt.

Scott wiped his palms against his jeans. 'Besides, you don't know that turning her down could end things.'

'True, I don't. Not for sure. But can I really take that risk? She's the only family that I have.'

'Sh-she doesn't have to be.' Uncertainty vibrated in his voice.

My head snapped up and I stared at him. 'What does that mean?'

Scott licked his lips as his gaze darted back and forth across my face. 'We could be a family. You and me.'

My heart soared at those three little words. *You and me.* The way he said them sounded special. United. Inseparable.

'You want that too, don't you?' His nervousness was endearing. It showed this was important to him.

I nodded rapidly. 'Of course I do.' I'd wanted it ever since I'd first laid eyes on him.

'I never thought I'd feel this way again, not after losing Sasha. The pain of it crushed me. It numbed me to everything. Nothing mattered any more. And then I met you.' Scott's eyes were bright and glossy as he stared into mine. 'You brought me back to life, Chloe.'

I cupped his face in the palm of my hand, speechless at his unaccustomed outpouring of emotion.

Scott's Adam's apple bobbed up and down as he swallowed repeatedly. 'The thought of you not being in my life, even just for a few months, terrifies me.'

'Oh, Sco—'

He pressed his finger gently against my lips. 'Let me finish, please. Before I lose my nerve.'

I nodded silently.

'I want this, Chloe. I want you. Us. Together. Not just for now, but for always. I know you'll say we haven't been together long enough for me to be talking like this. But time is irrelevant when you know. And I *know*.'

'You do?' I stared at him. How could he be so sure? Especially about me.

'We're good together, Chloe.'

I nodded. We were. Scott was everything I'd hoped for. Everything I needed. Solid. Dependable. Protective. Loving. He was good to me.

But more than that, he was good *for* me.

With him I felt like I mattered. My feelings, my opinions,

everything about me mattered. It made me feel like perhaps there could be something worthwhile about me after all. That maybe I could be worthy of that kind of love.

With him, I might finally get to be part of something again. Part of a family. A real one where I was accepted. Loved.

'So, what do you say?'

'I, I—' I stuttered. I didn't know how to answer. He wasn't actually serious, was he? He couldn't really mean—

'Chloe Philips.' Scott reached out and took my left hand in his. 'Will you marry me?'

I stared at him. Nothing about this was how I'd imagined. I'd longed to be asked that question. To be wanted that much. And I couldn't deny that since I'd meet Scott, I'd secretly hoped that it would be him. That one day he would propose. But in my mind, it was always somewhere beautiful and exotic. He'd get down on one knee with a delicate diamond ring in his outstretched hand.

This was nothing like that. It was too soon. Too impulsive. Too unprepared.

And yet, it was perfect.

A broad smile spread across my face as I found myself nodding. 'Yes,' I murmured. 'Yes, I'll marry you.'

41

NOW

October

I pivoted on my heel. I was wrong, avoiding Aaron wasn't the answer. I needed someone with me. Someone to distract me.

Aaron might just be the key to my survival here. Just like he had been before.

I hurried back past the apartment complex, refusing to pay attention to the seed of doubt that niggled in the pit of my stomach.

I was doing it again. Latching on to someone. Convincing myself that they would save me.

The problem was, I wasn't sure anyone could save me from myself.

I slowed as I approached Aaron's beach hut. Now that I was here, I had no idea what to say.

'Mia, hi,' Aaron called as he waved at me from in front of his beach hut.

It was too late to retreat now.

I walked towards him, attempting to look nonchalant and casual, while my heart raced.

How was it possible that after all these years he still had that effect on me?

Then again, given his beaming smile, it seemed I still had an effect on him too.

Reality hit me like an icy wave. It wasn't me that had an impact.

It was Mia.

She was the one who'd broken his heart. The one who'd caused him to abandon his decision to go to university and flee England instead.

The irony was, she was a large part of the reason I'd wanted to do exactly the same. And in the end, she'd been the reason I'd stayed.

'These early mornings are getting to be a habit, I see,' he teased as I reached him. 'You do know you're on vacation, right?'

Vacation.

Aaron assumed that was what this was for me. A temporary break from reality. A week or two and then I'd leave again. Another job. Another country. Another life.

Except this time everything was different. There wouldn't be any more jobs. At least not the ones Mia was used to.

I'd been so focused on leaving London, on escaping everything that happened there, that I hadn't actually considered what I would do once I was in Bournemouth.

'I guess I haven't quite adjusted to not having my usual routine yet,' I admitted.

'Don't tell me you worked weekends as well?' Aaron studied me dubiously. 'That doesn't sound like the Mia I know.'

He was right of course. Mia had a far too busy social life at the weekends to even contemplate working. Whereas for me, a day off was a rare occurrence. Sundays were my only chance for a lie-in, but even then, there were flower arrangements to create, or deliveries to make.

I'd longed for a break. A chance to slow down. To rest. And yet, the irony was, now that I could do exactly that, I missed my work. My purpose.

I'd always wanted to be Mia so badly, that it had never occurred to me that I might actually miss being me. And now I could never be me again.

That one spur of the moment decision to keep quiet when Ethan mistook Mia for me, had trapped me. I could have corrected him then. I *should* have corrected him. But the lure of being Mia was too strong.

I'd waited a lifetime for this moment. I'd thought it would be more gratifying. Instead, I was just treading water, trying not to sink.

'I'm not sure I am the Mia you know any more. At least, not completely.' I kept my gaze steady. 'I'm making some changes.'

Aaron arched his eyebrow. 'What kind of changes?'

'Well, for a start, this isn't just a vacation. I'm taking a career break. It will give me chance to reassess what I want to do with my life. Who I want to be.'

'Wow,' Aaron nodded. 'That sounds incredible.'

I smiled ruefully. 'Yeah, but it's also terrifying. For the first time in my life, I don't know what to do.'

'I can help with that,' Aaron said with a mischievous grin. 'You can give me a hand with these repairs.' He picked up a hammer and held it out towards me.

I stared at it. Part of me wanted to reach out and snatch it from his hands, eager to be productive again. But that part was Chloe.

Mia was different. She didn't do manual labour.

'You owe me, remember?' Aaron said, without budging.

'I do?'

Aaron laughed. 'Nice try, but you know feigning innocence doesn't work on me. I know you too well.'

I swallowed. He thought he did.

Scott had thought that once too.

'Do you have somewhere better to be?' Aaron asked, still not giving up.

I shook my head. The truth was, I didn't.

As confusing as this situation was, it was still more favourable to Mia's empty flat.

'Perfect,' Aaron said, as I took the hammer. 'Then you can be my Chloe for the day.'

'Your Chloe?' The hammer slipped from my grasp and thudded onto the wooden decking. 'S-sorry,' I stammered, as I lunged forwards to pick it up.

'Are you okay?' Aaron asked, his voice full of concern. 'Did it hit you?'

I shook my head.

'Sorry, I shouldn't have called you Chloe. I know you both hated it when people mixed you up.'

'It's fine,' I said, trying to muster a shrug.

'No, it's not. It's just—' he shook his head '—for a second there I guess I was sixteen again, repainting the hut with Chloe.'

'Do you miss her?' I asked.

'She was my best friend,' Aaron replied quietly.

I nodded slowly. That was the problem. I was *just* a friend.

* * *

'I'm doing it for you,' Mia insisted.

I stared at her; my jaw dropped. 'You're dating my boyfriend for me?' Even in Mia's warped sense of morality that declaration would never – could never – make sense.

'Of course; you're my sister. Why else would I go out with your ex?'

'Because you know I love him? Because you wanted to hurt me? Because you were always jealous of my relationship?'

Mia shook her head. 'I'd never want to hurt you.'

I studied her. Could I really believe that? She seemed to specialise in hurting me and yet, her words seemed so heartfelt. So genuine. But then they always did.

'But him on the other hand…' Mia grinned mischievously. 'No guy is going to get away with treating my sister the way he did.'

I frowned in confusion. 'So his punishment is to date you?'

'I'm going to make him fall in love with me, just like you fell for him. And then when he can't bear the thought of being apart, I'll dump him and ghost him the way he has done to you. I'll show him just how it feels to get his heart broken.' Her eyes glinted with a spitefulness that I was only too familiar with.

This time, though, it wasn't directed at me. She was doing it for *me*.

And yet, despite her declarations of sisterly solidarity, there was something that still didn't sit right about her plan.

She was the twin he would fall in love with.

It never even occurred to her that he could have ever loved me once. Her assumption was that Aaron would fall in love with her in a way he never could with me. That she could break his heart.

But leaving me hadn't.

42

THEN

September

'Mia wants to meet me for dinner tomorrow night,' I told Scott as I washed a dinner plate and handed it to him to dry.

'Again?'

I paused, my hands immersed in the hot, soapy water at his incredulous tone. 'She *is* my sister,' I said indignantly.

'Of course she is, I just meant, is it a good idea right now? She's going to be disappointed when you tell her you're not going on the cruise with her.'

Scott and I hadn't discussed Mia's invitation again. But after his proposal it seemed a moot point. Of course I wouldn't be going now.

I scrunched my nose. 'That's true.' I wasn't looking forward to that conversation with Mia.

'Maybe it would be better to just send her a text,' Scott suggested with a shrug.

'I can't send her a text about this.' I lifted another plate from the water, to hand to Scott, and my gaze locked on the sparkly diamond ring on my finger. More importantly, I didn't want to send Mia a text. This was news I intended to tell her in person.

I'd just leave out the part where Scott had abandoned me at the jewellery store, leaving me to pick out my ring alone because he'd had to work late.

'She invited you on holiday, it's not a big deal to say no. *We* have other plans.'

A warm glow radiated from me. I loved the way he said we. But he was wrong. 'It's not just a holiday,' I said sadly. Mia had finally given me the one thing I'd always wanted: an invitation into her life. To be her sister again. 'I have to handle this right and let her down gently.'

'Fine, but I'm coming too.' Scott slid the dry plate into the cupboard and planted a kiss on my forehead.

'Afraid she'll talk me into going with her?' I teased.

Scott chuckled. 'I'm more worried she'll make you feel bad for choosing me over her.'

I tipped my head to the right. 'Is that how you see it?'

'It's how she'll see it.'

I couldn't argue with that. There was no way that Mia wouldn't take my decision as a personal slight. But it wasn't really a case of choosing Scott over her. It was about putting myself first. My needs. My plans. Not just marrying Scott, but opening my flower shop, buying a house. Finally living the life I'd been dreaming about.

I let out a weary sigh as I watched Scott walk into the living room and drop down onto the sofa. As much as I appreciated his desire to be there and protect me, the thought of being a third wheel between Scott and Mia whilst they conversed in French for a second time was unappealing.

It meant nothing, I knew that. But what if Scott realised he'd asked the wrong sister to marry him? The quiet, boring twin, when he could have had loud, outgoing Mia.

I could always ask Mia to bring a date. She'd have no trouble finding one. There was no doubt in my mind about that. She loved flaunting her ability to meet guys when it suited her, but making me jealous because of her connection with my boyfriend probably had an even greater appeal. And asking her to bring a date would ensure she knew just how much it bothered me.

Which meant I needed to invite someone for her.

'Does Ethan have a girlfriend?'

Scott's head jolted up from his phone. 'No, why?'

'I thought we could invite him to join us for dinner with Mia tomorrow. It would be good for them to meet before the wedding. And I'd like to get to know your friend better too.'

Scott shifted. Was it my imagination or did he look uncomfortable?

'Plus, it will give you someone to talk to while Mia and I talk wedding stuff.'

Scott laughed and I knew I'd won him over. 'That's a good point. I'll send him a message now.'

I smiled to myself as Scott typed a message. Mia was wrong. Keeping Scott wasn't that difficult. I just had to give him a gentle nudge in the right direction occasionally.

43

October

'I guess I should probably get going,' I said reluctantly, as the sun started to set. I couldn't believe how quickly the day had slipped by. Working side by side with Aaron again had felt safe and familiar.

How was that even possible after the way he'd treated me at eighteen?

Aaron nodded. 'Meeting up with the girls?'

I frowned. 'The girls?' Realisation dawned on me a second too late. He meant Rachel and her little clique.

'I thought you were all still tight?'

'Yes. Yes we are. But, er, I came back kind of unexpectedly so, you know, we haven't really reconnected yet.' I swallowed, uncertain whether my rambling had actually made any sense.

'Ah, I see.' Aaron nodded. 'Well, if you're at a loose end and feel like some company, why don't we go for dinner?'

My heart rate quickened. Dinner with Aaron. I'd missed that.

'Let's head home and get cleaned up, and then I'll pick you

up and take you somewhere fancy. We deserve it after all our hard work. And it would be good to have a proper catch up. You can fill me in on all your exciting adventures in Rome.'

'Oh, right.' Of course he wanted to hear about Mia. Her adventures. Her life. I sucked in a deep breath. It wasn't ideal. It wasn't the way I'd hoped. But I could still make it work.

Besides, the one thing Mia loved to do was talk about herself. I'd heard all about her adventures. I flicked my hair over my shoulder. 'Actually, that would be great.'

I was getting better at this.

You'll still find a way to screw it up. You always do.

I shook my head.

Not this time. This time was different. I wasn't me any more.

I was Mia.

I had to be her. All of her. Every detail mattered. There wasn't room for error or embellishment. I knew her life almost as well as I knew my own. I should be able to do this.

I *was* doing this.

I had to.

I wasn't just playing dress-up in my sister's life out of a desire to satisfy a lifelong wish. It was a necessity.

My life depended on it.

* * *

'You look nice,' Aaron said as I slipped my coat off and draped it over the back of the chair in the Captain's Club restaurant.

Someone opened the door beside me to slip out onto the terrace for a cigarette and the October chill penetrated to my bones as I held my breath, waiting for him to continue. His eyebrows drew together as he studied me.

'Th-thank you,' I stuttered hesitantly as I slid into my chair, torn between waiting for the caveat to his compliment and the realisation that waiting any longer, or failing to acknowledge it at all, would appear rude.

'I was paying you a compliment,' he said slowly as confusion radiated from him.

'Thank you,' I repeated again. What else could I say? To explain my reaction would lead me back through a door to the past.

And that was a door that needed to stay firmly closed.

'Would you like some water?' the waitress asked as she handed us the menus.

'Yes, please,' Aaron and I replied in unison, and she smiled as she nodded and walked away.

'You've got to stop listening to that little voice in your head,' Aaron said as soon as she was out of earshot.

I swallowed, but my mouth felt dry. 'The voice...' I couldn't even finish the sentence.

How could he know?

'It's so strange, sometimes you remind me so much of Chloe.'

'Well,' I cleared my throat, 'we do look alike.'

I glanced behind me, hoping the waitress wouldn't be long.

Aaron shook his head. 'No, I don't mean your appearance. I mean the way you are. After your mum died, Chloe sort of shrank away within herself. She was always listening to that little voice in her head that told her she wasn't enough. Not good enough, not smart enough, not—' Aaron paused and gave a small, almost apologetic shrug '—Mia enough.'

His words sliced through me, and I stared at him speechless. But it wasn't the fact he'd so accurately identified the sense of inadequacy within me that surprised me. I'd never been very good at hiding my envy of Mia, especially in front of Aaron. He could always read me so well. But the sadness in his voice confused me.

Not Mia enough.

That simple fact had tormented me every single day for as long as I could remember. The difference now was it wasn't just me who thought it. Aaron thought it too.

'You have that same voice. Only yours has always told you you're not Chloe enough.'

I was vaguely aware that the waitress had returned with a jug of iced water and was filling our glasses. 'Are you ready to order, or would you like a few more minutes?' she asked.

My gaze dropped to the menu in my hands, but the words had no meaning to me.

'Yes, please.' Aaron's voice sounded far away even though he was sitting opposite me. 'We'll need more time.'

The waitress's shadow shifted from my menu, and I realised she must have left, but I still couldn't focus.

'Mia?' Aaron's voice was soft and gentle. 'Are you okay? You look a bit pale.'

I nodded mutely. Except I wasn't okay. I was questioning everything I'd thought I knew.

'What do you mean, not Chloe enough?'

'I'm sorry, I know you two hate to be compared to each other.'

'No, it's fine.' I leaned forward on the edge of my seat. 'But what did you mean?'

Concentration was etched on Aaron's face as he struggled to find the right words. 'I saw the way you used to look at her. The envy in your eyes.'

I snorted. 'Envious of Chloe?'

'You've always loved to be at the centre of things. You surrounded yourself with a big group of friends. People that looked up to you. Idolised you. But whenever I saw you, somehow you seemed lonely.'

'Seriously?' Mia wasn't lonely. She was popular.

'Chloe never needed that. She didn't have many people in her life, but the people she did have meant everything to her. I think you were jealous of that. That connection. That closeness.'

My mouth opened and closed as I tried to respond. But I didn't know how. Aaron's analysis of me was so accurate, was it possible he was right about Mia too? Could she really have been lonely?

'How can you be so certain?'

Aaron smiled coyly. 'Maybe you're not really as alone as you think.'

I blinked.

What had happened between them when Mia came back to Bournemouth in the spring?

Despite her claims that she'd only dated Aaron for revenge, for the pain he'd caused me, I'd never fully believed her.

I'd wanted to. I'd wanted her to care that much about me. But the truth was, Mia just wanted the attention. She'd hated that I'd had Aaron. That he'd chosen me. She just wanted to prove that she could get him to want her too.

Scott had been the same. She'd craved his attention. She'd wanted to draw him away from me, too.

I should have let her have him.

44

THEN

September

'So, tell me about yourself,' Mia said, as she edged her chair closer to Ethan.

I tried to restrain my beaming grin. Inviting Ethan to join us all for dinner had been a brilliant plan.

'All Chloe told me is that you're a police officer too,' Mia continued.

Ethan glanced back at Scott uncertainly. 'I thought Scott told me you were a translator?' he said as his gaze returned to Mia.

I frowned. Why had Ethan thought Mia had been referring to herself? He and Scott were the two police officers here. He knew that.

'I a—'

'She speaks three languages,' Scott announced loudly. 'French, Spanish and Italian.'

I drew back in my chair. He sounded so proud.

Of her.

The confusion didn't lift from Ethan's brow as he studied Mia. 'But you just sa—'

'We should get the drinks in, mate,' Scott said, scraping his chair back as he got to his feet. 'Red wine, ladies?'

I blinked. What just happened? It felt as though Scott was intentionally dragging Ethan away. But why would he do that? Was he trying to prevent him from finishing his sentence? And why was Ethan so confused about Mia's job?

Something didn't add up.

Mia smiled sweetly at him. 'That would be perfect, thank you.'

Scott nodded and ushered Ethan ahead of him as they headed towards the bar.

I stared after them. How come no one else seemed to have noticed Ethan's obvious confusion and Scott's strange behaviour? Then again, how come Scott knew that Mia drank red wine, but he didn't know I preferred white?

'So,' Mia said, immediately turning to me. 'Have you thought any more about my invitation?'

My knee bounced up and down. This was it. The moment I'd been dreading. Saying no to Mia never ended well.

'I have,' I said slowly. I glanced at the bar, thankful there was no queue, and Scott and Ethan were already being served. At least they would be back soon. 'It was a really lovely invitation, and it means a lot to me—'

'You're not seriously turning it down, are you?' Her eyes widened as she interrupted. 'I'm offering you a once in a lifetime opportunity here. And I'm not just talking about the world cruise.'

'I know,' I replied. Of course I knew. An invitation like this from Mia was monumental. It was a chance for us to change things. To be close.

And I was turning it down.

I crossed my legs beneath the table, shuffled and then uncrossed them again, conscious that Mia was watching my every move. I hated being the subject of her scrutiny. Her judgement.

I knew I would always fall short.

Except this time was different.

'Scott asked me to marry him,' I blurted out as I lifted my left hand and held it out in front of Mia's face.

'What?' Mia's voice was an octave higher than normal. '*You*?' she asked as she turned to stare at me.

My hand fell to my lap. 'Yes, *me*,' I replied, my words sharp and short.

'You told her the good news, then,' Scott said as he and Ethan returned with our drinks.

'I can't believe you're actually engaged,' Mia said, shaking her head as she stared at me, seemingly oblivious to Scott's presence.

My body tensed. I wanted to ask why? What about me being engaged was so unbelievable? Was it really so impossible that someone could love me?

I gritted my teeth, not trusting myself to respond at all. It was better to stay silent. To let Mia's barbed comments wash over me without impact.

'You barely know each other.' Her gaze shifted to Scott as she spoke. It felt wrong. As though her concern rested with him, instead of where it should have been. Where it always should have been.

'Congratulations, mate.' Ethan beamed as he slapped Scott on the back. 'I'm so happy for you both.'

'You've only been together five minutes,' Mia continued, drawing the attention back to her.

'Time is irrelevant when you know.' I repeated the words Scott had said to me the day he'd proposed. 'And *we know*.'

My declaration sounded so powerful. So certain. But somehow it failed to resonate within me.

Did I know?

I hurriedly pushed that thought away. Of course I knew. I was just letting Mia get in my head. I couldn't let that happen.

Ethan raised his glass. 'Here's to you both, I wish you a lifetime of happiness together.' His gaze shifted to me as he spoke. His smile still bright and his eyes kind and accepting, and yet, there was something else there too. A sadness that didn't fit with his outward appearance. 'Right, Mia?' Ethan added, shooting a meaningful look at her.

She nodded instantly. 'Of course,' she replied, holding up her glass.

I smiled. A sense of relief settled around me as we all clinked our glasses together. Ethan was a good influence on Mia. Perhaps my distraction scheme could actually turn into something more long term...

'Come on, then,' Mia said reluctantly. 'Let's see the ring.'

I held my left hand out cautiously, waiting for her disapproval.

'Oh, it's beautiful. You have excellent taste.'

Mia's compliment slithered through my defences and excitement surged within me. She approved.

'Thank y—' my words dissipated as I realised Mia's attention had shifted and she was smiling at Scott.

'Thank you,' Scott said, straightening his back. 'I wanted to get something that really reflected who Chloe is. Something understated and subtle.'

I stared at him. Nothing about his manner betrayed his lie. It was so convincing.

I swallowed.

He was so convincing.

Mia nodded. 'Yes, it's her completely.'

My gaze fell to my outstretched hand and I stared at my ring. Of course it was me, *I'd* chosen it. Not Scott.

He hadn't had any part in choosing my ring. He hadn't even paid for it. I'd done it all. I blinked as I realised the magnitude of the situation. I'd bought my own engagement ring.

A jittery sensation emanated from within me, and I gripped my hands together.

'So come on, how did he propose?' Ethan asked.

'It was in the park,' I said quietly as I lowered my gaze and studied the chipped wooden table.

I didn't need to see Mia's expression to know it would be a familiar mix of scorn and gloating. Scott's proposal had been anything but spectacular. It wasn't even romantic. And now Mia knew it too.

'The park?' Mia scoffed.

'It probably doesn't sound like much,' Scott said. 'Especially to someone who's travelled the world like you have. I wish I could have given Chloe something more.' My head jolted up and my eyes met his. 'Maybe I should have at least booked a fancy restaurant, like The Rooftop Bar at The Trafalgar St James, and asked you there.'

A wave of disappointment washed over me. The Rooftop Bar was famed for its stunning views of London. A proposal there would have been like something out of the movies. It would have been perfect.

'But—' Scott shook his head slowly '—I know it's silly, the park felt like the right place for us.' He reached across the table and squeezed my hand. 'I mean, where better to propose than the place we met?'

My lips parted and I stared at him open mouthed. His proposal in the park hadn't been impulsive. It had been thoughtful. Meaningful. I sat up straighter in my chair and grinned at Scott. It *had* been romantic.

'You mean, the park where you had your bag snatched? I wouldn't even want to set foot back in that park if it was me, let alone get engaged there.'

She was ruining it. My moment. My engagement. Why couldn't she let me have just this one thing without tearing it apart?

'But it's not you, is it?' I held my left hand out in front of me and wiggled my fingers. 'It's me.'

For once I had something Mia didn't and not even she could take this from me.

45

NOW

October

'Why did you come back to Bournemouth?' Aaron asked.

'I needed a change.' The words tumbled unfiltered from my lips. It was the most honest thing I'd said in days.

But now wasn't the time for honesty. I couldn't afford to let my guard down. I'd learnt that lesson the hard way.

I cast a nervous glance at Aaron, studying his reaction as I braced myself for the inevitable question that would follow my admission. But instead, he just nodded and allowed the silence to linger between us.

I hated silence. I needed to fill it.

'I travelled a lot for work and just wanted to stay in one place for a while,' I added. 'To feel a little more grounded.' I reiterated the reasons Mia had given for her return to London. Now, though, I couldn't help wondering why she had chosen London. Her flat was here in Bournemouth, and so was Aaron.

The only thing in London had been me.

'You came back to Bournemouth too,' I pointed out. 'It's not like you have family here any more either. Perhaps there's something about this place...' I let my words hang as curiosity bubbled inside me. I had to be careful, though. I couldn't come right out and ask why he'd returned. Mia should know the answer already.

'True.' Aaron's gaze drifted to the window and he seemed lost in his thoughts as he stared at the river. 'I needed to come home. I know it's not the same now. The people I care about are off living their lives elsewhere. But I'd been so happy here once and — ' he paused '—I really needed to recapture that feeling.'

'I get it,' I said, nodding slightly. 'Bournemouth is the place I've been the happiest.' I wrapped my hands around my arms, trying to bring warmth to them. 'But it's also the place I've experienced the most pain too.' I wondered if that was really still true. London had traumatic memories now too.

I gave myself a shake, desperate to free myself from the melancholy. I couldn't succumb to it. If I did would never find the strength to keep going.

'But we used to have far more exciting Sundays back then,' I teased. 'I think every muscle in my body aches from how hard I worked today.'

Aaron's face seemed to light up as he grinned at me. 'I don't know, I think today was pretty fun. Especially watching the concentration on your face when you were hammering in a nail.' Aaron stuck his tongue out slightly between his teeth and furrowed his brow in pretend concentration.

'I didn't look like that!' I objected, swatting his arm.

Aaron's impression crumpled as he laughed. 'I'm sorry, but you really did.'

I groaned as I buried my head in my hands in embarrassment.

'It was cute,' Aaron said, his laughter ceasing.

I dropped my hands and stared at him as my face burned. Had Aaron just called me cute?

I tore my gaze from his, and I reached for the glass of water. 'Don't you have anything else you'd rather be doing with your weekend, though?' I asked, eager to redirect the conversation. 'You'll be exhausted tomorrow. Monday mornings are tough enough as it is, without having spent the weekend doing manual labour.'

Aaron chuckled. 'This is pretty much just another day at work for me. I told you I run my own carpentry business, didn't I?'

I froze. This was something Mia probably should have known. 'I mean, yeah, I-I—'

'Don't worry about it.' Aaron shrugged. 'I wouldn't expect you to remember. It's not like it's anything exciting.'

'Of course it is!' I declared. 'Running your own business is hard. You have to juggle everything yourself. There's no safety net. You succeed or fail on your own.'

Aaron nodded slowly. 'Yeah, you're so right. Wow, you really seem to get it.'

'I do,' I told him firmly. I had years of running my own business to know enough about the hardships it entailed. 'So, how did you learn to do all this?'

'I did construction work during my gap year in Australia.'

My stomach lurched at the mention of Australia. How different our lives could have been if we'd gone together.

'I was pretty handy at carpentry at school, plus all the stuff I used to help my dad make at home, so I ended up being offered another job,' Aaron continued. 'I applied for a student visa and worked part-time while I got my qualifications.'

'How come you didn't come back after you'd finished your studies?'

'By that point I'd married Kiara, so it was natural for me to stay.'

'You got married?' My muscles went slack, and my focus blurred.

His revelation tore through me. Aaron was married. Except, it shouldn't have been a revelation. Mia would have known that too. I tried to relax the muscles in my face. I had to mask my surprise and try to explain my outburst.

Aaron's mouth contorted. 'Divorced now.' He held up his left hand, which was lacking a wedding ring.

His response was unexpected. He hadn't seemed to notice my faux pas. But more importantly, he was single.

I blinked away the fuzzy darkness, concentrating on his features. 'I'm so sorry.' My voice cracked with emotion. It was true. I was sorry. Sorry that he'd experienced that kind of pain and heartache. But that didn't stop a part of me from rejoicing in the fact he was no longer married.

'I know I probably should have told you when I first moved back to Bournemouth,' Aaron lowered his gaze.

'You didn't?' My eyes widened as I realised I'd said that aloud. 'I mean, why didn't you?' I fought to keep the smile from my face. Mia didn't know.

'I was embarrassed,' Aaron admitted.

'Oh.' My elation at Mia's ignorance slipped away. His reluctance to tell Mia wasn't due to a lack of closeness between them. In fact, it was the opposite. He'd been embarrassed to tell her, which meant he cared what she thought of him. 'I understand,' I nodded slowly. 'But there's no need to be embarrassed. You did something so brave.'

Aaron arched an eyebrow as he looked at me dubiously.

'You travelled to the other side of the world alone. Made a life for yourself. And invited someone in to share that life with you,' I explained. 'Love means taking a chance.' I shrugged. 'Sometimes that chance doesn't work out. It doesn't mean it was wrong.'

My words surprised me. They sounded so sincere. And yet, I knew without a doubt that taking a chance on love with Scott had been wrong.

Aaron's gaze met mine, and I realised, perhaps I wasn't talking about Scott, though...

Aaron tipped his head to the side, studying me. 'You're different.'

I swallowed. 'Am I?'

I'd always known it would only be a matter of time before someone realised my deception. Wearing Mia's clothes and styling my hair the same way wasn't enough to actually make me be her.

'You seem more genuine.'

My eyes widened. 'Really?' I was pretending to be someone I wasn't. Genuine was the last word that could be used to describe me these days.

'Sorry,' Aaron said, clearly interpreting my surprise as offence.

But then I should be offended, shouldn't I? Or at least Mia should be. His observation meant she hadn't seemed genuine before. And whilst as Chloe I agreed, as Mia I couldn't.

'It's just you always seemed so focused on putting on this show of confidence and being the centre of attention that sometimes conversations with you could feel kind of artificial.'

'You thought I was shallow and self-centred?' I asked, forcing my voice to stay flat.

I wanted to hear him say it. To recognise Mia for who she really was. Her manipulativeness. Her darkness. I wanted vindication. Reassurance that what had happened had been her comeuppance. Maybe then I could stop feeling guilty.

'I think that's what you wanted everyone to believe.'

No, this wasn't right. He didn't speak like someone who'd been cast aside and crushed by Mia's callousness.

I wanted him to hate her. To resent the way she'd treated him. To refuse to have anything further to do with her. But shunning Mia now meant shunning *me*. I already knew how much that hurt. And as much as I wanted him to hate Mia, I wanted to be in his life more.

* * *

'It worked. I got payback for you. I broke his heart, just like he broke yours. He's out of our lives, just like we wanted.'

I wrung my hands together. Was that what I wanted?

It was clear Mia believed it was for the best, but Aaron had never meant anything to her. Not like he had to me. I squeezed my eyes shut as I realised that despite the pain he'd caused me, Aaron still mattered to me.

I still loved him.

And now he was gone.

'You should come with me to London.'

My brain was unable to process Mia's statement. I heard the words. Individually I knew what they all meant. But her sentence was beyond my comprehension.

She couldn't really be asking me to go with her.

It wasn't possible.

'You're starting university next week.'

'So?'

'I don't have a place. The plan was always to go to Australia with Aaron. I never applied to any universities. And it's too late to go through clearing now.'

'I was going to stay in student accommodation, but we can rent an apartment together instead. I can study and you can get a job.'

'But—'

'Unless you'd rather go home to Reading with Dad?'

I shook my head automatically.

'Well then, that settles it. We're moving to London.'

* * *

'When I first saw you at Christmas, I wondered if you'd have changed since I left. I mean, it had been years,' Aaron said, disrupting my thoughts.

'Six,' I said automatically.

'You mean five,' Aaron corrected.

I nodded. 'Yeah, of course.' For me it had been six years, but for Mia it had only been five.

It was strange that Mia hadn't told me Aaron was back. It was unlike her to miss an opportunity to remind me of painful memories. Perhaps she had been saving that piece of information, waiting for the right moment when it would have had the most impact.

As far as I could work out, she'd seen him twice: at Christmas, and then again after Dad's funeral. I envied her that time. If I'd known Aaron was back maybe I'd have done things differently.

Or perhaps that was why she hadn't told me. With me ignorant of Aaron's return, it meant she got to keep him all to herself.

'Anyway, you were exactly as I remembered last time I saw you. But now...' He shook his head. 'You actually seem to care.'

'I do care,' I assured him. I always had. Even when he stopped caring about me.

Aaron nodded solemnly. 'Anyway.' He cleared his throat. 'The divorce was for the best. We got married so young. It was impulsive,' he said, with a half-hearted shrug. 'I met Kiara when I arrived in Australia, I was so cut up over everything that happened here, I kind of fell into the relationship too quickly.' He tutted. 'I think I was trying to block out all the painful memories with happier new ones.'

'Did it work?' My voice wobbled. If I was honest with myself, that was exactly what I'd tried to do too.

The difference was, while I'd been devastated over him, he'd been devastated over Mia.

'I thought it did.' He shrugged. 'But I realised eventually, it's not possible to be truly in love with two people at the same time.'

The sounds around us became muffled and distant as my thoughts whirled.

Aaron was still in love with Mia.

I'd been fooling myself thinking I'd been in love with Scott. It hadn't been love; it had been desperation. An overwhelming desire to not be alone any longer. To be part of something. A couple. A future.

Perhaps if he had been genuine, we could have made it work. I would certainly have tried to. But in the end, it would probably always have been nothing more than it was. A pretence.

The saddest part was that that would have been enough for me. I could have been content with that. Because I thought what I truly wanted was unattainable.

And it was, for Chloe.

But for Mia anything was possible...

There were advantages to being dead.

46

THEN

September

I shuffled down the stairs, tugging my robe tightly around me as the doorbell chimed again.

I winced at the piercing sound and pressed my hand to my throbbing head. 'Alright, I'm coming,' I grumbled under my breath.

So much for my hope of a Sunday morning lie-in. And I'd really needed it after lying awake most of the night.

I reached the door and swung it open, not even needing to check who it was. Scott stepped inside before I'd even had chance to say hello.

'You look terrible,' he announced, scrunching his nose as he appraised me.

I scowled at him. 'Geez, thanks. I have a throbbing headache.'

'Aww, poor you.' He kissed my forehead, before dropping the two bags he was carrying and shoving them to the side of the hall.

'What's all this?' I asked as I started to push the door closed.

'Hey, hold on,' a familiar voice called from outside and I pulled the door back open.

'Ethan?' I instinctively put my hand to my chest, checking my robe was still in place. I hadn't expected visitors. Not while I was in my pyjamas.

'Morning, Chloe. Where do you want me to put these?' he asked, holding up the bags he was carrying.

'Boxes go in the living room, and bags go upstairs.' Scott replied.

'What? But—' I started to object as Ethan took the stairs two at a time.

'Bedroom on the right, mate.'

I took a step forward to the bottom of the stairs. My bedroom. He was going in my bedroom. It felt weird and intrusive. That was my space. Personal and private. And now some guy I barely knew was just walking in there uninvited.

I glared at Scott.

'Don't worry, babe. We've got it covered. Why don't you pop the kettle on, though? I'm sure Ethan would love a cuppa when we're done.'

'Done?' I leaned out of the doorway and realised there was an unfamiliar car blocking the end of my drive. The boot was open, exposing bags and boxes. 'What is all this?' Even as I asked the question, I knew the answer. It was obvious, but it couldn't be. We would have talked about it first, wouldn't we?

'I'm moving in, babe.'

'Already?'

Scott's expression clouded over.

Perhaps it had been the wrong thing to say, but it was a valid question. Wasn't it? He'd literally only just mentioned the idea of him moving in last night. We hadn't actually agreed anything yet.

At least not in terms of timeline or logistics. I hadn't had time to prepare.

Ethan's footsteps thudded down the stairs and I stepped back to let him pass as he returned to the car for more bags.

'We discussed this, Chloe,' Scott said. 'We agreed that me moving in here made sense.'

'It does.' I nodded. 'I just hadn't realised you meant right now.'

'Why would we wait?' He looked so confused. So hurt.

I shook my head. It was a question I didn't have an answer for. We were engaged. We were intending to spend the rest of our lives together. Those lives could start right here, right now. And yet, were we ready for that? Was I ready for that?

If I was honest with myself, I knew the answer was no. I felt completely unprepared. 'I'm not even sure where the spare key is,' I fumbled.

Scott laughed. 'We can get a new key cut.' He wrapped his arms around me and pulled me to him. 'I'm so relieved, for a minute there I thought you were having second thoughts.'

Now was the moment to tell him. He'd understand. He loved me. He wouldn't want to rush me. Not if he knew that's how I felt. It wasn't that I didn't want *him*. I just wanted time to adjust to all of the changes.

He stepped back and stared at me intently. 'I couldn't bear the thought of us not being together.'

I clamped my mouth closed.

Was that what would happen if I told him the truth? If I told him I needed more time? Would that be the end for us?

'You're so important to me, and I just really want you to know that.'

I nodded. 'You're important to me too. I love what we have.'

I did love it. I loved it too much to do anything that might risk losing it. Even if I was starting to question what it was I truly loved: him or the idea of us.

'Me too.' Scott grinned at me. 'And I'm so excited to take this next step together.'

I nodded again as I watched him slip out the door and jog to the car. Except it didn't really feel as though we were taking this step together at all. It felt like I was just following behind. Just like I always did.

47

NOW

October

I spotted her too late. A few seconds earlier and I could have turned on my heel and ducked behind the row of beach huts. Instead, Rachel was waving frantically at me. And even more disconcertingly, so were the four other women huddled beside her.

Pasting on a smile, I pushed my shoulders back and marched forwards, hoping my body didn't betray my underlying desire to run away.

'Mia,' Rachel greeted me with air kisses. 'We were just talking about you.'

The other women took turns hugging me, whilst I tried not to show my confusion.

'We were so surprised when Rachel told us you were back,' one of the women informed me, as I rammed my hands back into my pockets out of the cold south-easterly wind. 'Sarah was all, "but our Mia only comes to see us at Christmas." But I knew all that travelling would get boring someday.'

There was a murmur of agreement amongst them, but I was too distracted to pay attention.

Our Mia.

Those two words repeated over and over in my head. No one had ever described me as 'our Chloe'. And yet Mia, the woman who barely spent time in the country, was such a part of this group that they claimed her as one of their own.

'Well, we do only see you at Christmas,' a woman on my right objected. Presumably she was Sarah, I decided. 'But Lisa's always been an optimist.'

'Come on, ladies.' Rachel clapped her hands together. 'We're supposed to be getting our steps in before it gets dark. We can catch up with Mia another time.'

'You should come with us,' a blonde piped up.

'Oh, er, thanks, but I've just walked all the way back from Hengistbury Head. Besides—' I glanced at the dark clouds overhead '—I want to get home before the downpour starts.' I'd worked outdoors on the flower stall long enough to learn how to judge when to take shelter.

The five women tilted their heads back and scrutinised the sky. 'Rachel says it won't rain for another hour yet,' Lisa said, somewhat dubiously.

'That's what the weather forecast said,' Rachel informed me. 'Which gives us plenty of time to walk along the promenade to Southbourne and back.'

Large drops of rain fell the moment she finished speaking. The women shrieked with laughter as they tugged their collars and hoods up. 'So much for that theory,' the other woman, whose name I didn't know, said ruefully.

'Well, enjoy your walk,' I said, deciding this was the perfect opportunity to beat a hasty retreat.

'We'll come with you,' Sarah announced.

'With me?' I repeated. 'Oh, but...' I grappled for an excuse. A reason to keep them out of Mia's flat.

'Oooh, yes,' Lisa gushed. 'We can have a cup of tea in the warm and you can make us all green with envy with your photos of Rome.' She hooked her arm through mine, and I found myself being escorted home.

* * *

The group piled into the flat, hurriedly peeling off soggy coats and shoes. My suggestion to go to Rachel's flat with her more spectacular view had been rejected en masse. It was hard to argue when I was so outnumbered.

I dropped my phone on the coffee table and headed to the kitchen to put the kettle on, while they all settled into the living room.

'Mia,' Sarah called. 'Your phone's ringing.' She glanced at the screen, as she held it out towards me. 'It's an Ethan.'

I swallowed as my heart pounded. 'I'll call him back,' I said, opening my hands, gesturing to my crowded living room. 'I'm busy.'

It was the second time Ethan had called. How long could I keep avoiding him? Or more importantly, should I keep avoiding him?

Perhaps I should answer and find out what he wanted. Ignoring him didn't ease my anxiety, it just prolonged it. I could tell Sarah I'd changed my mind. For once, I could face my fears instead of constantly running from them. Sarah smiled and hit the reject button as she settled back against the sofa. I let out a deep breath as I turned away to get the mugs out of the cupboard. But I knew the relief I felt at having avoided his call was only temporary. It wouldn't ease the growing sense of foreboding that weighed heavily in my stomach. I still didn't know why he'd called.

Or worse still, would he call back?

'So, come on Claire, tell us how it's going with that new guy you're seeing,' Lisa urged and I smiled, grateful for the distraction.

The blonde-haired woman's cheeks turned pink. 'It's good,' she said.

The others groaned. 'We're going to need more than that,' Sarah informed her. 'We're all married now, the excitement of first dates is a distant memory. We have to live vicariously through you.'

More laughter erupted.

'Plus,' Lisa added, 'we need to make sure he's good enough for our Claire.'

'Aww,' Claire murmured as she gave her a hug.

I watched the exchange in silence. I envied them the ability to share details of their lives, their fears and concerns. If I'd been one of them perhaps I could have talked to them about Scott. We could have analysed his behaviour, his words and theorised on what it had all meant.

I turned away, trying to focus my thoughts on the task at hand, as I made the tea.

'Mia's not married,' Rachel announced loudly. 'Though from what I saw yesterday, that may be temporary.'

My head jolted up as everyone's attention shifted to me. Their interest had definitely been piqued.

'You've only been back a couple of days, how have you managed to meet someone already?' Claire asked indignantly.

'It's a rekindled romance, rather than a new one,' Rachel informed them. A smug smile formed on her lips. 'I saw you,'

Rachel said, jerking her head towards the window. 'I never thought I'd see the day Mia Philips voluntarily did DIY.'

I tried to laugh. She was right of course. Mia wouldn't.

'The fascination you and Chloe had with that guy has always bewildered me.'

'What guy?' Lisa asked.

'Aaron. He owns one of the beach huts down there.'

Everyone raced to the window, as though they expected to catch a glimpse of him.

'It's the one with the new roof,' Rachel helpfully informed them. 'Mia helped fit it yesterday.'

'Wow.' Claire sank back into her seat. 'I've never done carpentry for a guy. Is this why I always seem to end up dating losers?'

'I thought you said things were good with this one?' Sarah asked, as I carried the tray into the living room and set it on the coffee table.

Claire shrugged, helping herself to a mug of hot tea.

'Well, I'm not sure Mia is someone to emulate, given her track record,' Rachel said, turning back to me. 'I'm not sure all that hard work agrees with you anyway. You're looking tired.'

'Oh.' I drew back at her bluntness. 'I, er, I didn't really sleep so well.'

'You need to start using eye serum. It would help with the puffiness.'

I patted my forefinger under my eye. Were they really that puffy? I'd never noticed.

Another way I'd failed to live up to the real Mia.

'I told you all that travelling was no good for your skin.'

Rachel's criticisms weren't directed at me because I was a poor imitation of Mia, they were directed at Mia and had been before my arrival. Her life wasn't the way I'd imagined. Her friendships weren't what I'd imagined.

I thought stepping into Mia's life would make me happy, but now that I was in it, I couldn't help but wonder had Mia even been happy? Why had she chosen London? Why not Bournemouth where her friends were? Or Europe where her language skills could have opened doors for her? The only thing she had in London was me.

Was it possible that was the reason? That I was the reason?

A lump lodged at the back of my throat. Had Mia been trying to rebuild our relationship? And if that was her intention, then was it me that had sabotaged it? Grief for what might have been welled up inside me. Had everything I'd dreamed of for us, finally been within our grasp? The worst part was that now I would never know the answer. I'd never know if I'd truly been the reason for her return.

But I did know I was the reason for her death.

48

THEN

September

'You'll have to let me know how much I owe you towards the bills,' Scott said as I shoved a box, attempting to move it to the side of the room. 'Now that I'm living here it's only fair we go fifty-fifty. I'm sure my parents will understand.'

I lifted my head as my progress stalled. 'Understand what?'

Scott waved his hand dismissively. 'Oh, they just helped me out with some financial difficulties I ran into a while back. I'm still paying them back for bailing me out.'

'I didn't know you had financial issues.'

'Sure you did, babe. That's why I was crashing at Ethan's. He wasn't charging me rent, so everything I earned could go straight back to my parents.'

'Oh.' I stared at him. I hadn't known that. Any of it.

But I *should* have known. My face tightened as my lips pinched. He should have told me.

'But now that I'm living here, I need to contribute.'

He was right, he should contribute. It's what couples did

when they lived together. They shared their resources. Their lives.

But he hadn't done that. He'd kept things from me. Again. Small details that he seemed to think were irrelevant. They weren't.

And yet, how could I be angry at him for his omissions, when I had outright lied to him?

I forced a smile on my face. 'I don't want to take money from your parents.' I didn't. I wouldn't.

But I would have liked to have had a conversation about it earlier. Instead, I felt backed into a corner. Insisting he contribute would be callous and insensitive to his difficulties. It would doom our relationship to failure.

Was that why he hadn't told me until now? Had he known springing this information on me in this way would make it impossible for me to object? Was he afraid that if he'd told me before moving in, I might not have let him?

Was he insecure and vulnerable? Or just dishonest and manipulative?

Then again, which was I?

'You're not, you're taking it from me,' Scott insisted.

'I can afford the bills here. You moving in doesn't really change much.' I shrugged. 'A few more groceries. A bit more council tax.' Somehow, I would manage. It would be a struggle for a little while, but when my inheritance was paid everything would work out. His omissions and my lies would all be put behind us.

Scott shook his head. 'That wouldn't be fair on you. It's not how I want to start our lives together. They are my financial issues, not yours.'

'We're a team, aren't we?'

Scott nodded.

'So that means we share everything. The good and the bad.'

Scott rubbed his jaw. 'It would only be temporary, just until I've paid them back.'

'Right.' I nodded. 'Like I said, it's not a problem.' Perhaps if I was accepting and didn't make a big deal of his failings, he would do the same for me if mine were ever revealed.

Or at the very least, it might help ease my own guilt.

Scott shook his head as he stared at me. 'You're amazing, you know that? You're so supportive and accepting.'

I grinned at him as his praise engulfed me like a warm embrace.

'We're in it together now,' I told him firmly. However, at the back of my head a tiny doubt whispered to me.

Shouldn't I have known exactly what 'it' was before I was in?

Shouldn't he?

What chance did our relationship really have, when we were both deceiving each other?

Loud music suddenly thudded through the living room wall, disrupting my thoughts.

'Do you want me to go and talk to them?' Scott asked.

I shook my head as I stepped around the boxes that covered my once spotless living room carpet. 'It's just one of the perils of a terraced house. Shared walls mean shared music.'

'Your neighbours should have more consideration,' Scott said as he pushed himself up onto his feet, abandoning the box he was unpacking and walking towards the hall.

'It won't do any good.' I dashed after him and put my hand on his arm. 'It will just antagonise them and they'll play it even louder.'

'I can be pretty persuasive, you know?' Scott said. He sounded offended that I doubted his ability to succeed. 'I am a police officer.'

'Yeah, I know. But I just don't think it's a good way to go. They'll turn it off soon. They always do.'

The last thing I wanted was a confrontation with my neighbours. If that meant I had to put up with a little bit of inconvenience, then so be it.

'Okay,' Scott said. 'We'll leave it for a while. But if they don't turn it down soon—'

'They will,' I assured him as I glanced nervously back at the wall.

'One day, we'll buy a detached house when we move,' Scott said as he started to head back to his half-emptied box. 'We'll need more space for the kids.' His eyes glazed over as he stared somewhere over my shoulder. 'We could move out of London. Find somewhere quieter. Maybe the countryside.' He nodded as though in agreement with himself. 'We'll have a large garden and an extra bedroom. They'll each need their own, don't you think?' His eyes met mine and I realised he was waiting for my input.

I nodded mutely.

He frowned. 'You don't look very sure. I mean, we did talk about this. We both want kids. Right?'

'Er, I guess so.'

'You don't sound very sure.'

I swallowed. Scott sounded so indignant. He thought I should be as eager as he was. I couldn't blame him. We were getting married. It was natural to think about the future. *Our* future.

This was exactly what I'd wanted. So why was I hesitant?

'I'm just...' I searched for the right words. Ones that would reassure him. And me too. 'I'm not used to being part of someone else's life. Someone else's plans.'

'You say that like being part of my life is a bad thing.'

I shook my head. 'No, it's not bad. Quite the opposite.' I paused. 'But it is a little bit scary,' I admitted softly.

'The thought of a future with me scares you?' Scott's shoulders crumpled.

'No.' I shook my head again, more frantically this time. I shouldn't have said anything. It wasn't coming out the way I meant it to. 'It's not you.' I cringed at my clichéd excuse. 'I mean, it's not a future with you that scares me. It's a future without you.'

Contempt morphed into confusion as Scott blinked.

'Everyone leaves,' I muttered weakly.

'Wait, so you think that because someone left you before, because *they* abandoned you, that means I'm the same? That I'll leave you too?' It was Scott's turn to shake his head now. 'Oh, Chloe.' Scott reached out and pulled me to him.

I buried my head in his shoulder, the warmth of his embrace slowly quietening the doubts that raged within me.

'I can't imagine how tough it's been for you losing your parents, and I know Mia isn't the most reliable person. Of course you've had to learn to be independent and protect yourself from being abandoned again. But I'm not them.'

He was right. And yet I still couldn't completely break free from the fear that this would all end badly.

'Perhaps I just need more time to adjust,' I said carefully. Everything was all happening at once. First the engagement, then moving in, now kids and a new house. It was all so fast. Too fast.

When you know, you know.

Scott's words repeated in my head.

I envied his certainty. That adamance that made every decision so easy. So solid.

All I had were questions and doubts.

There had been a time when I'd trusted my instincts. When I'd been decisive.

And someone had died as a result.

49

NOW

October

'Bye,' I called into the corridor, waving at the group of women as they huddled into the elevator. I closed the door and sucked in a deep breath, before summoning the courage to walk back down the hall to the living room.

'You know, there really isn't that much to do,' I assured Rachel. 'It won't take me long to wash a few mugs.' I silently prayed she'd take the hint and leave too. The last thing I wanted was for her of all people to insist on staying behind to clean up.

'We'll be done in half the time with two,' Rachel said brightly. 'Besides, it'll give us a chance to talk without the others.'

I tried to muster a smile. The prospect of making conversation with Rachel definitely didn't appeal. But what choice did I have?

Rachel sat back down on the sofa and signalled for me to do the same. I braced myself for more insults. Or perhaps she wanted to reiterate her concerns about me pursuing a relationship with Aaron.

'So,' Rachel said, crossing her legs and gazing at me intently. 'How long exactly are you planning to keep this charade going?'

I heard a gasp, but it took me a moment to register that it had come from me.

Rachel knew.

'I d—'

'Don't insult me any further by feigning innocence.' Rachel's words were harsh and detached. 'Clearly you underestimated my intelligence already. Don't make the same mistake twice.'

I clamped my mouth closed.

'My instincts told me something was off about you on Friday, but I didn't listen. I mean, you'd only just got back, you probably were just tired like you said. But today...' Rachel nodded. 'Watching you interacting with the girls, I knew.'

My heart raced. What exactly did she know?

'Do you really think I wouldn't spot an imposter when they are impersonating my best friend?'

The sound of my own breathing resounded in my ears.

I knew Mia better than anyone. Even when she wasn't with me, I knew what she'd say. What she'd think.

Her opinion had become a voice in my head, so loud that it drowned out my own thoughts. Everything was about Mia. What she would approve of. What she would do.

And yet somehow it still wasn't enough. I wasn't enough. Just a poor forgery of a masterpiece.

'I don't need other people to enable me to be myself, and neither do you. You are so much stronger than you think you are.'

Mia's words echoed in my memory.

She was right. I didn't need Rachel to believe me. She had no proof. It was her word against mine. I smiled, instinctively knowing what Mia would do right now.

'I always knew you felt threatened by me, Rachel. You were

afraid I would take your place at the centre of our little circle of friends. While I was only around for a few weeks a year that threat was tolerable. But now I've moved back. Now I plan to stay here permanently. You'd do anything to protect your empire, no matter how crazy it makes you sound.'

Rachel's eyebrow arched upwards. 'Impressive,' she acknowledged. 'That was very convincing. Very Mia. But I'm still not buying it.'

I shrugged. 'Then prove it.' I leaned back on the sofa nonchalantly, whilst inside my whole body trembled. Mia never backed down, and so now, neither did I.

Rachel's mouth twisted and relief surged through me. She had nothing. Just a hunch. An unprovable, improbable hunch.

And yet I still felt as though I was teetering at the edge of a precipice. Until now, everything had been gliding along. No one suspected anything. All it would take was for Rachel to start raising questions to her friends, to Aaron, and then...

What if Ethan heard her suspicions? Or the police? I wasn't sure which was worse. Either way, Scott would find out. And I knew how that would end.

I took a deep breath, fighting to steady my breathing. I couldn't let Rachel see me panicking like this. I was spiralling. Catastrophising. I had to think it through calmly.

Ethan was in London. All Rachel knew of him was his name. There was no way she could tell him her suspicions. And as for the police, Rachel was smart enough not to go to them with accusations she couldn't back up. She had her own reputation to think of. A reputation that she would protect at any cost.

'Tell you what, if you're so convinced I'm not her, then why don't I get "Mia" to call you?' I put air quotes around her name as I spoke. I was starting to enjoy this side of being Mia. It was terrifying but exhilarating. The power. The risk. It was intoxicating.

I picked Mia's phone up from the coffee table and scrolled through her contacts until I found Rachel. I hit dial and smiled smugly as Rachel's phone rang.

Rachel jabbed her finger at the phone, rejecting my call and stood up. 'I don't know what the two of you think you're playing at, but I deserve better. Especially from her.' She snatched her handbag up off the floor by her feet and stalked towards the hall. As she reached the door she swung back. 'You might want to remind your sister that I know her secrets. All of them.'

I followed Rachel to the door and watched as it slammed behind her.

What secrets did she know?

Every fibre of my being screamed to ask her. To fling open the door and demand she told me everything.

But that was probably her objective.

My curiosity would be my undoing. Right now, she just had suspicions. And as long as I kept my mouth shut that would be all she had.

I turned the lock, keeping her out and me in. My need to keep being Mia was stronger than my desire to know what secrets she may or may not have had.

The problem was, Rachel wasn't the kind of person to let things go. She wouldn't give up. I hadn't convinced her of who I was. I knew that. But what did she plan on doing with that information?

50

THEN

September

'You look nice,' Scott said as I walked down the stairs. 'But...'

I drew back. 'But?'

'The red dress looks better.'

'Oh.' I glanced down at my navy hankie dress. 'Does it?'

'Definitely.'

My head jolted up at the adamance of his tone. 'But this looks okay, doesn't it?'

He hesitated before he replied. 'Yeah, of course.'

It was only a fraction of a second, but it was enough to tell me that despite the conviction of the words that followed, he didn't mean them.

My dress didn't look okay. Not really.

I glanced at my watch. 'I can change really quickly.' I stared to turn back, but Scott caught my hand.

'It's okay,' he whispered with a smile.

Maybe I'd overreacted. He preferred the red dress, that was all. It didn't mean that this one was bad. I'd just remember to wear the red one next time. I felt my shoulders relax. It was okay. I was okay. I didn't need to change. He didn't expect me to. Didn't want me to. We were better than that. He was better.

'Take as much time as you need.'

My stomach plummeted. Then again, maybe he wasn't.

* * *

I clambered out of the taxi and teetered precariously on my heel.

Scott caught my arm and steadied me as he stepped beside me. 'You must be the only woman I know who can't walk in heels,' he teased.

'I told you I should have worn my flat sandals,' I hissed at him, frustrated by his tone. It was bad enough I'd had to change my dress, but then even my choice of footwear had been over-ruled as well.

'You're right, I'm sorry.' He kissed my cheek. 'You should have worn flats and not worried about what my parents think.'

I glanced down at my feet. Would my choice of footwear really have made a difference to his parents' opinion of me?

'I just wanted you to feel more comfortable tonight.'

'Comfortable?' I questioned. 'How can I be comfortable when I can't feel my toes?'

'I know how nervous you get about meeting new people,' Scott soothed. 'It's like they say, dress confidently and you'll feel confident.'

'Well, right now I can assure you that I feel neither comfortable nor confident.'

'I know this must all feel overwhelming for you, Chloe. Meeting your partner's parents is always a big step, but given what happened to yours...'

I jolted back, his words feeling like a physical slap.

'I don't want to talk about my parents.'

'No, of course not. But I just wanted you to know that I know you're thinking about them right now. And that's totally understandable. It's natural for you to miss them more at times like this. It would be weird if you didn't.'

I blinked. He was right. Of course I should be thinking about them. Regretting the fact that I wouldn't be able to introduce Scott to them in the same way that he was about to introduce me to his parents. That the six of us would never be able to sit down together and share embarrassing old stories.

There would never be any of that.

'I knew how important tonight would be for you, that's why I wanted to help you.'

I nodded slowly, desperately fighting back the tears that threatened to start flowing at any second.

I slid my hand in his and tottered up the driveway to his parents' house.

'Chloe, just one thing,' he said as he reached for the doorbell. 'Don't mention my job. You know how parents worry about that kind of stuff.'

I nodded automatically. Except I didn't know. It had been so long since anyone had worried about me that I had forgotten what that felt like.

I glanced across at Scott. But maybe I knew now.

51

NOW

October

'Why didn't you tell me?' Aaron's voice cracked as he glared at me as I opened the door. His voice had sounded strained on the intercom, when he'd asked to come up to the flat, I'd thought it was static. Now I realised it wasn't.

I could feel his hostility and yet there was an undercurrent of pain beneath it. I squinted at him. In fact, his eyes looked glossy as though he was fighting back tears.

He knew. I was sure of it.

Rachel. It had to have been her. She'd been so angry when she'd left last night, I should have known she would run straight to Aaron. Rachel wasn't the kind of person to let things go. I'd known she wouldn't just give up.

Aaron must feel so betrayed. Manipulated. I couldn't blame him.

And yet, I still wasn't ready to come clean. Ignorance was the best option.

'Tell you what?' I asked cautiously.

'About Chloe.'

Chloe.

My stomach lurched. He couldn't know. It wasn't possible. My life in London was a world away from here. No one knew where I lived. No one knew anything about me.

'We were worried about you,' Aaron continued. 'You've been acting so weird since you got back. You just didn't seem like yourself.'

'We?'

'Rachel stopped by the beach hut this morning; she kept going on about you not being yourself. I don't usually pay any attention to her ramblings, but...'

Mia was right. I wasn't good enough to pass myself off as her. Of course everyone had realised.

'I thought Chloe might know something that could help.'

'C-Chloe?' I staggered backwards, letting go of the door.

After all these years he'd finally tried to contact me. At any other moment that revelation would have filled me with joy. But he was too late.

Aaron put his hand out and stopped the door before it closed. 'I googled her,' he said, stepping into the flat. 'I was looking for her social media accounts, something I could use to message her. But instead, I found a news article.'

I closed my eyes. I couldn't bear to see the sadness contorting his feature. But the darkness was worse. Angry flashes of orange flames danced through my memory, I could practically feel the heat on my face, the heaviness in my lungs.

'Why didn't you tell me Chloe is dead?'

52

THEN

September

'What's all this?' I peered over Scott's shoulder at the mound of holiday brochures covering the kitchen table. 'Are we going somewhere?'

'Yep,' he said, grinning as he wrapped his hand around my waist and pulled me onto his lap. 'I was thinking, maybe Mia's on to something with that career break idea of hers. A year travelling the world would be an incredible adventure.'

I drew back. 'You want me to go travelling with Mia?' He'd been so offended when I'd mentioned it. Insulted that I'd even considered abandoning him, but now he wanted me to go?

Scott chuckled. 'Not with Mia. With me.'

'We can't.'

'Of course we can. Your store basically runs itself anyway, right? I mean, it's not like you ever go there that much. And with the inheritance we could afford for me to take the time off work and pay for our trip.'

The inheritance.

My inheritance.

The money that was going to get me out from under my own lie. That would finally legitimise my claims of owning a flower shop.

'We could sublet the house, so that would take care of the bills here.'

I shook my head. 'We can't.'

'Why not?'

I opened my mouth and clamped it closed again quickly. I couldn't tell him that my lease didn't allow for subletting. He thought I owned my house, which would mean I could do whatever I wanted with it.

'And what about your job? Could you really take a year off like that?'

Scott shrugged. 'I'll quit.'

I stared at him. He said it like it was nothing. But it wasn't. It was his job, his career, his livelihood. Without it he'd be completely dependent on me.

I gasped as the weight of that responsibility crushed the air from my lungs. I couldn't be responsible for someone else.

Not again.

Especially as his plan was dependent on resources that didn't even exist. Renting out a house I didn't own, and living on the profits of a shop that didn't exist.

I should never have lied to him. It was one thing to deceive Mia, to create the illusion of being more than I was. More successful. More important. More loved. But this was Scott. There didn't need to be any pretence between us. He would have loved me as I was.

'You'll never amount to anything.'

Dad's words reverberated through my brain. Perhaps he'd

been right. I hadn't amounted to anything. My lies didn't equal success.

The only thing that was real was my inheritance. But I needed that to buy everything he thought I already had.

It was impossible.

But Scott didn't know that. He couldn't. Not unless I told him.

'You can't just quit your job.'

'Why not?' Scott asked earnestly.

This was my chance. I could tell him everything. I *should* tell him everything. 'I...' I hesitated. 'How will you pay your parents back if you don't have a job?' I asked, as my nerve failed me.

'They won't mind waiting a little bit,' Scott said, wafting his hand in the air. 'This is important for us, they'll understand that. They like you,' he insisted. 'They were really impressed that I've managed to get a girl like you. When we were leaving, Dad told me not to screw this up.' Scott grinned. 'He'll appreciate that I'm actually listening to him for once.'

I frowned. Why would his dad say that? It wasn't as though he'd screwed his previous relationship up. Sasha had died.

'I've been thinking about it for a while anyway,' Scott continued. 'It's time for a change. This break would be the ideal opportunity to give me a chance to think about what's next for work. For us.'

Those two little words were like being thrown a lifeline. One I grabbed hold of with both hands.

'Having kids requires a big financial investment.' My words picked up speed as my thoughts raced. 'Two working parents and a solid business would give them a better start.'

'This is our only chance, though, Chloe. Once kids come along our lives will never be our own again. Every decision we make will have to consider them first. So let's make it about us while we can. It's not as though we're being reckless. We'll still have your business.'

Everything was coming unravelled. And the only way out was to tell him the truth.

'Scott.' I took a deep breath, trying to summon my courage. 'I can't—'

'You were willing to walk away from everything for Mia.'

I shook my head. 'It's not like that.' But my objection felt weak. It was exactly like that. But not for the reasons he thought. If I'd gone with Mia, she would have taken care of everything financially. If I went with Scott, the financial burden all fell on me. It wasn't viable.

'You know what? I think you're right. We're moving too quickly.'

I arched an eyebrow at Scott's sudden declaration.

'Maybe you should wait awhile before you expand and buy the new store.'

'Wait? Why would I wait?' This was what I'd worked so hard for. The moment I'd been dreaming of. Finally, it was so close. I was so close.

'Relocating to new premises, bigger premises, is going to be a lot of work. A lot of stress.'

I stroked his arm. His hesitation made sense now, he was concerned about me. He cared. 'I can handle it,' I assured him.

But Scott didn't look convinced. 'Are you sure you're ready?'

I heard it then, the patronising tone that seemed to penetrate deep into my bones. How had I never heard it before?

Because I hadn't been listening, I realised suddenly. But worse than that, I hadn't wanted to listen. Hadn't wanted to hear.

'We'll talk about it more once you've given it some thought,' Scott said as he closed the brochures and stood up.

I gritted my teeth as I nodded silently. Conscious that there was an edge to our relationship that hadn't been there before. Or perhaps I just hadn't been willing to see it before.

53

NOW

October

'Mia,' Aaron repeated. 'Why didn't you tell me?'

I knew I owed him an explanation. I owed him far more than that. 'I-I can't.' The tears I'd fought so hard to keep inside burst free. 'I can't,' I repeated between sobs.

Aaron sprang forward, his anger outweighed by concern as he wrapped his arms around me and pulled me to him. I sobbed uncontrollably into his shoulder, until my legs grew weak, and he guided me into the living room.

I curled up on the sofa, unable to look at him. If my eyes met his I knew I would fall apart again.

'Do you want a cup of tea?' he asked as he stroked my hair. But I didn't lift my head. Didn't answer.

The rhythmic stroking ceased, and I missed the warmth of his touch as his footsteps retreated. I heard doors opening and closing in the kitchen and realised he was making a cup of tea anyway.

I couldn't blame him. I used to do the same thing for Dad, in the days that followed Mum's death. It was something to do. Something to focus on. A tiny purpose. Even if it was insignificant.

Lifting my head I watched Aaron over my shoulder as he boiled the kettle and rummaged in the cupboards, searching for the tea bags. And I realised: I wasn't insignificant. At least not to him. A warm rush flooded to my chest, and I pressed my hand against it, desperate to keep hold of that feeling. To treasure it.

Making a cup of tea was a simple enough task. Too simple to actually solve anything. But then that wasn't the point. It was symbolic. A sign that someone cared. That someone wanted to help.

Just like I'd wanted to help Dad.

The difference was that I was grateful for Aaron's attempt. His presence. Whereas Dad had ceased to feel anything for me, except contempt.

I turned my head and stared out of the window. The same kind of contempt that I had for Bournemouth. The place that had stolen everything from me.

Aaron returned with two mugs of tea. He set them on the coffee table and sat beside me on the sofa.

'Thank you,' I said, avoiding his eyes as I reached for a mug. I perched it precariously on my knee. It was too hot to drink, but I needed something to hold. Something to ground me to the present.

My lip trembled. 'Why are you being so kind to me? I don't deserve it.'

'Hey.' Aaron shook his head. 'Don't talk like that. I shouldn't have shouted at you. I was so caught up in my own grief I didn't think about how hard this must have been for you.'

I shook my head. 'But I should—'

'It's okay.' He squeezed my hand. 'I'm just sorry that you were going through all of this alone. I just wish...' Aaron's voice cracked, and he stood up quickly. Turning his back he hurried to the window. I stared after him, watching his shoulders shudder as he kept his back to me.

I stood up and joined him at the window. 'You know I—' I froze. 'Chloe. Chloe wouldn't have got through losing Mum without you,' I told him, resting my hand on his shoulder. 'Maybe we can help each other get through this?'

Aaron nodded. 'Yeah,' he said, turning slowly. He gave me a small smile. 'We have each other.' We walked back to the sofa in companionable silence and sat side by side again.

'I understand now why you've seemed so different since you got back,' Aaron said softly.

'Y-you do?'

He nodded. 'Losing someone changes you, but to lose your twin...' He sucked in a deep breath. 'I can't even begin to imagine how devastating that must be for you.'

He was right. It was devastating. Not just the loss, but the reason it happened.

'Did you tell Rachel?' I asked suddenly.

Aaron shook his head. 'I almost did, but then I realised it wasn't my place. It's not like Chloe and Rachel were ever close. To be honest, I know she's your best mate, but honestly, I've never understood why. She's so...'

'Opinionated?'

'Yes, exactly.' Aaron squinted at me. 'That's the first time I've ever heard you say anything remotely negative about her. You're usually her biggest fan.'

He was right, Mia idolised Rachel. There was no way she would ever criticise her.

But I would. I always had.

'I guess she's starting to grate on my nerves a little recently.'

Aaron smiled as he shook his head. 'You really are different these days. I swear you get more like Chloe every day.'

I cringed.

'Sorry,' Aaron apologised immediately. 'I know how much you hated being likened to each other.' A lopsided grin formed on his lips. 'Although to be honest, I always had a feeling you secretly liked it.'

I smiled ruefully. 'Chloe did, but—'

'You did too.' He winked at me. 'Still do, I think.'

He was wrong. Mia had never wanted to be like me. I frowned. Although she did always chase after the guys I liked. But that was just her trying to take what I had, to prove she was better, that everyone would always prefer her. It wasn't her trying to be me, she simply wanted to make me suffer. To pay for my mistakes. As far as Mia was concerned there was no redemption for what I had done. It was probably the only thing we'd ever agreed on.

Silence filled the living room as we both slipped into our own thoughts. 'Can you tell me what happened?' Aaron asked eventually, his eyes pleading. He needed to understand. To process. To talk.

And yet that was exactly what I wanted to avoid.

It had been the same after Mum died. There had been questions at the time. So many questions. They'd felt relentless. Each one drawing me back to that moment.

And then they'd stopped and everyone moved on with their lives. Her death, her life, was forgotten. Except by Dad, Mia and me.

We remembered.

We mourned.

Then the questions were replaced by anger. By silence. By guilt.

I picked up my tea, and I took a tentative sip. 'I thought we were starting to reconnect. We talked, properly talked, for the first time in years. And then everything was gone. *She* was gone.'

'That's...' Aaron shook his head. 'I'm sorry.'

His words were filled with such emotion that I could feel his empathy, his support.

They were just two little words that couldn't change anything, but they meant so much.

Too much.

Because I didn't deserve them.

I lurched forwards, slopping my tea as I set it back on the coffee table.

'Are you okay?' Aaron reached for my hand. 'Did you scald yourself?'

'Don't do that,' I said, snatching my hand away.

'I'm just trying to help you.' Aaron stared at me in bewilderment. 'Why won't you let me help you?'

I gritted my teeth, trying to keep my emotions in check. But I couldn't. 'Because I don't deserve it. I don't deserve your help. I don't deserve your sympathy.' The admissions slipped from my lips as my body trembled.

I'd fought so hard for so long to keep everything locked away inside me. To not show weakness. To hide my failings. My pain. But being back in Bournemouth had made it impossible. The pressure of being Mia. The paradoxical joy and agony of being with Aaron again, and living with a constant reminder of what could have been. Of knowing at any moment the charade could all end. That Scott could find me. Or the police. It was all too much.

'Why not?' Aaron asked.

'Because it was my fault,' I finally admitted the truth that tormented me. 'They died because of me.'

54

THEN

September

'What the—' I stared at the notification on my phone screen.

'What's wrong, babe?' Scott asked as he sat across the table from me, a spoon full of cereal paused in front of his lips.

'It's—' I shook my head. 'It's a mistake. It has to be a mistake.' I opened the banking app and pressed my finger to the sensor, my heart pounding as I waited impatiently for the statement to load.

I inhaled sharply as I stared at the deposit.

£10,000.

I scrolled down the statement. There had to be more. This must just be an instalment.

My fingers drummed against the table waiting for another notification.

'Chloe?'

'Huh?' My head jolted up at the sound of Scott's voice.

'What's going on?'

I swallowed. I couldn't tell him this. Not yet. 'A customer

underpaid me,' I lied. It was worrying how easily the lies came these days.

'Seriously?' Scott reached his hand out for my phone. 'Let me have their details and I'll handle it. I'm not letting anyone get away with treating you that way. You work too hard.'

I pulled my phone close to my chest. 'It's fine,' I assured him. 'I'll handle it. It's probably just an oversight.'

Scott shook his head. 'You're too trusting. You always think everyone is as good and honest as you are.'

I froze. I wasn't good or honest. My gaze dropped back to the bank statement. And if this wasn't a mistake, Scott would soon realise exactly how bad and dishonest I really was.

* * *

I hammered on Mia's hotel room door so hard that my hand hurt. But I didn't care. I still kept knocking.

The door swung open, and Mia glared at me. 'What the hell are you playing at?'

'What am I playing at?' I scoffed. 'I should be asking you that question, don't you think?'

'What are you talking about?' Mia's anger morphed into confusion.

'This,' I said, thrusting my mobile phone in front of her face.

Mia squinted at the screen. 'Why are you showing me your bank account?'

'Look at the latest transaction.'

'Oh, great.' Mia smiled. 'You've received the proceeds from the sale of Dad's house.' Her gaze shifted from the phone to me. 'So why are you so angry?'

'Why am I—' I gritted my teeth. 'Are you kidding me? Where's the rest, Mia?'

'The rest?' She looked back at the screen. 'It's all there.'

'Dad's house was worth way more than this.'

'Well, I mean, yeah, that's just your share.'

'My share.' My eyes narrowed as the meaning of her words sank in. 'And what percentage is my share, Mia?'

'Maybe we should have this conversation inside my room, instead of in the doorway,' Mia suggested, turning away and walking towards the window.

'Why?' I demanded, but followed her inside, allowing the door to slam behind me. 'Are you afraid that everyone will overhear how you've stolen my inheritance?'

'I didn't steal anything from you.'

I snorted.

Mia held her hands out to her sides, her palms open. 'It wasn't left to you.'

I took a step backward, pressing my fingers to my temple as I shook my head. 'Dad wouldn't do that. He couldn't.'

'I'm sorry,' Mia said, her eyes wet and dull. 'I thought you knew.'

I staggered towards the bed and sank down onto the soft mattress. I'd already accepted that Dad's death had sealed my fate. I would forever be unforgiven for my mistakes. But I'd pacified myself with the knowledge that at least he hadn't cut me out of his will. That his disdain for me didn't reach quite that level of hatred and loathing.

I was wrong.

This was worse than if he had cut me out entirely. At least that would have been upfront and honest. I would have known where I stood, instead of thinking perhaps beneath his anger, he still loved me.

It wasn't just the final precarious fragments of our relationship that were shattered, though. It was everything.

All my hopes for my new store, for my future with Scott, evaporated in an instant. Dad had sabotaged it all.

There was no way I could keep the pretence going indefinitely. Scott would figure my deception out eventually. But what was the alternative? I couldn't tell him the truth. Not now. It had been too long. The lies were too big.

Even if I managed to explain it all to him, how would he ever trust me again? One way or another I was going to lose him. It was just a matter of time.

The mattress dipped as Mia sat beside me. 'You need me, Chloe. You've always needed me.'

She was right, of course. She would never have got into a mess like this.

'Come on the cruise with me,' Mia repeated her invitation.

'Scott—'

'Scott can manage without you for a few months.'

'I have my sta-store to run.'

Mia groaned. 'Chloe, I *know*.'

I frowned. 'What—'

'You don't have a store.'

I shook my head. No, she couldn't know.

'You don't even own your house. You rent it. The only things you do actually own are a second-hand van and a foldout table in a park. That's your business. Your life.'

My mouth opened and closed, but I couldn't find the words to deny it.

'It's okay,' Mia said gently. 'Take a breath.'

I inhaled deeply. 'How did you know?'

Mia smiled ruefully. 'I've always known.'

'And Dad?'

Mia nodded. It was a tiny movement, barely perceivable. But it was enough. It was everything.

Dad knew.

I closed my eyes.

All the years of pretending I was fine, that I was better than fine, that I was successful, were for nothing.

'I wanted him to be proud of me. I wanted both of you to be pr—' I hiccupped back a sob.

'I am, Chloe. I'm proud of how hard you tried. How you persevered no matter what. Financial success is irrelevant. It's who you are that matters to me.'

'And Dad?'

Mia licked her lips. 'He was worried about you.'

My body crumpled forwards. Worried wasn't proud, but at least it was an emotion. 'I thought he'd ceased to feel anything except contempt for me a long time ago.'

'That's why...' Mia hesitated. She swallowed. 'That's why he left almost everything to me. He was worried you weren't—' she lowered her eyes '—capable.'

The word echoed through me. I was wrong. It wasn't contempt he'd felt for me. It was pity.

My own father thought I was a failure.

55

NOW

October

'They?' Aaron asked, pulling away from me. 'Who died? And what do you mean, because of you?' His questions tumbled out rapidly.

'My mum and my sister,' I sobbed.

'I-I don't understand. Mia, your mum died years ago.'

I nodded. 'Because of me,' I repeated.

'How could that have been because of you? You were just a kid.'

'I should have done more. I should have done *something*.'

Aaron shook his head.

'And now my sister's dead because of me too. It should have been me in that house. In that fire.'

'Don't say that.'

'It's true. It was my fault. It was *all* my fault.'

Aaron reached for my hands and twisted me to face him. 'Start at the beginning, Mia. Tell me everything.'

'We argued. I-I told her I would never forgive her. That I was done with her. And then I left her there. In that house. Alone.'

'But you couldn't have known there'd be a fire, could you?'

I shook my head. That small detail didn't absolve my guilt.

'There, you see?' He smiled at me as he squeezed my hands, and I felt relief ebb away some of my panic. Even after everything I'd done maybe there was someone who believed in me. Someone could see something good in me. Something in me that made him want to spend time in my company. Something that made him want to help me.

Maybe there was still hope for me.

I imagined Mia's reaction if she heard my claims. My stomach contracted at the thought of her. What would she think about everything I had done recently?

'It's like I'm stuck in this suffocating darkness, and I can't climb my way back out,' I told Aaron quietly. 'I don't have the energy to do so. I'm not even sure I have the desire to. Not enough of one, anyway.'

'You're grieving,' Aaron said softly.

I shook my head. 'It's more than that. It's not just grief. It's guilt.'

'But why guilt? I still don't understand.'

I couldn't tell him. It was too big. Too irredeemable. But I needed to say something. He was waiting. Studying me with curiosity. 'I was so awful to her.'

Aaron's eyes widened. 'I've never heard you admit that before.'

'I don't think I've ever fully admitted it to myself before either.' I'd always told myself that I was the good twin. The overlooked one. But was I really so innocent? Hadn't I stolen far more from her than she ever had from me?

'She adored you, you know? I know you two were complete

opposites, but she always tried to find a common ground. She tried to emulate you. To make herself more likeable to you.'

'You saw that?'

Aaron smiled slightly. 'She didn't know that I knew. She would have said I was crazy. But yeah, I saw it. I saw her. I loved her.'

I closed my eyes as my tears broke free. He had loved me. Genuinely. Completely.

More than Scott had done.

And yet, it still hadn't been enough.

56

THEN

September

SCOTT

I miss you.

I smiled as I read the message before setting the phone back on the table beside me. Even with my world falling apart, a message from Scott could instil a sense of calm within me.

I needed that right now.

Although Mia was being supportive too. Uncharacteristically so.

'Let me guess, Scott?' Mia asked as she set a cup of tea down next to my phone.

My cheeks flushed. 'Is it that obvious?'

'Completely.' Mia rolled her eyes. 'It's like you're a love-struck sixteen-year-old again.' She pulled the chair out from under the desk, and dragged it across her hotel room, to join me by the window.

I laughed. 'I wasn't as bad as you.'

Mia frowned. 'Oh yeah. You were always the studious, serious one and I was—'

'Falling madly in love with a new guy every other week?'

'I was going to say, I was the spontaneous one,' Mia said with a pout. 'But—' she broke into a grin '—your version is accurate too.'

I nodded. 'I know. I was the one who had to deal with all the broken-hearted guys you left in your wake.'

Mia winced. 'Sorry about that.'

'No, you're not,' I laughed, and Mia shrugged before bursting into laughter too.

'I'm not like that now, though,' Mia said, suddenly becoming serious.

'You mean you haven't left a trail of broken-hearted guys across Europe?' I stared at her in surprise.

'No. I mean I let them down gently now.' She grinned mischievously and I groaned.

My phone pinged again, and I flipped it over to read the message, still shaking my head. 'You're a lost cause,' I told Mia. 'Those poor guys don't stand a ch—' I frowned.

SCOTT

Do you miss me?

'Everything okay?'

I glanced back at Mia. 'Yes, sorry.' I fixed my smile back in place as I put the phone down. 'All good.'

'Scott again?' she asked.

I nodded and cleared my throat. 'He misses me.'

'Aww, he's adorable.'

'Yeah, he is.' My smile wavered. At least his first message was. But his second...?

The phone pinged again.

I stared at it but didn't move.

'You can message him back, you know?'

I shook my head. 'I don't really know what to say to him at the moment, everything is just such a mess.' I picked up my cup of tea and took a sip, grateful for the quiet calmness.

'You're avoiding him,' Mia said bluntly.

Another ping.

I knew from the way her nose wrinkled that Mia's curiosity had been piqued, but she was too quick for me as she reached out and snatched my phone up off the table.

I lurched forward but she moved out of reach. Her eyes widened as she read the message.

'What?'

Mia shook her head.

'What does it say?' I demanded impatiently as I attempted to grab the phone again.

'"Or are you having too much fun without me, that you've forgotten all about me?"' Mia read. 'And then the next message wants to know where you are.'

I cringed.

'Chloe.' The concern in Mia's voice had ramped up further. 'Tell me he's not really serious, is he? Is he always like this?'

I bristled. 'Like what?'

'Clingy?'

I shifted uncomfortably.

'Controlling?' Mia added and my skin prickled.

'Scott's not controlling,' I objected. But I could hear that my voice lacked conviction.

Mia puffed out her cheeks and let out a long slow breath. 'I don't know. All I've seen are a couple of messages. The question is, if I was to scroll back would I find more messages like these?'

I swallowed.

Mia nodded with understanding. 'Then I guess you have your answer,' she said, handing me back my phone.

'He didn't used to do this,' I said, feeling the need to defend him when he wasn't there to speak up for himself. 'I mean, he might have sent me a message to say hi or tell me that he was thinking about me, but that was it. There was no follow up. No clinginess.'

It sounded such an awful word: needy and suffocating. And yet... I realised, that was exactly how things had felt between us lately.

'Things at work are tough for him at the moment. It's a difficult job at the best of times. But recently, I think he's found it more draining, physically and emotionally. And then there is some stuff going on with his—'

'Chloe.' Mia placed her hand on my arm. 'You don't have to defend him. Not to me. And not even to yourself.'

'But I'm just trying to explain that maybe this change in behaviour is just a reflection of his current situation at work. Maybe when things settle down...' My words trailed out as I registered Mia's horrified expression.

'Is that really how you want to live? Waiting for things to settle down? To get better?'

My breath escaped in a gush as I realised she was right. I'd done that before. I'd done it for so long that it was second nature to me now. Keep my head down. Say nothing. Don't complain. Just ride it out.

I'd been a kid then. I hadn't had any choice. But things were different now.

'It's just little things,' I said, still trying to dismiss the doubts that niggled within me. 'I feel like he makes all the decisions. What we do, where we go, what I wear.'

'Wait, what you wear?'

I shrugged again. 'It's not a big deal, he just thought I should wear a different dress when we went to meet his parents.' I frowned. 'And shoes.' I shook my head. 'But he was just trying to be helpful. He wanted me to look my best and make a good impression. He was probably nervous.'

Mia's face contorted as though she had a bitter taste in her mouth. 'Shouldn't he have been proud to show you off to his parents, not nervous? I mean, I've seen your wardrobe – your clothes might not be designer, but they are lovely. You have a gorgeous sense of style. Better than his.'

My cheeks flushed with pride, and I sat a little taller.

'That feeling there. That reaction,' Mia said, pointing at me. 'That is how Scott should make you feel when he sees you. Confident. Vibrant.'

'He does,' I replied automatically, but then frowned. 'He used to.'

'And how does he make you feel now?'

'I'm...' I hesitated.

'Confused?' Mia asked.

'Maybe a little,' I admitted quietly.

She nodded. 'You're having doubts, aren't you?'

I sucked in a sharp breath.

Mia smiled ruefully as she studied me. 'I thought so, I can see it.'

What was I doing? This wasn't a conversation I should be having with Mia. I didn't open up to her. I didn't share my vulnerabilities and fears. Not any more.

She nodded. 'We're twins, remember?'

She said it as though that meant something. But it didn't, did it? Not to her?

'It's not just about your relationship, though, is it?' Mia asked. 'It's more than that.'

'I...' I hesitated.

'It's okay,' Mia assured me. She squeezed my hand and sat patiently waiting for me to continue.

The strangest part was, I realised I actually wanted to continue.

Now that I'd started, the words were bubbling up inside me, desperate to escape. To be said. Or perhaps, to be heard.

'I guess I'm starting to have doubts about myself and who I am when I'm with him,' I continued in a rush. 'I ignored those doubts. Sidestepped around them in the hope they would simply dissipate.' I scrunched my nose. The truth was, I couldn't even claim ignorance. I'd known what I was doing. It was a conscious choice. Because it felt like it was the only choice. 'Because the alternative was a life without Scott,' I admitted quietly.

I'd thought that was what terrified me. That I loved him so much that I couldn't bear to be parted from him. But there was a tiny voice in the back of my head that kept repeating one question over and over: What if there was no one else?

Was it really the thought of life without him that scared me? Or just life without someone?

'Would that be so bad?' Mia asked.

I nodded instinctively. 'Our relationship isn't perfect, but it's the best I've ever known.' I heard the desperation in my own voice. The need to be loved. To be accepted.

'You've had other boyfriends. Other relationships that didn't last. You recovered. You moved on. You will again.'

She was right. I'd had boyfriends before Scott, but none of them had been serious. They were like Aaron, they never stayed.

'But Scott's different. I chose him.'

'All relationships are a choice.'

'Not like this.'

Mia shook her head. She didn't understand. She couldn't

understand. It wasn't surprising. My relationship with Scott had a unique beginning. I'd known he was special from the moment we first met.

He was good. He had principles. He followed the rules, did the right thing.

I could trust him in a way that I couldn't trust myself any more.

* * ⅄

I lingered a few steps in front of my flower stall. My gaze fixed on the path to the right.

That was the direction he always came from. I checked my watch again: 8.35 a.m. There was still time. Some Saturdays he didn't arrive until almost 9 a.m. If at all.

His routine wasn't as predictable as mine. Although, mine was less structured recently. Ever since the day he'd brought flowers for Mother's Day, he always took time to say good morning. It had become a ritual now. It was so small and insignificant and yet there was something about the way he smiled at me. Something more than just polite acknowledgement.

Wasn't there?

The only way to know for sure would be to have an actual conversation. All I knew so far was that his mother loved white lilies and he was a police officer. He was clearly very proud of that. He'd managed to work it into our short conversation even though he hadn't needed to. He'd wanted me to know. Wanted me to be impressed. To care.

And I did. More than I should, perhaps. But I always cared the most in relationships. I'd learnt not to mind. It was just how things were.

That's why the next move was clearly up to me. I couldn't be satisfied with a half wave and grunted 'good morning' as he jogged passed each week. I couldn't just wait around until he needed flowers for his mother's birthday, or for a first date... No, I'd learnt long ago not to sit idly by and do nothing. I was more proactive than that now.

I had to be.

'Do you have any chrysanthemums?' a voice behind me asked, and I turned to see an elderly lady peering at the stall.

'No, sorry,' I said automatically, as I fought to keep my gaze from drifting to the bucket full of chrysanthemums that were just out of her eyeline. I couldn't afford the distraction of serving a customer right now. Everything would be ruined.

'Oh.'

That one tiny word sounded so small and disappointed as she turned away that I immediately felt guilty for my lie. 'Come back in an hour and I'll have some then,' I assured her and was met by a beaming grin as she nodded enthusiastically.

'I'll do that, thank you, love.'

I smiled, though the guilt still lingered. I could have saved her the hassle of having to come back and just sold her the flowers now. But even as that thought furrowed my brow, my gaze drifted back to the path to my right. It wasn't worth the risk.

I sighed. Mia would tell me I was being pathetic if she could see me right now. She'd be right, of course. Like always.

There had to be another way to get his attention. A more effective way.

57

October

Aaron patted his back pocket and groaned. 'Can I use your phone?' he asked.

'Sure,' I replied as I handed it to him.

'Burgers okay for you?'

I nodded aimlessly. My protests of not being hungry had already been overruled. Aaron's insistence that we needed to eat was as sweet as it was irritating. But I decided to go with it.

It was easier that way.

'I made a friend today,' Aaron said with a brightness to his voice that didn't match his pained expression as he tapped our order into my phone. 'She owns the beach hut next to mine.'

I made a friend.

The words circled in my head. But it wasn't Aaron's voice I heard. It was Scott's.

I forced a smile onto my lips, resisting the overwhelming sense of possessiveness that had descended over me. Aaron could make friends. Of course he could. It was a good thing.

'She's been so sweet, making me cups of tea and chatting to me as I work.'

'That's so kind of her. It must get lonely working by yourself all the time.' I felt a rush of pride at how well I was handling this. My tone gave no indication of the jealousy that flowed beneath the surface.

My brow twitched as I suddenly wondered why Aaron was telling me this. Was he just sharing his day with me, or was my jealousy exactly what he had been hoping for?

I wanted to ask, but if dating Scott had taught me anything, it was that I couldn't believe everything I heard. Lies sounded like truths when you wanted it badly enough.

'Actually, I think she's the one who's lonely. She kind of reminds me of my own grandmother.'

'Your grandmother?'

A flash of understanding passed across his face. 'She's in her eighties.'

'Oh.'

I waited for his laughter. His mockery. It was obvious that he knew what I'd been thinking.

'I feel bad for her being on her own.' Aaron spoke as though he hadn't noticed my reaction. He just kept talking and my heart expanded. 'She said she'd lost her husband last year. They'd been married fifty years. Can you imagine losing the person you had shared the majority of your life with? It must be like losing a piece of yourself.'

'I think that's how Dad felt when we lost Mum.' The words slipped from my lips. 'Not that they had been together for fifty years, but—'

'She was his other half,' Aaron finished for me.

'She was his everything.'

'It must be incredible to experience a love like that. That

strong. That certain.' He shook his head in awe. 'Love is a powerful thing.'

My thoughts drifted to Mia. Our relationship was different. It might not have been a marriage, but we'd spent our lives together. Admittedly not always in the same country, but we were still connected. Aaron was right. Despite my doubts about whether I'd loved my sister when she was alive, her death made the truth inescapable. I loved her. Even if that love was complicated.

'And painful.' I blinked as I realised I'd said that out loud.

'Are you still talking about your dad or someone else?'

I hesitated. I didn't have to answer. Didn't have to have this conversation. And yet, some part of me wanted to. Needed to.

'Both,' I admitted. 'When someone's your everything, who are you without them?' As much as I'd tried to deny it, Mia had always been the centre of my world. Living in her shadow I'd felt inferior, but now I just felt incomplete.

Aaron tipped his head to the side. 'Who are you?'

'Someone different,' I said slowly.

'And the person who was your everything?' Aaron asked tentatively. 'Do you miss them?'

Did I miss her? I inhaled slowly. Admittedly, I did. I missed the sister she could be sometimes. Interested. Supportive. Funny. But those times were fleeting. Their absence left a void inside me. A loneliness I had been so desperate to avoid that it had driven me to Scott. I'd made him my everything, then. And I'd become his.

'Do you wish you could go back?'

'No. Never.' My words were short and certain. It was the one thing I knew without question, there was no going back. 'I idolised what my parents had. Dad's love for Mum was unrelenting, even after she'd gone. I'd wanted that kind of love. I'd wanted to be someone's everything. Until I was...'

'It wasn't what you'd thought?'

I shook my head. 'Maybe my parents were unique. Or maybe I was just with the wrong person.' I shrugged. 'Either way, it wasn't what I'd thought. It was intense. Powerful. Suffocating.'

'Suffocating?'

I shifted, feeling the past weighing down on me. 'It's like being under a microscope. Every move is monitored. Every decision assessed. At first it seems sweet. It makes you feel important. Like you matter.' My lips curved upwards at the memory of how that felt. 'But slowly you start to realise, you're never alone. Never allowed to be.' My smile withered. The flat suddenly felt small and claustrophobic as my heart raced. I wanted to escape, except I couldn't. Wherever I went, I carried the memories with me. I would never fully be free from Scott now.

How had I not seen who he was from the start? How had I justified his behaviour for so long? With hindsight it all seemed so clear. The warnings were always there. And yet I'd been blind to them. Or perhaps, more accurately I'd chosen to ignore them.

Had I been so desperate to be part of something that I was willing to live in feigned ignorance? Or had a lifetime with Mia taught me to second guess myself, and believe what I wanted, what I thought, was somehow inferior.

'You become an extension of someone else,' I continued as Aaron tipped his head to the side, listening intently. 'Not sure what decisions, what thoughts, are theirs and which are yours. If *any* are yours.'

'That sounds awful,' Aaron said earnestly.

I nodded. 'Yeah, but that's one good thing about being here,' I said, turning away as I tried to make my voice sound normal. 'I got to leave all that behind. And all this space is so—' I took a deep breath as I gazed out of the window at the long stretch of beach below '—freeing.'

'Maybe it was a good place to come after all,' Aaron said. 'It's giving you a chance to find yourself again.'

'Yes.' I nodded slowly. 'I think you're right. I'd thought coming here would be a chance to reinvent myself. To be someone new. But it's not really working out that way. Now that I'm here I realise you can never really escape your past. Yourself.'

'I'm glad,' Aaron said, and this time his smile was genuine.

I'd missed that smile. I'd missed everything about him. More than I'd even realised. But I didn't have to miss him any more.

'And being back here has brought me back to you, too,' I said softly as I cupped his face in my hand and leaned towards him.

58

THEN

September

'If you're not happy in this relationship, you need to leave,' Mia said flatly.

I shook my head. It was so easy for her. She was used to walking away from everything and everyone. I wasn't like that. People mattered to me. Scott mattered.

'I am happy. Scott makes me happy,' I assured her.

'Then you at least need to talk to him.'

I puffed my cheeks out as I let out a breath. She was right. I knew she was. I'd been feeling for weeks that things had changed. His messages that used to be cute and loving, now felt like I was being monitored and needed to check in. And yet the thought of broaching the subject tied my stomach in knots.

'You need to talk to him about *a lot* of things,' she said firmly.

Bile rose in my throat, and I swallowed.

'You're worried about how he'll react,' Mia said, watching my reaction. Her eyes narrowed. 'You don't trust him.'

'I never said that,' I objected.

'Then why did you lie to him about owning a store?'

'I lied to everyone about that.' Somehow, my argument didn't sound like a particularly strong defence when I said it aloud.

'Everyone? Or just Dad and I?' Mia asked knowingly.

It was true. There were only three people who I'd told that lie to. The three people I should have been the most honest with. My brow creased. Or perhaps, more accurately, I should have felt *more able* to be honest with.

'I get why you lied to me,' Mia said, her tone softer. 'I can come across a little judgemental.'

I stared at her in silence, too stunned by her admission to pay much attention to her attempt to downplay the level of her criticalness as 'a little'.

'And Dad?' Mia shook her head. 'I know all you've ever wanted was for him to be proud of you again. Like he used to be before.'

She didn't clarify before what. She didn't need to.

'But Scott?' Mia continued. 'Why lie to him? Whether you owned a store or just a flower stall in the park shouldn't have mattered to him, or his opinion of you.'

'It was never about him,' I admitted, surprising both of us with my confession.

'It was about you,' Mia realised.

It felt strange hearing Mia voice the words I'd never been able to admit to myself.

'There's nothing wrong with having a stall, though,' Mia assured me.

'I know,' I replied automatically. I loved my stall. I loved that it was mine. That I had built it from nothing and turned it into a viable business. And perhaps most importantly, that I'd done it all alone.

But at the same time, that was the saddest part. It hadn't been through choice that I'd done it alone. But necessity.

'I've never told you, but I've always been kind of envious of the life you've created for yourself here.' Mia's voice was barely a whisper.

I scoffed. For a brief moment I'd thought we were reconnecting. Being honest with each other for the first time in years. Maybe ever. But Mia was patronising me now. There was no way she could be jealous of my little life when she had so much more.

'I'm serious,' Mia insisted, louder now. 'You broke out on your own. You decided what you wanted to do. Unlike me.' She shook her head sadly. 'It was Dad's dream for me to go to university and study languages.'

'Because you were good at them. Because he wanted you to have a solid foundation. To have options and financial stability.'

'And happiness?'

I froze. 'He wanted that too. For you.'

Mia's happiness had always been Dad's priority. Even when he'd cared about mine, Mia's had still taken precedence.

Parents always claimed they didn't have favourites. But they did. Some just hid it better than others.

Dad tried. At least when we were younger. But there was always a bond between Mia and him that evaded me and shut me out even more.

Perhaps their bond was what drew Mum and I closer together. She'd always treated Mia and I the same but the closer Mia and Dad grew, the more Mum and I found ourselves abandoned together.

Mia nodded. 'He did, but...' She shook her head, leaving her thought unfinished.

I wanted to ask her to continue. I wanted to know what she was struggling to say. To know *her*.

But I wouldn't rush her. We'd come so far today; I didn't want to jeopardise that progress by pushing for more.

'What about Scott?' Mia asked. 'Doesn't he want you to be happy?'

'Of course he does.' I didn't have to think about my reply. I knew it without hesitation.

'So tell him the truth.'

'I want to,' I admitted, my voice small and uncertain.

'You're afraid he wouldn't understand why you lied.'

I didn't respond. I didn't need to.

'So you're just going to keep pretending you already own a shop and hope he doesn't question why you don't work there? And that he never tries to visit it?'

I shrugged. 'I've got away with it so far.'

'And that's what you want? A relationship dependant on what you can get away with?'

'I thought it was temporary. With Dad's inheritance I was going to open the store for real.'

'Well, I guess now you have no choice but to come clean.'

'Or...' I nibbled my lip. 'You could give me the money.' I tried not to squirm. It felt a big ask. I was grovelling for money which legally I had no right to. It had been Dad's to do with as he chose, and he'd chosen to leave me next to nothing.

The magnitude of that realisation was like a punch in my gut. Dad had made his resentment of me perfectly clear in the past. I wasn't sure why his actions now affected me so much. But they did. I'd been naive to think I would be treated equally with Mia. Perhaps I should just be grateful he'd left me anything at all.

Why had he done that, though? Was it a token gesture to show me that he didn't hate me completely? Or was it simply to clear his conscience, so he could pacify himself that he hadn't cut me off entirely?

Either way, I'd lost and Mia had won.

But Dad was gone now. What happened next was up to Mia. If she truly had any love for me, she would split the inheritance. I would have done it for her. And I wouldn't have made her ask for it. But this was Mia. And one heartfelt conversation in twenty-four years, didn't mean our sisterly bond was strong enough to expect her to suddenly start doing the right thing by me.

'Dad might have cut me out, but you don't have to,' I pointed out. 'We could still share the money.'

Mia didn't respond, she just took another sip of her tea.

Her silence stoked the resentment that smouldered within me. 'You have the flat in Bournemouth already. You don't need the money from the sale of the house. But I do. *You* could help me.'

'But even if I did, Scott would think it's your second shop and that you still own the first,' Mia said flatly.

I shook my head. 'No, I'm moving to bigger premises in a better location.'

Mia stared at me, her eyes wide. 'You talk as though the store is real. It's like you've fallen for your own lie.'

I shrugged. Perhaps on some level I had. The lie was my illusion. An image of the life I wanted to live. I wasn't ready to give up on that.

'A loan then,' I suggested, desperation overriding my anger. 'I could pay you back in instalments.' It wasn't a fair solution, but it was *a* solution. And right now it was the only one I had. My future rested in Mia's hands.

And she knew it.

59

NOW

October

'What are you doing?' Aaron asked as he leapt to his feet.

'I-I'm sorry. I-I—' I clamped my mouth closed. This wasn't right. I was reacting the way Chloe would. But I wasn't her any more. I was Mia. And Mia wouldn't run away apologising. She would stand firm. Say what she wanted. *Get* what she wanted.

I turned back, lifting my chin as I stared Aaron straight in the eyes. 'Actually, I'm not sorry.' My voice trembled but I pushed on. I couldn't run away from him. Not this time. 'I love you, Aaron. I always have. Always will. Being here. Being close to you again has reminded me of that.'

'Mia...' Aaron shook his head.

'I screwed up. Letting you go was one of the biggest mistakes I've ever made. And believe me, I've made a lot of mistakes.'

'You didn't let me go, Mia. We were never really a couple.'

My eyebrows lifted. 'Of course we were!'

Aaron scoffed. 'That was never real.'

It's not real, Chloe.

Aaron's words from six years ago sprang into my head.

His denial had cut deeply. It was bad enough that he'd discarded me for Mia, but then to lie to me about it had been devastating.

I frowned. Except, why would he keep the lie going now after all these years? It made sense to do so when I was Chloe, but I was Mia now. He had no reason to pretend.

'I should never have let you talk me into that,' he added.

So Mia had instigated the relationship. It wasn't surprising. Even back then Mia had always been clear about what she wanted and had gone after it. She never let anyone stand in her way.

'Deep down I'd known it wouldn't work.'

'Ah,' I murmured with sudden understanding. That was it. Aaron didn't view them as a real couple because he'd know Mia well enough to know that it wouldn't last. He'd been nothing more than a passing phase. Just like everyone else.

Aaron shook his head. 'Chloe wasn't the jealous type.'

I stifled a laugh. Not jealous? Me?

Had I hidden my feelings that well? Or perhaps he'd simply never known me as well as he'd known Mia. That thought was like shards of ice slicing into my heart.

'I should have just talked to her, told her I would give her space, time, whatever she needed.' Aaron's words ran into one another. 'Faking a relationship to make her jealous was never going to win her back.'

I blinked. 'W-what?' I couldn't have heard right. Their relationship wasn't fake. It had meant so much to him, that he'd been completely devastated when she'd dumped him. That's why he'd ended up running away to Australia, broken-hearted because of Mia.

Hadn't he?

'But I love you,' I repeated the truth I had carried in silence for years. 'I've always loved you.'

'Mia.' Aaron shook his head sadly. 'I know you better than that.'

'But it's true,' I pleaded.

'You only wanted to be with me because Chloe was with me. You wanted everything she had. You still do.'

I shook my head. No, this couldn't be happening. Everything I'd ever wanted had been right in my grasp and yet somehow it was slipping through my fingers.

Again.

I should have known better. I'd built my relationship with Scott on so many lies, and where had it got me? I'd selected him. Manipulated him.

Our entire relationship had happened because Scott had come to my rescue and helped me when that kid tried to steal my bag. Except, there was never any danger. I'd set the whole thing up. I'd created the situation to get his attention, and it had worked perfectly. It had ignited a spark between us which would never have existed without my intervention.

And I'd done it again to Aaron. I'd thought I could win him back by being what he wanted. By being Mia. But it wasn't what he wanted.

'I've changed,' I told him urgently. 'I'm different now.'

'Yes.' Aaron nodded. 'You are. I can see it. I can feel it. But...'

I drew back. 'It isn't enough,' I realised slowly. 'I'm not enough.'

Aaron shook his head.

'But I can be,' I said as I stepped towards him. 'I can be better. I can be—'

'You'll never be her.' Aaron's words cut through me.

I froze. My heartbeat thudded so forcefully I could feel the vibrations in my head.

'You'll never be Chloe.'

60

THEN

September

'Chloe!' Scott bellowed from the hall as the front door slammed behind him. 'Chloe!'

I raced from the kitchen. 'What's wrong? Are you hurt?' My gaze darted over his body from head to toe, checking for any signs of injury. With the dangerous job he did, I lived in fear that something would happen to him.

'Only my pride,' Scott spat the words at me.

My relief was deadened by confusion. His anger seemed to be directed at me. But why?

'I had coffee with a new friend today,' Scott said, pacing the hall floor. 'She had some interesting things to say.'

She.

Jealousy prickled at me. He'd had coffee with another woman.

His pacing stopped abruptly, and he swung round to face me. 'About you.'

'Me?' My confusion deepened. Who would be talking to him about me? I didn't really have any close friends. Acquaintances, yes. People I said hello to every day. Regulars who bought flowers from me. But no one who really knew me, except...

'And all the lies you've been telling me.'

'Mia,' her name slipped from my lips in a rush of clarity. It had to be her. No one else knew. No one else would even care.

Scott crossed the hall in two strides and loomed at me. 'She made a fool of me, and now you think you can do the same.'

I shook my head. 'It wasn't like that. I didn't mean to lie. I just—'

I gasped, my fingers instinctively clawing at Scott's hand as he grabbed me by the throat and rammed me backwards into the wall.

My brain fought to process what was happening, but it didn't make sense. Nothing made sense.

Scott's movement had been so fast. I hadn't seen it coming. I hadn't expected it. How could I have done? This was Scott. My Scott.

As angry as Dad had been at me, his retaliation had been silence. He'd never once physically hurt me. And I'd failed him far worse than I'd failed Scott.

I squirmed against his grip, whimpering in a desperate plea for him to release me as I struggled to breathe.

'You're just like her.' He spat the words at me, before letting his hand fall from my throat and pushing me aside.

I fell to the floor, discarded, gasping for air, unable to summon the strength to scramble to my feet. I stared up at him in bewildered shock. His words had been filled with such hatred. But not just for me.

'Sasha thought she could mess with me too.'

Sasha.

I shook my head. It didn't make sense. Sasha had been the love of his life. Their relationship had been cut short by the accident that had taken her away from him, and that loss had all but destroyed him. That's what he'd said.

But the man towering over me now wasn't mourning for his lost love. He was angry at her. And angry at me for reminding him of her.

My lie had made me like her, which meant Sasha had lied too.

The questions about his past relationship that before had felt like none of my business, suddenly seemed critical. Perhaps if I'd asked them sooner, we wouldn't have ended up here.

I reached for the phone in the pocket of my jeans, but Scott kicked it from my hand. I cried out in pain as I nursed my fingers to my body.

'Who are you planning on calling?' he demanded. 'The police?' A twisted smile formed on his lips. 'You really think that they'll help you?' He drew close, his face only a few centimetres in front of mine. 'That *we'll* help you?'

I flinched at his mocking tone. He was right. He was the police. Someone who was supposed to protect me. Not hurt me.

I shook my head. He was bluffing. He just wanted to scare me to protect himself. His career. His freedom. 'They'll help me,' I said evenly.

I waited for Scott's angry explosion. I was being defiant which was reckless. There would be consequences.

Scott shrugged and stood up.

I frowned. His reaction wasn't what I'd expected. It was so calm and nonchalant. He bent down to retrieve my phone. 'If you believe that then I guess you'd better call them,' he said, holding the phone out to me.

I stared at it. It was so tempting to snatch it from his outstretched hand and call for help, but something felt wrong. That one call could destroy everything for him and yet he wasn't afraid. He was almost taunting me to do it.

I lifted my hand tentatively towards the phone.

'They didn't do Sasha any good, did they?'

61

NOW

October

I turned away from Aaron and staggered to the window. I rested my forehead against the window frame as I stared down at the newly repaired beach hut.

'I've always loved her. Every time I look at you, I see her. You speak and I hear her. It's weird but that feeling is stronger than ever this time.'

'I can be her.' I turned to face him, my watery eyes pleading with him to realise the thing I couldn't tell him.

Aaron shook his head. 'It's not the same.'

My lips quivered as I search for the words to tell him that it was. It was exactly the same.

I was Chloe. His Chloe.

I shook my head. 'No, this isn't right. If you loved her this much you wouldn't have ended it with her.'

'I didn't.'

I frowned. 'Yes, you did. In fact, it was worse than that. You stopped talking to her. It was as though you just erased her from your life. How could you do that to someone you love?'

'Being around her was too hard. I couldn't speak. I couldn't breathe. It was crushing me to be near to her and know that she didn't love me. Didn't want me.'

'What are you talking about? I lo—' I shook my head. 'Chloe loved you. She loved you more than anything.'

'Then why did she break up with me?'

'She d—' I stopped as my denial withered on my lips. I hadn't broken up with him. I knew that. And yet, I could see from his expression that he truly believed I had.

Which meant only one thing.

It was Mia.

I shook my head. I had to be wrong. It couldn't have been her. Not even Mia would have done that. Not to me. Not to her sister.

Yet something deep inside told me she would.

She had.

Aaron's eyes clouded over as he stared into the distance. 'I can still see her standing at the end of the pier telling me it was over. We were over.'

I followed his gaze as though trying to see what he was seeing. But I couldn't. It wasn't real. It had never been real.

'I...' I searched for the words to tell him he was wrong. It hadn't been me. Mia had taken away the one person who'd loved me. The only good thing I'd had in my life. He needed to know that. To know that I had always loved him too.

But it was too late.

Revealing Mia's deception wouldn't help me now. Chloe was dead. And I was trapped being the person I despised. Telling Aaron the truth would only make him despise me too.

I couldn't bear that. I'd already lost him as Chloe. I couldn't lose him as Mia too.

My lie had brought me back to Bournemouth. Back to Aaron. But it was also now the reason we could never be together.

'I thought she'd come back one day. London never seemed like her. She used to talk about buying a cute little whitewashed bungalow in Mudeford someday.'

I blinked. 'You remember that?'

Aaron nodded. 'Of course, that was before everything happened, but still—' he shrugged '—that dull, grey, end of terrace house in Hammersmith didn't feel like her.'

My body tensed as a chill seeped into my bones. 'How do you know what the house looked like?' I'd built my life in London after he'd abandoned me for Australia. He'd never been a part of it. And yet somehow he knew where I lived.

Panic flashed across Aaron's face. 'Y-you told me.'

Even as kids I'd always been able to tell when Aaron was lying. His nervous stammer gave him away back then, just as it did now.

My eyes narrowed. 'Y-you said it didn't *feel* like her.' I struggled to get the words out. I wasn't sure what it all meant. But something in the pit of my stomach told me it was important.

And worse still, it was connected to what happened to Mia.

'From the w-way you described it.' Aaron tried to shrug but it looked heavy and awkward.

He was lying.

But why?

62

THEN

September

My pulse quickened as the alarm clock beeped and Scott stirred. I'd lain by his side, staring at the ceiling all night, too afraid to move.

Every instinct screamed at me to crawl out of bed while he slept and run away. But it wasn't as though I could call for help, he still had my phone. He'd tucked it under his pillow out of my reach last night. And if I tried to run, I doubted I'd make it out of the house, let alone the bedroom, before he woke up. Even if I did, where would I go?

I had the money from my inheritance. It was less than I'd hoped but it would at least be enough to rent somewhere for a while until I could get back on my feet. But he was a police officer. Wherever I went, he would find me.

I'm never letting you go.

Scott's words repeated, causing bile to rise in my throat.

At one time those words had made me feel so safe and loved, but now...

Was that what Sasha had done? Tried to leave him?

'Morning,' he said groggily as he reached out to silence the alarm.

The familiarity of his morning ritual grated against me. This was *my* home. *My* safe space. And yet, it felt like his presence suddenly dominated it.

'M-morning.' I was surprised how relatively normal my voice sounded. Only a slight tremor betrayed the fear and anger that vibrated within me.

'Ugh,' Scott groaned. 'I feel awful.'

I turned my head, surveying him in the dim morning light. Hope fluttered in my chest. He felt bad. Remorseful for his actions last night. It didn't make up for it. It didn't redeem him. But it was something.

Wasn't it?

'Best not to get too close,' he said, as though he'd expected me to roll towards him for our typical morning hug. 'I think I'm getting the flu.'

'Oh.' My hope evaporated. 'I'm sorry.' But the words lacked compassion. I wasn't sorry. Not for him. Only for myself.

Beneath my disappointment, though, I felt a sense of relief. I was grateful for the reason to have a little space. To avoid having to hug him and pretend that everything was normal. When nothing could never be again.

'My head feels awful,' Scott said, rubbing his forehead.

Resentment simmered inside me. It took all of my strength to keep it contained. Keep it quiet.

I was suddenly angry. A fire raged within me. But my resentment wasn't about him feeling unwell. I raised my hand to my throat and winced as my fingers touched the tender spots where his hand had gripped me last night. He knew nothing of what real pain felt like. Our relationship was in crisis and the only thing affecting him was a cold. It felt like a sign. Proof that I'd cared more about our relationship than he did.

Was I angry with him for that?

It wasn't the first time. In fact, I was always the person who cared the most.

Mum used to tell me it was a good quality. A sign of my big heart. Of how much love I had to give.

But she'd failed to warn me of the consequences of it. The pain. The loneliness. It was tough being the one who cared, when everyone else remained ambivalent.

I sat up and swung my legs out of bed, eager to get up and escape the house that had once been mine. 'I'll bring you a Lemsip,' I said generously. Except I knew my offer wasn't motivated by kindness, but self-preservation.

Keeping him happy kept me safe. At least for now.

'Nah, don't bother, babe,' Scott said, throwing the duvet off. 'I'm meeting the guys this morning. We're going paintballing, remember.'

I nodded. 'I didn't think you'd feel up to it.'

'I don't but I already paid, so I'm not going to miss it now.'

He'd paid? The question formed on the tip of my tongue, but I bit it back. He'd told me Ethan had a spare ticket, that was the only reason he was going. After all, he was broke.

I watched as he padded to the bathroom. Everything seemed so normal. For a moment I wondered if last night had really happened. Perhaps it had just been an intensely vivid nightmare.

Flicking the bedroom light on, I peered at my reflection in the full-length mirror. My fingers traced the dark bruises on my neck.

The tentative sliver of hope evaporated in an instant. It wasn't a nightmare.

I scrambled across the bed and grabbed my phone from under Scott's pillow.

'Hey, babe,' Scott said as he poked his head out of the bathroom.

I froze, my phone still in my hands.

'What are you doing?'

'I-I have orders to deliver this morning,' I stammered.

Scott swung the door open and strode towards me. He held out his hand for my phone. 'Show me.'

I tapped the screen, pulling up the order page from my website, before handing the phone to him.

He studied the screen, and then gave a shot sharp nod of approval.

I let out a breath, thankful that I hadn't had to lie.

'Look, Chloe,' Scott said, 'about last night...'

This was it. He was going to apologise. Tell me he overreacted. That he still loved me and wanted to work through this.

My fingers automatically traced the bruised on my neck. Was that what I wanted?

'I think it's best if we put the whole episode behind us, don't you? As long as you never lie to me again, everything will be fine. We'll be fine.'

I nodded mutely. Except we weren't fine. We never would be. Not now.

Anger surged through me as Scott started to turn away. 'Sasha wasn't,' I spat the words at him.

His head jolted back, and he glared at me. 'Sasha never listened.' His features relaxed, and he half smiled. 'You're smarter than she was.'

I wondered how true that statement was. After all, we'd both fallen for him.

He jerked his head towards the phone in my hand. 'I'm trusting you here. Just don't do anything stupid, okay?'

I swallowed.

'It really wouldn't do you any good. It just makes Ethan and I more work.'

'Ethan?'

Scott's smile grew into a sneer. 'He helped me cover it up after Sasha died. Do you really think he won't protect me now, too?'

The temperature in the bedroom plummeted as I watched Scott disappear into the bathroom again.

I flung the wardrobe open and quickly changed into a pair of jeans and a polo neck jumper. I pulled it on and rolled the neck down, checking it covered my bruises.

I wasn't sure why I did it. Was I trying to shield him from seeing the result of his actions? Or was I protecting him from awkward questions from the neighbours if I happened to encounter them outside?

Either way he didn't deserve my loyalty.

I heard the shower start and I sprang back into action and sprinted down the stairs. I loaded a few buckets of flowers into the van, leaving half behind in my hurry so I could slip out of the house before Scott finished his shower. I took just enough to ensure I didn't arouse suspicion, but it wasn't as though I needed them. I wasn't going to the park this morning.

* * *

My body trembled as I walked towards the police station.

I was doing the right thing, I assured myself. The only thing I could do.

I wanted Scott gone. Wanted him out of my home. Out of my

life. I snorted at the irony. I'd thought getting him was the hard part.

From the moment I'd first met him when he bought flowers at my stall, I'd been infatuated with him. I'd fantasised about him, envisaging our lives together. But they'd looked nothing like this.

I hated him for destroying the illusion. But the truth was, I was as much to blame. After all, I'd contrived our meeting. I'd given him the opportunity to be the hero. *My* hero. How was I to know he was a villain in disguise?

I pushed the door open and stepped inside. Unfortunately, getting rid of him was going to be a lot more difficult.

'Chloe, what are you doing here?'

I swung around from the reception desk. 'Ethan?' Panic gripped my chest as my eyes darted to the open door behind him. 'Is Scott with you?'

'Scott? No.' A puzzled frown creased his brow. 'Why would—'

'I thought you were going paintballing today?'

Ethan let out a short chuckle. 'I wish!'

'But Scott said—' I stopped as I suddenly realised the obvious explanation. Scott had lied.

Anger bubbled inside me, and I gritted my teeth as I fought to hold it back. Another lie. Another betrayal.

'Is everything okay?' he asked, his gaze drifting to the reception desk where the officer was patiently waiting.

'I...' My mind went blank. The only reason I'd found the courage to do this was because I was certain Ethan wouldn't be here. I was taking a risk, hoping that Scott had been bluffing about the willingness of the other officers to cover for him. But he'd been very clear about Ethan's involvement. I shook my head. 'Sorry, this was a bad idea.' I turned on my heel and yanked the door open.

'Chloe, wait,' Ethan called after me.

I ignored him and kept walking, but he was faster. He sprinted ahead of me and stepped in front of me, blocking my path.

'I shouldn't have come here,' I said, attempting to sidestep around him.

Ethan placed his hand on my arm. 'Why did you come?' His voice was soft and soothing as though he was trying to calm a spooked animal.

'I just... I thought...' I glanced back at the police station behind me. 'I needed help.'

'You're worried about Scott.'

My head jolted back, and I stared at him. He knew.

'Things have been really tough for him, Chloe.'

I frowned. His words weren't what I had expected. They sounded like a justification. An excuse.

'Because of what happened to Sasha?'

Ethan took a step back, the colour draining from his face. 'Scott told you about her?'

'That surprises you?' I frowned. 'Why? We're engaged, of course he'd tell me about his previous fiancée.'

'But we don't talk about her,' Ethan said bluntly.

We.

My breath caught in my chest; Scott had been telling the truth. Whatever went down between him and Sasha, the police were involved too. *Ethan* was involved.

I clenched my jaw. 'Scott told me everything.'

Ethan's eyes widened and he looked as though he was about to throw up. I'd seen that reaction before. Dad had looked the same way, when he'd arrived home to find two paramedics in the flat.

'Chloe, you have to understand, what happened to Sasha

was...' He glanced back at the police station behind him. 'Unthinkable.'

A wave of nausea rose from the pit of my stomach. What exactly had happened to Sasha? And how much was he involved?

'There's nothing more we can do for her,' Ethan continued. He turned back to face me, and his eyes met mine. 'It's the people who are still with us that we have to focus on now.'

My stomach lurched. What did that mean? Was it a threat? Was I the subject of his focus?

'I should go.' I stared to turn away but stopped. 'You won't tell Scott I was here, will you?'

Ethan shook his head. 'Everyone deserves a second chance.'

A chill seeped through my body that didn't match the bright sunny October morning. Was he giving me a reprieve, or a warning?

I nodded slowly. 'Yes.' My voice was hesitant and croaky. I tried not to wince. I'd spent years longing for exactly that. A second chance to prove I was better than my worst moment.

I shouldn't have come. I couldn't trust Ethan. I couldn't trust anyone.

Yet even as I fled the police station, I couldn't help feeling jealous. Scott and Ethan had the kind of bond that I'd always wanted. One that would withstand anything.

Even death.

63

NOW

October

Mia's phone rang and I dashed out of the bathroom to answer it, praying it was Aaron. He'd left so abruptly after my foolish attempt to kiss him earlier, that I hadn't had chance to find out how he really knew what my house looked like.

As I reached for the phone, I realised that wasn't entirely true. I could have sought the truth. I'd chosen not to. I was afraid I might push him even further away.

I'd only just got him back in my life. I couldn't bear the thought of losing him again.

Disappointment pressed down on my chest as I read Ethan's name on the screen. I threw the phone back onto the bed and started to turn away, but I paused.

Perhaps I'd ignored his calls for long enough. He clearly wasn't going to give up.

Reluctantly I picked the phone up, and pressed it to my ear as I perched on the edge of the bed. 'Hello,' I said tentatively.

'Mia.' Ethan sounded relieved to hear my voice. 'I've been calling for days. I was afraid I was never going to catch you.'

'Sorry, I've...' I tried to think of an excuse, but I couldn't.

'It's okay, I understand,' he assured me. 'With everything you've gone through, it's natural to want some time to yourself.'

'Yeah,' I agreed, even though that wasn't the reason I'd been ignoring his calls. I wasn't avoiding people. I was avoiding *him*.

'I went to the hotel to see you, but they told me you'd checked out.'

'I just needed to get away for a little while. It was too hard to stay in London without Chloe.'

'Of course,' Ethan said. 'I, er, I just wanted to check on you. See how you're doing.'

'I'm okay,' I lied. I was getting good at that.

'Have you—' he cleared his throat '—haveyou spoken to Scott?'

'No.' At least I could answer that question truthfully.

'Did Chloe talk much about him?'

'What do you mean?' I asked cautiously. Was he afraid Chloe had told me about Sasha?

'About their relationship. Or—' Ethan paused '—his previous one.'

'I think Chloe said he'd been engaged before,' I answered vaguely. 'Sasha, was it?'

'Yeah,' Ethan confirmed. 'She didn't say anything to you about how Sasha died, then?'

I swallowed. It was obvious I would need to be careful here. If Mia had died because of what I knew, I could easily be next.

'No, why?'

'Oh, I was just curious.' Ethan sounded disappointed.

That was strange, wasn't it? He should have been relieved. As far as he knew, his involvement in Sasha's death remained a secret.

'What was Sasha like?'

'Fiery,' Ethan said. I could practically hear his smile as he spoke. 'Passionate.'

I swallowed. He spoke about her with such affection. Too much for someone else's fiancée.

'She was so stubborn.' He sniffed. 'Though she preferred to call it determined.'

'What happened to her?' I felt like I should ask. It would be expected, wouldn't it?

'She was out clubbing with some friends. They said she was kind of wasted. Not that that was unusual for her.' Ethan sighed. 'She separated from her friends and started hanging out with a group of guys. Being in a committed relationship wasn't what she thought it would be.'

'What do you mean?'

'I'm not sure she said yes to Scott's proposal for the right reasons. I mean, Scott, he adored Sasha. He always had, right from when we were teenagers. But Sasha...' Ethan groaned. 'I'm not sure she loved him, but rather—'

'The idea of him.'

The phone fell silent. Perhaps I shouldn't have said that.

'Yeah,' Ethan said slowly. 'I think she believed being with Scott would fill a void in her life.'

The air suddenly felt thick and heavy. Breathing became harder and harder.

'Mia? Are you okay?'

'Uh-huh.' But I wasn't okay.

I was just like Sasha. I tried to shake that thought away. But instead, Ethan's words sprang into my head.

Since we were teenagers.

They'd all known each other back then. He said Scott had adored Sasha, but had Ethan loved her too?

If that was the case, why would he help cover up Scott's involvement in her death?

64

THEN

September

I pulled the van up at the curb and stared across the street at the park. I wasn't sure why I'd come here. I'd been on autopilot after leaving Ethan at the police station. But then I didn't have anywhere else to go. Only home, and that no longer felt safe.

I wasn't in the mood to go through the motions of setting up the stall and feigning interest in other people's lives today. I usually loved being part of my customers' world. It was what made me set up my business in the first place. The ability to catch a glimpse of their special moments. From first dates and anniversaries to apologies and sad farewells, I was a part of it all. A tiny part, but a part that counted.

I should have been satisfied with that. If I'd ignored that relentless desire to have what they had, I wouldn't have set my sights on Scott.

'There you are!' Mia's voice startled me as I walked through the entrance to the park. 'I've been waiting for you for ages. I was starting to worry.'

'Worry?' I scoffed as I marched past her. 'You've never worried about me in your life, why would you start now?'

'Don't be ridiculous.' Mia's high heels tapped against the pavement as she hurried after me. 'You're my sister, I always worry about you.'

I swung round and glared at her, my hands on my hips. 'Really? You're so worried about me that the second I confided in you, you went behind my back and told Scott.' I spat the words at her. Twenty odd years of resentment unleashed from their restraint. Of all her betrayals this was the one there would never be any coming back from.

'Someone had to.'

My eyes narrowed. 'And you decided that should be you?'

Mia lifted her chin defiantly. 'Yes.'

She wasn't even contrite. She had no remorse. No guilt. I wasn't sure why that surprised me. I should have been used to her methods by now. I should have known better than to hope for more from her. To hope for a shred of decency or compassion.

But no longer.

Everything made sense now. She'd been trying to drive a wedge between me and Scott since she'd arrived. Wanting me to go on the world cruise with her had all been part of her ploy. She'd *expected* me to choose her over Scott. And once I had, she would have bailed on me. It wasn't me she wanted. It was him.

But she hadn't counted on him proposing.

This was my punishment. She'd intentionally sabotaged my relationship. She couldn't have known how Scott would react. What he was capable of. But that was irrelevant.

She'd wanted to hurt me, and she had.

'I will never forgive you for this,' I told her, repeating the words that Dad had said to me years ago.

Mia's mouth formed an 'O' shape as her body contracted. I felt a small sense of satisfaction watching her reaction, knowing I'd inflicted pain on her. I wondered if Dad had derived the same fulfilment from my reaction when his words had torn a hole in my heart that had never healed.

Perhaps I should be grateful to her. Without her intervention I would have remained ignorant of Scott's true character. Not that that brought me any comfort right now. I was still trapped.

Only now I didn't even have my sister to turn to for support.

'Chloe, I—' Mia reached her hand out towards me and my body jolted as I leapt backwards.

I watched as her expression morphed from surprise to confusion. 'What just happened?' she asked, studying me intently.

'Nothing,' I replied, aware of how defensive I sounded.

'You were scared.'

'I'm not scared of you, Mia. I just don't want anything to do with you any more.' I turned on my heel and started back towards the van. Coming here had been a mistake. Nowhere was safe any more. The places that had once been mine had been taken over by people I couldn't trust.

'No.' Mia jogged ahead of me and blocked my path. 'I'm not buying that. Your reaction wasn't anger, it was fear.'

I tried to veer around her, but she sidestepped, preventing me from passing.

'Tell me why?'

'Talking to you is what got me into this mess. That's a mistake I never intend to make again.'

'Something happened with Scott, didn't it?'

I clenched my teeth together.

'Something more than you two just breaking up?'

'We didn't break up, actually. So I guess your plan failed.'

There was something strangely satisfying knowing that she had been thwarted. Even if it was at my own expense.

'I don't understand. Something happened between you two. Something bad. I can feel it.'

'As if you actually care.'

'I do care, Chloe. You're my sister. Let me help you.'

'Help me? You've never helped me, Mia. You've pretended to, but when it came down to it, you never followed through. And yet foolishly, I kept hoping that this time it would be different. That you would be different.' I was done hoping for a sister. For family. We always failed one another in the end. 'But it's all irrelevant now. You won't break us up. It doesn't matter what you do. He's never going to let me go.'

65

NOW

October

I wandered from the bedroom, my mind racing. Ethan's call had made me feel nauseous and confused, my thoughts spiralling.

My gaze automatically drifted out of the living room window as I started to walk past it. The row of beach huts nestled at the foot of the cliff were like a beacon, drawing me in. There was something comforting about watching over Aaron's beach hut even when he wasn't there. It made me feel closer to him.

I frowned. Except tonight it literally was a beacon. My feet veered towards the window as I tried to get a closer look. A soft yellow glow emanated from Aaron's beach hut. I checked my watch. It was late for him to be there.

Then again, given how distraught he was about Chloe, about *me*, perhaps he wasn't ready to go home yet.

I glanced at the phone still in my hand. This was a perfect excuse to call him. It was what a friend would do, what a neighbour would do, when they saw a light on at an unexpected time. Right?

Peering back out of the window, I pressed the phone to my ear as I listened to it ring.

'Sorry, I'm not able to answer the phone right now, but if you leave a message, I'll call you back soon.' I sighed impatiently as waited for Aaron's message to finish.

'Hi, Aaron, it's, erm, Mia. I was just, erm, closing my blinds for the night and noticed a light on in your beach hut. I-I know it's probably just you, right? But, well, I thought I should let you know, just in case...' I nibbled my lip, aware that I was rambling.

Perhaps I shouldn't have called. He didn't need me checking up on him. And now he would know I was up here spying.

'Oh wait.' Movement below drew my attention back to the hut and I leaned closer to the glass as someone stepped out of the beach hut. 'I think you're leaving.'

The door of the beach hut closed, and the figure retreated into the distance along the promenade.

'Is it you?' I asked as I kept watch, hoping the figure would turn back, so I could catch a glimpse of his face in the light from the streetlights that lined the promenade, but he didn't.

I let out a sigh. 'Well, whoever it is has gone now, so, erm, I'll say goodnight. Hope everything's okay.' I hung up, but lingered at the window, still keeping watch.

I shook my head. This was crazy. It probably was just Aaron. It wasn't as though he had anything valuable in there. There wasn't much of anything in there at all thanks to the fire. Besides, there was no point standing here staring at the promenade all night.

Aaron's beach hut was none of my business. And yet, even as I picked the mugs back up and walked to the kitchen, I knew that still wouldn't stop me peering out the window at his hut again in the morning.

It was part of my routine now. He was part of my routine.

Bournemouth was having an effect on me. I paused as I filled a glass with cold water. It had had an effect last time too.

66

THEN

September

I paced the kitchen, fleetingly wondering if Scott was really paintballing, and if he was, who was he with? I shrugged, it was irrelevant. The key thing was, he wasn't here.

I grabbed my phone as a bolt of inspiration struck me. I could call a locksmith while he was out. I could reclaim my home. My life.

Except I knew it wouldn't really be that simple.

I sank into a chair and set the phone back on the table. A new lock wouldn't stop him. It would only anger him further. At some point I would have to leave the house, and he would find me, assuming he didn't force his way in first.

The only thing I could do was bide my time until I could find a way out. I'd done it before. I could do it again.

The doorbell chimed, disrupting my thoughts. I ignored it. I wasn't in the mood for dealing with other people.

It rang again. I let out a frustrated sigh. Why couldn't they just leave me alone?

The letterbox clattered. 'Chloe!' Mia's voice called from outside.

Mia.

She was the last person I wanted to see. Well, maybe not quite the last. Scott held that position. But that didn't mean I wanted anything to do with Mia. I was done with her.

'I know you're in there. I'm not leaving until you speak to me.'

Shoving my chair back, I stalked to the front door and swung it open. 'Haven't you done enough already?' I snapped at her. 'Can't you just leave me alone?'

Mia shook her head. 'I'm sorry.'

I snorted. 'It's not enough,' I said as started to close the door.

Mia put her hand out to stop it. 'Please, let me come in and we'll talk.'

I snorted again. I'd already learnt my lesson. I wasn't about to repeat that mistake.

'And then if you still want me out of your life, I'll go. I'll leave and won't bother you again.'

I hesitated. A few minutes wouldn't hurt. Not if it meant I would be free of her for good.

That thought reverberated through my body as its meaning sunk in. Was it really what I wanted? I'd worked so hard to keep her in my life. Desperately trying to build a closeness in our relationship that had never really been there. And now it was over.

Despite my anger, there was a sadness to the finality of it all. I'd lost everyone. First Scott, now Mia. Or at least, I'd lost the fictional versions of them that I'd wanted them to be. It seemed getting rid of them in person wasn't so easy.

Stepping backwards I pulled the door open and let her enter. She lingered in the hall. For the first time in my life Mia actually seemed nervous and lost.

'Go through to the living room on your right,' I told her.

Mia placed her Gucci handbag at her feet as we sat at opposite ends of the sofa, both of us perched on the edges of our seats, as though ready to flee at any moment.

I understood my reluctance to be here, but I didn't expect it from her. She always seemed to look at ease before, regardless of the situation.

What made this so different?

Mia licked her lips as she shifted uncomfortably. She put her phone down on the sofa in the space between us and tugged at her short black skirt. 'I screwed up,' she said finally. 'I'm sorry.' Remorse emanated from her, not just the passion within her words, but the way she sat, small and withdrawn. 'I know it doesn't seem like it, but I did what I did because I was worried about you. I wanted to help you.'

I scoffed. 'You sabotaged my relationship to help me?'

'I could see how besotted you were with Scott. You were never going to leave him. But that was exactly what you needed to do.'

'You've been back in my life for a few weeks and you think that means you know what I need?' I shook my head. 'You don't know me, Mia. You've never wanted to.'

Mia flinched. 'I'll admit, there may have been an element of selfishness too. With Scott in your life, there wasn't as much space left for me. I guess I'm used to being your priority. But I truly thought I was doing the best for both of us.'

Part of me wanted to believe her.

'I am worried about you, Chloe. More so now. Please let me help you. No matter what's happened between us, you have to know I'm always here for you.'

I didn't move. Didn't speak.

Usually, I'd nod and assure her that I knew. We were sisters no matter what. But this time the words wouldn't come. I no longer believed them. If I was honest with myself, I hadn't for a long time. Mia had been everything to me. I'd hoped to one day be that for her too. But I never would be.

I shook my head slowly.

Mia drew back, her expression stunned and pained. A ripple of satisfaction made my skin tingle. It had taken me twenty-four years, but she finally knew how it felt to be rejected.

It was empowering.

Her gaze dropped to the floor, making her appear timid and unsure. For the first time, looking at Mia was like looking in a mirror.

My sense of satisfaction was instantly replaced by guilt. I'd hurt her.

I knew how it felt to be on that side of our relationship. Did I really want to be responsible for that kind of pain for Mia? Hadn't I caused enough heartache to our family already?

'I—' My apology was cut off before I'd even fully worked out what I was going to say.

'I need a drink, do you have any wine?' Mia asked, overly brightly.

'Er, y-yeah,' I stammered, thrown by the sudden shift in conversation. 'I think there's a bottle of white in the fridge.'

I started to get up, but Mia waved her hand as she leapt to her feet. 'You stay there. I'll get it.'

I complied and leaned back on the sofa as I watched Mia scoop up her handbag and disappear into my kitchen.

'We should go away this weekend,' Mia called above the sound of cupboards opening and closing.

'We?' I asked. 'As in the two of us? Together?'

'It will be good for you to get out of London for a little while and let things settle.' There was a pause filled as the cork popped. 'But I think it would also be good for us to spend some time together. To reconnect.'

She was finally offering me the one thing I had always wanted, a proper relationship with my sister.

But did I still want it now?

I shook my head slowly.

'Where would we go?' The question slipped from my lips. My head might no longer want Mia in my life, but apparently my heart hadn't quite caught up.

Mia poked her head around the door and peered at me. 'Bournemouth.'

I inhaled sharply as my body tensed.

'I know how you feel about it,' Mia continued. 'But I think that's why it's important we go there. It's time to finally deal with the past, Chloe. Neither of us can keep running from it.'

'Is that what you've been doing?'

'It's what we've both been doing. And for the same reason.'

'I don't understand.' My guilt had driven me from Bournemouth. Mia didn't carry that burden, so how could our reasons be the same?

'I know you don't. But I think it's time you finally did. And that's why it's important we go back together.'

I frowned at the empty doorway as she slipped back into the kitchen. What on earth did she mean?

Mia's phone pinged loudly beside me, and I jumped.

'Can you see who that is?' Mia called.

I rolled my eyes, but obediently picked up her phone and tapped her PIN in. That was one thing about Mia, she trusted me with her PIN for her credit card and her phone. It wasn't a level of trust that I reciprocated.

I stared at the name that appeared on the screen.

It couldn't be.

My hand trembled at I opened the message.

SCOTT

Hey babe, it was so awesome to spend time together yesterday.

I can't wait to see you again tonight.

I've reserved a table for 8 p.m. at The Rooftop Bar.

Scott.

My Scott.

Our restaurant.

Or at least it could have been ours. If he'd actually proposed there instead of the park.

'Who was it?' Mia asked as she emerged with two glasses of wine in her hands. She froze as she saw me. 'Chloe?'

'This is why you wanted me to leave him.' I stared at her, my eyes wide. 'I knew you hated me, but this...' I shook my head. I couldn't even find the words to describe the level of betrayal I felt.

Mia rushed forwards, set the glasses on the coffee table and took her phone from my hands to read the message.

'You always take everything from me. Everyone.' My voice shook as I spoke.

'You took Mum from me.'

Mia's accusation hung between us, sucking the oxygen from the room. 'It wasn't like that.'

'You took her long before she died.' Her tone was venomous.

My lip trembled as I fought back my tears. 'So this is your revenge?'

She shrugged.

'What happened to all that talk earlier about how you are always here for me?'

'You didn't want that. If you had...' Her words trailed away.

I stood up, straightening my back and lifting my chin as I fought to repress the overwhelming sense of loss that welled within me. 'Well, the two of you deserve each other,' I said finally.

There was a truth to my words and yet even as I said it, guilt pressed down on me like a heavy weight. Mia had no idea what she was getting into. No idea who Scott really was.

I could warn her.

I *should* warn her.

She might have betrayed me, but I was better than that. Better than her. At least, I could be.

'It's a shame you won't be there to see it for yourself,' Mia taunted.

'See what?' I cursed myself for my curiosity.

'The way he looks at me.' Mia closed her eyes, and a wistful smile passed across her lips. 'It's so full of desire and lust.' She opened her eyes and glared at me. 'A way he's never looked at you.'

I shook my head. 'That's not true.'

'Isn't it?' Mia's eyebrow arched. 'Are you sure about that?'

She was right. I wasn't sure.

'Aren't you curious how he is with me?'

I shook my head. I didn't want to know.

'Really? If I was you, I'd want to know. I'd want to see it. How different it is to how he is with you. How much better he is. More thoughtful. More caring. More romantic.'

'It doesn't matter,' I insisted. None of it mattered. I already hated him, I didn't need to know the details of his latest betrayal.

Mia chuckled. A smug little sound that taunted me. 'But it does matter, don't you get it?'

I stared at her blankly.

'Scott would never treat me the way you let him treat you. No one would.'

I opened my mouth to object, but I couldn't. What if she was right? My hand shifted protectively to my throat. If Mia had been in my shoes last night, would Scott have attacked her? Or would he have been too in awe of her to risk losing her?

'It's a shame you'll never know what Scott and I have that you didn't.' She smiled coyly. 'What I have that you don't.'

I shook my head. She was wrong. There was a way I could know.

67

NOW

October

I staggered to the kitchen and flicked the light switch on. The sun hadn't even started to rise yet, but I couldn't lie in bed any longer. I'd given up hope of sleeping hours ago.

The stench of burgers filled my nostrils, and I scrunched my nose as I glared at the unopened bag of takeaway sat on the worktop. After Aaron's revelations last night, he'd beaten a hasty retreat, and I hadn't been able to stomach eating anything. Let alone the meal we had planned to share together.

Aaron hadn't answered my call or bothered to call me back. He'd made it clear he wasn't interested. Not in me. Not even as a friend. Regardless of what changes I made, I couldn't erase the image he held of me. Held of Mia. It was always there in the back of his mind, influencing his thoughts, his opinions. And it always would be.

I'd thought Mia's life was so perfect. So exciting. So full. Now I had everything I'd ever wanted. But it was a life without purpose. Without meaning. It was as lonely as my own life had been.

Perhaps it was time to move on. Mia had planned to take a world cruise. Maybe that had been the right decision for her.

The last few days had made me realise that I wasn't Chloe any more, but I wasn't Mia either.

'I don't know how you could ever move away,' I said as Mum helped me carry my hired surfboards onto the beach. 'It's perfect here.'

Mum lowered her end of the surfboard, and I let go, allowing her to dig it into the sand. She leaned against it as she stared out at the sea. 'Sometimes you have to leave everything behind to figure out who you really are.'

I frowned. 'I don't understand.'

'I know, honey.' Mum reached out and stroked my hair, just like she used to when I was a little kid and had a nightmare. 'But one day you will.'

I sucked in a deep breath and let it out slowly. She was right. I did understand now. Leaving London, leaving the person I had been there, had freed me.

I was different here. For the first time in twelve years, I felt more like myself again. But that was the very person I could never be.

It was time to leave again. Staying in Bournemouth was too difficult now. Surprisingly, it wasn't the painful memories that were chasing me away. It was the realisation that being here would forever trap me in my sister's shadow.

Regardless of how much I perfected my imitation of her, I would always know that's all it was.

68

THEN

September

'Switch places with me,' I demanded, as I glared at Mia across my living room.

'What?'

'Switch places with me,' I repeated more firmly this time as the idea solidified in my brain.

Mia was right, I didn't know what she and Scott had together. Part of me didn't care. I wasn't jealous of Mia stealing the man I loved from me. Not this time. After all, I didn't want to be with him any more. But there was another part of me, a curious part, that wanted to know why. Why did he prefer her? Why did he treat her differently?

Maybe if I knew what it was that Mia had that I didn't, I could be different. Better. Maybe my next relationship would be stronger. Longer.

Sometimes you can't move forwards until you look back. My future didn't include either of them, I knew that now. But before I was ready to embrace that future, maybe I needed to understand my past. That way I could learn from it. I could ensure I never repeated it. That a guy never treated me the way Scott had.

'You want to switch? You never want to, usually.'

'Because you only ever wanted to switch when you had something to gain. When you could get me to pass a test for you, or pin the blame on me for something you'd done.'

'That's not—'

'Are you really going to try and deny it?' I scowled at her, daring her to attempt it. I'd been a pushover for too long. It was time I fought back.

Mia snorted. 'So now you have something to gain, deception is suddenly okay?'

'Deception?' I scoffed as I waved her phone in front of her. 'This message tells me that Scott isn't who he pretended to be. He acted like an honest, committed partner. Talking about our future together. Our kids.' I shook my head. 'Our entire relationship has been a lie. Switching places now is simply levelling up the playing field.' At some point I needed to end things with him. The restaurant was the perfect place. It was public. Safe. I could learn what I needed to and then dump him. He and Mia were welcome to each other.

'He'll never believe you're me.'

'If I cut my hair a little and change my make-up, he will.'

Mia scoffed. 'You think that's all that differentiates us? A bit of make-up?'

'Then prove it isn't.' I was challenging her. It was the only way to get her to help me. And I needed her help.

Mia smiled slightly and I knew she was caving. She'd spent a lifetime outmanoeuvring me for her own advantage, but finally I was playing her at her own game.

And I was winning.

Her agreement was fuelled by her desire to see me fail.

Further evidence that I would never be as good as her. I could never *be* her.

But like Mum always said: pride comes before a fall. Mia's pride was the one thing I was counting on to make this work.

And it needed to work.

I didn't need to see Scott's betrayal for myself. The text message was enough proof of that. And his behaviour in the last week had already shown me there was another side to him.

But perhaps confronting Scott wasn't really about him. It was about me. About proving to myself that I was as good as Mia. Otherwise, I would spend my whole life living in her shadow, always feeling inferior.

I'd wasted enough of my life doing that.

Mia glared at me. 'You'll never pull it off.'

I bristled. The words were a taunt. Another way of reminding me that I wasn't as good as her. But today her words felt like a challenge. This was no longer just about learning from her. It was about proving her wrong.

I *was* as good as her. I was good enough to be her.

I lifted my head and met her stare defiantly. 'Maybe you don't know me as well as you think you do.'

* * *

I set my phone down on the table in the hall next to a crystal pyramid that cast colours across the small hall in the sunlight. I lifted my head and examined my reflection in the mirror, feeling the unfamiliar bounce to my new shorter hair style. Mia had done a surprisingly good job in her first attempt as a hairstylist. Dressed in her clothes, and with her skills at applying make-up, even I didn't recognise myself any more.

'Well?' Mia asked, and I turned to face her. It was strange

seeing her in my jeans and Primark sweater. I hadn't seen her in anything other than a designer label since she got her first part-time job and started buying her own clothes.

'Looking at you feels more like I'm looking in a mirror than the actual mirror does.'

Mia chuckled. 'Yeah, it is eerie. Kind of fun, though,' she added hesitantly. 'It's been such a long time since we've done this.'

I had to admit she was right. If I overlooked the reason behind our afternoon makeover session, it was probably the most enjoyable time we'd spent together in years.

It was sad that it couldn't have been like this before. A heavy weight descended on me, as I realised that it never would be again either.

'I need your phone,' I said, holding my hand out.

Mia hesitated for a second, before reluctantly handing it over.

'And your bag,' I added. If I was going to be Mia, then I was going to look the part.

'It's in the kitchen,' Mia said, turning towards the door. 'I'll fetch it.'

'I'll go,' I said firmly. We might look like each other right now, but it was still my house.

I tottered to the kitchen in Mia's high-heeled boots and picked up her Gucci bag from the kitchen counter. I frowned slightly, recalling the way Mia had grabbed her bag and taken it with her to the kitchen when she'd gone for the wine. There was something about her manner, something uncharacteristically protective about her belongings. Not that it mattered, there were bigger things to worry about right now.

'Don't forget to leave your ring,' Mia said as I walked back into the hall.

I nodded, and automatically twisted my engagement ring off my finger and then paused. Even though our engagement had never been what I'd imagined, there was something so final about taking my ring off. But the ring had never really been about us. I'd chosen it alone. Bought it alone.

Perhaps I was nothing more to him than a possession. A source of income. And a place to live. Meanwhile he was free to pursue other women. To pursue Mia.

I hesitated. Shouldn't that have been a reason to be faithful? Why would he risk jeopardising his newfound financial stability? Especially with Mia? Someone who had every opportunity to tell me everything. And from what little he knew of our relationship, even he should have realised Mia would relish doing so.

Maybe it was the challenge. Or the thrill of risking everything for something forbidden. Or maybe it was just that he could. Because he didn't really think it was a risk at all. He thought I needed him too much to leave him. He thought I was too afraid to stand up to him.

He was partially right. Chloe was the quiet twin. Shy and obedient.

I placed the ring down on the table beside my phone and turned my back.

Chloe was staying home tonight.

I reached for the door handle and hesitated.

'Having second thoughts?' There was something different about Mia's tone. It lacked its usual taunt. She almost sounded anxious.

I turned to face her, and the corner of her mouth twisted upwards with familiar smugness. Whatever I'd thought I'd heard, clearly I was wrong.

She leaned against the corner of the stair-rail. It felt strange to leave her in my home. Before this visit she'd rarely even set foot in my house, and now she was wearing my clothes looking as though she completely belonged here.

I could ask her to leave. But the last thing I wanted was for her to run into anyone who might mistake her for me.

I started to turn back to the door, but as I did so, something about her stance shifted. 'This isn't what I'd wanted, you know?' she said quietly, lowering her eyes to avoid mine.

I tipped my head to the side, scrutinising her. Something was off. She was too subdued and uneasy. But why?

My feelings clearly didn't matter to her, otherwise she wouldn't have started a relationship with my fiancé. Guilt was an emotion Mia had never seemed to suffer with. Why would that suddenly change now?

She'd taken pleasure in telling me how much better their relationship was than mine. How much better Scott thought she was than me. After all, that was the reason I was doing this. To understand those differences.

But now she seemed almost regretful.

I wanted to ask her why, but I knew I wouldn't get a straight answer.

I shrugged as I reached for the handle and pulled the door open. It didn't matter anyway. After tonight I would never see either of them again.

69

NOW

October

It didn't take long to pack. I only needed enough to get me through a few days. Once I was out of Bournemouth, no one would know me. I would no longer need to dress like Mia. I could change my hair, make-up and clothes. I would be a new me.

Completely new this time. Not an impersonation of someone else.

I scanned the living room, checking I had picked everything up. I wouldn't be coming back for anything I'd forgotten. My gaze drifted out of the window and settled on the beach huts below for one final look.

Aaron was at work again. My heart did a little somersault as I realised he was painting the beach hut. Bright pink. *My* pink.

I turned away, unable to watch, as my desire to tell him the truth intensified. But what good would it do? It wasn't as though it would change things for us. Once he knew of my deception he wouldn't forgive me. He still wouldn't want me in his life.

Besides, it wasn't safe to tell anyone. Not even him. Not if I wanted to keep them and me safe. I couldn't risk Scott ever learning that I was alive. Not if I wanted to stay that way.

If he thought Aaron had helped me or knew where I was... I swallowed. I might not be able to share my life with him, but I wasn't going to endanger his.

I glanced back over my shoulder. But there was one thing I could do for him.

* * *

I strode across the courtyard of the apartment complex towards the gate. Talking to Aaron was the right thing to do, I told myself again. I owed him that much.

Nerves bubbled in the pit of my stomach as I tugged the gate open. What kind of reception would I get after last night? Heat crept into my cheeks at the reminder of his rejection. It would be easier for both of us if I just left without saying goodbye.

But we'd done that before.

'Mia!' Rachel's voice called behind me.

I sighed but didn't stop. I couldn't face dealing with her. Not today. I needed to see Aaron. I couldn't tell him who I was, but I could tell him I'd always loved him, and Scott had been nothing more than a costly mistake.

'Chloe!'

I stopped dead and spun around. 'I already told you—'

'Yeah, yeah, I know,' Rachel said, between breaths as she ran to catch up. 'You're not Chloe.'

'Right,' I started to turn away.

'So in that case, you won't care if I go and tell Aaron my theory, will you?'

I hesitated, fighting to keep my expression neutral. I couldn't let her see my fear. Mia wouldn't. She'd call her bluff.

I shrugged. 'Sure, if you don't mind him knowing you're completely crazy.'

Rachel smirked. 'Nice try.' She nodded approvingly. 'Very Mia-like.'

I arched an eyebrow. 'You know there is a reason for that?'

'Hmm,' Rachel murmured. 'I'm still not buying that.' She marched past me, down the slope towards the promenade. Rachel paused. 'Are you coming?' she called back over her shoulder. 'Surely you wouldn't want to miss the chance to disprove my theory, do you?'

My heart pounded. This was bad. I'd been so certain that Rachel wouldn't do anything without proof, her reputation was too important to her to risk looking foolish. Did she really care about Mia so much that she was willing to chance it? Or was she bluffing?

I wiped my sweaty palms against my jeans. I had to stop this. Stop her. But how?

I could just go back up to the flat, grab my bag and disappear. But I if I did that, then I would look guilty, Rachel would know she was right, and then what would happen?

'I guess not, then,' Rachel said with a shrug and resumed walking.

My stomach lurched. Right now, Rachel had thought Mia and I were playing some twisted game. That we were both involved. The moment Aaron told her that Chloe was dead, that would change everything. It wouldn't just be Aaron she told.

One phone call to the police and everything would come unravelled. Especially if anyone started looking too carefully into the fire.

And then there was Scott. Once the truth about who'd really

died that night was revealed, it wouldn't be long before he came looking for me then. Even if I wasn't here, what about the people I left behind? I'd made that mistake with Mia. I couldn't do it again.

I wouldn't.

'Wait for me,' I shouted as I sprinted after her. I had no idea how I was going to stop her, but I certainly wasn't going down without a fight.

* * *

'What on earth?' Rachel said as we turned the corner and saw a police car parked on the promenade ahead. 'That's Aaron's beach hut.'

I froze as we watched a police officer guide Aaron to the car.

Rachel's head jerked back. 'Have they arrested him?'

'I don't know, but—' I shook my head again '—why would they? I mean, it's Aaron.'

'Come on,' Rachel tugged at my arm. 'Let's go and find out what's going on.'

My feet refused to budge. I couldn't go over there. Not with the police there. They were the people I needed to avoid. Scott had taught me that.

'I thought he was your friend.'

'He is,' I replied weakly.

'Then how come right now, I seem to be more concerned about him than you do?'

She was right. Aaron deserved better than this from me.

I allowed Rachel to pull me forwards. I could do this. I could do it for him.

A uniformed officer stepped out of the beach hut, followed

by another man. 'Ethan.' The name was a whisper on my lips, but Rachel heard it.

'Ethan? The guy who was calling you the other day?' Rachel asked, spinning back to face me as we drew to a halt again.

My breathing became raspy as my mind raced. What was Ethan doing here?

And if he was here, did that mean Scott was too?

I scanned the promenade, searching for his familiar build as my hand trembled. My brain screamed at me to turn around and run before it was too late, but my feet wouldn't let me.

Aaron was involved now. I couldn't just run this time.

Rachel looked back and forth between the police and me. 'Start talking or I'm going over there and telling them everything I know.'

I didn't speak. I couldn't.

None of it made any sense. If Ethan had come to Bournemouth looking for me, why was he at Aaron's beach hut? It wouldn't be hard to find me, not when I was living in Mia's flat. The police should be upstairs banging on my door, not out here on the beach.

I rubbed my forehead, but it did nothing to ease the throbbing as I tried to figure out what was going on. Everything was so messed up. Why would Aaron be of any interest to the police?

'Fine.' Rachel pivoted on her heel.

'Wait.' I grabbed her arm, fear controlling my reflexes. 'Please,' I added desperately. It was a risky move allowing Rachel to see how terrified I was. But there was no way I could mask my emotions now. Channelling Mia wasn't going to be enough to get me though this. I needed more than her. I needed Rachel.

'Why should I?' she demanded.

'Because...' I swallowed. 'Because I need your help.'

70

THEN

September

It'll never work.

Mia's voice repeated in my head like a rhythmic chant, in sync with the click of my high-heeled boots as I weaved my way through Trafalgar Square. I lengthened my stride, in an attempt to outrun her voice of doubt. But it continued to follow me. I crossed the road and my gaze locked on the building ahead of me. I'd arrived.

I strode to the door, but as I caught a glimpse of my reflection in the glass, the determination that had carried me this far wavered.

It'll never work.

There was still time to back out. I could simply walk away. Do what I had always done and pretend everything was fine. Or at least, that it would be in time.

I shook my head. I had to know.

I pushed the door open and stepped inside. There was a

sadness to the finality of it all. I'd fought so hard for so long to keep both Mia and Scott in my life, and now...

* * *

I stared out of the window at the impressive view of central London as I drained the last drop of water from my glass and set it back down on the table.

What was I doing here?

I already knew Scott wasn't the man I'd thought. The man I wanted.

Common sense told me I needed to focus on figuring out how to escape from him, not witness his infatuation with my own sister.

I wasn't sure what was driving me. Possibly some sense of morbid curiosity. Or perhaps, despite all his flaws I was hoping that his interest in Mia was just fleeting. That when I saw him, I would know from the way he looked at her, at me, if anything we'd had had ever been real. Not because I wanted him back. But because, if he had loved me, really loved me, then maybe it was possible that eventually, someone else could too. Someone better than him.

I drummed my fingers against my empty glass. He was late again. However, my irritation at being kept waiting was overshadowed by a smug sense of satisfaction. It wasn't me he was keeping waiting. It was Mia.

At least that's what Scott thought.

I often wondered if it was something about me that made Scott feel like my time wasn't important. That *I* wasn't important. Perhaps if I was more like Mia, maybe he would treat me differently. He'd treat me like a priority instead of a backup. And yet here I was, as Mia, still waiting.

It seemed even changing who I was couldn't change who he was at his core: unreliable.

I rummaged in Mia's bag and pulled out her phone. No new messages.

I set the phone down on the table. Eventually he would call or turn up. Until then, I would sit and wait.

I glanced at my watch again. It felt wrong for him to be late for her. Mia wasn't the kind of woman anyone kept waiting. She wasn't the kind of woman to stick around if you did.

Unlike me.

I touched my fingers to the bruises on my neck, discreetly hidden beneath a layer of make-up and a carefully positioned scarf. I stayed no matter what.

However, if Scott wouldn't keep Mia waiting, where was he?

A sinking feeling weighed heavily in my stomach as Mia's words replayed in my head.

I tapped the contacts icon on Mia's phone, scrolled to the S section and selected Scott's name, but just as I was about to hit the call button I froze.

It wasn't right.

I couldn't remember the whole of Scott's number, but I knew it ended in III. That part was so memorable. So distinctive. And also, completely missing from the number displayed on Mia's phone.

Did Scott have a separate number?

My heart pounded as implications swirled through my head. Did he have a separate number just for Mia, or were there more women in his life?

But Scott wouldn't be as careless as Mia had been to allow me to see his messages.

Careless.

My stomach tightened. Mia had never been careless before.

Everything she did had always been meticulously thought out to get exactly the outcome she wanted.

Events of the afternoon replayed in my head, like a movie on repeat. Everything about it had felt odd. Mia's unannounced arrival. Her insistence on getting the wine. The way she'd taken her bag with her to the kitchen and yet left her phone sitting right beside me. The way she taunted me, almost dared me to switch places and pose as her.

She wanted me to be here.

But why? To catch Scott in the act? To see for myself that she still had the ability to lure away any boyfriend she chose? I glanced around the restaurant. If that was the case then Scott would be here.

There was only one way to find out what was going on. I sucked in a deep breath and hit the call button and pressed the phone to my ear.

A repetitive buzzing resounded from Mia's bag on the chair beside me. I rummaged one-handed in the bag and pulled out a basic small phone that vibrated in my hand.

With a shaking hand I pressed the call answer button and the ringing on the phone in my other hand stopped as the line connected and sounds of the busy restaurant echoed through the phones.

I stabbed at the button and instantly the other phone fell silent. I dropped them both on the table in front of me, suddenly unable to bear the weight of them in my hands.

I glared at them in turn.

The message had never come from Scott at all.

Mia had faked the message. It wasn't her carelessness that had caused me to see the message. She'd planned it.

I grabbed Mia's phone and scrolled through the contacts list, checking each name. I frowned as I reached the end of the list. Scott's other number wasn't here.

Without my own phone, I didn't have any other way of contacting Scott.

But Mia did.

I'd left my phone at home. With her.

My stomach churned. Had switching places really been my idea, or had she goaded me into it? Switching places had not only given Mia free access to my phone and my home, it had given her access to Scott.

Suddenly everything fell into place, like a row of dominos cascading into each other.

There had never been anything between them. Scott had played on my insecurities and feeling of inferiority to disrupt my already fragile relationship with my sister. He wanted me to cut Mia off. To ensure I was isolated and fully controlled by him.

And Mia, well, I was never sure what motivated her. Perhaps she wanted to break Scott and I up just to hurt me. Or perhaps Scott was right all along, and she did want him for herself.

They both deserved each other. They'd both manipulated me for their own advantage. She was welcome to him as far as I was concerned.

All I had to do was sit back and let Mia's plan unfold. Scott would undoubtedly prefer to have the more adventurous, more glamourous sister, and Mia would get to bask in her success of having taken a second boyfriend from me.

The difference this time was that their betrayals would benefit me. It would give me an opportunity to escape from a man whose idea of love terrified me and a sister whose presence in my life would always be disruptive. Perhaps they held the key to my freedom from both of them.

They would be so distracted with each other, I could just fade into the background and disappear. I could move away. Start over. This time would be different. *I* would be different.

Mum had always believed in karma. It was her motto. Her compass.

'Positive energy towards others will bring positive energy back to you,' she assured me whenever someone had wronged me. 'Their negative energy will come back to them.'

That belief had always been enough for her. It had given her the strength to rise above the hurtful behaviour of others. It was a quality I had strived to emulate my whole life.

But what if this time it wasn't enough? What if sometimes karma needed a little help?

71

NOW

October

'I can't believe I'm doing this,' Rachel said, as she paced her living room, while I peered cautiously out of the window. She'd certainly been right about the view from her flat being superior. 'Explain to me why you couldn't go back to your own flat?' Rachel demanded as her pacing paused.

'It's complicated.'

Rachel shook her head. 'Not good enough. I deserve an actual explanation, or I'll march out on that balcony and signal those police officers.'

'You can't,' I told her gently.

'You want to bet?'

'They've already gone.'

Rachel joined me at the window and grunted. 'Then why are you still standing here staring down there then?'

I shrugged. 'Because I don't know what else to do.'

Rachel inhaled deeply. 'You asked for my help, the least you could do is tell me what I'm helping you with. Why have you and

Mia switched places? Why are the police questioning Aaron? And who was that guy with them, the one you called Ethan?'

I dragged my gaze away from the beach hut and nodded. 'You're right. I owe you an explanation.'

'Finally,' Rachel exclaimed. 'So, out with it. What are you and Mia into?'

'We're not into anything.'

Rachel's hands flew to her hips. 'You said you were going to explain.'

'Mia...' My voice wobbled. 'Mia's dead.'

It was the first time I'd said those words aloud and they tore my heart apart. I didn't even try to stop the tears that flowed freely. I couldn't. It was as though admitting the truth at last had finally allowed me to grieve for my sister.

'W-what?' Rachel staggered backwards.

'I'm s-sorry,' I stuttered between sobs. 'I know how close you two were. Closer than she and I ever were,' I added, envy creeping into my words.

'How? When?' Rachel shook her head, as though trying to clear her thoughts. 'Why didn't you tell me? And—' her eyes narrowed '—why are you pretending to be her?'

'Because everyone thinks it was me who died.'

Rachel blinked. 'And you just decided to let them?'

I nodded. 'I had to.'

Rachel scoffed. 'You've always been jealous of Mia. Her life. Her friends.' She jerked her head towards the window. 'Her boyfriend. Of course you'd relish the opportunity to step into her shoes and finally be her.'

'It's not like that.'

'Isn't it?' Anger flashed in Rachel's watery eyes. 'Then what's with this charade?'

'I'm pretty sure she was murdered,' I blurted out the fear that had bubbled away inside me from the moment I saw the smoke rising from my home.

'Mur...' Rachel couldn't finish the word. 'W-why?'

'Because whoever killed her thought she was me.'

72

NOW

October

'I need to speak to Mia,' Aaron's voice demanded through the intercom.

'Then why are you buzzing my flat, instead of hers?' Rachel asked.

'I already did. She's not answering.'

'Then I guess she's out.'

I stood on the other side of Rachel's hall, watching her in awe. She didn't like me. She'd never liked me. She was the last person I would have ever imagined would come to my aide.

But she had.

And she was still protecting me. Hiding me in her flat. Shielding me from Aaron.

Except, did I want to be shielded from him? Did I need to be?

'Is she with you?' Aaron asked and Rachel glanced at me uncertainly. 'Come on, Rachel. I saw you two together on the promenade.'

'When the police arrested you, you mean?' Rachel asked.

'They didn't arrest me. They just wanted to ask me some questions.'

'Why?'

'Let me in and I'll explain.' There was a long pause. 'Or at least, as much as I know, anyway.'

'How do we know you're not involved?'

'We?' Aaron's sigh of relief vibrated through the intercom. 'I knew she was there with you.'

I rolled my eyes. 'This is ridiculous, just let him in,' I told Rachel.

I sighed and pressed the buzzer to open the door myself, pacing impatiently as we waited for Aaron to climb the stairs. As soon as I heard footsteps outside, I swung the door open.

Aaron and I stared at each other across the threshold. 'I think it's about time you told me what really happened to Chloe,' Aaron said.

'Just as soon as you tell me why the police wanted to talk to you,' I batted back at him as he followed Rachel into the living room silently. We stood in the middle of the room, awkwardly glancing at each other.

'Are you okay, Rachel?' Aaron asked, as he dropped his rucksack on the floor by his feet. 'You look like you've been crying.'

Rachel sniffed. 'Of course I'm not okay. Mi—'

'Do you think you could give Aaron and I a few minutes?' I interrupted. 'It's important,' I assured her.

Understanding flashed in Rachel's eyes. 'Then you'll fill me in?'

I nodded.

'Okay,' Rachel conceded and reluctantly walked out of the room.

I waited to hear the click of the bedroom door closing, before

I turned to Aaron. 'Why did the police want to talk to you?' I demanded.

'They were looking for something.'

I frowned. 'Some*thing*?' I'd expected him to say someone, not something. 'What?'

'The murder weapon that killed your sister.'

My eyes widened. 'W-weapon?' I shook my head. No, he was wrong. 'She died in the fire.'

'Apparently not.' He crossed the living room and stared out of the window, looking down on his beach hut.

I stared at the back of his head, trying to make sense of his revelations. If the fire hadn't killed Mia, then what did that change? I'd always suspected she was murdered. The method was irrelevant to that. Wasn't it?

And yet, one thing didn't make sense. 'Why were the police here? Why would they be interested in your beach hut? In you?'

'They received an anonymous tip off. So they turned up this morning with a search warrant. Looking for that.' Aaron turned back and pointed at the rucksack he'd left in the middle of the living room floor.

My jaw dropped as my gaze darted to the bag. 'Wait, you have it? You have the weapon?' I stared at the bag, unable to move. Whatever had killed Mia was in that bag. But how?

'I found it in the beach hut this morning.'

'You found it?' My eyes narrowed as I studied him. 'Just like that, it just happened to be in your beach hut?' His statement was too convenient. Murder weapons didn't just appear like that. Which meant...

Aaron shook his head. 'Someone must have planted it there.'

I shuffled backwards. 'In a locked beach hut?'

'Ah, that's the interesting thing, though. I couldn't find my key yesterday. I looked everywhere for it, but nope.' Aaron shrugged.

'My parents have the spare, so I had to use bolt cutters to cut the lock off this morning.'

I froze. 'What are you saying?'

'It's a bit convenient, isn't it? I mean, what are the chances that I would happen to lose my key and right after that a key piece of evidence finds its way into my locked beach hut?'

Was it possible he was telling the truth? Was he innocent?

My gaze shifted back to the rucksack. 'What is it? How did she...' I couldn't finish my question. It was too painful.

'Take a look,' Aaron said, nodding to the rucksack.

I edged towards it and crouched down. Slowly I reached my hand out and unzipped the main compartment.

I frowned. All I could see was a balled-up sweater. I glanced at Aaron uncertainly.

'It's wrapped in the sweater,' he told me.

I reached into the bag, pulled the sweater out, and slowly unravelled it as my heart pounded. My mouth opened as I revealed a crystal pyramid. It caught the sun as I held it in my hand, turning it slowly, sending a rainbow of colours dancing across the walls of Rachel's living room.

'This is—'

'Your mum's,' Aaron said flatly.

I stared at him, stunned that he remembered that.

'She gave it to Chloe,' he added, and my heart swelled. That's why he remembered. Because it was special to me.

I turned back to the crystal. I squinted at a stain on the one edge. 'What is that?' I asked pointing to it.

Aaron came closer. 'I don't know, it looks kind of like—'

'Blood,' I realised, as my breath caught in my chest. I'd seen the bloody gash across Mia's forehead as the paramedics had tried to revive her. I hadn't thought to question what had caused it. All my questions had been focused on the fire.

If she'd been hit with this... My hands trembled as the crystal grew heavier. I was holding the cause of her death in my hands. 'How did it get in my beach hut, Mia?'

My head jolted up, and my eyes met his. He looked so different. The calm, friendly expression he usually had, was hostile and accusatory. I blinked. 'You think it was me? You think I planted it?'

Indignance coursed through me. How could he suspect me of such a thing? It hurt.

And yet, I couldn't ignore the fact that part of me still suspected him...

'It's a bit of a coincidence, isn't it? You suddenly taking an interest in helping with the repairs and then a murder weapon turning up in my hut? You and I have been spending a lot of time together since you got back. You could have swiped the key.'

I shook my head. 'I wouldn't do that to you. I couldn't.'

'You really expect me to believe that, Mia?'

I closed my eyes. That was the problem. Aaron still thought I was Mia. Lying and manipulating were part of who she was, of course he would think I was involved.

Except...

'If you really believed it was me, then why didn't you turn me in to the police?'

Aaron rubbed his jaw but didn't answer.

'And come to think of it, how do you even still have it? Why didn't the police find it when they searched your beach hut?'

'Remember I told you I'd made a friend?' Aaron asked.

'The lady who owns the beach hut next to yours?'

He nodded. 'She was there this morning and saw me cutting the lock off. She suggested I store my tools in her hut until I'd bought a new lock. When I saw that—' he pointed at the crystal in my hands '—I knew I couldn't just leave it in the unlocked hut either. So I put it in my rucksack and stored it with my tools until I could talk to you. I was planning to come and see you today, anyway.'

'So it was next door before the police arrived.'

Aaron nodded.

I frowned. 'Hang on, why were you planning to see me today?'

'I didn't like how we left things last night.'

'Me neither,' I replied.

'I might not have romantic feelings for you, but I do still care about you, Mia. I still want us to be friends.' He let out a weary sigh. 'I thought we needed each other. That we understood the loss each of us has experienced. The void her absence has left. But—' he paused '—that was before...' His gaze rested on the crystal.

'I didn't kill my sister,' I said firmly.

'I know you wouldn't,' Aaron said, and relief washed over me. 'Not intentionally. But if you two argued—'

'No!' I shook my head. 'Not even then.' I closed my eyes as tears ran down my cheeks. 'Despite everything she did, everything we did to each other, we were still sisters.'

Aaron nodded slowly. He believed me. Even as Mia, he believed me.

'She never got over you, you know?' I blurted out. There, I'd said it. I'd told him the truth. I just hope it brought him some comfort.

Aaron snorted. 'She looked pretty over me with that policeman and all those stupid candles.'

My heart thudded. 'You saw her with Scott?' Questions raced through my mind. How? When? It didn't make sense.

'In the p-photo you showed me, remember?'

Even without his stammer I would have known he was lying.

I fought for breath as my body shook. It felt as though my world was crashing around me. 'I don't have a photo of them together.'

'Sure you do.' There was a nervous wobble to Aaron's voice.

I shook my head. 'I don't.' It was the one thing about Mia's life I knew with absolute certainty. I had never sent her a photo of Scott. 'Besides, Scott and Chloe met while I was in Rome. I haven't been back to Bournemouth until now. There was no way I could have shown you a photo, even if I'd had one.'

Scott and I had never been to Bournemouth together. Which meant Aaron had been to London. But what did that mean?

'I, er...' Aaron looked helpless as he fidgeted in front of me.

'You knew what the house looked like. You knew Scott was a policeman. You've been there. Been to London. To her house.'

'I—'

'Don't even think about denying it!' I glared at him. All the tension I had been keeping bottled up inside me erupted in anger. Everyone I cared about had deceived me in some way. And now Aaron had too.

Aaron's shoulders slumped forwards.

'Wait,' I said suddenly as Aaron's earlier words circled in my brain. 'What candles?' My temperature rose as my skin became hot and clammy. I didn't need to hear his answer, I already knew. And yet, I stood there, praying for a different explanation.

Aaron shrugged. 'They were all around the living room.'

'I've never put candles around the living room,' I said quietly as my anger morphed into disillusionment.

'You?' Aaron frowned. 'Why would you—'

'The police said the fire was caused by a candle setting fire to the curtains in the living room.' My lower lip wobbled as I fought the urge to cry. 'When were you there?'

Aaron's eyes widened as his lips parted, but no sound escaped.

'You were there the night of the fire, weren't you?' I'd spent days living in fear of Scott. My body constantly on edge. My eyes instinctively searching for him in every darkened corner. But what if I'd been afraid of the wrong person?

'She called me.'

'Chloe called you?' I spoke slowly, trying to understand the words he was saying. I'd never called him. I wanted to. Longed to. But I never had.

He closed his eyes. 'She said she needed to see me.'

'So you drove all the way to Hammersmith?'

Aaron's eyes flew open. 'Of course I did. It was Chloe.'

I stared at him. He still loved me. After all these years apart, nothing had changed.

Except Chloe was dead.

And Aaron might have killed me.

73

NOW

October

I shook my head. 'I thought it was Scott. I thought he'd killed her. But it was you.'

'Me?' his eyes widened as he stared at me, horror distorting his features. 'I haven't killed anyone. Why would you even say that?'

'Then where did this come from?' I demanded, holding up the crystal as I edged towards the door.

'I keep telling you, I don't know.'

'It was in my house when I left that evening. It was on the table in the hall where it always sat. You were there. In my hall. You... You...' I couldn't finish my sentence. My accusation.

It was impossible. Of course it was. He couldn't really have killed Mia. This was Aaron. My Aaron. But then the truth was he wasn't really my Aaron at all. He hadn't been for a long time.

How much had he changed in the years that had passed? After all, I knew how much I'd changed. What I was capable of now. So what about him?

He'd said it himself, he still loved me. He'd wanted me back. Just how far would he have gone to get me?

All the little things that hadn't quite added up since I'd got back to Bournemouth whirled around in my head. Aaron knew what my house looked like. He knew about Scott. He was there that night after I'd left.

He'd seen Mia dressed as me.

What had she said to him? She'd broken his heart posing as me once before, how much had she hurt him this time? Enough to make him mad? To lose his temper? To kill her?

'Your house? But that was Ch—' Now it was Aaron's turn to back away from me. 'You're Chloe.'

My secret was finally out. I'd dreaded this moment. I'd worked so hard to prevent it. But now that it had happened, I felt a strong sense of relief. I didn't have to pretend any more.

And yet, with the truth revealed, the fallout was inevitable. Mia was dead because she was dressed as me. Which meant... Aaron and I stared at each other. Neither of us were who we'd thought.

'Why?' he asked, his voice coarse and ragged.

'I thought Scott had killed her. I was afraid if he knew he'd got the wrong sister, he'd come after me too. I thought I'd be safe here. As Mia.' Silent tears streamed down my face. 'I didn't know I was running from the wrong man.'

Aaron stepped forward. 'I didn't do anything, Mi—' He cringed. 'I mean, Chloe.' He closed his eyes. 'I thought you were dead. You let me grieve for you.' His legs crumpled beneath him and he dropped to his knees. 'I was out there this morning to paint the beach hut the same damn pink that you chose. Because I just wanted to keep a little bit of you still with me. And all the time, you were right here. Alive.'

I studied him though my tears. His pain seemed so vivid, so

real. Surely it couldn't be an act. If he'd killed Mia thinking she was me, then he'd need to rectify that mistake, wouldn't he? He'd be focused on silencing me before I could turn him in.

The man sobbing on his knees before me seemed too overwhelmed by emotion to be interested in preventing me from leaving or calling the police.

What if I was wrong? What if Aaron was innocent? Tears welled in my eyes. I'd been so focused on protecting myself, I hadn't thought about how my lie would affect anyone else. How it would hurt them. Hurt Aaron.

'W-when did she call you?' I asked, desperately trying to make the pieces fit together. If Aaron hadn't killed Mia, then why was he there?

Aaron took a deep breath as he leaned back against the sofa. 'She called that afternoon. She begged me to meet her. Gave me her address. I jumped in my car and headed straight there. I tried really hard to be there on time.'

'On time?'

'She been really particular that I arrived after 7 p.m. but before 8 p.m. It had to be in that window.'

'I left the house just before 7 p.m.,' I said, as clarity seeped into my brain. 'She wanted to make sure you arrived after I'd gone.'

Aaron sucked in a deep breath. 'And clearly before her policeman friend arrived.'

'At 8 p.m.' I closed my eyes. That entire evening had been a set up. Manipulating me into switching places. Getting me out of the house. Convincing me Scott would be at the restaurant, when all the time he was headed home to meet her.

But why?

'Why did she want you there?'

Aaron shook his head. 'I never found out.' He flopped into

one of the deckchairs. 'Traffic was horrendous. An accident on the M3 delayed me. I rushed to the door as soon as I arrived, scared of what might have happened given I was late. The guy, Scott, opened the door. Chloe made the introductions, and the whole time she acted as though she was surprised to see me. That my arrival was unexpected, and unwanted. The hall and living room were filled with candles, I'd clearly interrupted a romantic evening. So I left.'

'Just like that? After driving all that way, you just left?'

Aaron shrugged. 'What was I supposed to do? It wasn't as though I could stay. Or I even wanted to stay. They couldn't keep their hands off one another. The whole thing was just some bizarre, twisted game to make me jealous, I suppose. But the weird thing is I would never have expected that from Chloe, that was more like something—' Aaron clamped his mouth closed.

'Something Mia would do,' I finished for him. He was right, of course. The whole episode was typical of Mia. The manipulation. The games. The lies.

But to what end? Mia never did anything without a reason.

'I didn't have your number,' I realised suddenly. 'You said she called you. But we switched phones.' I'd deleted his number from my phone the second Aaron had left for Australia. I had no way of contacting him. Not until I took Mia's phone.

'So she must have called me before you switched. I can check the time,' Aaron said, reaching to his back pocket of his jeans. He groaned. 'But I don't have my phone. I lost that when I lost the key.'

I studied him uncertainly. Could I believe him? There were no calls showing in the call history. I'd already checked. But Mia could have deleted it before I took her bag.

'I messaged her back a few days later, when I'd calmed down

a little bit. She never replied.' He shook his head. 'I know now that she was already dead, but—'

'You messaged her?' I grabbed Mia's handbag from the sofa and rummaged inside. I'd never emptied her bag. I hadn't been able to bring myself to do so. Which meant Mia's other phone was somewhere inside.

I pulled the phone out, turned it on and checked through the missed calls.

An unknown number had messaged the night I'd arrived in Bournemouth.

I grabbed Mia's other phone and found Aaron's number. They matched.

My legs felt weak as relief washed over me and I clung to the phones as though they were a lifeline. Aaron was telling the truth. Mia had sent him the message from her second phone. The same one she had used to send the fake message from Scott to her own phone.

I closed my eyes and uttered a silent prayer of thanks. Aaron was just another pawn in Mia's game.

And yet, I still had no idea what she'd been up to.

74

NOW

October

'When did you lose your phone?' I asked Aaron.

'I don't know, sometime on Monday.'

Understanding seeped into my brain. 'That's why you didn't return my call on Tuesday.'

Aaron peered up at me, confusion and contempt etched into his features. 'What call? And what does an unreturned call even matter right now?'

I crouched down in front of him. 'It matters,' I said firmly. 'It was Tuesday night, after you left here. I called you when I saw a light on in the beach hut.'

'At night?' Aaron frowned. 'I haven't been to the beach hut at night.' He wiped his eyes roughly with the back of his hand.

We both turned back to the crystal. 'It *was* Scott,' I realised with a gush of relief. It felt strange to be relieved by that. Not that long ago, Scott was everything to me. I wanted to spend the rest of my life with him. And now...

'Why would he—'

'Because you were there that night.' I turned back to Aaron. 'He's trying to frame you.' Excitement and fear battled within me. Aaron was innocent. He was good. And yet whilst they were reasons to celebrate, they also meant he was in trouble now. Scott was after him, and I knew what happened to people who he took a disliking to. Even if Aaron managed to avoid arrest, Scott wouldn't let it end there.

'We need go to the police,' Aaron said firmly.

I flopped to the floor, my legs no longer possessing the strength to hold me. 'Scott *is* the police.'

'That doesn't matter.'

'They've covered for him before. He told me so himself.' It all felt hopeless. It was hopeless. I'd known all along that running away to Bournemouth as Mia had been the only possible escape from Scott. And now that had failed.

The only thing my performance over the last few days had done was entangle Aaron in this mess too.

Aaron looked apprehensive. 'He could have been bluffing.'

I shook my head. 'Ethan, his best mate, is also a police officer. He all but confirmed it. He was trying to be subtle but...' I shrugged.

'So we go to the police here.'

My breath caught in my chest. 'Ethan's here.' Rachel's spacious living room felt suffocating and claustrophobic. Everything was closing in on me. 'He was with the uniformed officers this morning. He's working with them. He's one of them.' I hit my fist into the carpet. My careful plan was spiralling out of control and I was helpless to prevent it. 'They all look out for each other, that's what Scott said. They would never believe me over one of their own.'

'Once you've filed a report they'd have to investigate.'

I nodded. 'They'd investigate us.'

'Us?'

'You have that.' I jerked my head towards the crystal. 'And as for me – she died in my house, dressed as me, while I was out pretending to be her.'

'You switched places? But you hated doing that.'

'Mia tricked me into it. I was such an idiot for not seeing through it. But then when I got home, the flat was on fire and she was dead. I panicked and kept that pretence going when I was interviewed.'

'Why would you do that?'

'I was scared if Scott knew I was alive, that it was Mia he'd killed, then he'd come after me to rectify his mistake.'

'But the police could have protected you.'

'I had no proof about him! He's a police officer, it's not like he wouldn't know how to clean up a crime scene. And even if he had left any evidence, the fire would have destroyed it. It would be my word against his. And as far as everyone else was concerned, I had a lot more to gain from Mia's death than he did. So I did the only thing I could do. I ran.'

'You couldn't have had motive to kill your own sister.' Aaron said, dismissing the idea.

'She inherited practically everything from Dad. He barely left me anything.' Saying those words out loud still hurt. I'd had access to everything Dad had left Mia now. It was all in my grasp and had been for days, and yet I hadn't touched it. It wasn't really mine. 'I'd been counting on the money I thought I was getting to help me out of a bind. Mia had a good job, a high salary, and I had a tiny flower stall that was just scraping by.' I closed my eyes, hoping to hold back my tears. 'And yet she talked Dad into basically cutting me off.'

'You don't know that.'

I opened my eyes and looked directly at him. 'I do.' Those

two simple words almost broke me to say. But the truth was undeniable now. 'You told me so yourself.'

'What?' Aaron shook his head. 'I did no such thing.'

I smiled ruefully. His confusion was adorable. He had no idea the depths of deception Mia had been capable off. Then again, I'd known her better than anyone and she'd still fooled me too. 'The day I arrived, when we met on the pier, you told me Dad had changed his will because I'd talked to him. That I'd told him I didn't want the flat.'

'Yeah, so—' I saw the moment understanding dawned on him. 'That wasn't you.'

I shook my head sadly. 'She stole my inheritance.' My own sister had done that to me. She'd done it knowing the financial difficulties I was struggling with. And worse still, knowing I would believe it had been Dad's idea. That he'd intentionally cut me off. I'd never forgive myself for Mia's death, but I also wouldn't forgive her either.

Assuming Scott didn't get to me first, then I would have a long time to think about that in prison. I took a deep breath. 'I think the police would deem that to be a pretty strong incentive for murder.'

75

NOW

October

'We have to do something,' Aaron insisted. 'We can't just let Scott get away with it. And we can't sit around and wait for him to make his next move.'

'The police wouldn't believe me,' I repeated.

'They might.' Aaron shook his head. 'I did.'

A long pause expanded between us. I could feel him willing me to change my mind, as though he thought his belief in me should be enough to persuade me to go to the police. To risk everything.

For him.

But I couldn't. It wouldn't work.

Aaron had been on my side once before. It hadn't made any difference then either. If we hadn't been able to persuade my own father that I was a good person, how could I expect the police to believe it? They didn't know me. But they did know I had been present at the deaths of two members of my family.

First Mum. Now Mia. Scott would make sure they viewed that as more than just a coincidence.

'I see,' Aaron said, his voice barely a whisper. He scooped the crystal up in the sweater and shoved it back into his rucksack. 'Well, I'm going to the police station, with or without you.'

He paused. Clearly still hoping I would choose to go with him.

I didn't.

'You know I'm going to tell them everything you've told me? The police will come looking for you after I do.'

I nodded. I was counting on it.

Aaron shook his head slowly. 'I guess you're not planning on sticking around though.'

He turned and I watched as he walked out the door. I followed after him, searching for the words that would make him understand.

But I knew he wouldn't. He still trusted the police. As flawed as his plan was, he was doing the right thing.

He didn't realise it wouldn't be enough.

I'd abandoned so many people in my life. Failed them when they had needed me the most. Aaron thought I was sacrificing him now, too. He had the crystal that had killed Mia. If I didn't step forward and tell the police about Scott, Aaron could end up taking the blame. I'd lose him too.

Turning myself in to the police wouldn't do any good though. Not yet. Not until I had proof.

I nodded slowly, casting one last lingering gaze at the beach below. I knew what I had to do now.

76

NOW

October

I stood at the end of the pier, the heavy rain already soaking through my coat. My gaze drifted to the choppy waves. I hadn't even hesitated before slipping past the chain-link fence this time. Perhaps I was becoming more like Mia after all.

'Hello, Chloe.'

I froze at the use of my old name. But it wasn't the name that sent tremors through my body. It was the voice.

I turned slowly.

'Did you really think I wouldn't figure it out?' Scott asked as my eyes met his.

I shook my head. I'd always known it was just a matter of time before he realised I was alive.

Even through the rain, I could see his frown. 'Aren't you surprised to see me here instead of Aaron?' he asked.

I shook my head again. 'Did you really think *I* wouldn't figure out that you'd stolen his phone?'

'So the message you sent Aaron, asking him to meet you here...'

'Was for you,' I confirmed, brushing my hair from my eyes as the wind whipped around me.

'I always said you were smart,' he said, nodding approvingly. 'Where is he?' Scott glanced around him, as though he expected to see Aaron lurking in the shadows.

'On his way to the police station to tell them everything.'

Fear flashed across Scott's face. I froze. I hadn't expected that. Why had that scared him?

Scott shrugged. 'Well, you know that won't help either of you. We look out for our own. It's only a matter of time before he's arrested.'

'When the police find my crystal, you mean?'

Scott's jaw dropped. 'You know about that?'

'Aaron found it before the police turned up to search his beach hut. We know you're trying to frame him.' My eyes narrowed. 'Why did you do that? Why him? Just because he's my friend?'

'Don't try to trick me. He's more than a friend, Chloe. I see the way that you two look at each other. But once the police arrest him and you see the kind of guy he really is, then you'll realise how lucky you'd been to have me.'

'The kind of guy he is?' I stared at Scott in disbelief. He spoke as though he was rescuing me from Aaron. 'You aren't exposing his criminal activities. You planted evidence. You set him up.'

'I was protecting you, don't you see that?'

'Protecting me from what? A nice guy who'd done nothing wrong?'

'He was there the night Mia died.'

'So were you.'

Scott let out a defeated sigh. 'He told you that, did he?' He shrugged. 'He won't be able to prove it, though. It'll be his word against mine. And who do you think my colleagues will believe? Especially given the evidence stacking up against him.'

'You're framing an innocent man.'

'Collateral damage,' Scott replied, without emotion.

'Like Mia?'

Scott's expression clouded over. He looked as thunderous as the dark sky above us. 'That was your fault. She wasn't supposed to be there.'

I grimaced. 'No. It was me you'd wanted to kill.'

'No.' Scott's shoulders hunched forward. 'Things got out of hand. It was an accident. I didn't mean to kill her.'

I knew I should scream. Run. Do something. Anything. But instead, I waited silently for him to continue. This was what I'd come here for. I pushed the waves of panic down inside me. Fear wasn't going to prevent me from seeing this through.

'She thought she could fool me. That turning out the lights and burning a few candles would make me think she was you.' Scott sneered. 'I know you better than that.'

'So that's it? You got mad once you realised she'd lied to you?'

'Not at first. I decided to play along for a while. See what she was up to. Then that guy turned up, convinced she'd called him. He kept apologising for being late, and saying how he knew it had been important he was here before 8 p.m.'

'Let me guess, she'd told you to be there at 8 p.m.?'

Scott nodded. 'Yeah, intriguing, right? Of course, I wanted to know why. She denied it at first. She was a pretty good liar; her protests of her innocence were almost convincing.'

'Except you already knew she was lying about being me.'

'In the end she explained her whole crazy scheme. She'd sent you off somewhere out of the way, and had called that Aaron guy, pretending to be you. He was supposed to arrive before me.'

'Why? To scare you off?'

'Partly. But only after she'd rekindled their, sorry, *your* relationship. That was another reason for all the candles and rose petals: to make me think you two had got back together. That you'd replaced me.'

'She thought Aaron would protect her when you lost your temper. That he'd throw you out.' The realisation crashed down on me. Mia wasn't trying to steal Scott. She was trying to get rid of him for me.

'Instead, he was the one that walked in on us in romantic candlelight.'

'Why didn't she stop him? She could have told him what was really going on. He would have stayed. He would have helped.'

'She tried.' Scott snorted. 'But I don't think he even heard her calling after him. Or maybe he didn't want to hear.' He shrugged. 'Besides, I don't think she was too concerned at that point. She still thought I believed she was Chloe. She probably figured everything was fine. That she could get out of the situation without me ever realising.'

That sounded like Mia alright. She never admitted defeat, even when everything was falling down around her, she simply carried on with her charade.

'We argued after he'd left. She made me so mad. She...' Scott ground his jaw.

'She fought back.'

'Yeah, you two really were nothing alike.'

His words stung and I cursed my weakness even more. If I'd fought back when Scott had attacked me, Mia wouldn't have had to.

'She came at me and I just grabbed what was in reach and swung it at her. I didn't think I'd hit her that hard. I'd just wanted to make her stop.'

'And the fire?' I fought back my tears. I wouldn't let him see me cry, not again. I would be stronger this time. Like Mia.

'I had no choice. I had to cover it up. There were so many candles, it was so easy.'

'And now, Scott? Is there a choice now?'

He nodded. 'There is. But the choice isn't mine to make. It's yours. You get to decide what happens next. It's not too late for us.' His eyes met mine, pleading and desperate. 'That's why I came here. I needed to see you. To talk to you. To take you home.'

'Take me home?' I stared at him. I couldn't believe what I was hearing. He was here because he wanted me back. 'And if I refuse? What then? You'll kill me too?'

Scott pulled a face, as though my words were sharp and bitter. 'You make it sound so—'

'Crazy?' I asked. 'Because that's exactly what it is. You really think I would go back to you now I know who you really are?' I was amazed at how calm I sounded. The tremors that vibrated through me, didn't register in my voice.

Was I running on adrenaline? Or determination?

'I told you, Chloe. I'm never going to let you go.'

I nodded. I knew that. I'd known it from the moment he'd pinned me to the wall in my own home. There was only one way this would end.

Death.

'So you're going to set another fire? Burn me too?'

Scott shook his head. 'That would be too suspicious. Besides —' his gaze drifted past me to the sea behind me '—why over-complicate things?'

77

NOW

October

I stared at him. Who was this man I had brought into our lives? Not just mine, but Mia's and Aaron's too.

They had both been impacted by my poor judgement.

Memories flashed through my brain like a movie played at high speed. The things he'd said. They way he'd acted. All the tiny details that had seemed unimportant at the time suddenly seemed critical.

'Why did you ask me not to mention your job when you took me to visit your parents?'

Scott blinked. 'What?'

'And how come when you introduced me to Ethan, you called him an old school mate, but not a colleague?'

'Did I?'

'And I've never seen you in your uniform.'

'It's not as though I wear it to go on a date.' Scott's tone was condescending, but I could see a flicker of panic in his eyes. 'What's your point, Chloe?'

'You're not a police officer.' My accusation hung between us. I waited for him to deny it. But instead, Scott just smiled and in that instant I knew my crazy theory was right.

'You made me believe you were invincible. That I couldn't report you for attacking me because Ethan and your mates would protect you. You wanted me to believe they'd covered up your involvement in Sasha's death. You wanted me to be scared, not just of you, but of them. Your friends. The police.' I took a shaky breath. 'And I was. You killed my sister and instead of seeking justice for her, I ran. Because I was so terrified of you.'

Scott looked so smug. He seemed pleased that I'd figured it out. That I finally understood how impressive his manipulation had been.

'Was Ethan part of it? Does he know you pretended to be a police officer?'

Scott laughed. 'Ethan? He would have arrested me himself for impersonating a police officer if he'd known.'

His revelation jarred against me. If Ethan wouldn't have stood by Scott for impersonating a police officer, then surely he wouldn't have stood for murder either.

Anger twisted my stomach in knots. Scott had deceived me. He'd made me distrustful of the police. Worse than that, he'd made me fearful of them. The people I could have gone to for help. Who I *should* have gone to.

'Ethan's a good guy, though,' Scott continued. 'He offered me a place to stay rent-free when my own parents gave me an ultimatum: find work and start paying them back or find somewhere else to live.'

'But you all seemed so close when I met them. I didn't sense any hostility.'

'They thought you were a sign I was getting my life back on

track. I told them I was going for interviews. That I would be able to start paying them back any day now. And they believed me.'

I nodded. Of course they'd believed him. They believed him for the same reason I had believed all his lies. Because we'd wanted to. We'd needed to.

'Why did you pretend to be a police officer? Why lie?' It should have been irrelevant to me now. His reasons didn't matter. Only his actions did.

And yet, some part of me still wanted to know. *Needed* to know.

Scott shrugged. 'Why did you lie?'

I hesitated. I knew the answer. I'd always known it. But saying it aloud was different. It felt more foolish. Weaker. 'I wanted you to think I was more than I am,' I admitted finally.

He nodded. 'You see, we're not that different.'

A familiar pull of connection tugged at me. Perhaps that was what had drawn me to him in the first place. A sense that on some level we were the same. Both lost and lonely. Desperate to be accepted.

'When I stopped to see if you were okay after that kid tried to grab your bag, you looked at me with such gratitude and adoration. I wanted to keep that.' Scott's voice was thick and gruff. He coughed and cleared his throat. 'Sasha had never looked at me like that. Not even at the beginning. Not even when things were good.' He gave a half-hearted shrug. 'I was still Ethan's loser friend.'

Scott snorted. 'Of course, that's what attracted her to me in the first place. She wanted to rebel from the family. Ethan's the latest in a long line of police officers in their family. But Sasha never wanted that life. She was too much of a free spirit to conform to that.'

'Their family?' I questioned, suddenly realising why Ethan had spoken so fondly of Sasha. She wasn't a romantic interest, she was family.

'Sasha was Ethan's little sister. She was two years younger than us.'

'That's how you met? Through Ethan?'

Scott nodded. 'She might have rebelled against her family, but she still respected them. Unlike me.' Scott snorted. 'She was only with me to rile them. Our engagement was just another part of it. It meant nothing more to her beyond that. And she took great delight in ensuring that I knew it. With Sasha it was always about being the centre of attention. It didn't matter what kind. Good, bad, it was all the same to her. She fed off it.'

I understood so much more now. Scott's need to be engaged to me was a way to pacify himself that I would stay with him. But he'd been hurt too much before to believe that I actually would.

'Losing Sasha changed me,' Scott continued. It was as though now he had started to open up, he couldn't stop. He needed to share his pain. His frustration. 'I lost my way for a long time. I gave up. Drink and gambling were the only things that made life tolerable. But eventually, I started to claw my way back out of the darkness. I knew I had to find a way to start again. Find someone new to replace her. I vowed this time would be different. I would never let anyone make me that weak again. I would never let anyone leave me.'

'So you killed Mia.'

Scott lurched at me. His face centimetres from mine. 'That was your fault. I tried to get you to get rid of her. She wouldn't have been there if you had done what I asked.'

Scott seemed to run out of energy and drew back. 'I didn't want to kill her. I didn't want to kill anyone.'

'But you did. You've killed two people. And now you're planning to make that three.'

'You think you're so much better than me,' Scott said with contempt. 'But really we're not so different.'

I shook my head. 'I'm nothing like you.'

'Would your mum agree with that?'

78

NOW

October

I froze. The unexpected reminder of Mum unbalanced me. Tears pooled in my eyes, threatening to overflow. It was too much. Especially here, on the pier. This was her place.

'Mia blamed you for her death, didn't she? Your dad too, I think.'

I closed my eyes.

Mia.

Tightness gripped my chest. Dad and Mia were the only people who'd known what had happened that day. Dad was too ashamed to tell anyone. But Mia...

'What did you do?' Scott asked.

I frowned. 'Mia didn't tell you?'

Scott shook his head. 'I could sense your guilt and self-loathing when you talked about your mum and the rift with your family. You blamed yourself and so did they.'

My breath escaped in a gush. Mia hadn't told him.

She'd spent years reminding me of the imbalance in our relationship. Tormenting me with my guilt. Ensuring that I never forgot what I'd done. Not that I could. Not that I ever would.

It had become a precarious tightrope walk, between living in fear that she would expose my secret and hope that she would eventually forgive me. In the end, she'd done neither.

* * *

'Sorry, girls,' Dad said as he came into the living room. 'No surfing this morning, your mum's not feeling well.'

Mia pouted. 'But Mum never comes with us anyway.'

'I know, sweetheart, but it's not very nice of us to all leave her here alone when she's sick.'

'What's wrong with her?' I asked.

'She just a bit short of breath,' Dad said. 'She's probably just got a cold, and needs some rest and lots of hot drinks.'

'Can I make her one now?'

Dad nodded. 'I'm sure she'd appreciate that.'

'Maybe I can read with her for a bit, like she does for me when I don't feel well?'

'Perfect,' Dad said, ruffling my hair.

'Great, so if Chloe's looking after Mum, we can go surfing, can't we, Dad?'

I padded to the kitchen and filled the kettle.

'That wouldn't be very fair to Chloe,' Dad said, shaking his head.

'I don't mind,' I assured him as I flicked the kettle on. 'I'm happy to stay and look after Mum.'

Dad hesitated.

'Pleeease,' Mia urged. 'We don't have to surf for long. Just a few minutes.'

* * *

'It wasn't what I did that was bad,' I told Scott. 'It's what I didn't do.' My admission felt like a relief. After all these years of avoiding it, I'd finally voiced my failure.

'I don't understand.'

'Mum's breathing was so bad and her skin was cold and clammy, but she told me she was just tired. She needed to sleep and then she'd be fine.' I took a deep breath, fighting the nausea that churned my stomach. 'I shouldn't have left her alone so she could sleep. I should have called an ambulance straight away.' Tears streamed down my face. 'When I went back to check on her, I knew something was wrong. She looked grey.' I swallowed. 'I called an ambulance then, but it was too late. I was too late.'

I choked back a sob. 'The doctors said it was an acute pulmonary oedema. I didn't know what that meant. But they said if she'd received treatment sooner...' My voice cracked and I couldn't finish my sentence. I didn't need to. We both knew what my lack of action had done.

'No wonder your dad and Mia blamed you. You let your own mum die.' Scott's accusation sliced through me.

'I didn't know,' I cried out above the roar of the crashing waves. My words were full of pain and desperation, but suddenly I realised they were also full of truth. 'I didn't know,' I repeated softly. I was only twelve years old. How could I possibly have known?

I clung to the railing as something inside me shifted. The memories that had tormented me for years replayed in my mind. The same pain. The same outcome. And yet, it felt as though I was viewing them through a different lens. Before, they had seemed so clear. I could see my mistake, my failing, without question. But now everything was hazy. My guilt no longer seemed as obvious as it once had.

'Why was I the only one who'd stayed with Mum when she was sick?'

'You chose to,' Scott reminded me. 'And your dad trusted you to look after her.'

I frowned. 'If I should have known how critical Mum's condition was, then why didn't Dad? He was the adult. I was just a child. He and Mia knew Mum was sick and they still went surfing. They abandoned her. They abandoned both of us.'

'Because they didn't know it was serious,' Scott pointed out.

I nodded. 'Right, but in that case, how could I?' What if it had simply been easier to be mad at me? To blame me to avoid their own guilt?

What if my actions had been an understandable mistake, rather than neglectful?

What if it wasn't my fault? And if Dad and Mia had been honest with themselves, what if they knew it too?

My knees buckled beneath me, and I crumpled against the railing, struggling to hold myself up.

Scott stepped towards me, his arms outstretched. 'Chloe, are you okay?'

'Don't,' I snapped. My revulsion at his presence summoned a strength within me I didn't know had. 'Don't touch me.'

Scott glared at me. The hatred I'd seen in his eyes the night Mia had told him of my lies was back.

I lifted my chin defiantly. I'd always known when he found me, he would kill me. There was no way that he would let me live. Not when I would accuse him of attacking me and killing Mia. I might not have been able to prove it. But he wouldn't take that chance. Especially not now that I knew he didn't actually have the support of Ethan and his police mates.

My eyes darted up the pier. The only chance I had was to outrun him and get help.

'You know you'll never get by me,' Scott said. 'I'm stronger than you.'

I nodded. He was. But that didn't mean I wouldn't try.

I couldn't stand back and accept my fate.

I took a step to my right, hoping to dodge past him and back up the pier. But he sidestepped in front of me.

I shook my head. 'How did I ever love you?'

Scott's chin lifted. 'You did really love me, then?' I heard the hope in his voice. That desperate need to be wanted. To be loved.

It was so familiar to me. There was a time when I would have done anything to have been loved too.

Except kill.

And yet, that might be exactly what I needed to do now.

I swung to the left, hoping to be faster than him. But I wasn't. Scott caught hold of my arm, his grip crushing me.

He swung me back against the railing. I cried out in pain, but the sound was drowned out by the crashing waves beneath the pier.

I edged sideways along the railing, squinting as I searched the shoreline through the heavy rain, praying someone would be out despite the weather.

I winced as I slammed my right arm against something hard. I turned to my right and realised it was the tubular bell, part of the musical trail along the pier. Maybe I could use it to signal for help.

'I'm sorry, Chloe,' Scott said, and I turned back to face him just as he lunged at me.

I dropped to my hands at the base of the bell and swung my leg out, kicking his shin. He lurched forward, banging his head against the bell.

Scrambling to my feet I slammed my body into him, sending

him flying into the railing. His body folded at his waist over the railing as his head lolled forwards.

My gaze shifted to the water and in a split second I knew what I had to do. If I tried to flee, he would come after me. He'd said it himself: he was stronger. Faster. Which meant I had to be smarter.

I pulled my phone from my pocket and hit the stop button as he pulled himself back upright. I turned the phone towards him and held it up, showing him the screen.

He squinted, his body swaying. 'What are you doing? What is that?'

I smiled. He was clearly disorientated from hitting his head. 'Oh, did I forget to mention I was recording our conversation?'

'What?' Scott lunged forward, trying to grab the phone from my hand, but I twisted out of his reach. 'Turn it off,' he demanded.

I laughed. 'Don't worry, it's off now. I've already saved the recording.'

Scott snorted. 'So I'll just throw the phone in the sea, and it's no longer a problem.' He shook his head. 'I thought you were smarter than that.'

'Oh, I am,' I assured him. 'And thanks to you, I finally believe that about myself. You see, all of Mia's recordings are automatically saved to the cloud. So if you damage the phone, the only thing you actually destroy is your chance to access the cloud and delete the file.'

Scott paused for a second. 'But once you're gone, no one will even know the file is there.'

'Do you really think I haven't already thought about that? I've scheduled an email to Mia's contacts.' I lifted my chin defiantly. Scott had to believe he still had a chance to save himself. That there was still time. 'If you don't let me walk away, in a few minutes they will all receive her password, and know what file to look for.'

Fear flicked in his eyes. He believed me. I fought the urge to scoff at his naivety. He really thought I would allow him the very thing he had taken from Mia: time. He hadn't given her a chance to save herself, and I wasn't about to give him one either.

'Delete the file,' he shouted, lunging forwards again. 'Now!'

'I wouldn't do that,' I said, dashing to the railing. 'One wrong move and I drop this into the sea,' I taunted him as I dangled the phone over the water. 'Then you'll never be able to delete it.'

'You're bluffing,' Scott said, shaking his head. 'The second you drop that in the water all your leverage is gone. Then there will be nothing to stop me throwing your body in after it.'

I swallowed. My body. That's all he saw me as now. Not a person. Not his fiancée. Just a body to be disposed of.

And he was right. We were trapped in a stalemate. If he came at me, I could destroy the phone. But equally, he wasn't going to let me leave the pier with it.

I edged sideways along the end of the pier away from him. The anger and determination that had driven me to this point, evaporated as the reality of situation I had put myself in crashed down on me.

A flash of red and white caught my eye and I my gaze shifted to the long strands of tape that fluttered in the wind, leaving a gap in the railing.

My mind raced as the storm raged around us. The first day Aaron and I had met on the pier I could tell he'd been afraid I'd sneaked through the barrier to do something desperate and dangerous.

But what if right now desperate was the best option?

Bile rose in my throat. As a child I'd been too afraid to dive into the swimming pool, and now I was actually considering jumping off the pier. The current was strong. There were no guarantees I would make it safely to shore. First though, I had to get into the water. If I tried to scramble over the railing, Scott would stop me. But if I could make it to the gap…

'What are you planning to do?' Scott asked, looking completely bewildered, as his gaze darted back and forth between me and the gap. 'Jump?'

I cursed myself for letting him see what I was planning. I'd been counting on the element of surprise to make this work. Without that…

Scott snorted. 'You don't have the guts to do it.'

Hatred surged through me. Scott thought he knew me so well. It was time I showed him just how much he'd underestimated me.

I sprinted to my right, my gaze locked on the opening as it drew closer. I braced myself, ready to jump. There wasn't time to allow fear to take hold. Two more strides and then…

'Ugh!' My breath was forced from my lungs as Scott collided with me, flinging his body on top of mine, slamming me against the wooden floor. The impact shook the phone free from my hand and Scott gasped as it scooted across the pier towards the edge.

He lunged forward, clambering across me as he reached for the phone. I gritted my teeth, blocking out the pain in my ribs as I clawed at him, pulling him back. I couldn't let him reach that phone.

I wriggled free from the weight of his body, frantically swatting at the phone, desperately trying to knock it into the water. I had to destroy it, even if that meant giving up any chance of escape. One way or another, everyone would know what he'd done.

My fingers brushed the side of the phone, and it slid closer to the edge. Scott clambered to his feet, his gaze locked on the phone as he lurched forwards to grab it.

It was out of my reach now. There was no way I could stop him.

A smug smile formed on his lips as his fingers wrapped around the phone. 'You failed,' he taunted as he started to straighten up. 'Who's going to stop me now?'

My gaze shifted to the opening that was now directly behind him. 'Me,' I told him as I lunged at him, slamming my shoulder into his legs.

Scott cried out, his arms flailing, trying to find something to grasp, as he and the phone plummeted into the sea below.

79

NOW

October

I leaned over the edge, watching as Scott hit the water below.

It was over. I was free. I could run back down the pier, call for help. I could clear Aaron's name.

And yet I couldn't move. I couldn't look away from the water. I stared at it, watching, waiting for him to surface.

He didn't.

I'd heard his head hit the pier as he fell. The thud had reverberated through me. If he was unconscious, he'd drown.

Let him.

The voice in my head screamed at me.

I closed my eyes. It was what Scott would have done to me. Let me drown.

But I wasn't him.

I opened my eyes, wriggled out of my coat, kicked my trainers off, and stood at the edge of the gap.

I wasn't Mia either.

I jumped feet first into the icy water. I kicked frantically, desperately fighting my way back up to the surface. I gasped for air before diving back down. I fought against the current as the water made my clothes heavy and awkward to swim in. I had to find him.

I surfaced again. Took another deep breath and dived back down.

The salt water stung my eyes as I searched. It had been a long time since I'd been in the sea. I dived again and again. And then, there he was.

I grabbed his arm, pulling him upwards to the surface. I floated him onto his back, keeping his face out of the water as I kicked frantically, determined to get us both to shore.

My feet kicked the bottom, and I realised it was shallow enough to walk. I staggered forward, dragging Scott with me.

'Chloe!'

I lifted my head and squinted at the beach.

'Chloe!' Aaron's voice grew closer as he waded into the water towards me.

'He's unconscious,' I told him as he reached me and grabbed Scott from the other side.

People rushed out of the restaurant on the edge of the promenade and they took him from me. I followed them up the beach and watched as someone started CPR.

'Are you okay?' Aaron asked as he appeared beside me again.

My teeth chattered as I stared at him. 'What are you doing here?' I asked, bewildered by his concern and his presence.

Aaron slipped his coat off and wrapped it around my shoulders, hugging me to him. 'I got your email from Mia's account. I'd just arrived at the police station, but when I read your message I came straight back. I couldn't let you do this alone.'

'I needed to do it alone,' I told him. 'I'd got you caught up in this nightmare too much already.'

'It's not your fault,' he assured me.

'You're wrong. It's all my fault. I'm the one who'd got involved with Scott. I'm the one who'd failed to report him to the police when he attacked me. I let him get away with killing my sister. And enabled him to set you up.'

A police car pulled up behind the ambulance and I took a deep breath as I unwrapped myself from Aaron's arms. 'But now it's time to do what I should have done from the beginning.'

Aaron slipped his hand in mine. 'We'll do it together.'

We started walking up the beach towards the police car but I stopped dead when I recognised one of the men.

'Ethan.'

'Scott's friend?' Aaron asked beside me. 'The one who helped him get away with murder?'

I shook my head. 'I don't think he really did.'

'Mia? Are you okay?' Ethan asked, his voice full of concern.

I nodded slight. 'I think so. A bit sore but...' I shrugged.

'I'm glad,' he said, his shoulders relaxing.

'Why are you here?' I asked tentatively. When I'd thought he had been helping Scott, it made sense why Ethan would be in Bournemouth. But if he hadn't been involved, then what had brought him here?

'I followed Scott.'

My eyes widened. 'You did?'

'When Chloe died, I started to get suspicious. I mean, a second fiancée dying in dramatic circumstances felt too much of a coincidence,' Ethan said slowly. 'And then a couple of days ago Scott disappeared. I was afraid Chloe must have told you something that would endanger you and he was coming after you now, too.'

'You mean that he killed Sasha?'

'He really did it, then?' Ethan asked. 'I kept telling myself I was wrong. He couldn't have done that. But I had to come here. I had to be sure.'

'I'm sorry,' I said. 'I know how it feels to lose a sister.'

Ethan nodded. 'I wish I'd realised what Scott had done. I couldn't save Sasha, but maybe...'

I shook my head, as I reached out and placed my hand on Ethan's shoulder. 'It's not your fault.'

'Isn't it? I'm a police officer and I had no idea that my best friend had murdered my own sister. I felt so sorry for him when he lost everything because he was so cut up about her death that I took him in and let him crash on my sofa. Sasha deserved better from me than that.'

'Scott was good at deceiving people. At being whoever they needed him to be. You shouldn't beat yourself up for wanting to see the best in someone you cared about. Sasha did the same, and so did I.'

'You?' Ethan frowned. 'I could have understood if you'd said Chloe, but you?'

I glanced at Aaron beside me and he nodded.

'Ethan, there's something I need to tell you.' I took a deep breath. 'I'm Chloe.'

80

NOW

October

'You saved his life, you know?' Aaron said, as we walked side by side along the pier. It felt so different here now. The storm had died down and I was with Aaron again. Things were the way they should be. 'Scott would have drowned if you hadn't jumped in after him.'

I nodded. It felt strange knowing I'd saved the life of the man who'd killed my sister and tried to kill me.

'Not many people would have done what you did. I don't think I would have done.'

'You don't know that,' I said, shaking my head. 'It wasn't as though I planned to save him. Up on that pier I'd known it was going to be him or me. And I would have done anything to survive.'

'But you didn't. You found a way to save you both.'

'I just wish—' My voice cracked. 'I wish I could have found a way to save Mia too.' Whatever transgressions Mia had committed against me in the past, she was still my sister. I would still miss her. Still love her.

Aaron wrapped his arm around my shoulders. 'I know. I wish you could have done too.'

'I'm sorry I lied to you.' My apology felt too small. It wasn't enough. There was no way it could be.

'I understand that sometimes you have to make difficult choices in life. And it's not always easy to know what the right decision is. You were doing what you thought was necessary to be safe.'

I nodded. 'I was.' And yet somehow that didn't feel like it was enough to excuse my actions.

'And the CPS aren't pressing charges, so even they think your actions were understandable.'

'True.' But it still didn't erase all the mistakes I'd made.

My gaze locked on the tubular bell at the end of the pier and my body tensed.

'We don't have to be here,' Aaron said. 'I know they say you're supposed to get straight back on the horse after a fall, but I'm not sure the same principle applies to revisiting the place where someone tried to kill you.'

I smiled despite the circumstances. 'I want to be here. This was Mum's place. Scott has taken Mia from me, I won't let him take my last connection to Mum too.'

Aaron nodded and we carried on walking, but he held my hand a little tighter as though signalling I wasn't in it alone.

'Do you think Mia was trying to reunite us?' I asked suddenly. 'She called you to London to help me, and she'd wanted me to come back to Bournemouth with her at the weekend.'

'Maybe realising the danger you were in with Scott made her remorseful for the way she'd treated you,' Aaron suggested.

'Yeah,' I agreed, deciding that whilst I would never know her true intentions for sure, I could choose to believe he was right. That Mia had done it for me.

'What will you do now? You could go back to London. Be you again.'

I froze. The thought of going back terrified me. That job. That life. I couldn't cope with it again. I barely survived it last time. It had driven me to make crazy choices out of desperation and loneliness. It had almost cost me my life. It had cost Mia hers. That wasn't something I could just forget.

'I'm not sure I'm that person any more.'

Too much had changed. I'd changed. The past was no longer a world I fitted into.

Aaron nodded. Somehow, he understood. 'So stay here, then.'

'But this isn't me either. It was an act. A lie.'

'Was it?' There was something about the way he asked, the doubt in his tone, that made my head jolt back up and I stared at him.

'This was Mia's home.'

'Maybe in the beginning. But I think somewhere along it became your home too. You might have lied about your name. But in many ways, you were still you. This is still your life.'

'How can you be so sure?'

'Because I know you.'

I cringed. 'You said that before and I think I've proved you didn't really know me at all.'

'Didn't I?' He arched his eyebrow. 'I'm still here, aren't I?'

I nodded. 'Yes, for some inexplicable reason you do seem to be.'

Aaron smiled. 'The question is, will you be?'

'I'll never be able to forget what happened, though. The mistakes I've made.'

'Healing doesn't mean the past doesn't exist any more. You're not going to be able to click your fingers and suddenly everything will be fine. There will be difficult moments. Hard days. You'll still experience sadness, pain, regret. But the important thing to remember is that's not all there is.'

I nodded.

'You are stronger than you think. Look at all the changes you've made to your life. And you did it all on your own. Just you,' Aaron assured me. 'You can do this too.'

'I was running away. That wasn't strength. That was fear.'

'Maybe,' Aaron conceded. 'Or maybe it was hope.'

Hope.

Perhaps he was right. I'd stayed in Bournemouth despite the painful memories. I could have run away from them and from him.

But I hadn't. I'd tried to make a life here. To reconnect with Aaron. To make peace with the past.

I smiled slightly. 'I like that way of looking at it.'

'So is that a yes? You'll stay?'

You can't heal in the place that broke you.

Mum's words replayed in my head.

Perhaps she was wrong. Perhaps sometimes the place that broke you could also be the place that healed you.

'Maybe,' I said slowly. But even as I spoke, I knew that I would. At least for now. I had more healing to do here. I inhaled deeply, allowing the cold, salty air to fill my lungs.

Mia was right, I wasn't her. I never would be. I inhaled slowly, feeling a weight lift from me as I realised I was okay with that. For the first time in my life I was content being me.

* * *

MORE FROM ALEX STONE

Another unputdownable psychological thriller from Alex Stone, *The Good Patient*, is available to order now here:

www.mybook.to/GoodPatientBackAd

ACKNOWLEDGEMENTS

It never ceases to amaze me when I get to hold the printed book in my hands, knowing that it started out as a vague idea in my head. Particularly for this book. Written through a difficult time with family health issues and my own illness too, this book has been a long time coming. So it's even more of a thrill to see it to fruition.

Thank you to my incredible editor, Emily Ruston: your patience, unwavering support and feedback made this book possible. Thanks as always to you, and the whole Boldwood Books team, for making my dreams become a reality.

Huge thanks to my writing mentor, Jonathan Eyers, from Cornerstones Literary Consultancy, for your encouragement and helpful feedback. Somehow you always manage to help me find a way to stitch all the threads together, and weave a story. Thanks once again to Yvonne Hazell-Webb for your medical expertise and friendship, and Stuart Gibbon for your continued expertise on all the police matters.

Thank you to my parents and Ahl for your support and encouragement.

Thanks to all my fantastic writing buddies: Ellie Henshaw, Sophie Beal and Alice May, to name but a few. To Alison May, Lucy Waldron and Beth Lord for keeping me (relatively) sane when my world was falling apart, and Kath McGurl, whose brainstorming beach walks once again came to the rescue. And to the bookshops, libraries and festivals, who have made me feel so welcome. Particularly to The Bournemouth Writing Festival; it is an absolute delight to see Bournemouth grow into a thriving writing community.

None of this would be possible without all of you, and of course the wonderful readers and book bloggers who have supported my books with your purchases, reviews, social media posts and lovely messages. Thank you never feels big enough to express the gratitude I have for you all.

ABOUT THE AUTHOR

Alex Stone, originally an accountant from the West Midlands, is now a psychological suspense writer based in Dorset. This beautiful and dramatic coastline is the inspiration and setting for her novels. She was awarded the Katie Fforde Bursary in 2019.

Sign up to Alex Stone's mailing list for news, competitions and updates on future books.

Visit Alex Stone's website: www.AlexStoneAuthor.com

Follow Alex on social media here:

 facebook.com/AlexStoneWriter
 x.com/AlexStoneAuthor
 instagram.com/AlexStoneAuthor

ALSO BY ALEX STONE

The Perfect Daughter

The Other Girlfriend

The Good Patient

The Quiet Sister

THE

Murder

LIST

**THE MURDER LIST IS A NEWSLETTER
DEDICATED TO SPINE-CHILLING FICTION
AND GRIPPING PAGE-TURNERS!**

**SIGN UP TO MAKE SURE YOU'RE ON OUR
HIT LIST FOR EXCLUSIVE DEALS, AUTHOR
CONTENT, AND COMPETITIONS.**

SIGN UP TO OUR NEWSLETTER

BIT.LY/THEMURDERLISTNEWS

Boldwⓞⓞd

Boldwood Books is an award-winning fiction
publishing company seeking out the best
stories from around the world.

Find out more at www.boldwoodbooks.com

Join our reader community for brilliant books,
competitions and offers!

Follow us
@BoldwoodBooks
@TheBoldBookClub

Sign up to our weekly
deals newsletter

https://bit.ly/BoldwoodBNewsletter

Made in the USA
Las Vegas, NV
01 March 2025

18863888R00223